PRAISE FOR TH

"Fans of the Expanse series will enjoy this engaging and fast-moving combination of corporate machinations, police procedural, and interstellar naval combat."

—*Booklist*

"A series you should start if you are a fan of grounded space opera with a military lean. The Palladium Wars comes at straight-up military fiction from an angle that keeps it interesting."

—*Locus* magazine

"I gulped down *Ballistic* in one long read, staying awake half the night, and now I want the next one!"

—George R. R. Martin

CITADEL
THE.PALLADIUM.WARS

Also By Marko Kloos

Frontlines

Terms of Enlistment
Lines of Departure
Angles of Attack
Chains of Command
Fields of Fire
Points of Impact
Orders of Battle
Measures of Absolution (A Frontlines Kindle novella)
"Lucky Thirteen" (A Frontlines Kindle short story)

The Palladium Wars

Aftershocks
Ballistic

AUTHOR OF THE FRONTLINES SERIES

MARKO KLOOS

47NORTH

This is a work of fiction. Names, characters, organizations, places, events, and incidents are either products of the author's imagination or are used fictitiously. Any resemblance to actual persons, living or dead, or actual events is purely coincidental.

Published by 47North, Seattle

www.apub.com

ISBN-13: 9781542027250 (hardcover)
ISBN-10: 154202725X (hardcover)

ISBN-13: 9781542027243 (paperback)
ISBN-10: 1542027241 (paperback)

Cover design by Shasti O'Leary Soudant

Printed in the United States of America

First edition

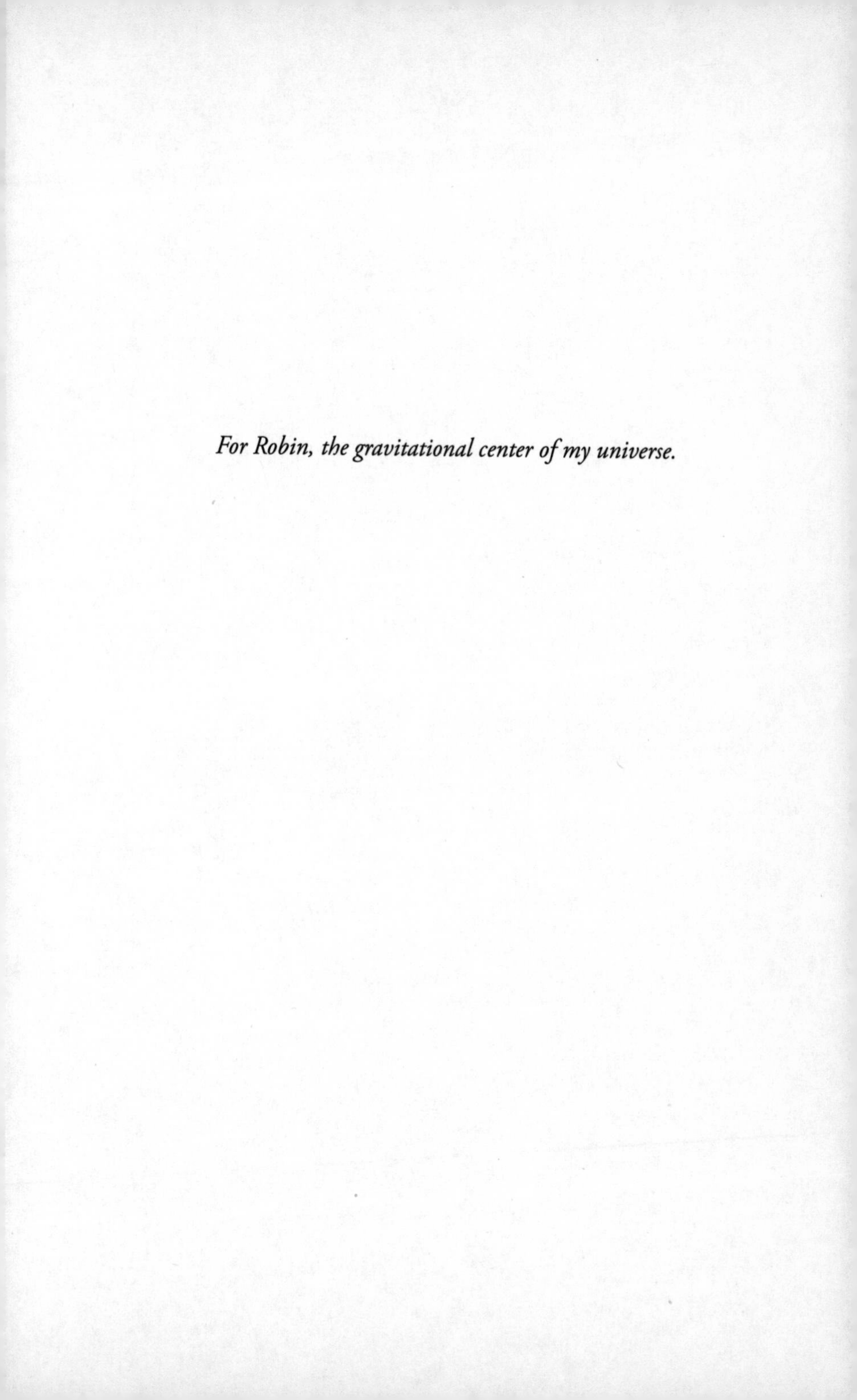

For Robin, the gravitational center of my universe.

Chapter 1

Aden

"I remember you," the voice said from the back of the room.

Aden turned around to look at the only other customer in the shop, an older woman who had been glancing at him ever since he had walked into the place a minute ago to buy breakfast. It was an automated shop, prepared food placed in transparent compartments along three of the four walls for customers to browse, so there was no clerk to overhear them. But Aden still felt an unwelcome rush of anxiety.

"Excuse me?"

"I remember you," she repeated. "I remember your face. From liberation day."

"I'm not sure I know what you mean," Aden said, careful to keep his discomfort out of his voice.

"I scanned ID tags at the spaceport for the prisoner transport," she said. "I don't remember your name, but I am pretty good with faces. You were with the Blackguards. I assigned you to one of the shuttles."

Aden forced a surprised smile that he hoped looked nonchalant.

"I think your memory is playing tricks on you. I'm a local. I was home on Chryseis on liberation day. Getting drunk with the rest of the city when the last fuzzhead left."

The woman's eyes narrowed. He had inflected his Oceanian with just enough of his mother's Chryseis timbre that it must have shaken her conviction at least a little.

"Which part of the city?" she asked.

"Second canal belt, right off Civic Square."

"Fancy part of town," the woman said. She seemed to appraise him anew with the fresh information in her mind. "I lived on Chryseis for three years. Out on the eighth belt."

"By the university quarter," he guessed, and she nodded.

"Well," she said. "Maybe my memory *is* playing tricks on me. Maybe I remember your face from there. Either that, or you have a twin who was in the fuzzhead military. My apologies. Nobody wants to be mistaken for one of *those* people."

Aden shrugged with a smile.

"No offense taken. It was a strange time. Seems like a bad dream after all these years."

She nodded and mirrored his smile, but hers didn't quite reach her eyes. Aden returned his attention to the wall of food compartments, but having been identified by a local had unsettled him, and he just wanted to get out of the shop as quickly as possible without looking like he was running away. He picked two meals in what he hoped didn't seem like a random fashion and opened the compartments with his ID pass, making sure to be obvious about it so the woman behind him could see his Oceanian identification. He collected the trays, stacked them on top of each other, and walked out, giving the woman a friendly nod as he passed her. When he was outside in the sun, he glanced back and saw that she was following him with her gaze, the suspicion still evident on her face. He turned right and strolled down the leaf's main artery, doing his best to make his walk casual and unhurried.

Out by the ocean wall of the nearby seaside park, he saw a warship for the first time since the end of the war.

It was a hydrofoil cruiser, a sleek and ominous dagger shape that was carving a silver line through the shallow waters a few kilometers outside of the city, and it stood out between the smaller leisure craft and commercial fishing boats like an eagle in a chicken coop. Aden watched it glide past the seaside park at the tip of the northeastern leaf. During the war, which had been brief for Oceana until Gretia had subdued and occupied the planet, the Oceanians had used these hydrofoil cruisers to good effect against the attackers, as highly mobile seaborne anti-air platforms and artillery support. The mood in Adrasteia had changed a little in the two weeks since the insurgent attack on Rhodia, but the hydrofoil cruiser off the coast was the first visual indicator that Oceana was preparing for conflict. The tourist crowds from all over the system were thinner than usual, and the chatter on the streets was more subdued.

Aden stepped around a cluster of Palladians who were showing off the panorama to some far-off friends or relatives via comtab projections, chattering and gesturing. Palladian was the one language in the system in which he could not even guess at the content of a conversation, but the laughs and the facial expressions supplied that information clearly enough. He returned a few smiles from the group and continued his path along the seawall, following the far-off warship with his eyes until it disappeared behind the skyline of the neighboring leaf. The sight of it reinforced the unwelcome memories of the end of the Gretian occupation that had been triggered by his encounter with the suspicious woman at the food shop. An Alliance fleet had shown up in orbit, chased off the garrison force, and landed troops on every Oceanian city to pry off the Gretians. It had been Aden's last day of freedom for the next five years. The Alliance had achieved complete surprise—the morning had started out like this one, a perfect, sunny twenty-degree day with a light breeze, and by noon, the sky had been dark with troop landers and attack craft. Some of the Gretian detachments on other cities had put up brief and futile fights, but the garrison commander on Adrasteia had surrendered almost immediately. After four years of war, Adrasteia had been mostly an R & R area for the troops coming back from the meat grinder at Pallas and the fleet actions in space, and they'd had neither the numbers nor the will for a pointless fight. Before the end of that day, Aden had marched his entire signals intelligence company onto the central island into detainment, past jeering Oceanian civilians and grim-looking Alliance soldiers. The sight of the gunship cruising on the tranquil waters just off the outer edge of the city brought back the feelings of that day—the fear, shame, and anxiety.

Someone had run up to their column and spit at him that day, and the memory of it came back as vividly as if it had happened an hour ago. The man had meant to spit in his face but had hit the collar of his Blackguards uniform instead, where the spit had trickled down the branch insignia and onto the fabric of the tunic. It was strange—he could clearly remember everything about that incident, and how he had left the spit to dry on his uniform because he didn't want to smear it into a bigger blotch trying to wipe it off, but he couldn't remember any encounter that day with the woman he'd just met in the food shop. He barely recalled the registration procedure at the spaceport, where the Alliance marines had corralled them into groups by rank and searched them for contraband before letting the civilians assign them to shuttles.

Aden shook his head and tried to clear the unwelcome recollections from his mind. The breeze out here on the tip of the northeastern leaf was clean and pleasant, and the warm food in his hands smelled appetizing through the perforated lids of the containers. This was the present, the here and now, and he tried to return his focus to what was in front of him. But as he walked back toward the place where he was staying, he could still feel the gaze of the woman from the shop on the back of his head, and he had to turn around to make sure she wasn't following him, alerting passersby that a fuzzhead—an occupier, a warmonger—was walking among them again.

The suite he had rented here on the most scenic part of the leaf was probably a little extravagant for a rookie spacer, but the advice of his friend and crewmate Tristan had been never to be stingy with accommodation, food, or drink, and just be miserly with everything else instead. The room was shaped like a rounded flower petal, jutting out from the side of the resort building in a way that offered a 180-degree view of the ocean without looking into any neighboring suites. Most importantly, resorts that catered to well-to-do people had much enhanced security over budget hotels in the busy part of the city, the sort of places where half a dozen graduating university kids from Rhodia or Acheron would split a basic room to rest their heads in between their drinking or pharmaceutical expeditions into town.

When he unlocked the door and walked into the suite, the blinds were still drawn, and the place was bathed in semidarkness.

"Room, open blinds," he said. "And the balcony door."

The blinds silently retracted upward at his command, and the balcony door slid sideways to admit a light gust of sea air from outside.

"Too *bright*," a muffled voice said from the bed in the middle of the main room.

"It's midmorning," Aden said. "I brought some breakfast."

The covers on the bed moved, and a tousle-haired Tess raised her head and squinted at him.

"I don't think I can get anything down this morning," she said. "But I do need some water. My mouth tastes like the inside of a wastewater tank."

Aden walked over to the kitchen nook and put the meal containers on the counter. Then he pulled a cup off the rack and filled it with cold water from the in-wall dispenser. He walked to the bed and handed the cup to Tess, who took it and emptied it in one long gulp.

"Food's over there if you change your mind." Aden nodded at the counter.

"Right now, my mind isn't so much on *intake* as on *output*," she replied. She threw back the covers and swung her legs over the edge of the bed with a groan. Ever since Aden had met her, he had seen her mostly in the artificial illumination of *Zephyr*'s compartments or the interiors of space stations. Here in the natural sunlight streaming through the windows, she looked more vivid somehow. Her skin had a different tone, and her tattoos looked brighter and more colorful. He watched as she got onto unsteady feet and walked over to the wet cell, past a low table that held the evidence of last night's indulgences—empty food containers and several bottles of liquor. They hadn't really made a spoken arrangement to get together after the *Zephyr* crew disembarked and came down to Adrasteia yesterday, but then their paths had crossed on the northeastern leaf a few hours into their customary twenty-four–zero solitary time, and things had developed rapidly from there.

"This bathroom is bigger than my whole berth on the ship," Tess said from the wet cell over the sound of running water.

"I think it's bigger than both our berths put together," Aden replied. He walked over to the balcony door and stood in the opening to enjoy the breeze. Fresh air, the wind ruffling his hair, was what he missed most when he was on the ship, where all the air was continuously recycled. Then his stomach growled and reminded him why he had gone for a morning stroll in the first place. He turned and walked over to the counter to get one of the breakfast meals, then took his food out onto the balcony to eat.

A few minutes later, Tess came out to join him, the other meal tray in her hand. She was wearing clothes he had never seen on her before, sleek dark trousers and an airy sleeveless tunic that showed off the artwork on her arms.

"I didn't think you even owned any clothes that aren't flight suits," he said.

"I got these on Coriolis City before we left," she said. "You showed up at our bar evening with a new outfit. It made me want to step up my shore-leave game a little. It's easy to get lazy when you're on the ship or on a station most of the time. Spacers don't give a shit about looks."

Tess sat down and opened her food container, then propped her feet up on the low railing of the balcony and blinked into the sun. "You know, every time I'm home, I think about how much I've missed this place, and that I never want to leave again. And after a week down here, I usually can't wait to get back into space."

"We may be down here for a lot longer than just a week," Aden said.

"I know. Until the dust settles."

"Or until we run out of money. Whichever comes first," he replied.

"We won't make a killing with just Acheron-to-Oceana runs. That's only a lucrative route if you're a 100,000-ton bulk hauler. Protein one way, graphene the other. Not a job for a ship the size of ours."

"Then let's hope the dust settles quickly."

Tess gave him an amused glance and took a bite of her food.

"How likely do you think *that* is? They're still putting out the fires on Rhodia."

"Not likely," Aden admitted. "Nukes kick up an awful lot of dust."

"Like you said, we may be here for a while. So you may want to think about downgrading your suite a little. Not that I don't appreciate the amenities."

"It's just for a few days. And if it's down to a few hundred ags, I'm in deep shit anyway."

"Do you have family here you can lean on?" Tess asked.

Aden thought about her question. His mother was from Chryseis, one of Oceana's floating cities, but she hadn't been back in a long time, and her family had all but disowned her when Gretia had gone to war with the rest of the system. Whoever was still around wasn't likely to give him a warm reception.

"Maybe," he said. "But I didn't exactly leave on good terms. I'll save that option for desperate times."

To his relief, Tess seemed satisfied with his answer and didn't probe any further. As far as most of the crew knew, he had grown up on Oceana and visited Gretia during the long summers, when in truth it had been the other way around. Only Captain Decker knew that he was Gretian, and he hadn't told her that he had been a Blackguard. Every time Tess asked a question about his personal history, no matter how innocuous, formulating an answer felt like having to walk a tightrope. He tried not to lie to her, to make his answers as ambiguous as possible without arousing suspicion, but he felt bad every time he had to be evasive.

"One bad contract," Tess said. "That was all it took. One quick show of hands, and a few weeks later we're down to one low-profit trade route. If we ever decide to get underway again, with this sword hanging over our heads."

She looked up at the cloudless blue sky overhead and sighed. High above them, contrails curved toward Adrasteia, announcing the imminent arrival of another orbital shuttle ferrying travelers and cargo down to the spaceport in the center of the city.

"It doesn't feel right."

"What's that?" Aden asked.

"*Zephyr*," Tess replied. "Up there, tied up at the station. She's not built for that. She's built for ten-g dashes on the transfer routes. Not for racking up parking fees. She needs to earn her keep."

"You're not just talking about the ship, are you?"

She looked at him, and the corners of her mouth turned up in the hint of a smile.

"Could be," she said. "Maybe I'm not built for that either. She's just a bunch of alloy and graphene, after all. She'll weather it better than I will."

He watched as she took another bite of her breakfast. By now, he was used to her little idiosyncrasies and habits, like the way she preloaded her fork in between bites, or the way she wiped the corners of her mouth with the inside of her wrist on occasion. She caught him looking at her and gave him a quizzical look.

"What?"

"Nothing," Aden said. "Just wondering if this is going to be a problem when we're back up on the ship again."

"If *what* is going to be a problem?"

"This," he said. "Whatever we are right now."

"Whatever we are right now," she repeated. "We're crewmates, Aden. Crewmates who find each other attractive enough to duck out for a little fun together on shore leave. Let's not overthink it."

He wasn't sure whether to feel relief or disappointment at her assessment. But before he could think of a response, his comtab back in the room let out a cheerful little chirp, the notification of an incoming private message. A second later, Tess's comtab did the same. She transferred her food box to her left hand and pinched a screen projection into existence with thumb and forefinger. Aden did likewise and made a new message window appear above his palm. He smiled when he read the name of the sender.

"Tristan?" she asked, and he nodded.

"Same here," Tess said.

The message just had an address link and a door access code, followed by a directive to Bring drinks at 1600.

"Guess we're getting together at his place," Aden said.

"There'll be food. Lots of it. He likes to go all out with fresh stuff when we're home on shore leave. Don't eat lunch. You'll need your appetite later."

He checked the time.

"That's still eight hours away. What are you doing until then?"

Tess shrugged.

"I haven't thought about it yet. Maybe I'll go race some tube pods at the subsurface track out on the eastern leaf. What about you? Want to come?"

"I don't know the first thing about pod racing."

"I'll show you. Come on, get a bit of adrenaline into your system."

"All right," he said. "Let me rinse off and get dressed."

He got out of his chair and turned to walk back inside. When he was at the door, Tess let out a low whistle. He turned, thinking that she had directed it at his backside, but she had her hand above her eyes to shield them from the sun, and she was looking out at the water. Aden followed her gaze to see the Oceanian hydrofoil cruiser he had spotted earlier. It was heading back out to sea, and now it was moving at high speed, standing up on its foils and spewing a hundred-meter rooster tail of water spray from its propulsion jets.

"They're really hauling ass," Tess said. "Two hundred klicks per hour, at least. Wonder what the trouble is."

"Probably just an exercise," Aden replied. "Or maybe some leisure craft needs rescuing."

The assertion seemed to satisfy Tess, but it didn't quite tamp down the discomfort the sight of the warship had stirred up in Aden's own mind again. It was a visible reminder that armed strife had returned to the system, that conflict had been rekindled. And small fires had a way of growing out of control and turning into conflagrations.

Today, the hydrofoil cruiser off the coast was probably just making a high-speed training dash. But there was a chance that tomorrow or the day after, those missile silos in its hull would start to ripple-fire their payloads at unseen attackers or incoming ballistic missiles, and the anti-air ordnance on that ship would paint bright white trails across the sky with dozens of exhaust plumes. The possibility was small, but the presence of that warship was a reminder that the odds were greater than zero again, just five years after the system had almost burned itself up. Adrasteia was well protected, but Aden knew that it needed to have strong defenses because it was the only city on Oceana with a fixed location, the only one that could be reliably targeted with a ballistic missile or a kinetic impactor from millions of kilometers away.

At least I'll be at ground zero if that happens, Aden thought. *I won't have time to care.*

Tess yawned and stretched out in the sun, and the sight made him shake off the dark thoughts. Tomorrow was just that, and he had no control over what happened in the system. But Tess and Tristan and the rest of the crew were today, and he reminded himself to pay attention to the here and now, the things that were in his power to influence.

"You going to rinse off or what?" Tess asked. "If we're going to hit the track, we need to get there before the noon crowd. Early in, early out."

"Yes, ma'am," he said and returned her smile. Out on the ocean, the hydrofoil cruiser had disappeared, leaving only a long wake of disturbed water that was slowly dissipating in the gentle currents. He turned to walk to the wet cell.

CHAPTER 2

IDINA

Being around generals and politicians gave Idina more anxiety than being on a battlefield, and in the mornings, the streets of Sandvik's government quarter were full of both.

It wasn't the custom to exercise in fatigues, but the current security level required every Pallas Brigade trooper to be armed at all times, and the one-piece exercise suit had no provisions for a holster. So she did her runs in boots and combat dress, which earned her more than one reproachful look from the Alliance officers she passed along the way.

It was late summer, and the mornings had turned a little chilly, which suited her fine. Seasons were still strange to her, but after experiencing all of them over the course of several deployments, she had decided that summer was her least favorite, a wretched succession of sweltering days that were good for nothing except seeking refuge in climate-controlled buildings and vehicles, too hot to comfortably exercise. Autumn felt perfect to her, and the late-summer morning felt enough like a preview of that season to put her in a good mood as she ran, despite her discontent at being pulled off joint patrol duty with Dahl and the rest of the Gretian police. But the Joint Security Patrol cooperation had been suspended in the wake of the attack on Rhodia, and the powers in charge had decided to use the JSP for shoring up security for the Alliance commissioners in the diplomatic quarter. She had started this tour of Gretia as an infantry soldier, then they had turned her into a military police officer, and now she was a glorified gate guard.

At this rate of regression, I'll be serving tea in the general officers' club in another month, she thought sourly.

By now, she knew the area well enough to not have to think about her route or consult her wrist comtab. She turned the corner by the Rhodian embassy, which put her back onto the central axis, a fifty-meter wide avenue that was lined with tall, ancient-looking trees. This was her favorite part of the run, which was why she always went counterclockwise to save it for last. The trees shaded her from the morning sun, and the air underneath their leafy canopies felt clean and pure.

On the roadway, a steady procession of transport pods hummed along, Gretian government functionaries and Alliance military personnel on the way to their offices. Idina ran to the little park that was right across the road from her destination, then stopped and waited for a gap in the pod columns on the road to cross. There was an official crosswalk just fifty meters ahead, but she didn't like to take those precisely because the Gretians seemed to have a natural aversion to crossing a street any other way than the designated method.

"Color Sergeant!" a voice called from behind. "Could you wait a moment, please?"

Idina turned around to see a Pallas Brigade trooper trot toward her across the little park. He was in combat fatigues, and he carried a deployment bag on his back. She looked for rank insignia and didn't see any. He huffed a little as he made his way toward her. When he halted in front of her, he dropped his bag and began a salute, and Idina waved him off with a sharp, dismissive motion of her arm.

"Belay that. We don't salute around here."

"Sorry, Color Sergeant." He dropped his hand. To Idina, he looked impossibly young, a good-looking kid with the sharper-than-usual jawline that was the hallmark of someone who had finished the grueling brigade training not too long ago and was still recovering from the caloric deficit.

"You go around saluting, you give the insurgents an idea who's worth shooting," she explained. "Not that they're picky with their targets. What's your business, Private?"

"Private Khanna, ma'am. I just got assigned to Fifth Platoon. But I don't know where to report. I was hoping you could tell me."

"You're in luck today, Private. I'm Color Sergeant Chaudhary. I'm the NCO in charge of Fifth Platoon. So you're supposed to report to me."

She looked at his uniform more closely. He had no rank sleeves, no armor, and no weapon except for his kukri, which looked like it had been issued to him just yesterday.

"Where's your sidearm, Khanna? We're in Condition Two security posture right now. You need to be armed at all times."

"I just got off the shuttle an hour ago, ma'am. They didn't issue me one yet. Or armor. They just put me on a ground transport and told me to report here."

Idina stopped herself from muttering a curse out loud.

"Is this your first deployment to Gretia?"

"Yes, ma'am. First time off the planet. If you don't count Pallas One."

"Have you had your occupation force training yet?"

"We got that before we left," he said. "Back on Pallas."

"Well," Idina said. "You're going to have to throw out a lot of what they've taught you. Things have changed in the last few weeks."

She sighed. The brigade had started to bring its strength up to wartime level, and they had begun to funnel every available trained trooper to Gretia. The emergency buildup had saved her from having to take a shuttle home for medical leave, but she wasn't quite sure if having to integrate green troopers into her JSP platoon was worth the trade. Inexperienced young privates belonged in a line company out in the field, not in a security platoon tasked with the protection of dignitaries and installations.

"First things first," she said. "See that building over there?" She pointed at the Palladian embassy across the street.

"Yes, ma'am."

"Report to the gate guard, then go straight down to the armory in the first sublevel and have them issue you scout armor and standard light armament. They know the routine. When you are done, go to the security detachment briefing room on the ground level and claim a seat. Team briefing is in twenty-five minutes. I will be there in twenty-three. And stop at the dining hall on the way and grab some portable food."

"Armory, first sublevel, standard-issue kit. Briefing room, ground level, briefing in twenty-five. Understood," he repeated in the by-the-book form that was particular to troopers just out of training. He straightened his spine for a salute, then caught himself and relaxed the hand he had started to raise.

"Quick learner," she said. "That will serve you well around here. Off you go."

Idina watched as the young trooper crossed the roadway. The heavy gear bag on his back seemed almost as tall as he was, but she knew that brigade members just out of training were in the best shape of their lives, stronger and fitter than any other demographic in the entire system, and that he could carry that bag around all day if someone gave him an order to do just that.

I was that young and strong once, she thought. *And just as fresh-faced and eager.*

She waited for another gap in the flow of pod traffic and followed Private Khanna across the street toward the embassy.

When she walked into the briefing room on the embassy ground floor twenty-two minutes later, freshly showered and dressed in clean fatigues, her platoon was already present, eschewing the chairs as usual and standing in neat rows by section. The senior NCO, Sergeant Noor, called the room to attention with a raspy clearing of his throat, and all of Fifth Platoon's troopers snapped to attention in perfect synchrony. It was a point of pride for her section leaders to spot her and call the platoon to attention before she could get out an "as you were" as she entered, and she was happy to let them have their little contest with her every day.

"At ease," Idina said. All the troopers switched to parade rest. She scanned the room and saw that Private Khanna was standing with Red Section next to Corporal Shakya.

"Good morning," she said. "Before we get to today's section assignments, let me introduce our new platoon member. Private Khanna over there joined us this morning fresh off the shuttle from Pallas. It's his first time off-world, so I expect you to fill him in on how things are done here on Gretia and in this regiment. *Useful information only*, please. If you send him to the quartermaster to fetch red shower tokens for hot water like you did the last new trooper, we're going to have words. *Stern* words."

From the platoon, a mixture of smiles and low chuckles came in response. Hazing the new troopers was a time-honored tradition, and she knew they'd let him have at least a little bit of that. But all Pallas Brigade troopers were brothers and sisters for life once they got their kukri, and she also knew that they would take Khanna under their wings and get him up to speed quickly and thoroughly. Today, he was the new blood, but this afternoon, the life of anyone in the platoon might depend on him. Making him an efficient member of the team as quickly as possible was in everyone's best interest.

"All right," she said when the moment of levity had passed. "The current security situation is unchanged. All Alliance forces remain at

Condition Two planetwide. You all know the routine. Nobody goes off base, nobody walks around unarmed. We're having daily run-ins with the civilian protesters at the Green Zone gates, but the insurgency hasn't popped up since the IBIS intercept three days ago."

IBIS was the new Ballistic Intercept System, a network of sensor-controlled point-defense energy emitters that protected the Green Zone against attacks from insurgent munitions. It scanned the airspace around the government quarter continuously, and if it detected an incoming projectile, it blew it out of the sky with megawatts of directed energy. Until three days ago, IBIS had only worked in theory and at the test range, but then the insurgency had taken a few shots with a rail gun from the top of one of Sandvik's tall buildings. The ability of the insurgency to aim direct fire at the government quarter had unnerved a great many people, but the ability of the IBIS arrays to shoot down tungsten slugs traveling at several thousand meters per second made Idina feel a little less like she was walking around in a shooting gallery whenever she stepped outside in the government quarter.

"Patrol assignments," she continued. "Red and Blue, you are on perimeter patrol. Shakya and Noor, work out your own team schedules. The fence is all yours from 0800 until 0800 tomorrow morning. Green Section, you have the main gate today. Yellow Section, rooftop overwatch. Purple is with me for close protection detail. The Quick Reaction Force team is on standby if we need them. Don't get jumpy out there because we can only ring that bell once. But I trust the section leaders to know when things get too hot for us to handle alone. Any questions or concerns?"

She looked at the assembled platoon for a moment. When nobody raised a hand, she nodded.

"All sections, draw weapons and armor up. Final gear and comms check out front in fifteen. Let's get it done."

The platoon stirred, and the low din of conversation filled the room again as the sections coalesced around their leaders.

"Corporal Shakya," Idina called out, and the corporal came trotting over.

"Yes, ma'am."

"I know they assigned you the new private to fill in the vacancy in your section, but I think I am going to take him with Purple Section and keep him close on his first day. Why don't you take Lance Corporal Bodhi in his stead for today?"

"Affirmative, ma'am. He's all yours," Shakya said. "Khanna, over here. You get to stick with the color sergeant."

Khanna stepped up and stood in front of them, obviously a little nervous and unsure. Around them, the members of the platoon streamed past and out the door on the way to armor up and receive their weapons.

"To the *armory*, Khanna," Idina said. "Get what everyone else is getting. Go where everyone else is going. Just like in Basic."

"Yes, ma'am," Khanna said and joined the throng.

She waited until the entire platoon was out of the room, then followed them to bring up the rear. The security situation had deteriorated in the last few weeks, and the streets were now more dangerous than they had ever been since the very beginning of the occupation. But she was profoundly glad that these new circumstances had kept her with her troops on Gretia instead of putting her on a slow transport home to Pallas, to spend the rest of her service time in a desk job. The troop buildup would end sooner or later, and then she wouldn't be able to avoid the attention of Major Malik anymore. But for now there was soldiering business to be done, and she was happy for the purpose.

Outside, Idina watched the section leaders go through their last-minute equipment and comms checks. All the sections were wearing soft spider-silk armor instead of the hardened composite plates of battle armor, as a compromise between adequate protection in an attack and what Alliance command had determined to be a gentler and more "de-escalating" appearance here in the administrative heart of the planet. The sections on guard duty were armed with universal combat rifles, set up with both lethal and crowd-control modules. Her Purple Section, the group tasked with the protection of the Palladian high commissioner, was equipped with personal defense weapons, small automatic machine pistols that were less capable than the standard rifles but easier to handle in the confines of vehicles and hallways. They were also far more discreet, and better suited to environments where dignitaries and government functionaries got together for meetings and social events.

"Purple Section, listen up," she said when the other sections had marched off to their respective duties. "There's nothing on the PHC's schedule for the day as far as travel is concerned. That means we'll have a quiet day staying in reserve for the principal protection team. But that doesn't mean we let our guard down. I know it's not the most exciting duty in the world to stand around and wait for trouble to come to us. Stay sharp, keep alert. Remember, watch hands and pockets. You see anything out of the ordinary, you call it out. Got it?"

They nodded their affirmations.

"All right. Section, move out," Idina ordered.

They walked across the big square in front of the Pallas embassy. The transport pod traffic crossing the square halted to let them pass. To their left, the edge of the square was delineated by a beautiful arch, seven bright white pillars curving at the top thirty meters above street level to come together in slender points and form six tall archways. The first time she had been deployed to Gretia for occupation duty, someone had explained to her that there was one archway for each planet of the Gaia system, and that the entire arch was supposed to celebrate the successful colonization of this world and the other five. Beyond the arch, the wide roadway led out of the government quarter and across a vast green park that stretched out for a full kilometer and bordered Principal

Square in the middle of Sandvik on its other end. Far in the distance, halfway across the expanse of the park, Idina could see the electric-blue plasma shimmer of the security field that created a wide buffer of empty space for the Sandvik Green Zone.

If we need to put up walls between us and them to protect us from each other, we probably shouldn't be here, she thought. *But none of us wanted to be here in the first place. That is something they brought onto themselves.* She glanced at the arch to her left as they marched past, a lofty symbol of a system-wide unity that no longer existed.

In the center of the government quarter, the Council Hall loomed over the smaller structures that surrounded it. To Idina's Palladian sensibilities, it seemed excessive and ostentatious, but she could not deny that it was an imposing and important-looking building. It was a hundred meters on each side, with slender spires at each corner that were fifty meters tall. The exterior was clad in white stone that looked brilliant in the rays of the morning sun. In the middle of the structure, a transparent pyramid rose almost to the height of the corner spires, graceful titanium latticework with immense slabs of Alon in between. The Council Hall had been the seat of Gretian political power before the end of the war. The Alliance had dissolved the government and negated the building's original purpose, and now it housed the headquarters of the Alliance High Commission and the parts of the Gretian civil system that had been allowed to operate under the supervision of the occupation forces.

They crossed the square in front of the Council Hall and headed for the entrance. Out on the sunlit plaza, Alliance officers and Gretian civil servants were congregating in small groups, but Idina could see that the Gretians were mostly keeping to themselves. A quartet of Gretian police officers caught her eye as they came down the steps of the Council Hall, and she felt herself hoping for a brief moment that one of them would have captain's stars and wear her silver-white hair in a tight braid. But as they got closer, the Gretian officers exchanged respectful nods with her, and none of them were familiar faces from her JSP patrols with Dahl's contingent.

In the atrium of the Council Hall, she always felt out of place. It wasn't just that most of the Alliance troops here were staff or flag officers—majors and colonels and generals. The building was designed as a showpiece of government, and every floor of it served as a gallery to observe the legislative chamber in its center, a huge open space located directly underneath the translucent pyramid in the middle of the roof. Gretian architecture was sparse, economical, and elegant, and this place was clearly built to erase the scale of the individual and showcase the dynamics of the group working on common goals. She imagined it had worked as intended when the legislative floor was busy, but now that the big chamber was empty and quiet, it felt more like a tomb to her, a silent memorial to a way of life that no longer existed.

The offices of the Alliance High Commission were on the top floor of the Council Hall, in the rooms previously occupied by the highest tier of the Gretian government. Idina and her section stepped off the skylift platform and walked into the wide North Gallery that was home to the Palladian delegation. When they got to the ready room for the security detachment, a familiar Palladian color sergeant came down the gallery floor toward them.

"Colors Chaudhary," he called out when he was in talking range.

"Colors Norgay," she said. "I was about to report in with your detail."

"Change in plans today, I'm afraid," he said. Norgay was the leader of the Palladian High Commissioner's permanent bodyguard detail, a four-trooper detachment that always accompanied the High Commissioner wherever he went on Gretia. Idina's JSP troopers were there to augment the security detail, but only as backup. The bodyguard detail were brigade military police specialists who were trained for the personal protection job, and they did nothing else all day.

"Nobody's updated my schedule," she replied. "I was about to settle in for a day at the office with the section here. Where are we going?"

"The principal's staying right here with me," Norgay said. "But I am going to have to loan you out today. The new deputy high commissioner just got in. And he wants to do an in-person visit to Camp Unity today." He lowered his voice a little. *"By surface transport."*

"What?" Idina shook her head. "I take it you explained the current security situation to him."

"We did. Twenty minutes via gyrofoil, low risk. Or four hours on surface roads, medium-to-high risk. He chose the surface route."

"But *why*?" she asked.

Colors Norgay smirked. "It's his first time on Gretia. He says he wants to get a *personal impression of the situation on the ground*."

"You've *got* to be joking."

"Diplomatic corps," he said. "I checked his background. Never wore a uniform in his life."

"Fabulous." Idina sighed. "So we're doing a road trip today. Fine."

"It gets better," Norgay said. "The armored assets are mostly tied up today. The armor pool has *one* transport available. He still wants to go."

"He wants to make a single-vehicle run through a hot security zone."

Norgay nodded.

"Well, fuck." Idina looked back at her section. "He's got his detail with him?"

"He's got two on duty right now. Colors Sirhan and Sergeant Kapoor."

"We won't all fit into one transport. I'll take half my section along and leave the other half on call for you here."

"You sure you want to do that, Chaudhary?"

"I'm pretty sure that I don't," she replied. "But that's all the bodies we'll be able to squeeze into the armor. I'm not going to send ahead half a section to play ambush detector in a soft-skinned ride. Did you ask about air support? I'd feel better if we had a combat gyrofoil keeping an eye on things from above."

Norgay shook his head.

"I suggested it, but he turned it down. Says that he's not going to tie up an air asset if he's not going to be riding in it."

Idina checked the time and sighed again.

"All right. He's the boss. He gets to play it however he wants. Did you request the armor already?"

"Affirmative. They'll be out front at 0900."

"Please let his detail know that we won't be able to send an advance command, and that we won't have overhead coverage except for drones. Maybe they can talk the deputy high commissioner out of it and convince him to take the gyrofoil instead."

"I'll tell them, Colors Chaudhary. But I wouldn't count on it. The DHC seemed pretty set on this."

"Aren't they always." She nodded her thanks and watched the color sergeant walk off to convey the information to the other security detail. Then she turned to look at her section.

"Corporal Rai, you stay here as the ready reserve for the high commissioner's detail. I'm going out with the DHC on his field trip. Let me take along Arjun, Raya, and Condry. And Khanna, you're coming along, too. Told you I'd keep you close on your first day."

"Yes, Color Sergeant." Khanna looked like he wasn't quite sure of himself, and she didn't blame him. He'd barely set foot on Gretia, the first foreign planet he'd ever been on in his life, and he was already having to adjust to being in the center of planetary high command, about to do a combat patrol. It was enough to give anyone mental whiplash, which was why she wanted to have him nearby, to assess his resiliency under the unfamiliar stress of a real-world deployment.

"You heard Colors Norgay. Ground transport will be here at 0900. Do your last-minute checks and hit the head, whether you think you need it or not. There won't be any stops along the way for a few hours," she told the other troopers. They acknowledged and set off down the gallery toward the skylift.

"If he has never served, you would think he'd take the advice of people who have been here for a while," Private Khanna said next to Idina.

"You haven't been around bureaucrats a lot, have you, Khanna?"

"No, ma'am."

"They're some of the smartest people you'll ever meet. Most of them could sell seawater to an Oceanian. But when it comes to military life, most of them are clueless toddlers."

She sighed and gestured for him to follow her down the gallery.

"And our job today, Private Khanna, is to keep the deputy high commissioner from burning his hand on the stove."

Chapter 3
Dunstan

The new stripe on his rank insignia still looked like it didn't quite belong there. Dunstan had been a lieutenant commander since the end of the war, and he was used to seeing two silver stripes with a thinner gold stripe between them on his rank sleeves. Now there were three silver stripes of equal width, denoting that the wearer of the uniform was a commander of the Rhodian Navy.

A commander without a command, he thought as he straightened out the front of his service uniform. Technically speaking, he was still the master of RNS *Minotaur*, but his ship was on the way to the reserve yard, destined to be scrapped and recycled. The heavy Gretian gun cruiser they had engaged several weeks ago had broken *Minotaur*'s back, and to the navy, she was too old and too full of holes to be worth repairing, even though she had served faithfully through the war with distinction. But in the end, she had brought her crew home safely one last time and taken a few chunks out of the enemy ship in the process. Dunstan knew there were worse ways to end a military career. Still, now that he no longer had a crew under him, the command star on his uniform that marked him as a ship's captain felt a little fraudulent.

His wife was standing at the large living room window when he walked out of the bedroom to get his morning coffee. Seeing her in front of the big glass pane gave him a brief pinch of anxiety. In normal times, their living quarters were a privilege of rank and seniority, a lovely three-bedroom suite in the top half of the arcology, with a marvelous view of the mountains. But after the nuclear attack on Caledonia-4 two weeks ago, Dunstan was newly aware of the fact that his family's home only had a ten-centimeter thick sheet of hardened glass between it and the rest of the world, and that an evacuation in case of disaster meant a long way to the ground level and the shelters below.

He walked into the kitchen nook and took a mug from the rack to place it under the beverage dispenser. The coffee was steaming hot and fragrant, and just the smell of it made him want to step into an Action Information Center and look at a tactical plot. He took his beverage and went to join Mairi in the living room.

"You can't see the smoke plume anymore," she said when he walked up next to her. In front of them, the northern highlands stretched out into the distance, toward the central mountain spine of Rhodia that bisected the continent.

"You mean it was visible all the way over here?" he asked.

Mairi nodded and vaguely indicated a spot to their left.

"We could see it rising above the mountains," she said. "It was a clear day. Can you imagine? Eight hundred kilometers away, and we could see the cloud from the explosion. The smoke from all the fires. It was the strangest sight. Like someone tore a wound into the planet, and it was just bleeding out into space."

"What did you tell the girls?"

"They knew before I did. They were in school. Their teacher turned on the network feed when the news came across all the comtabs."

He wrapped his arm around her, and she leaned her head against him.

"You look good," she said to his reflection on the window. "Commander."

"I haven't worn this uniform in a while," he said. "It feels a little loose around the middle. I'll have to take it in to get fitted again. I thought people were supposed to put on weight in middle age."

"Normal people," Mairi said. "With desk jobs and low-impact hobbies. Not people like you."

"People like me," he repeated.

"People who don't know how to sit still. It's been three days, and you're itching to head out again."

"I just want to know what I'll be doing next. I brought home a wrecked frigate. With the shortage of hulls we have right now, they may just decide to give me command of a supply depot for the next year and a half."

"You'd be home a lot more," Mairi replied. "Don't hold it against me, but I hope you do get a desk job. Even if I know that it would drive you a little crazy."

"The navy will put me where they need me. If they decide that's shore duty, then that's what it will be."

"But it's not what you want."

"No," he conceded. "It's not."

Dunstan took a sip of his coffee, and they let the next few moments pass in silence.

"I hate the navy," Mairi said. "I know it's heresy to say that as an officer's wife, but I do. I hate that we only get a few days with you. They're treating you like hardware. Rearm, refuel, and back into space."

Dunstan sighed.

"We don't get to choose the times we serve in. You know that."

"I know. But I thought I was done with all of that when the war ended. Watching the network news every evening, hoping to get news and wishing I don't. Having my heart jump in my chest every time a message comes in on my comtab. But most of all, I hate the navy for having such a hold on you that you'd rather go out there and chase down pirates than come home to your family every night."

He turned and walked back to the kitchen counter, where he put down his coffee and checked the front of his uniform to make sure he hadn't dripped any on it. Mairi watched him, arms crossed in front of her chest.

"I'm sorry I'm putting you through all this again," he said. "I thought we were done with this, too. I figured I'd have a few quiet years before retirement. But these people are looking to get us all into a shooting war. If I don't do what I can to stop them, I won't be able to live with myself if there's another mushroom cloud."

He nodded at the window.

"Especially if the next nuke lands eight kilometers from my family instead of eight hundred. It's not the navy that has a hold on me."

She smiled and shook her head. Then she crossed the space between them and kissed him.

"That last sentence was horseshit. But it was nicely packaged horseshit."

She disengaged and smoothed out the front of his uniform, then gave him an appraising look.

"Everything looks sharp and straight. Go and be Commander Park. Just promise me you won't mope too much if they do give you a shore assignment. And I promise I won't sulk if they give you a new ship and send you out again."

"Now see, that last sentence was horseshit as well," Dunstan said and leaned in to kiss her.

His flight across the central mountain spine of the planet was emptier than usual, and half the passengers on the atmospheric shuttle were service members in uniform. Rhodia had been at PLADEC-1 for a full week after the attack before stepping down the military alert level a notch, but it still felt uncomfortably like wartime again, skyports full of uniformed people wearing grim expressions, and a general sense of anxiety in every public space.

When the shuttle descended into the skyport on top of the Caledonia-2 arcology, Dunstan tried to get a glimpse of the attack site through the observation windows on the portside. It was just far enough away, and the day was just hazy enough for the damaged arcology to be just a vague pyramidal outline against the volcanic rock of the Kelpie Peninsula. The fires were out, of course, but he knew that recovery crews and engineering teams were still combing through the thousand-meter tall building even weeks later. Rumor had it that the arcology wasn't going to be repaired, that the radiation from the nuke had rendered it too dirty. There were calls to leave the structure standing as a memorial, but the idea seemed ghoulish to Dunstan. Nobody needed a thousand-meter commemorative marker of the attack, a giant gravestone for forty thousand dead that would remind everyone of the trauma anew whenever they were within line of sight. He wouldn't need any external prompts to remember that day, and he doubted that anyone else would either. Mushroom clouds and burning cities were not something people could witness and then let the images fade from memory, overwritten by the trivialities of normal life.

The shuttle descended into the semicircle of the spaceport on top of Caledonia-2, and his line of sight to the gutted arcology on the horizon broke. Dunstan focused on his breath for a few moments to put his mind back on the task at hand, his impending meeting with the navy's operations chief.

—

"Commander Park, reporting as ordered, ma'am," Dunstan said.

"Do come in, Commander," Admiral Holmes said from her desk. "Take a seat, please."

"Yes, ma'am." Dunstan stepped into the office and sat down in one of the empty chairs in front of the admiral's desk. He looked around at the decorations on the walls. Every flag officer had an ego wall, but Rear Admiral Holmes's version of it was refreshingly modest, just a neat row of ship crests from previous commands and a few mementos from her time as a warship captain. The list of ships told him that she had seen combat during the war—a frigate, a light cruiser, then a battlecruiser, the ship class that was widely considered the crown jewel of command assignments.

"Would you care for some tea, Commander? We have a lovely strong Palladian blend if that is your sort of thing."

"It is, ma'am. Thank you."

"Edmund, would you get us some tea, please? And do activate the security field when you close the door."

"Aye, ma'am," the orderly said and stepped out of the room. The door closed behind him, and the red indicator lights on the door panel flashed three times to show that the anti-eavesdropping security protocol was now in place.

"Congratulations on your promotion," Admiral Holmes said. "Commander was always my favorite rank. High enough up the ladder for a consequential command. Not so high up that most of your day is spent checking boxes on admin forms."

"Thank you, ma'am," Dunstan replied. "I wasn't expecting it so soon. I barely had the time in grade for the promotion." He shifted a little in his chair and glanced down at his uniform to make sure it was still wrinkle-free.

"You seem a little uncomfortable. Everything all right this morning?"

"To be entirely frank with you, I wasn't expecting to see the navy chief of operations this morning," Dunstan replied. "I get a little jumpy when I am ushered into flag rank offices without warning. It usually means my day is about to become more complicated. No offense, Admiral."

Admiral Holmes chuckled.

"None taken. Keep that healthy sense of paranoia. It'll serve you well. But you can stop worrying. You're not here for a dressing-down."

She touched a control on her tabletop, and a screen projection opened in front of her. He could see that it was an excerpt of his personnel file. The admiral flicked through the data and opened another screen next to the first one, this one a little smaller and overlapping his personnel data.

"I'm sorry about *Minotaur*," she said. "It's a bad reward for her to be sent to the wreckers. But she did well. And so did you."

"I don't know about that," Dunstan replied. "I brought back a broken frigate. I was hoping she could be fixed. But I was sure that if she did go out again, it wouldn't be under me."

"I went through the after-action report with my deputy chief of operations and a few of my other people, Commander. Every one of us thought that you fought that ship as well as anyone could have hoped. You took on an enemy that was punching well above your weight class, and you fought them to a draw."

"We should have won that fight. We had a ship with new AI algorithms and a better Point Defense System. That fuzzhead cruiser hadn't seen any updates since the war. And whatever crew they had over on that ship, they were still getting used to their jobs."

"That fuzzhead cruiser was almost three times your mass. And you were outgunned from the start. That ship was designed to kill ships like *Minotaur*. Now stop the modesty and accept that command thinks you did just fine in that fight. And your ballistic intercept saved Rhodia One. I don't know if they told you yet, but the missile you destroyed had a nuclear payload as well."

The revelation gave Dunstan an unpleasant jolt. A nuclear detonation on Rhodia One would have obliterated the station and disabled or destroyed every ship docked there at the time. Almost forty thousand people perished on the ground when the second nuke hit close to the civilian arcology, but if the first one had hit the station, it would have killed fifty thousand more, crippled Rhodia's civilian space trade, and wiped out a quarter of the navy.

"We're not looking good out there right now," Admiral Holmes continued. She flicked aside the screen with his personnel file and brought up a strategic chart of the system.

"We're close to Hades and Pallas, so the transit lanes are as low energy as they've been in years. But we're not really making use of that advantage because the navy has taken a defensive posture around Rhodia. We can't keep a lid on the entire system, so we've decided to focus on the home sector. That nuclear strike threw everyone into a panic."

She magnified the view of the space around Rhodia, where the vast majority of red dots representing Rhodian Navy units was concentrated at the moment, guarding transit lanes and patrolling the space between them. But even this close to the planet, there was a lot of empty space between the little red dots.

"Five years I've been warning people that we need more hulls to do our jobs. But the war's over, and the Gretian fleet is gone," the admiral said. "Warships cost a lot of money to run. Too big a target for budget hawks to leave alone. And now look at us. Trying to spread a knife tip of butter over a slice of bread. And gods forbid we leave any spot uncovered, or people start screaming and calling for heads to roll."

"That cruiser is still out there," Dunstan said. "And so is that little stealth ship that launched the nukes. They'll have a harder time getting close to Rhodia now. But if they want to get another missile or two through our defenses . . ."

"You know as well as I do that it's all just a matter of how willing you are to die to get the kill," Admiral Holmes said.

She pointed to the clusters of red icons that were concentrated near the transit lanes, where the Rhodian Navy now turned a bright light on anyone entering Rhodian space on the way to the planet.

"Ship inspections take a lot of time and personnel. You know that. And I can't help but think that this was the point of that attack. To make everyone panic and draw us back home."

"I've had the same thought," Dunstan said. "It's the only way that missile strike makes sense."

"We can't lock down Rhodian space and patrol the transit lanes at the same time. Not with what we have right now. And the fewer ships we have out there, the more brazen the pirates get. Then the whole system gets destabilized. The Oceanians can look after their own space. So can the Acheroni. But that leaves a lot of empty space in between."

"What about the reserve fleet?" Dunstan asked. "I know they're reactivating a lot of ships. It's old wartime hardware, but it's plenty to do merchant lane patrols."

"We've got hulls, Commander. We just don't have enough people to crew them. You know the haircut the fleet got after the end of the war. It takes three months to pull an old frigate out of the boneyard and get her ready for action. It takes a *year* to train someone to serve on her. And that's just the rank-and-file enlisted crew. We don't have enough lieutenants and commanders around anymore. No space warfare officers, no engineers, no network specialists. It takes years to expand a fleet. The civilians think you can do it with the stroke of a pen."

Admiral Holmes sighed and turned off the screen with the chart projection.

"But we still have a job to do. And I'm the chief of operations, so I get to figure out how to do it with what we have."

By the door, a warning tone sounded, and the red indicator lights on the security panel flashed.

"Come in," Admiral Holmes said. The door opened to admit the orderly, who was carrying a small tray with two teacups. He brought it over to the admiral's desk and put it down carefully.

"Thank you, Edmund. That will be all for a while."

"Yes, ma'am." The orderly left the room again, and the security lock reactivated. Even here at fleet HQ, there were different layers and magnitudes of secrecy, and just because someone was cleared for one layer didn't mean they were fully trusted with the rest as well.

"That brings me to you," the admiral said. She offered a cup to Dunstan, and he took it with a nod of thanks. It was a fragrant Palladian tea with quite a bit of spice to it, enough to make his throat tickle a little.

"You are a bit of a rarity right now. You're a fully trained and experienced ship commander without a ship. And after what happened on your last deployment, there's no doubt that you're one of the best we have left. I've handpicked you for a special job."

"A special job," Dunstan repeated.

"I know, I know." Admiral Holmes sipped her tea and made a satisfied little sound. "Whenever you hear that word from a superior, you know you're about to get handed a shovel and pointed at a giant hill of shit."

Dunstan chuckled at her blunt statement. The admiral looked like she was close to retirement age, and her gray hair and stocky build made her look a little matronly. But he could tell that despite her grandmotherly appearance, she was as blunt and straightforward as any officer he had met out in the fleet.

"Well, I won't lie to you. I am about to point you at a giant hill of shit. But I am about to hand you a very nice shovel."

His interest piqued, he put his teacup down and watched as she tapped away at her desk surface. The screen that opened above the desk a moment later showed the longitudinal profile of a spaceship hull. It looked utterly unfamiliar to Dunstan.

"This is RNS *Hecate*," the admiral said.

Next to the ship profile, a short list of general parameters scrolled down the screen. The hull looked like nothing he had ever seen in the fleet. It wasn't an elegant ship. No two lines on her seemed to meet at right angles. She had a blunt, wide cylindrical shape, but he could tell that the hull didn't have the efficient, regular round or octagonal cross-section of most spaceships. Something about her shape seemed off, but he couldn't quite put his finger on it without examining the schematics in detail.

"*Hecate*," he repeated. "I've never heard of her. What class is she?"

"You won't have heard of her unless you have a level-one security clearance and a need to know. She's the lead ship of her class. The only ship of her class," the admiral added. "In the construction budget, she is listed as Multipurpose Corvette 212. We have two more on the way, but one's still getting fitted out and the other one is a month past having her hull spine laid."

"That's a 212 class," Dunstan said. The sinking feeling from earlier had returned to the center of his stomach. "A two-thousand-ton hull, if I recall correctly. Lightly armed."

"Eighteen hundred tons, actually. Fifty-six meters long. Five officers and twenty-two enlisted."

"*Minotaur* was three times that mass," Dunstan said. "I wasn't hoping for a battlecruiser command, Admiral. But that's a corvette hull. Corvettes aren't built to stand up to capital ships. You know what's still out there and waiting for us."

What am I going to do with that little nutshell against a heavy gun cruiser? he wanted to add.

The chief of operations looked at Dunstan with a wry smile.

"By all means, speak your mind, Commander. After all, you've worn the rank for—what, three full days now?"

Dunstan felt his face flush. He considered his reply and bought himself an extra moment by taking another sip of tea.

"No disrespect intended, ma'am. But a minute ago you were praising my performance, and now you're putting me from a frigate into a corvette. Forgive me if it feels a bit like a demotion."

"Size doesn't always matter, you know. And from your personnel file, I thought you would know not to make judgments on a situation until you have sufficient intel," the admiral said.

"Yes, ma'am." He put his teacup back onto the desk. "I did speak out of turn. My apologies."

Admiral Holmes increased the size of the screen in front of her and flicked the schematic of RNS *Hecate* around to send it into a slow spin around her dorsal axis. The ship had the mass and overall length of a corvette, but it didn't really look like one. Corvettes had external arrays, weapon mounts, and all the other trimmings of a warship, just on a smaller scale. *Hecate* had no visible hatches, comms equipment, or gun mounts. As the model on the screen spun to show a stern-on view, he could see why her hull shape had looked strange to him at first glance.

"Prismatic cross-section," he said, more to himself than to the admiral. "That's a stealth hull if I've ever seen one. What is this thing?"

"When the war started, we had a lot of the same problems we have now. Too few hulls, too few people to crew them. And that was when the fleet was four times as big as it is now. So we started an accelerated building program. But you know that we could barely keep up with the attrition rate. It was bankrupting the Gretians, but it was killing us, too. After the war, the navy put a bunch of their best R & D brains in a room and had them figure out how to break the meat grinder. Go away from the arms race of bigger hulls, thicker armor, more missiles. Find a way to dominate the battle space other than bringing bigger guns to the fight."

Admiral Holmes leaned back in her chair and nodded at the screen.

"They called it 'Project Athena.' That's the result right there. The first ship wasn't scheduled to be launched until next year. After the internment fleet incident, they put a lot of energy into getting her out early. She just came back from her shakedown cruise three days ago."

Dunstan studied the schematic as it kept up its slow rotation on the screen, trying to deduce her capabilities from the shape of the hull and the few external fixtures in evidence.

"I've never heard of Project Athena. And I try to stay on top of the rumor mill."

"It was a little easier to keep this under wraps because it's a small hull. It doesn't get the attention that a new battleship would get. From what I understand, the hardest part was hiding the insane amounts of money we sank into this thing without anyone noticing. And trust me that we don't want it noticed. Not even by the rest of the Alliance. If they knew what this ship can do, there would be discord."

"What *can* she do?" Dunstan asked.

"She's not a corvette, Commander. She's an information warfare cruiser. She has the latest in electronic warfare gear. We designed her as a space control ship. She has the sharpest eyes and keenest hearing of any ship in the system. And she's the most expensive ship in the navy, by a fair margin. One hundred tons of her mass are just the palladium for her AI processor. Her computing core can do more operations per millisecond than all the rest of the combined AIs of all the navy ships."

Dunstan sat up straight and looked at the hull schematic with new eyes.

"There are a *hundred* tons of palladium in that ship?"

"That is correct."

"Gods," he said. Every warship had a few tons of palladium built into it, most of it used for the gravmag rotor at the nose of the ship that generated gravity whenever the ship wasn't burning its drive at one g. The palladium that went into those rotors constituted a fair percentage of a warship's construction costs, and salvaging palladium from destroyed warships had been a dangerous but highly lucrative business during the war. Dunstan did the math and shook his head in disbelief.

"Ten billion ags," he said. "Good gods. A battleship costs half that."

"And that's just the material value of the palladium in the AI core and the data pathways. Throw in the costs for R & D and the construction, weapons systems and electronics . . . you get the scope of it. The total price tag was considerably higher. That's why we only have one of these right now and not fifty. As it is, she just about eviscerated our budget for a few years."

Dunstan tried to reconcile the shape of the ship on the screen with its monetary value. Palladium was used in small quantities all over the system. Whittling down the amounts of it needed for any product was the most important part of the design process. A comtab had just a gram or two, and consolidating the pathways to shave off half a gram could save hundreds of millions on the cost of manufacture. A hundred tons of palladium was an obscene amount. A merchant known to carry that much of it would be the juiciest piracy target in the system, and Dunstan would not put it past most of the planetary governments to try to claim it as well.

"And you want me to command her," he said. "I didn't even know that ship existed until just now. I don't know her layout, her capabilities. And if she just got back from her shakedown cruise, her crew barely had time to get familiar with her."

"I know you're a quick learner, Commander," Admiral Holmes said. "And you'll have an excellent first officer to show you the ropes."

"What about her current commander?"

"He had to take medical leave. I do not have the time to wait for him because I need that ship out there right now. That means you'll have to jump in and take over. I realize I'm making you hit the ground running. Your first officer knows the ship. I want someone in charge who knows how to fight. Who has shown they can keep their head when it counts."

Dunstan looked from the admiral to the schematic of RNS *Hecate*, which was still spinning in the space above the admiral's desk to show off all her angles. It seemed risky to take responsibility of a ship that was unknown to him, brand new, and unproven in battle. But there was a sort of excitement in the challenge—to be trusted with the most expensive unit in the navy. If the admiral wasn't overselling the *Hecate*'s capabilities, she had the potential to be a much greater force against the insurgency than any destroyer or cruiser they could hand him.

I knew that shiny new stripe would come with a shiny new cart to pull uphill, he thought.

"If that's where the navy needs me, that's what I'll do," he said.

Admiral Holmes rewarded his statement with a satisfied nod.

"Very well, Commander. I'll have the data for your new command sent to you so you can familiarize with her as much as you can before you take over."

"How much time do I have?" Dunstan asked.

"The crew are on their two-week leave. I thought about cutting their leave short, but I need a fresh and motivated contingent for *Hecate*'s first combat patrol. You have a week to prepare."

"Yes, ma'am. I'll make the best of it."

"I know you will."

Dunstan got out of his chair and straightened his uniform.

"I appreciate your confidence in me. I'll do my best to live up to the navy's expectations."

Admiral Holmes turned off her screen, and the schematic of RNS *Hecate* disappeared. Then she touched a control on her table, and a few moments later, the security light blinked and her orderly entered the room. Dunstan put his cap under his arm and walked over to the door.

"One more thing, Commander," the admiral said. Dunstan turned around.

"Yes, ma'am."

"You'll be out there by yourself, with nobody else to lean on if things get tough. You will have a great deal of leeway. But with that comes a great deal of responsibility. However things shape up out there, your first priority is that ship. I hope it never comes down to it. But *Hecate* is the most important asset in the navy right now. Whoever has her can dictate the course of the next war. You need to be prepared to do whatever it takes to keep her from falling into the wrong hands. *Whatever it takes*, Commander Park."

The directive sent an unpleasant little trickle down Dunstan's spine.

"I'll see to it that it doesn't come down to that, ma'am," he replied.

"I know you will. Good luck and fair skies."

He turned to follow the orderly out of the office, eager to get back outside and let the sunlight in the atrium disperse the sense of foreboding that had settled on his mind at the admiral's parting words.

CHAPTER 4

SOLVEIG

On the forward bulkhead of the Ragnar yacht, Gretia's northern hemisphere took up most of the viewscreen, a sunlit tapestry of green, blue, and brown hues spread out before the ship. It was a clear summer day above much of the northern continent, and Solveig could make out the geometric lines of the Sandvik city grid and the spiderweb of transportation arteries spreading out from the capital.

To think that some of us felt all this wasn't enough, Solveig mused. *That we needed more, when we had so much already.* Now they were all paying the price. Gretia was still itself, but it was no longer in charge of its own fate. The Alliance planets were in control now. And in times like these, they made sure to remind the Gretians of that fact as often as possible.

"We are now coming alongside the Rhodian Navy ship for our pre-docking inspection," the pilot announced from the maneuvering deck. *"Please return to your seats and buckle in just in case we have a bumpy rendezvous sequence."*

Solveig was already in her seat, and now she reached up and pulled down the harness of the restraint system to strap herself in as directed. In the seat next to hers, Gisbert made a generalized noise of discontent and started doing the same. The vice president of operations for Ragnar Industries was no longer bothering to fake the congeniality he had worn like a thin veneer at the start of this trip. They were over a week late for their return because all flights into Gretia had to be inspected now, and the yacht had to delay its departure from Acheron because they'd had to wait for a security clearance slot.

"This is our *home*," Gisbert grumbled as he struggled with the locking tabs of his restraints. "*Our* world. It's shameful that we have to ask permission to return."

"They won the war," Solveig said. "They get to make the rules."

"That was *five years* ago. Half a decade. At what point do we let the past be the past?"

I wonder if he voted for the war, Solveig thought. She concluded that she likely knew the answer. Gisbert wasn't one to go against the grain. He was one of her father's handpicked executives, elevated from the ranks for loyalty rather than ability. And Falk Ragnar had voted in favor of the war when he was on the High Council, Gretia's committee of 128 plot holders who had charted the course for the entire planet right into ruin. Half a million dead, a system economy in tatters, and Gisbert was offended that the Alliance wouldn't let bygones be bygones already.

On the forward bulkhead, the viewscreen changed to a different exterior angle. It showed the Rhodian corvette that was now alongside the yacht to starboard, only a few dozen meters away. The Ragnar ship was sleek and elegant, all flowing lines clad in silver and white. The warship was a study in contrasts, angled armor plating painted in matte black, bristling with sensor arrays and weapons. The rail-gun mount on the stern section of the Rhodian ship was aimed at the Ragnar yacht, a gesture of dominance and intimidation that made Solveig uneasy. It seemed a gratuitous display to her, pointing weapons at an obviously unarmed civilian leisure craft, but she supposed that was the point.

They get to make the rules, she reminded herself. *And nobody can blame them for being jumpy after what happened on Rhodia.* A few weeks ago, someone had gotten a missile with a nuclear warhead through the planetary defenses in the biggest act of terrorism ever committed in the history of the system. And now the war that had started to feel like the memory of a bad dream was threatening to flare up and set the whole system on fire again.

A few minutes later, Anja and Inga, the two executive assistants on the delegation, came up the ladder from the passenger deck below, followed by the bodyguards, Cuthbert and Fulco. Behind them, a Rhodian marine in full armor appeared, then another. They had their helmet visors open, but the vision slits only revealed their eyes and the bridges of their noses. Solveig put her translating bud in her ear. Next to her, Gisbert made no attempt to follow suit as he looked at the newcomers with a sullen expression.

"Apologies, Miss Ragnar, but they want us all in the same compartment while they look over the ship," Anja said.

"It's fine, Anja," Solveig replied.

"Do not sit down," one of the Rhodians said when Inga made to claim one of the empty seats in the VIP compartment. "Everyone line up over there and remain standing."

He gestured over to the back of the compartment, where there was some open space between the seating arrangements and the refreshment station.

Solveig unbuckled her harness and got out of her seat to do as instructed. Gisbert looked from her to the marines and back uncomprehendingly, and she nodded at the space they were told to occupy.

"Put your translator in, please," Solveig told him. "This will take twice as long if Inga has to relay everything they say."

Gisbert hesitated, obviously displeased, then fished his earbud out of his pocket and put it in. He got out of his seat in no particular hurry and moved to join the rest of the group. Solveig felt her own irritation rising. She had mildly disliked Gisbert before the business trip to Acheron, but two weeks with him had intensified that dislike into antipathy. The man had added no value to the mission, and his arrogance and tone deafness had been a constant source of irritation to her.

Over by the ladderwell, another pair of Rhodians came up and continued on to the flight deck above the VIP compartment. All the marines were armed with pistols, which they carried in holsters attached to their chest armor. From the way Cuthbert and Fulco were tracking the Rhodians with their eyes, Solveig could tell that the bodyguards were not at all happy to have several armed Alliance marines in the room with their protectee. But this inspection was the price of admission back onto Gretia, and there was nothing left to do but to bear the inconvenience.

"ID passes," one of the soldiers said.

"ID passes, *please*," Gisbert replied. "This is a Gretian ship in Gretian space. Let us not forget courtesy."

The Rhodian soldier took a half step toward Gisbert.

"ID passes," he repeated.

Gisbert took his pass card out of a pocket and handed it to the marine, who snatched it from his fingers in an aggressively quick move. The marine passed it back to his comrade without taking his eyes off Gisbert.

"Only say 'yes, sir' or 'no, sir' to me from now on, or I'll put this ship at the back of the clearance queue. Understood?"

Gisbert opened his mouth to reply, and for a second Solveig thought he would continue with his haughty attitude and buy them all three more days of waiting time in orbit. But then he seemed to catch himself, even though Solveig could see that his jaw muscles flexed with suppressed anger.

"Yes, sir," he replied with carefully precise diction.

The marine turned to his comrade and chuckled.

"Courtesy," he said. "Did I hear this one right?"

The other marine's eyes narrowed. He gave Gisbert a long up-and-down look.

"Courtesy," he repeated. "You've had courtesy for five years. Now we have thirty-seven thousand dead. A quarter million injured or still missing. The time for courtesy is over."

Solveig had to wait a second for the translation to arrive in her ear, but she knew the Rhodian word for courtesy, and the way the marine pronounced it made it sound like an obscenity.

"That wasn't us," she said. "Nobody on this ship had anything to do with that."

The marine shifted his gaze from Gisbert to her. He looked at her for a long moment.

"Unfortunately, I can't just take your word for that," he said.

"This is a business craft," she replied. "We have no weapons. No cargo other than our luggage. Surely the Rhodian Navy can tell a corporate yacht from a warship."

"Whoever dropped a nuclear weapon on our planet two weeks ago didn't use a warship," the marine said. "They sneaked in with a quick little civilian ship. Much like this one. Now get out your ID passes and submit to a search. Unless you want a few days to think about it. Or turn around and go back to where you came from."

Solveig knew that their ship didn't have the fuel to make the trip back to Acheron, and she suspected that the Rhodian marine was well aware of that fact. They had no choice but to jump through whatever hoops the Alliance had set up to obtain docking clearance. She couldn't begrudge the Rhodians their anger—*thirty-seven thousand dead!*—but it still felt like collective punishment to her, and for the first time, she felt herself agreeing with Gisbert on something, even if it was just a fleeting impulse.

She handed her ID pass to the marine, who handed it to his colleague. She watched as the second marine scanned her pass and brought up a screen to read the results.

"Ragnar," he said. "Same as the company name. You must be the VIP."

"I'm nobody important," she said.

"Important enough to have your name on the side of this ship."

"We were all on Acheron when the attack happened. You can check the movement data on our passes. We spent the last two weeks in Coriolis City on business."

He replied without taking his eyes off the screen.

"Movement data can be faked. ID passes can be counterfeited. Ship transponders can be duplicated. I don't trust anything except my own eyes right now."

The marines went down the row of Ragnar people, taking ID passes and scanning them one by one. When they had finished with Fulco at the end of the line, one of the Rhodians pointed to the seating in the center of the deck.

"You may sit down now while we perform our inspection of your vessel. Do not leave this deck or interfere with Rhodian military personnel. We will return your ID passes to you when we have completed the inspection."

They did as they were told. When Solveig sat down again and strapped herself in, she felt a little like a chastened schoolgirl. One of the Rhodian marines went down the ladder to the deck below. The other one took up position by the staircase and stood in a relaxed posture, hands clasped over the sidearm holster on his armor's chest plate. Gisbert exchanged a look with Solveig, his face still showing sour distaste, but a glance at the marine standing watch seemed to convince him to keep his mouth shut.

That's the smartest thing you've done in two weeks, Solveig thought.

Thirty minutes later, the marine returned from belowdecks, this time with three more of his comrades. Solveig got out of her chair when she saw them coming up the staircase, and the rest of the delegation followed her lead.

"We have almost finished our inspection," one of the marines said. "Please step over to the rear bulkhead one by one for a physical scan."

The Gretians exchanged looks.

"You want to search us?" Solveig asked. Next to her, Gisbert let out a nonplussed little gasp.

"Just a pat-down, miss. And a brief scan with a handheld unit. You may refuse, but—"

"I know," she said. "Back of the line."

She walked to the rear bulkhead, waving off Anja in the process, who had been about to do the same.

"I'll go first. Let's get this done so we can all be on our way."

Two of the marines followed her to the bulkhead. One mimicked for her to extend her arms away from her body, which she did. He produced a handheld scanner and ran it down her front, then her sides and back. When he was finished, the other marine stepped forward and patted down the front of her body. He wasn't particularly gentle, and he didn't even try to give her an explanation or ask for her consent. When he switched to patting down her back, he did so without asking her to turn around. Solveig thought that his hands were lingering on the curve of her ass for just a little longer than required for the professed task, even though she was sure he couldn't feel much through the gloves of his armor. Cuthbert, her bodyguard, seemed to have the same thought because he perked up and took a step toward the two soldiers.

"Hey," he said, anger flaring up in his voice. "Watch where you're touching her."

The marine who was patting her down stopped his search and turned around. His hand went to the butt of the pistol strapped to his chest.

"Please," he said to Cuthbert. "Give me a reason. Put some fun into my day."

Cuthbert froze in place and looked from the marine to Solveig and back. The struggle was evident in his expression. It was his job to keep her safe, and seeing an armed stranger touching her without her permission would go against all his instincts and his training. But Marten had picked him well enough, because he raised his hands in acquiescence and stepped back even though Solveig could still see the anger on his face.

"You have already scanned her," he said. "What are you hoping to find on her backside?"

The marine slowly moved his hand off the pistol's grip. Then he tapped the Rhodian insignia emblazoned on his chest armor next to the gun.

"This says I can do whatever I want up here," he said. "Because we won the fucking war. Don't forget your place."

"The scanner doesn't see everything," the other marine explained. "Pat-downs are standard procedure."

"Do we look like smugglers to you?" Cuthbert asked.

The first marine let out a humorless laugh.

"The fuck do smugglers look like, huh? Bunch of rogues in dirty flight suits? Flying some rusty shit pile?"

He made a gesture that vaguely encompassed the whole VIP deck.

"People who travel like this," he said. "People who can afford adaptive AI shielding that can defeat a handheld scanner. She could have three hundred grams of weapons-grade plutonium in a Class VI capsule strapped to her thigh and the scanner wouldn't see shit."

"Let him do his job, Cuthbert," Solveig said. "I'm fine. I just want to go home."

The first marine looked back at her.

"Listen to the smart one here," he said to Cuthbert. "Let me do my job. You think I get some kick out of doing scans and pat-downs up here for three months straight?"

"Please," Solveig said. "Forgive my security detail. I'm sure he meant no disrespect. It's his job to be protective."

The marine looked back at her, and she held eye contact when he did, doing her best to look contrite and worried. She found that she didn't have to fake the worry. The last thing she wanted to do right now was to spend three more days up here in Gisbert's company, eating meals from the ship's limited variety of galley food and not being able to stretch her legs properly. After the days-long journey from Acheron, she was yearning for some fresh air and a long, sweat-inducing run along the lake back home.

The Rhodian regarded her for a few seconds, his expression unreadable behind the impersonal facets of his matte black helmet.

"Right now he would serve you best by shutting his mouth and standing still in that spot until it's his turn," he finally said.

Solveig shot Cuthbert a cautioning look.

"We aren't here to cause you any problems," she said to the soldier.

He repeated his pat-down. The second one was every bit as rough and invasive as the first, as if he wanted to provoke Cuthbert into reacting again. But her security officer took the unspoken warning to heart because he didn't stir from his spot this time even though Solveig could practically hear his teeth grinding. Finally, the marine seemed satisfied that she wasn't hiding any contraband on her body. He motioned for her to step back and pointed at Anja.

"You next. Let's go."

Solveig watched the frisk of her entourage, which took several minutes. It seemed excessive and punitive despite the Rhodian marine's explanation of the necessity. If she had doubted the reasoning before, watching the Rhodians at work just reinforced that doubt. This was security theater, put in place to make the Rhodians feel like they were in power and show the Gretians that they weren't.

When they were finished with their search, the marines had them sit down again. From her seated perspective, the lead marine looming above her seemed huge and almost inhuman in his bulky armor.

"You are required to surrender your communication devices for inspection," he said.

"Our *comtabs*?" Gisbert said with renewed pique in his voice. "Those have personal information on them."

"The Rhodian military isn't interested in your private little secrets," the marine replied. "We will merely copy the location history and compare it with the movement records from the Mnemosyne. Again, you are free to refuse. But you will be denied docking clearance if you do."

For some reason, having to hand over her comtabs felt more invasive to Solveig than having her ass groped by a stranger. A good chunk of her personal life was on her device—finances, workout routines, message history between her and most people she knew. She was sure that if the Rhodians could get into her device and past the commercial encryption, they wouldn't limit their intelligence gathering to just her location history. But she was used to covering her tracks when it came to the stuff she didn't want anyone else to read. She doubted that the Rhodian intelligence services were any better at snooping than her father's own corporate security division.

She took her comtab from the Rhodian and authorized the device, then handed it back to him.

"This one, too," he said and held out her corporate comtab.

Solveig hesitated briefly. Then she authorized the device for limited access. The Rhodians would be able to get the basic information off it, but the executive comtabs were secured with the most advanced encryption money could buy, and if they wanted to dig deeper than just mere location data, they'd need a lot of time and computing power.

The marine took the second comtab and handed it back to one of his comrades, who placed it in a data scanner.

"Thank you for your cooperation," he said to Solveig.

"Of course," she said, giving him a curt smile that she had to force. Being courteous to these marines felt a little like being nice to a hostage taker to make sure he wouldn't hurt her, and she didn't like the way it made her feel: powerless, cowardly, self-abasing.

They surrendered their devices to the marine one by one, and the scans of all the personal and business comtabs took almost as long as the physical searches. Finally, the Rhodians seemed to be satisfied with the inspection.

"You may take your personal devices and return to your business," the lead marine said. The Rhodian troops filed out of the compartment and went down the staircase, leaving relieved silence in their wake.

"I am going to have corporate file a complaint with the occupation authority," Gisbert said when the last soldier was out of sight.

They have 37,000 reasons to tell you off, Solveig thought. *They'll do whatever it takes to feel less scared.* And a nuke on a civilian target out of the blue was a perfectly understandable catalyst for fear. But as much as she understood that, being on the receiving end of the Alliance reaction didn't serve to make her sympathetic to it.

A few minutes later, the bulkhead display showed the docking collar retracting from the side of the Ragnar yacht and withdrawing into the hull of the Rhodian Navy corvette. Solveig saw that even after the thorough inspection, the rail-gun mount of the warship was still pointed at them, the Alliance crew leaving nothing to chance. Whatever trust had been rekindled between Gretia and the rest of the system since the end of the war seemed to have been thoroughly doused by the insurgent attack on Rhodia.

"We are free to maneuver again. Please take your seats, buckle in, and prepare for our final docking approach into the spin station," one of the pilots announced from the flight deck.

Cuthbert got up and mentioned for Fulco to follow, and the two assistants got out of their seats as well. Cuthbert nodded at Solveig and went to lead the Ragnar staff back down to the deck where they had their assigned seating. On the viewscreen, the Rhodian corvette fired its bow thrusters to nudge the ship away from the Ragnar yacht. Solveig felt a swell of relief when the warship disappeared from her field of vision.

The gravmag system of the yacht compensated for the thrust inertia so effectively that she couldn't feel the ship moving at all when the pilot reactivated the main drive, but the changing visuals on the viewscreen left no doubt that they were now finally on the last leg of their long trip. Solveig took a sip of water and looked out over the expanse of blue and green that was unfurling below the ship as they made their approach into the station. Right above the planetary horizon, the position lights of dozens of ships were blinking against the backdrop of space like fireflies in a night sky. In a slightly lower orbit, much closer to the yacht and clearly outlined against the cloud cover above the main continent, two more warships were floating in a loose formation, slowly arcing across her field of view like a pair of guard dogs patrolling a yard.

"At least we're finally going home," Gisbert said next to her and took a sip from the drink he'd had to put aside at the start of the inspection. Solveig made a noncommittal noise and returned her attention to the viewscreen.

It doesn't really feel like going home right now, she thought. *It feels like checking into a prison.*

Chapter 5

Aden

The place where Tristan had set up station was one of the posh resorts that catered to well-to-do tourists. It jutted out into the sea near the tip of the southeastern leaf. Each of the individual condominium pods had its own floating pad out on the water, and the pads were connected to a central access pier with a network of long, slender bridges and suspended walkways that were just wide enough for two people to walk on them side by side.

"When Tristan goes all out, he does not screw around," Aden said. He watched a service drone flit overhead on silent rotors and head out over the water to one of the nearby condos. It circled the top of the dome and then disappeared inside to deliver whatever food or drink the guests in residence had ordered.

"This is how he likes to spend his money," Tess said. "I can't really criticize him. I spend mine on things that go fast. We all have our vices, right?"

They were following the directions on a screen projection of Aden's comtab. Tristan had sent them the location and told them that he'd added their comtab IDs to the security locks of the condo, and now they were out on the water, following the branches of the bridges and walkways that connected all the floating buildings of the resort. Everything was oriented so that each condo had an unobstructed view of the ocean. The units were all shaped like seashells, irregular fanlike designs with huge 180-degree windows facing the water. Aden had no idea what one of these places cost to rent for a week, but he suspected it was probably enough to fuel *Zephyr* for a no-holds-barred speed run from Oceana to Acheron. This wasn't the sort of resort for people who fixed spaceships, it was for people who owned them.

The walkways above the water were all made from a metal latticework, painted with brilliantly white corrosion-resistant paint, and the space between the struts was covered with wooden slats that afforded glimpses of the water through the cracks between them. To Aden, this was the most ostentatious display of casual wealth he had seen in a while. To someone from Gretia, tree wood was not a precious commodity, but there were no trees on Oceana. Every single one of these wood slabs had to have been delivered from somewhere else via space freighter at ludicrous expense. He stopped in the middle of one of the walkway segments and crouched down to touch the surface with his fingertips. Tess looked down at him with mild amusement.

"Those aren't real," she said. "They can't be."

"I don't know," he replied. "I can't really tell from the feel."

"They make really convincing synthetic wood. It's better than the real stuff in every way. And a twentieth of the cost."

"I guess you're right."

"Think about how wasteful it would be to spend twenty times the money on something that's not half as durable. With the seawater, they'd need to replace these every ten years. Or repaint them one by one."

And that's how I know they're real wood, he thought. *The wastefulness is the point. This is the sort of place my father would choose for his stay if he ever came here.* But Falk Ragnar had only grudgingly spent a few weeks every summer here on the planet of his wife's birth, and Aden's sister, Solveig, had told him that when their mother had left him, he had never returned here again. Aden looked up and smiled at Tess. His crewmates were much more knowledgeable than he was when it came to spaceships and spin stations, approach vectors and burn rates, but with the possible exception of Tristan, they didn't know anything about how rich people thought or why they did what they did. Tess was thinking like a pragmatic engineer, not like someone who could build an estate and spend a few million ags on a private lake and a floating bar just for the purpose of impressing other rich people.

"Come on," Tess said. "It's a little hot, and I'm a little thirsty. I don't want to crack those bottles open before we get to Tristan's place. Even if he's probably drinking already."

"There's no *probably* about it," Aden said.

Tristan's condo was at the end of a long walkway branch in what looked like the most secluded and private part of the resort, a full ten-minute walk from the main pier. His clamshell had a wide balcony that wrapped around the building, and as they walked up, they could see lounging furniture on it, and a metal staircase and catwalk that led to the water below. Tess walked up to the door and touched the security panel. It changed from red to green with a warm and friendly sounding chime, and the door opened silently.

"Tristan," Tess called out when they stepped through the door. "We're here. You better be somewhat dressed. And a towel doesn't really count."

Inside, the condominium pod was mostly one big, open room. The design language of the resort's buildings was continued in here as well, with flowing lines, soft lighting, and hues of mostly white and light blue. The middle of the floor was lowered to form a small pit, which was lined with seating arrangements. In the middle of the pit, a large transparent table was already set for six. On the other side of the living area, there was a kitchen nook that looked like it was about three times the size of the galley on *Zephyr*. Aden saw that Tristan had been busy preparing ingredients for whatever he was planning to cook for them. A row of little bowls sat on the counter between the kitchen nook and the living area, each with a different chopped or sliced ingredient: peppers, vegetables, seafood, and plenty of stuff Aden didn't recognize. The tall wraparound windows had no visible frames, and the view of the ocean was unspoiled except for the waist-high Alon rail on the edge of the balcony outside. There was soft music playing over an unseen sound projection system, the jaunty jazz-fusion style that Tristan liked to listen to whenever he was busy in the galley.

Tess walked into the living area pit and let herself drop onto one of the cushy-looking couches.

"This is nice," she proclaimed. "I have no idea how he always finds these posh places. Can you believe some people live like this all the time?"

"I've known a few," Aden replied. Any of the guesthouses on his father's estate were every bit as nice as this one, even if they lacked the ocean view. And as posh as this condo was, just the Old Earth antiques lining the hallway to his father's study were probably valuable enough to buy half a dozen of these seashell pods outright.

There was a little sanitary alcove on the wall to the left of the kitchen nook that looked like it led to a bathroom. Next to the alcove, another door stood halfway open. He walked over to it and lightly knocked on the frame.

"Tristan? We're here. I brought some Rhodian single malt."

There was no answer from the room. Aden pushed the sliding door open and looked inside. The windows were tinted to their semi-opaque state, and the bedroom was shrouded in semidarkness. Tristan was stretched out on the bed, one arm behind his head to prop it up, the other on his chest. His eyes were closed, and he looked like he was comfortably asleep. On the table next to the bed, there was a glass that had two fingers of an amber liquor and a few ice cubes in it.

Aden walked into the bedroom.

"Wake up, man. Henry and Decker will be here any minute. I see you got a bit of a head start on the whisky."

When he was two steps closer to the bed, the feeling that something wasn't right asserted itself in his brain, and the sudden, unwelcome burst of adrenaline felt almost like an electric jolt.

"Room, turn off the window tint," he said. The suite's AI obeyed and reduced the opaqueness of the windows until the sunlight streamed into the room unfiltered. In the light, Tristan still looked like he was sleeping, but Aden's heart skipped a beat when he saw that Tristan's chest wasn't rising and falling with his breath.

"*Tess,*" he shouted. Then he rushed over to Tristan and put his hand on the cook's chest to stir him awake. The fabric of Tristan's dark robe felt wet under Aden's fingers. His first thought was that Tristan had spilled some of his drink, but when he turned his hand to look at it, his palm had red smears on it.

Tess barged into the bedroom behind him.

"What's wrong? What is it?"

"Something's wrong with Tristan."

She went to the other side of the bed. When she saw the blood on Aden's hands, she let out a shaky gasp. She touched Tristan's neck and held her hand there to feel for a pulse.

"He's warm, Aden. But I can't feel a pulse. Gods, I can't feel a *pulse.* What the hells happened?"

Aden grabbed Tristan by the shoulders and tried to pull up his upper body. When Tristan's body shifted slightly, they both saw the blood underneath that had been pooling there for a little while, a dark splotch that looked almost black even in the bright sunlight. The front of Tristan's robe shifted, and Aden saw where all that blood had originated—a small wound in his chest, just below the sternum. Blood was pouring out silently and without drama, running down both sides of his chest and toward his back.

"Call emergency services," he said to Tess. "See if there's a medkit in the bathroom. Grab whatever towels you can find."

She groaned in despair and let go of Tristan, then ran off toward the living area. Aden looked around for something he could use to staunch the steady flow of blood that was coming from Tristan's wound, but there was nothing around that seemed suitable except for the pillows, and by the time he had ripped one of the covers into strips, Tess would be back with the proper medkit, which would have a few packets of quick-clot thermal wound sealer in it. Rental places always had medkits in them, and even the basic ones had far better ways in them to plug wounds than torn-off strips of fabric.

He held one hand on Tristan's wound and put the other one on top to apply pressure. The last time he'd had to practice his medic skills had been in the Blackguards, where all military intelligence field operatives had received the basic combat medic course. He had always wondered how useful all that knowledge would be under stress, but it had come back to him as if his brain had been waiting for an opportunity to dust off those neuron groups so they could finally fire again in the same pattern. Now he had a reason to be grateful for the constant drills, even if his younger self hadn't fully appreciated their utility.

"Aden," Tess called out from the next room. He looked back at her and saw that she was standing just beyond the doorway in the living space area. He opened his mouth to shout back that he was busy, that he was keeping Tristan's life from seeping out of him any further, but something about the tone of her voice made him hold his tongue.

He put Tristan's hand in place of his own to cover the wound just the way it had been when he walked in. Then he stood up and rushed over to Tess to see what was rooting her in place.

There was someone else in the condo with them. He was lightly leaning against the wall by the bathroom, putting himself between Tess and the way out. Aden recognized him right away, and from the way Tess had stiffened, he knew that she had as well. He was wearing different clothes, but the handsome face and the haircut were not hard to remember from that night in the Halo 212 club on Acheron two weeks ago. If there had been any doubt about his identity, the two ceramic knives in his right hand were incontrovertible final proof. He held them loosely, like someone would carry a set of silverware, but that didn't mitigate the threat of their appearance in the slightest. One of those knives had poked a hole in Maya's side right in front of the whole crew, and even Henry had gauged the man as dangerous enough to stay his own hand on the hilt of his kukri.

For a moment, time seemed to slow—a second or two stretched out into perceptual infinity. Aden looked around for some way of escape, but Milo stood between them and the only way out, and there was no way for them to make the balcony beyond the lounge pit without getting stabbed, even if they could wish the sliding doors open on the way.

"Is there something about me that seems insincere?" Milo asked. His expression was one of light puzzlement. Despite their dire situation, it seemed to irritate Tess enough for her to let out an exasperated little huff.

"I'm not going to play this game," she said. "The one where I set you up for clever one-liners."

"Because I keep having this problem where people seem to doubt the veracity of my statements. And then they seem shocked and surprised when I come to do what I told them I would do," Milo continued, as if he hadn't heard Tess's refusal to answer.

Despite his fear, Aden felt his anger flaring up. Tristan was lying in the room behind them without a heartbeat, and every moment that passed before medics reached him reduced his chances of coming back. But he knew that Milo wouldn't be moved by any pleas, and Aden was under no illusion about the outcome if he gave in to his anger and tried to fight his way out of this condo, so he had to save that option for last.

"When we met, I gave you two options," Milo said. The way he was leaning against the wall was infuriatingly casual, his body language that of a mildly bored party guest instead of someone who had come to kill everyone in the room.

"One option was to do as you were told and fly your ship to the coordinates we provided. The other option was to refuse and pay in blood instead. I told you there would be no third option. And now I'm here to collect the payment."

Out of the corner of his eye, Aden saw that Tess had shifted her weight almost imperceptibly. On the counter to her left, Tristan had laid out his prepared ingredients, and his knife roll sat at the edge of the countertop, the cooking knives neatly lined up and ready to use for the next step.

He'll never finish cooking that meal for us, Aden thought.

"'Pay in blood instead,'" Tess said in a mocking voice. "The *veracity* of your statements. Who the fuck talks like that? You want to kill us, get on with it. But spare us the pretentious shit."

Aden's mind cycled through possible solutions, trying to find a way out of this that didn't end with more blood on the floor, but there was nothing he could think of that could either convince Milo to put his knives away or see him on the losing end of a fight. But Tess seemed to be set on a last-ditch act of defiance, and the only way he saw to keep that from happening was to distract Milo and draw his attention. Every second they could draw breath was one where they still had a shot at fate or chance intervening in some way. He decided to follow the hunch he'd had since he first heard Milo talk, the one that had just now become stronger as the other man had kept up his overly precise and formal diction.

"I know what you are," he said in Gretian. "I know where you learned foreign languages. I'm fairly sure we had some of the same instructors."

The surprise on Milo's face seemed like the first genuine emotion Aden had seen out of him. He smiled thinly and looked at Aden as if he were reevaluating him.

"So you're one of us, then," he replied. "I never would have guessed. You talk just like one of the shell munchers. Your instructor must have been better than mine."

From the way Milo spoke, it was obvious that Gretian was his first language, and Aden was once again reminded what made someone sound like a native. Milo's Gretian had a regional inflection, the slightly softened consonants common in the capital region. His Oceanian had been clean and neutral, without any trace of an accent.

"Some people have an ear for it," Aden said.

"It was never my favorite subject. But go ahead. Take a guess. You've got me curious now."

"Military language institute," Aden wagered. "You don't seem like someone who was on the diplomatic track. But I don't remember your face from the branch training. So you were covert. Special activities division. Or maybe counterintelligence."

Milo nodded. "Not bad. You're pretty close. So you're field intelligence."

"I was," Aden said. He didn't want to glance over at Tess and give her away, but he could tell that she was tensing up for something, and the distance between them had increased ever so slightly. "In the 300th Signals Intel. But that's long in the past. I'm someone else now. The war's been over for five years, you know."

"Has it really," Milo said with that thin smile of his. He was a handsome man, and Aden would have guessed that his face was too distinctive for covert fieldwork. He certainly would have remembered him from the service. The military intelligence community was small, and he had run into the same people over and over. But training in the regular signals division didn't focus heavily on combat, and whatever this man had done in his time in the service, it had involved more than just standard hand-to-hand training. Every planet had covert intel operatives, and the Special Activities Division of the Gretian intelligence service heavily recruited from the top 10 percent of the military's elite commando units.

"It has," Aden affirmed. "And we got what we deserved."

The smile on Milo's face faltered a little. He turned the knives in his right hand idly, rotating the handles against each other.

"Maybe it was over for *you*," Milo replied. "You turned in your flags and you let them take your guns. March you off into internment. Fill your heads with guilt and self-loathing. But maybe some of us never quit. Maybe only you got what you deserved. For giving up when you still had fight in you."

To Aden's left, Tess darted for the counter and Tristan's knife roll. If Milo was surprised, it didn't show in the speed of his reaction. He rushed toward her, shifting one knife into his other hand as he went. Aden reacted reflexively. He dashed into Milo's path and slammed into him with all the force he could muster. Milo was fast and agile, but he was half a head shorter than Aden and probably a good ten or fifteen kilos lighter. They collided, and the force of Aden's impact hurled them both over the edge of the padded couch lining the rim of the dinner pit. One of Milo's knives fell from his hand and clattered to the floor somewhere nearby. The men hit the glass dinner table and flipped it off its legs, and all the dishes and utensils went flying. Aden tried to grab Milo's other arm to control the knife, but Milo was already squirming his way out from underneath him, and Aden felt a sharp, bright pain along his left arm as the blade sliced the length of his forearm.

He punched Milo with his right hand and tried to pin him to the ground, to immobilize the arm that held the remaining knife, but Milo knew more about ground fighting than Aden did. They struggled for leverage over each other for a moment, and then Milo was out of his grasp, and Aden scrambled backward to avoid the knifepoint that was lashing out at him. He kicked at the arm that held the knife to deflect the tip of the blade. For a few seconds, they engaged in a high-stakes contest of jabs and feints and kicks. Then Tess was there, one of Tristan's cooking knives in her hand, and Milo jumped to his feet to meet her charge.

Tess held her knife with the tip down, and the way she handled it made Aden think that she was no stranger to defending herself with a blade, but he knew that this would not be an even contest regardless of how many drunken spacers she may have nicked in seedy dive bars over the years. He struggled to his knees and scooped up the object on the ground that was closest to his hand, a beverage tumbler that had fallen off the table when they had turned it over. He hurled it at Milo, who was squaring off against Tess, and it hit him in the shoulder and made him raise his left arm reflexively. Aden grabbed whatever else was littering the floor around him and flung it at the other man—spoons, plates, cups, anything to distract him and keep him from giving Tess his undivided attention.

She jabbed her blade at Milo's chest, but he turned aside and avoided it, and when her arm was committed and extended into the attack, he flicked the tip of his own blade upward and jabbed it into her arm. She withdrew with a pained shout, and he followed up with another quick stab to her shoulder. Aden launched himself at him again, but this time Milo dodged the tackle and danced backward with infuriatingly light-footed ease. Aden tried to withdraw, but Milo darted forward and stuck him with the knife twice, quick and shallow jabs to his side and upper thigh, then retreated a step and gave his knife a little twirl.

He's playing with his food, Aden thought. *We are going to die right here and now, once he decides that he has had enough amusement.* Next to him, Tess had shifted her knife to her left hand, and her face was contorted in pain. Her right arm hung limply from her side, splattering big globs of blood on the white flooring. Aden's own arm felt like someone had set it on fire from elbow to wrist, and he could feel the warm slickness of his blood as it ran down his hand and added to the mess on the floor.

Something caught his eye on the ground near the overturned tabletop. It was Milo's second knife, the one he had lost in their initial collision. Aden lunged and scooped it up from the floor. The blade was made of white ceramic, and his hand left a bloody smear on it as he shifted it in his grip. Tess looked over and saw what he was doing, and she brought up her left hand in a guard position again, ready to join the attack even if they both knew it was foolhardy. But two knives were harder to block than just one, and going out swinging was a better option than waiting to die.

Milo looked at the knife in Aden's hand and repositioned himself, keeping his distance as he prepared to take them on. There was none of the earlier contempt in his face now. It was all just focus and concentration, the expression of a professional at work who was fully engaged in a challenging but manageable task. Tess moved to his left, and Milo adjusted his angle to keep them both in front of him. Aden took the tactical clue and moved to the right to increase the separation. If they managed to catch him from two sides at once, they would have a fleeting chance at hurting him enough to level the field a little.

Aden exchanged a look with Tess. She appeared frightened and frantic, but he could tell that she was also infuriated and determined. Dying in her company would not be the worst end he could imagine, not by a long shot.

They both went for Milo at the same moment, but Tess had been a little closer to him, so she reached him first. She had switched her knife from an upside-down grip to a blade-first one for more reach, and her blade was aimed right at Milo's middle. He turned into the strike and deflected her arm with his left hand, then pulled her forward so she was mostly between him and Aden. Her free arm came down reflexively just as he thrust his own knife. The blade had been aimed at her heart, but now it bit deep into her side, right above the hip bone. Tess yelled, but she sounded more pissed off than hurt.

Milo used Tess's momentum against her, pulling her by the wrist to get her off balance, then he shoved her against Aden. Their collision took most of the energy and all the aim out of Aden's own knife thrust, and Milo easily sidestepped it. Then Aden felt a blow against his rib cage, and all the air went out of him in an instant. He stumbled and fell onto the floor. When he looked back, he saw that Tess was also on the ground. The fingers that still held Milo's second knife were suddenly feeling numb.

Milo stepped on Tess's arm and wrenched Tristan's knife out of her hand, then tossed it aside. He looked over at Aden and the knife he was still holding.

"I'm going to want that back when you're done with it," he said.

"Come and get it, then," Aden mumbled. He tried to transfer the knife from the numb right hand into the left, but that one didn't work much better. The knife slipped from his grasp and tumbled to the floor, where it landed with a dull clinking sound. Milo shook his head.

"You really *were* one of those Signals wimps, weren't you? Can't even hang on to a knife in a fight."

Tess rolled over and kicked at Milo with both feet. He deflected the blows with his knees. Then he kicked her in the side of the head. She fell backward and went still, blood pouring from her nose and the corner of her mouth. The sight gave Aden a fresh rush of adrenaline and anger, and he got to his knees to launch himself at Milo again.

Then that's it, he thought. *But to all the hells with it.*

There was a new sound somewhere in the room behind him, an inarticulate vocalization of surprise and anger. Milo looked away from Aden and off to the side, and his body tensed as he shifted into a defensive stance. Before Aden could turn his head, Henry leaped into the dinner pit, his kukri a silvery blur in front of him.

Milo dodged the attack and swatted the blade of Henry's big knife aside with his own, and the two knives clashed with a harsh clicking sound, metal against ceramic. Milo avoided Henry's backhand swing as well, but only barely, the edge of the kukri missing the bridge of his nose by a fraction of a centimeter. Milo launched his own attack, a slash-and-jab combination that was almost too fast for Aden to follow.

Henry jerked away from the slash and parried the jab with the spine of his kukri. Milo danced away from Henry's counterblow, and each man assessed his opponent for a moment, their knives pointed at each other. Aden looked at Tess, who was rolling over onto her side with a groan. Milo's second knife was on the floor in front of Aden, and Aden tried to scoop it up with fingers that no longer wanted to obey him. Whenever he breathed in, it felt like Milo was stabbing his side all over again. A few steps away, Milo and Henry had ended their momentary détente. They were engaged in a rapid clash of quick strikes and parries, each trying to get their blade past the defenses of the other. Aden had no knife-fighting experience beyond the hand-to-hand combat training he'd received a long time ago in the Blackguards, and none of that had looked anything like this fast and violent dance of death. Even without experience, he could see that Henry had the longer reach and the bigger blade, but Milo had speed and agility, and the smaller man avoided the arcs of Henry's curved blade with what looked like practiced ease. Still, the sheer momentum and ferocity of Henry's attack forced Milo back step-by-step until he was at the edge of the dinner pit, his legs bumping up against the cushioned bench that surrounded the sunken area. He parried another one of Henry's blows and launched a lightning-fast counterattack, and this time his blade made it past the Palladian's guard.

Aden couldn't see exactly where the blow had landed, but Henry grunted and pulled his arm back, barely deflecting Milo's follow-up jab aimed at the side of his chest. Milo used the momentary breathing room he had created with the attack to jump over the low bench behind him and out of the dinner pit. Henry twirled his kukri and followed suit, crossing the knee-high barrier in a quick leap before Milo had the chance to exploit the momentary vulnerability. Then they circled each other again, two predators looking for an opening to strike a swift killing blow on a rival. But whatever blow Milo had landed on Henry moments earlier, Aden could tell that it was slowing the big Palladian down, and the arm that held the kukri wasn't quite as steady as before. They clashed again as if they had simultaneously obeyed an unheard signal. Once more the knives flashed and made contact. Henry grimaced in pain, but this time the exchange had been mutual.

Aden could see that the kukri had carved an ugly red gash along Milo's jawline from his chin to his earlobe. Henry seemed to have gotten the worst in the trade again because when he pressed a hand against his side, Aden saw bright-red blood welling up between the first officer's fingers. They went at each other once more, another flurry of jabs and slashes, steel against ceramic, dark skin against white. They were in front of the open balcony door now, and the tranquility of the ocean and the peaceful sounds of the water lapping against the piers below made the violence in front of Aden look offensively out of place.

Behind Aden, there was more commotion in the room, movement and voices. Distracted, Henry missed a swing with his kukri and left himself open for a fraction of a second. The little bit of air Aden was able to force into his lungs with every breath felt like it was on fire, and he could not shout the warning that was on his tongue, but it wouldn't have mattered. Milo kicked the outside of Henry's right leg, and the Palladian dropped to his knee with a pained shout.

Aden put whatever strength and willpower he had left in his body into hauling himself back onto his feet and over the low rim of the dinner pit toward Milo just as the other man flipped the knife around in his hand to plunge it into the back of Henry's neck. They collided for the second time today, and once again the physics were in Aden's favor, aided by the element of surprise. They plowed across the balcony together, and Aden felt a wild burst of satisfaction when he heard Milo's other knife hitting the floor. Then they crashed into the waist-high Alon barrier on the edge of the balcony, and the force of the impact squeezed the last bit of remaining air out of Aden's lungs. For a few heartbeats, the world spun madly in front of his eyes, sky and sea and white-painted composites trading places in brief flashes.

The water below the balcony felt as hard as solid ground when he hit the surface and plunged in. He was still holding on to Milo with his left hand, and the other man struggled to free himself from Aden's grasp. Aden's lungs were burning with their need for oxygen, and he could feel the darkness descend on his mind already, but he held on as they thrashed around in the warm ocean water, sinking deeper with every passing second. He had spent three months out of every year on Oceana all the way through his childhood, and swimming and diving had been the only forms of exercise he had ever truly enjoyed, the only sport he'd ever been good at. He grabbed Milo with the other hand as well and dragged him deeper, away from the sunlight reflecting on the surface. Once you were a few meters down, it was hard to tell which way was up if you weren't an experienced diver. The gradient of the ocean floor was shallow as it reclined from Adrasteia, but this far out in front of the southeastern leaf, the water was already twenty meters deep or more. Milo punched and clawed at him, but Aden hardly felt the blows, the water resistance robbing them of much of their energy.

Wherever I am going, you're coming with me, you piece of shit.

He felt a grim sense of triumph at the thought, even as he was slipping into unconsciousness.

Chapter 6

Idina

On a normal day, the sight of the armored transport rolling up to the bottom of the Council Hall's main staircase would have cheered Idina up, but right now it just amplified her anxiety. On a normal day, Red Section would be riding in a column of these vehicles, providing mutual protection and overwatch, strength in numbers. The security details would be riding in front of the VIP and behind, in the positions most likely to be hit first in an insurgent ambush. A single Badger was still formidable firepower and protection, but it left no doubt where the high-value target was riding.

It's been mostly quiet away from the demonstrations. Chances are good we won't even need the armor, she thought to put her mind at ease a little. Immediately, she chided herself for indulging in complacent thinking, even for just a moment. The last time she had allowed her edge to get dulled by complacency, her entire section had died in the span of two minutes.

At the bottom of the staircase, the Badger armored carrier silently rolled to a stop, a thirty-ton wedge of laminated armor riding on eight huge, knobby honeycomb wheels. The tail ramp opened and lowered to the ground with the soft hiss of pneumatics.

"Ride's here," she said on the team comms. "Purple Section, take up perimeter security for departure. Colors Norgay, we are ready to roll out when you are."

"Copy that," the close protection team leader replied. *"Coming down in two minutes."*

Behind Idina, the four troopers of her half section came out of the Council Hall's main entrance and made their way down the steps toward the Badger, where they took up guard positions around the vehicle. Idina surveyed the plaza below again, but nothing was out of place, no unusual circumstance caught her eye. Everybody here in the Green Zone had been checked and vetted, and the only access to the area was through a pair of security locks whose sensor tunnels could detect micrograms of explosives and any sort of weapon no matter how artfully it was concealed. But the grudges between Gretia and the rest of the system ran deep now, and she was not willing to bet her life on the security clearances of any of the Gretian civil servants here in the government quarter. There were only a handful of Gretians she fully trusted, and all of them wore green-and-white police uniforms.

The deputy high commissioner was short even for a Palladian, and he had the slight build of a desk warrior. The light scout vest they had scrounged up for him and managed to fasten over his civilian suit looked out of place on him and made him appear like a kid playing soldier with his father's work equipment. He came down the steps to the waiting Badger, flanked by his full-time security escorts. The DHC didn't acknowledge Idina as he walked past her vantage point at the top of the stairs.

Never mind me, she thought sourly as she watched him descend the staircase. *I'm just here to take a bullet for you if I must.* The top-down authoritarianism of Gretian society had steered them headlong into a war with the rest of the system, but in her time here, she had found that the relationship between soldiers and civilians was a lot less schizophrenic on Gretia. On Pallas and Rhodia and the other system planets, people understood the need for armed protection on an abstract level, but many instinctively seemed to loathe the people who committed concrete and necessary violence on their behalf, thought of them as unsavory and less worthy somehow. On Gretia, they respected their servants in uniform, even if that needle swung over to uncomfortable levels of reverence sometimes. She'd had those discussions with Captain Dahl during months of nightly patrols, and they had concluded that while the perfect society was cobbled together with the best aspects of all the planets, societies didn't evolve in that way, and that it was futile to try to make Gretians do things the Rhodian way and vice versa.

And yet here we are, trying it anyway, she thought. *Maybe all interplanetary diplomacy should be handled by two old soldiers from the opposing sides doing joint patrols in dangerous places.*

She fastened the chin strap on her helmet with a sigh and followed the deputy high commissioner and his bodyguards down to the waiting armored transport.

—

The commander and driver of the Badger left their vehicle for the mission briefing, and Idina walked over to them with Colors Norgay while the other bodyguard chaperoned the VIP into the armored box of the Badger's mission module.

"It's not the worst time for that run, if we have to make it at all," the Badger commander said when they had gone over the route and the contingency plans. "We have the usual rabble outside the main gate. Holding signs and chanting slogans. Once we're through the angry folks at the gate, we can punch it and head for the southern peripheral road. From that point, I don't want to get off the throttle unless I have to."

"What do we have for crowd control?" Color Sergeant Sirhan asked.

"Forty mil nonlethal. Stink bombs, and a full cassette of shit balls for the hard cases."

Sirhan and the commander exchanged a grin. "Shit balls" was the highly unofficial nickname for a particularly awful "soft force" option, a gel-capped grenade filled with a sticky slime that stank like rancid vomit and itched for days once it contacted the skin. On paper, it was better than getting shot, but Idina had been on the receiving end of a shit ball for education purposes during her occupation training, and on the whole she'd almost rather take her chance with a bullet wound instead.

"What's the lethal load out?" she asked the commander.

"Uh, the usual. Six thousand rounds for the tri-barrel, three each of hi-ex and armor-piercing. Plus whatever you are bringing along."

"Just rifles," she said. "And a *really* foul mood."

The mission module of the Badger was set up for eight passengers, two rows of four seats facing each other, each seat suspended from the sidewall of the hull in an elaborate anti-shock system. Idina strapped herself into the position that was directly across from the deputy high commissioner, and she watched him as he fumbled with the restraints until his chief bodyguard leaned over and fastened the padded straps properly. Her own section was already buckled in and ready to roll, weapons neatly stowed in the brackets between the seats. On a normal patrol, there would be some banter in the troop compartment to cut down on the tension, but with the high-ranking guest on board, everyone was uncharacteristically subdued.

The tail ramp closed, and the sudden lack of natural light made the compartment feel more claustrophobic than it already was. The battle lights inside came on after a moment, increasing their luminescence and color temperature to match the outside lighting conditions so the troops' eyes wouldn't need to adjust if they had to leave the vehicle quickly.

"Passengers secured and ready for movement," Colors Norgay said into his headset.

"Moving out," the vehicle commander announced from his station in the front of the Badger.

The armored transport started rolling on a nearly silent drivetrain. In front of Idina, the deputy high commissioner tried to appear blasé as if the whole thing were just routine for him, but the way his eyes darted around the interior of the compartment when he thought nobody was looking at him told her that he wasn't used to riding in war machines at all. He looked like he was in his late forties, lean like most Palladians but lacking the hard edges of military training. The high commissioners and their deputies were expressly and intentionally civilian. The Alliance leadership recognized that soldiers were good at breaking things, but that they had little expertise in rebuilding a functioning civil society from the rubble of a defeated planet. The people they sent from the diplomatic corps of the Alliance worlds were experts in law, civil engineering, economics, government, and a hundred other subjects that went mostly over Idina's head, so she was grateful for the fact that she didn't have to help figure out all those things for the new Gretia. But whenever she interacted with these academics and career civil servants, it was always clear that their minds were in different worlds even if they came from the same planet.

The Badger made its way across the square and onto the central avenue that bisected the government quarter. The way out led down the avenue and toward the main security lock that was the only entry and exit point for the Green Zone. Idina connected to the Badger's external optical arrays and brought up a screen to see what was going on outside. They passed underneath the commemorative archway at the edge of the government quarter, and she changed the view angle of her screen to look up at the tops of the arches coming together thirty meters above. The deputy high commissioner looked at her screen as she panned the view upward, and she enlarged the projection so he could get a good view.

"First time on Gretia, sir?" she asked. He shook his head.

"I was stationed here at the embassy once," he said. "Back when I was just out of training. Long before the war started. Haven't been back here in twenty years."

She acknowledged his reply with a nod.

"What about you?" he asked.

"I'm on my second consecutive tour now. The brigade rotates regiments in for occupation duty twice a year."

"Your second one in a row. How many in total?"

She had to think about her reply for a second.

"Five, I believe. Maybe six."

"You must know the place pretty well by now," he said.

"I thought I did," she replied. "But everything's gone upside down here in the last six months."

"You've been on the ground here. Tell me about that insurgent group. Odin's Wolves."

"I'm just a color sergeant, sir. I'm sure you have way better intel on them than I do."

The deputy high commissioner smiled curtly.

"Humor me. I know the official reports. I'd be interested to hear your impressions from the field."

Idina shrugged. "They came out of nowhere six months ago. No testing the waters, no slow escalation. The first time we ran into them, I lost my whole section. One moment we're doing a routine peacetime patrol, the next moment we're getting rail-gun fire and a coordinated ambush."

"You were there at the first attack?"

She nodded. "I was the platoon leader. I was the one who blundered into it."

"I'm not a military man, Color Sergeant. But I read the report. And I understand that nobody could have anticipated that sort of ambush. Not when there hadn't been a shot fired in five years."

"They had better gear than we did," Idina said. "Stealth suits and a rail-gun mount. And they didn't think twice about turning that gun into slag when they were done with us. That means they had the hardware to spare."

"Who do you think these people are?"

Idina glanced at her fellow troopers. Everyone in the hold was listening to their conversation and trying not to be obvious about it.

"They were wearing special operations gear. They had the training to use it. And they damn sure knew their ambush tactics and their explosives. If I had to guess? Blackguard commandos. Or some of their hard-case marine raiders. I'm quite sure these people have tangled with the brigade before. But that's the obvious answer, isn't it?"

"But why now? Why wait five years to start an insurgency? You're a soldier. If the Gretians had won the war and occupied Pallas, would you have waited that long to fight back?"

"No," she said without hesitation. "That's not the Pallas way. When they invaded, we didn't give them a minute to catch their breath. We attacked until we had kicked them off. And we would have fought to the last soldier. Not hidden ourselves away to bide our time. But they aren't Palladians. They don't think like we do."

The Badger slowed down to pass through the security lock at the main gate. The inbound lock was a tunnel of sensor arches and blast panels that scanned every incoming vehicle, and Idina saw a short line of transport pods waiting their turn to enter the tunnel from the other direction. The outbound portion of the lock was a short ramp that was separated from the inbound lane by another layer of reinforced blast panels. Nearby, the security field that bisected the park glowed a foreboding electric blue. It was an ugly setup that looked intrusive and out of place in the sunlit serenity of the environment.

"Passing out of the Green Zone," the vehicle commander said. "Going live on point defense and weapons."

The road out of the Green Zone cut through the middle of the park and ran for another half kilometer straight to Principal Square. The protests that had slacked off in size and intensity over the hot summer had exploded a few weeks ago when the Alliance had blocked all traffic onto and off the planet in the wake of the nuclear strike on Rhodia. It had been a reflexive reaction borne of fear and anger, and high command had lifted the total lockdown a few days later because it had greatly inflamed public opinion without yielding any security benefits. But the action had been a strategic error because it had given all the arguing factions on Gretia a common target for their discontent. Now the lockdown had been softened into a security and customs blockade, but the protests hadn't slacked.

When they approached the square, Idina flipped the screen projection in front of her around so the deputy high commissioner could see the mass of people nearby. The square was huge, a hundred meters on each side, but there were enough protesters out today to make it look a little crowded.

"There's the situation on the ground you wanted to see, sir," she said, careful to keep the irritation she felt out of her voice. *You could have seen that in a much safer way from five hundred meters up in the air.*

The protesters near the road to the government quarter were usually the loudest and most aggressive, and that didn't change today. They had seen the single Badger rolling across the open ground of the park up the road toward them for a few minutes now, and they'd had time to prepare a welcome. They blocked the road across both directions of traffic just before it led out into the plaza, shouting slogans and waving signs that refreshed their messages periodically, cycling through a preset repertoire. The visual translating software turned the slogans from Gretian into Palladian, but even with the AI's bias toward softening coarse language and erring on the side of politeness, Idina understood many of the crude invectives perfectly well.

"Riot shield up," the Badger's commander said. In front of the armored vehicle, two panels extended from the hull to form a V shape in front of the nose, then flashed blue as the commander activated the repulsor field. It was a much larger version of the riot shields the JSP troopers carried to repel crowds, and with its greater size and the thirty tons of the Badger behind it, it was much more effective. Idina could tell that the protesters were experienced with the vehicle-mounted zappers because they instantly started to move aside to form an alley for the Badger to pass through the crowd. It had only taken a few demonstrations in the beginning to educate them on the physics involved. It didn't matter how many people linked arms and tried to block a roadway because anyone who let the riot plow get close enough would get stunned and then shoved aside by the shape of the panels more or less gently depending on the speed of the vehicle. Today, their driver extended the protesters the courtesy of slowing down to a brisk jogging speed to give them ample time to clear the path. Beyond the initial ring of demonstrators, the crowd was thinner, and the driver accelerated a little once they were through the roadblock and on the square.

The riot plow kept the crowds from blocking their way, and the electrified skin of the Badger in crowd-control mode kept them from jumping onto the hull, but they could still show their defiance in other ways. As the armored vehicle moved across the square toward Sandvik's main north-south thoroughfare, things started to hit the hull, first a trickle and then a steady hail of objects able to be thrown that the Gretian protesters had brought with them just for the occasion. Next to Idina, Private Khanna looked a little concerned at the sound of rocks and drink containers hitting the outer hull.

"They usually hit each other about as often as they hit the ride," Idina said to him. "But I guess everyone needs to find a way to let off steam."

"They're lucky the PDS can tell the difference between a rock and a grenade," Color Sergeant Sirhan grumbled.

"Can you imagine?" Private Condry said. "One of them tossing a rock, and *pow*. Half a megawatt to the hand."

Some of the other troopers chuckled, and Idina shot them a stern look.

"Not funny. That would be terrible for our image."

"Doesn't sound like they have the greatest opinion of us anyway, Color Sergeant," Condry replied. The near-constant thudding of objects pelting their armor seemed to underscore his point.

"They're going to calm down at some point," Idina said. "And then we'll still be here, and we'll still need their cooperation. This is just a few thousand out of ninety million. If they *all* start actively hating us, we won't be able to keep a lid on this city, let alone the planet. Not if we start vaporizing hands for throwing a rock."

"Yes, Color Sergeant," Condry replied with a chastened expression.

The deputy high commissioner smiled at Idina.

"You said that like a diplomat."

Now it was her turn to chuckle.

"I don't have the temperament for a diplomat. The last time I had an argument with the locals, I had to let my kukri do the translating."

Next to the VIP, his main protectors kept a close eye on their own screens to monitor the crowd. None of the protesters dared to come closer than five meters to the Badger, which told Idina they knew what happened when someone touched the electrified outer layer of the armor. On the roof of the vehicle, the remote weapon station swiveled from left to right and back in a continuous slow sweep. Finally, they were through the ring of the most dedicated protesters, and the fusillade of objects glancing off the hull gradually lessened, then stopped altogether. They drove across the square, and the driver sped up once they were on the southern avenue and on the way out of the center of the city.

Private Khanna looked over at her.

"That wasn't so bad," he said.

"We haven't even gotten close to the dangerous part yet, Khanna," she replied.

—

"We have airborne coverage," the Badger commander told them a few minutes later. They were moving through the city at double the speed of the regular traffic now, passing pods to the left and right.

"That's good," Idina said. "Let's see what's up there."

She connected to the tactical network and queried the asset. A thousand meters overhead, one of the military surveillance drones had broken out of its regular patrol pattern above the city and changed course to follow them from above. It didn't give Idina the warm and friendly feelings that an armed gyrofoil with a backup squad would have, but it was better than nothing, and it made her feel just a little less exposed out here in a single and very obvious military vehicle.

"All right, we have one of the long-range patrol drones tracking us," she told her section. "It'll scan ahead of us for a few kilometers, so we should see trouble coming. But keep your own eyes on your screens. That drone isn't all-seeing."

If we get blown up, at least command will have high-resolution footage of the event, she thought.

—

On the outskirts of Sandvik, away from the high-rise buildings of the center, the city seemed to spread out and flatten before them, bustling commercial districts giving way to residential neighborhoods interspersed with cultural centers, wide plazas ringed with museums and concert halls. Every few blocks, there was open space or greenery or both, parks and promenades that broke up the neighborhood clusters. Even after three tours on this planet, it was still strange to Idina to see so much flat ground here. On Pallas, every square meter of level rock had to be claimed from the mountains the hard way, with mining lasers and explosives and backbreaking labor. Here the flat ground was just there, the default state of the surface, ready to be molded into shape or cultivated with trivial effort.

Overhead, the drone tracked their progress through the city, scanning the road ahead for any signs of danger. She watched the imagery closely. However good the AI in the drone's computer brain was, it would never be able to fully replace an experienced soldier's instincts.

"Bridge coming up," she told her section.

"Once we are across, the real fun starts," she added in Private Khanna's direction. "Two hundred kilometers of countryside. Anyone who wants to do anything to us will see us coming a long way out. And they won't have to worry about collateral damage."

The bridge ahead carried several automated traffic lanes across the river that wound its way around Sandvik in a wide arc. In front of the Badger, the civilian transport pods sorted themselves into a single lane and then filed onto the bridge in precise AI-controlled intervals. The driver of the armored vehicle took his place in line for the crossing, then slowed down to force a gap in the interval that would be wide enough for them to cross the bridge at high speed. The traffic AI switched the color of the roadway behind the Badger from green to red, and all the pods on the red portion came to a stop to give the military transport priority. Idina saw that the faces of the passengers who bothered to look up from their work or morning entertainment seemed less than happy when they spotted the reason for the delay.

They rolled up the access ramp and onto the bridge, and the driver accelerated. The bridge was a slender and graceful structure, elegant in its simple functionality like most Gretian architecture. Twenty meters below the road surface, the water of the river glittered and sparkled with reflections from the morning sun. The stream was roughly two hundred meters wide at this point on its way to the far-off ocean, and the embankments on either side were wide strips of grass interspersed with walking paths. On both sides of the river, residential buildings lined the waterfront, their architecture taking advantage of the view with a multitude of terraces and balconies. Behind them, the traffic AI turned the roadway from red back to green, and the civilian traffic started to flow onto the bridge behind the Badger.

"Have you ever seen so much flat water in one—" someone said to Private Khanna just as the front of the Badger heaved up in a violent jolt. For just a moment, it felt to Idina as if they had run up against a solid object on the road, but then the familiar smell of burning propellant spread out in the mission module, and the fire suppressant system removed all doubt when it activated near the front of the vehicle. The Badger nearly flipped on its side, and Idina's stomach churned with the motion. Then the vehicle dropped back onto its honeycomb wheels and skidded sideways. They came to a stop with a grinding sound from the front of the hull.

I fucking told you so, Idina thought wildly. *Gods, I hate it when I am right.*

Chapter 7

Dunstan

Assuming a new command always felt a little like meeting a prospective new partner for the first time, but in the presence of their entire extended family and all their friends. And as with first dates, Dunstan knew that first impressions set the tone when meeting a new crew. Every leader had a different command style, every crew had a different dynamic, and starting off on the wrong foot could introduce a sort of harmonic dissonance that would take weeks or even months to settle.

Hecate was docked in the military section of Rhodia One, and her crew was still on leave for another two days, which gave him the perfect opportunity to get to know the layout of his new ship without having the eyeballs of the entire crew on him. The standard uniform for reporting in was the service dress, the smartly tailored tunic that had all the decorations on it, but Dunstan dressed in shipboard utility dress on the morning of his trip up to Rhodia One. It made him look less like he was trying to impress the crew with his pins and ribbons, and he intended to check out every nook of the ship and maybe get a little dirty in the process.

Her docking location was all the evidence he needed that *Hecate* wasn't just a regular corvette. She was moored in one of the station's space docks, the cavernous interior maintenance sections inside Rhodia One's hull. Ships that got a space dock spot were either in need of more extensive service than was possible with EVA facilities, or they were sensitive technology the navy wanted to keep out of view as much as possible. The final verification of her special status was the gauntlet of security checks he had to pass just to get close to Space Dock 5.

"Sorry for the delay," said the officer in charge of the final checkpoint just outside the dock's main access door when he handed Dunstan's ID pass back to him. "You are cleared for entry, sir."

"No problem. I know how the classified business works, Lieutenant." He took his ID pass and pocketed it. "Do I need a guide? I haven't been to an air dock up here in a long time."

"No, sir. There's only one ship docked in SD5 now. You can't miss her."

"I suppose I can't."

The armored access door opened to admit Dunstan, and he walked through it and into the vast space beyond. The dock wasn't a place for anyone with a fear of heights. It was a vault-like compartment that measured sixty meters from the deck to the massive bulkhead above, and the access walkway he stepped out on was more than halfway up. There were three docking spaces alongside the curve of the compartment's wall, each designed to hold an entire ship upright and aligned with the gravmag field generated at the top of the station. Two of the spaces stood empty, their massive hull clamps retracted and their service catwalks folded up. The third space, directly in front of Dunstan, held a ship unlike any he had ever seen. It was so tall that the blunt nose of the ship almost brushed the ceiling bulkhead.

Hecate was modest in size, a little larger than an escort corvette and only a third the size of his old frigate, but standing in a cavernous air-filled room with her and seeing the hull standing on end right in front of him put the scale of even a small warship into perspective. All space-ships had the same basic shape dictated by physics—a blunt cylinder with a heavily shielded pointy or chisel-shaped top and a massive drive cone at the bottom. This one didn't quite break the mold, but it managed to look more like a sinister piece of munition than a crewed vessel. The hull had thick protrusions on four sides that looked vaguely like guidance fins for a missile, but they were irregular in length and width, so they gave the ship a strangely asymmetric appearance. The coating on the exterior armor plating was so nonreflective that it seemed to swallow the light from the many overhead lamp arrays.

As Dunstan walked toward the ship on the metal service catwalk, he tried to spot hull markings, but failed to find any. A normal warship hull had the pennant number painted onto the armor, along with dozens or even hundreds of various smaller labels and service directives: No Step, Access Panel, Danger: Class Iv Radiation Emitter. The hull of *Hecate* was devoid of any such visual clutter. When he was in front of the ship's main airlock, he looked at the coating on the hull. Dunstan reached out and put the palm of his hand on it. It felt soft and slightly warm, and he pushed against it to find that it was slightly yielding to the pressure of his touch. The sensation was not unlike touching a living thing. He withdrew his hand and walked into the airlock.

Inside, *Hecate* was so obviously new and pristine that it felt slightly disorienting. He had never served on a brand-new ship. His newest unit had been RNS P-7501, the orbital patrol ship that was his first command assignment, and she had already been in service for half a decade when he took her over. On *Hecate*, every surface looked like the titanium dioxide paint had just dried on it yesterday. The interior of the ship even *smelled* new to Dunstan, a distinctive blend of air from new filtration systems and deck liners that were still outgassing the residue molecules from the manufacturing process.

He brought up a projection of the ship's deck layout and let it float slightly to the left of his field of view so he could glance at it and use it as a guide. With the crew gone, the ship was peacefully quiet. Even the ever-present hum of air exchangers and powered-up electronic equipment was far more subdued than he was used to from his old frigate. He looked around in the airlock deck. The walls were crammed with equipment lockers and control-panel screens. *Minotaur* had two main ladderwells to traverse the ship from top to bottom; *Hecate* only had one, and it was narrower than the ones he was used to.

Dunstan climbed up the ladder to the next deck. It was the ship's command deck, the section that would have been called the Action Information Center on a bigger warship. Here, the schematics labeled it the CONTROL DECK. He rarely stepped into a ship's nerve center without someone else present, and seeing the compartment devoid of personnel felt a little eerie. *Hecate*'s control deck was much smaller than *Minotaur*'s had been. On the old frigate, the helm station was on a catwalk-like half deck above the AIC. Here, it was integrated into the control deck, and it was a single station tucked into a nook by the compartment wall instead of a double station in the middle of the deck. All the distances and scales in this ship seemed half the ones he was used to from other ships. Space was always at a premium in a warship, but this one felt far more confining and cramped than any other he had ever seen.

Guess I'll get to know my new crew really well, he thought.

Dunstan consulted the schematic from his comtab. There were only two more decks above the control room, the officer berthing deck and a compartment labeled AI CORE CONTROL. He went back to the ladder and resumed his climb. The berthing deck was the usual arrangement of sleeping compartment modules, ten cubic meters of private space per segment, each only slightly bigger than a capsule bed in a transit hotel. He climbed past the berthing deck without pausing. The hatch to the next compartment was locked, and the access pad next to the latch was blinking red, indicating a security protocol was in effect. He used his biometric signature to unlock it. The status field changed from red to green, and the hatch unlocked with the authoritative click of retracting titanium bolts.

A waft of cool air greeted Dunstan as he climbed up into the top compartment and stepped off the ladder. When he turned around, there was someone in the middle of the compartment, and the unexpected sight startled him a little. It was a woman in a shipboard flight suit, with the two stripes of a senior lieutenant on her shoulder sleeves. She looked over at him and straightened up, and the screen projection she had been looking at disappeared at once.

"Didn't mean to interrupt you, Lieutenant," he said. "I didn't realize someone was already back on the ship."

"Not at all," she said. "Just running a stress test on this beast before we go live again."

"And how is it going?"

She looked around the compartment and ran a hand through her hair.

"This ship has some wrinkles to iron out. But the AI core isn't one of them. I've never seen anything like it. Haven't had the slightest bit of trouble since we left for the shakedown cruise."

She wiped her hand on her overalls and offered it.

"I'm guessing you're the new CO. I'm your first officer, Bryn Hunter. And also the information warfare officer."

He shook her hand. Her grip was firm and purposeful. There was a faint but recognizable accent to her speech, marking her as a nonnative speaker of Rhodia despite her perfect diction.

"Dunstan Park," he said. "I've taken over from Commander Stone." He looked around at the various control consoles and the unfamiliar equipment in the compartment. "You're the expert. Give me the basics on this kit. I know it's a big deal. The admiralty gave me the big picture. But I'm a space warfare guy, not an AI specialist."

If she thought he was trying to gauge her expertise, she seemed happy at the opportunity to demonstrate it. She brought up a screen and flicked through a few data pages until it showed a diagram of the ship, with the AI components highlighted. A stern red warning flashed across the top of the projection: OPSEC LEVEL 1—AUTHORIZED COMMAND PERSONNEL EYES ONLY.

"I'd try to compare it to another ship, but like I said, there's really nothing like it. Four data cores with one thousand independent segments each. Forty-five tons per core. And every single digital pathway in this ship also runs on palladium, not just the emergency systems."

"Layman's terms, Lieutenant," Dunstan said. "I'm afraid that AI and network theory wasn't my strongest suit at the academy." He hoped she thought he was playing dumb just to keep checking how much she knew about her business, but the reality was that he really didn't know more than the academy basics about the magic and alchemy that was modern artificial intelligence.

"Right," she said after a moment of consideration. "I guess I will compare it to another ship after all. What was your last command, sir?"

"RNS *Minotaur*," he replied. "Olympus-class frigate."

"Olympus class," she repeated. "Not too many of those left around. Fourth-generation data cores, I think, with supercooled nonemergency trunks."

"That sounds familiar," Dunstan said even though it didn't. He had her accent figured out, but he wanted her to keep talking just to be absolutely positive.

She brought up a subscreen and queried for the data processing values of his old ship. Dunstan noticed that every bit of information popped onto the screen instantly, as if it had been waiting for the mere touch of her fingertips to reveal itself.

"All right. If an Olympus-class AI core is the baseline at a value of one hundred, this ship is a four point six million. And that's per core. We have four of them, and they can run in parallel."

Dunstan let out a low whistle.

"I may not know much about AI cores, but I understand 'forty-six thousand times better.'"

"She has more processing power than all the rest of the fleet put together. I still can't believe all the things this ship can do."

He smiled at the obvious excitement on her face.

"I'm old-school, Lieutenant. I like ships with lots of ordnance in the launch tubes, and lots of gun barrels to point at the enemy. I know that faster AI gives our point defenses an edge. I don't know what it's going to buy us when we stare down a heavy gun cruiser that's ten times our mass. But I'd like to think I'm teachable."

"The point defenses are amazing," Lieutenant Hunter said. "But if we use this boat right, we won't need them. We can break encryption on a missile's AI while it's still in the launch tube. We can make it inert. Or take it over as soon as it launches and turn it against the launching platform. You don't need a lot of ordnance in the launch tubes if you can borrow theirs."

"If it all works as promised," Dunstan replied. "Under combat conditions."

Lieutenant Hunter shrugged and slipped her hands into the side pockets of her overalls.

"That's what we're here to find out, isn't it?"

He nodded. "That's what our deployment orders say. Tell me more about the wrinkles that still need to be ironed out. How about you give me the bow-to-stern tour and point them out along the way? Unless you're tied up right now, of course."

"Nothing that can't wait an hour or two," she said. "Follow me, sir."

They went through the ship from top to bottom, stopping in every compartment so Lieutenant Hunter could list the features and tell him the little bumps and deficiencies she had identified. *Hecate* had ten decks for a crew of five officers and twenty-three enlisted personnel. The general layout was like every other ship he'd ever served on, dictated by the physics and the technologies involved. The airlock deck was always the equator of the ship, with the command and executive decks above the airlock and the crew and technical decks below. The engineering and propulsion deck was always at the bottom of the ship because it sat closest to the radiation shielding for the fusion reactor and the ship's drive section. There was little freedom for designers to mix up what was in between the nose cone and the drive cone. The crew berth decks were usually split above and beyond the medical deck, where the ship's sanitary facility was located, or the mess deck where everyone ate, to limit traffic jams in the narrow confines of the ship and allow for the division of crew into rest and watch cycles.

"Crew deck A," Lieutenant Hunter said when they were climbing past it on the way down. "That's the choice one. Sits right between the mess and medical, so it's only one hop to either. Crew deck B is below medical, and they have to climb up three decks to get to the mess. But they're close to engineering, so that's where we put the propulsion and reactor crew."

"What's the watch cycle?" he asked.

"Two watch crews. Six hours on, six hours off. They pulled most of the shakedown crew from recon and long-range escort ships, so they're used to the six-hour cycle. Got some from bigger ships, and they needed some time to adjust. But it's all smooth cruising now."

"Glad to hear it. I may need a little time to adjust myself. We ran triple eights on *Minotaur*."

"I'd much rather do those," she said. "I tried to figure out how to split the crew that way in the beginning. But we don't have the numbers or the facilities for triple eights. This ship's a weird size. Just small enough to lack the amenities of the bigger ships. Just big enough to lose the advantages of the smaller boats."

They stopped on the medical deck, which held three treatment stations and the sanitary capsules where the crew could take showers. Just like on the other decks, everything was designed in the most efficient way he'd ever seen when it came to maximizing the use of available space, without a cubic centimeter of volume wasted on decoration or frivolities. It was like someone had built the prototype of the ship, then gone through the entire hull deck by deck to mark up spots where weight could be shaved off or storage space added.

Below the medical deck, there was another crew berth deck, rows of individual bunk capsules stacked on top of each other like the honeycomb cells in a beehive. The officers on the ship got actual cabins, small as they were, but the same deck space that was divided into six private spaces on the officer berth deck had to accommodate twelve crew bunks down here. Being an enlisted crew member on a Rhodian Navy ship was not a job for anyone who put a premium on privacy, and serving on a small vessel also filtered out anyone with claustrophobic tendencies. On deployment, everyone lived and worked in close quarters, and it took a very resilient personality to cope with the hardships of this kind of duty.

"Ship's gym," Lieutenant Hunter said on the next deck down. This was the storage deck, loaded with supply modules for the three-month deployment, secured in neat rows along the walls. There was a small open space in front of the compartment's refrigeration locker, and someone had installed a compact treadmill and a strength-training machine in that spot.

"I'm afraid it may not be as extensive as what you're used to from *Minotaur*. But it's what they could squeeze in."

"Looks cozy," Dunstan said.

"It's a popular spot. Quiet and private. I hate the treadmill. But I come down here to hear myself think."

The bottom compartment of the ship was the engineering and propulsion deck, the control center for the ship's fusion reactor. Dunstan knew that below the deck flooring, a few tons of dense radiation shielding separated the fragile crew from the reactor and the ship's fusion rocket drive.

"How did the acceleration trials on the shakedown cruise go?" he asked.

"Fourteen and a half g at ninety-five percent," Lieutenant Hunter replied with pride in her voice, and he rewarded the statement with a low whistle.

"Not bad. Not bad at all. That's a lot of zip for a two-thousand-ton hull."

"Once we have her all tuned in, we can probably make her kiss up to fifteen at full throttle."

"I like the sound of that. There's always another half g in the drive somewhere if we don't mind a few nosebleeds."

Dunstan looked around the compartment. It was the most modern engineering section he had ever seen, and most of the control elements were unfamiliar to him—new consoles to steer and monitor millions of ags' worth of experimental technology.

"Thanks for the initial tour," he said. "I'll repeat the process with the chief engineer and the weapons officer. But you left out an essential piece of information, Lieutenant."

"What's that, sir?"

"How's the coffee on this boat?"

She grinned.

"Best I've had in the fleet. You want to give it a try, the dispenser is in the galley. I dialed in a fresh batch when I came aboard this morning."

Dunstan nodded at the ladderwell.

"I'll put it to the test right now. Join me for a cup if you would."

They climbed up to the mess, where Lieutenant Hunter took two mugs out of the vertical rack and filled them with coffee from the galley's dispenser. The scent of the hot brew displaced the smell of new plastics and paint and made his ship feel more real somehow. Dunstan took the offered mug from Hunter and sat down at one of the mess tables.

"Have a seat. I want to ask you something."

She sat down across the table from him. From her body language, he could tell that she had a good idea what he was about to ask her, but when she looked at him, there was no anxiety in her expression.

"I've never heard anyone with your accent in the fleet," he said. "It's Gretian, isn't it?"

She nodded.

"I still can't pass for a native," she said. "Don't think I ever will. Some people have an ear for it, but I don't. Comes with learning the language later in life. The mouth is already too used to making sounds in a particular way."

"So what's your story? I know you're Rhodian because you're wearing the uniform. And you're cleared to serve on a classified ship. How did you get that accent?"

"I was Gretian once," she said. "In a previous life. I met my mate when she was on Gretia as an attaché with the diplomatic corps. Then I moved to Rhodia with her. We got married, I got naturalized three years later. That was two years before the war started."

She took a slow sip of coffee and looked at him impassively.

"She was in the navy, so I joined, too, once I was a citizen. Figured our lives would be easier that way. I made middie and got into the fleet just in time to see the whole system blow up all around us. Not much to tell after that. Four years of combat deployments. I came home. She didn't."

"I'm sorry to hear that," Dunstan said. The blunt, matter-of-fact way in which she had recalled her loss threw him off a little. From the way she looked at him to gauge his reaction, he knew that she had intended it exactly that way, to preemptively put him on the defensive a little. "I wasn't implying that you had divided loyalties."

"Yes, you were," she said. "But I don't take offense. I'm used to it. And I can't say I wouldn't do the same. If I came across someone else in the navy with a Gretian accent, I'd feel the same way. They started a war with us, after all."

Lieutenant Hunter turned her coffee mug in her hands and took another sip.

"The first two years of the war, they wouldn't let me serve on a frontline unit," she said. "I spent a lot of time on supply freighters and rear-guard patrol boats. Had to prove myself to every new crew. Hear the same stupid comments over and over. Third year of the war, they were finally running low enough on junior officers to have to put me in the AIC of a proper warship."

"Which one?"

"RNS *Laconia*. Light cruiser, Hellas class."

"Lost in 916," he recalled. "At the First Battle of Pallas."

She nodded, and he could see the pain of the memory darken her expression.

"With two-thirds of her crew. We took a missile hit in the aft magazine that blew the ship in half. Nobody below the airlock deck made it to the pods. Luckily, we had a battlecruiser nearby that took the time to come about and pick up pods. I don't know how the Gretians would have treated me as a prisoner of war, but I have my suspicions."

She shook her head lightly as if to cast off the recollection of that day.

"Commander, I served on three frontline ships during the war. Had two of them shot out from underneath me. Those three ships got a total of seven enemy ship kills and four assists. I don't care if anyone questions my loyalties at this point. They can check my service record. And if they still doubt my allegiance after that, then it's their problem, not mine. I think I've earned the right to be left alone about the way I talk, or my planet of birth."

Dunstan knew commanding officers who would have taken her last sentence as a challenge, evidence of a personality conflict that would give them an excuse to have her replaced with a different first officer. Five years ago, he might have done just that. But he appreciated candor and courage, and whatever emotions were swirling behind Lieutenant Hunter's pale-blue eyes, he could tell that fear or duplicity were not among them.

"If I gave you that impression, I apologize," he said. "I'm not going to tell you that I'm fond of the Gretian accent. But you are right, Lieutenant. That's my problem, not yours. You put on that uniform and stepped into harm's way for Rhodia. You did earn that right."

She nodded.

"Thank you for saying that, sir."

They sipped their beverages in silence for a few moments. Dunstan looked at the walls of the mess deck. This was usually the place on a warship where the memorabilia from deployments was displayed, but *Hecate* was so new that she didn't have any trinkets or trophies yet.

"We're taking out an experimental ship," he said. "An *unproven* experimental ship. And we'll be using untested tactics. I hope you are comfortable with writing the manual as you go, Lieutenant. Because we are leaving day after tomorrow."

"Any word on what we're going to be doing out there? I figure they didn't press this boat into service early to babysit merchants on the Pallas run."

"We're not." Dunstan leaned back with a sigh. "You figured correctly."

"So what's the mission? I mean, I can wait until you brief the command staff tomorrow. But I am curious."

"If we come across any pirates, we'll bag and tag them for the patrols," Dunstan said. "But that won't be our main job. We're going to find the ship that dropped a nuke on our home three weeks ago. And if we run into the fuzzhe . . . the *Gretian* gun cruiser that's out there somewhere, I'll consider it a bonus. I'd love to get a rematch with that bastard."

"So we're going to look for trouble," Lieutenant Hunter said. "Good."

"They were the ones who were looking for trouble," he replied. "We're just delivering what they were seeking."

He swirled the coffee around in his mug and took another sip. Hunter hadn't oversold the stuff. It really was exceptionally good, better than any he could remember having on a navy ship.

"Of course, our orders say that we are not to engage in combat except for self-defense. We are to find them and call in the heavy guns when we have a fix," he said. "So if you were looking to add to your kill tally, this deployment may disappoint you."

She smiled wryly.

"You fought in the war, too," she said. "You know as well as I do that 'self-defense' can be a pretty flexible term out there."

Chapter 8

Solveig

The gyrofoil settled down on the landing pad so gently that Solveig could barely feel it when the skids contacted the ground. She had dismissed her bodyguard Cuthbert just before the flight home from the spaceport to get fifteen minutes of solitude before meeting her father again, and the brief aerial hop had not been long enough to quell the anxiety that had started to well up in her when they had arrived planetside.

There's no telling what two weeks of silence has done to his anger, she thought as the sound of the engines faded and the soft cabin illumination came back on. *Maybe it died down. Or maybe he used it to keep the coals red-hot all the while.*

"We have arrived, Miss Ragnar. It was a pleasure to fly you again this evening," the pilot said over the intercom. The door at the front of the passenger cabin opened and let in a gust of warm summer air. Solveig unbuckled her safety harness and got out of her seat.

Outside, the late-summer heat and the blazing sun felt like an assault after spending more than three weeks in climate-controlled environments and steady twenty-degree temperatures. It was her least favorite time of the year. She suspected that part of her dislike for summer originated during her school years—summers were for going home and spending time in her father's company, away from her friends and the safety of relative anonymity.

"Where would you like me to bring your luggage, Miss Ragnar?" the pilot asked.

"Just inside the front hall would be great. I don't know yet whether I'll be staying at the house tonight."

"As you wish, ma'am." The pilot moved to the rear of the gyrofoil to get her baggage out of the cargo compartment. Solveig walked to the pathway that led from the landing pad to the house through a little grove of young trees that stood barely taller than she did. It was early evening, and the low sun was bathing the estate in a soft golden light that made everything resemble the slightly gaudy landscape paintings her mother used to like.

Inside, the main house was cool and quiet. She walked through the foyer and down the central hall to her suite. When she passed the lounge, she peered inside to see if her father was sitting in his usual spot at the bar, but the room was empty, and the screens were dark. The house had felt huge even when they had lived here as a family. Now, with her mother and Aden gone, it seemed like an enormous waste of space—twenty rooms and enough social space to entertain hundreds of people, all sitting mostly empty, her father paying for a dozen domestic staff to maintain a house with only two residents. They used to have parties and social functions constantly, an almost steady stream of guests and drop-in petitioners, but her father seemed to have lost all interest in having people over when the war ended and he no longer had control of Ragnar Industries.

Back in her suite, Solveig took off her business clothes and stepped into the shower for a long and thorough rinse to rid herself of the smells of travel. Then she got into her workout clothes and went off to find her father.

When she stepped through the wide patio doors, Falk Ragnar was sitting outside on the patio underneath a sun canopy, sipping a drink from a tall glass and reading something on his compad. He looked up and smiled.

"Hello, daughter of mine. You finally made it home."

Solveig walked over to her father and sat down in one of the empty patio chairs. Out over the manicured grounds, watering drones made their quiet passes above the artfully arranged flower beds, misting the plants in regular intervals.

"I wasn't prepared for the system catching fire while we were on Acheron," she replied. "They made us wait a week for a clearance slot. And Cuthbert almost got himself shot by some Alliance marine in the end."

"Oh?" Falk raised an eyebrow. "How did this happen?"

"They did a pat-down, and Cuthbert thought the marine who did mine got a little too handsy."

Her father's expression darkened a little. "And did he?"

Solveig shrugged.

"I don't like it when anyone puts their hands on me. Once they get to do that, the rest is just semantics. But they had the guns and the armor. I told Cuthbert to stand down. I didn't feel like spending any more time waiting in orbit."

"This whole blockade is a bunch of chest-beating nonsense," Falk said. "So someone dropped a nuke on Rhodia. What did we have to do with that? We don't even have a navy anymore. It's all just pretext to squeeze us a little harder. Punishing a whole planet just because they can't keep a watch on theirs."

"Well, they were enjoying their jobs, I can tell you that," Solveig said. "They had us give up our comtabs for a data dump, too. They're going to have a fun time trying to get through the encryption."

"Nosy bastards. Just looking for a hook to hang you from. Now you know what we've been dealing with since the end of the damned war. One little cut and pinprick after another, just to keep us bleeding."

She nodded at his glass. "What are you drinking?"

Falk looked at his beverage.

"I'm trying something new. Synthetic distillate, without ethanol. I'm not sure I'm wild about it. But it's better than I had expected."

"Can I try?" she asked.

He handed her the glass.

"You just want to check if I am telling the truth about the drinking. But here you go."

She took a sip. The drink had the smell and flavor of alcohol, but there was something undeniably different about it. It lacked the sharp bite of her father's regular fare, and she didn't feel her face flush like it usually did whenever she had her first taste of a strong drink.

"Not bad," she said. She didn't ask why he was suddenly drinking cocktails without alcohol, despite her surprise at the shift. Falk Ragnar did nothing on a whim. Whatever the reason for his sudden abstinence, she was sure that it was part of a larger strategy, but she knew better than to ask about it and give him what he wanted.

She handed his glass back to him. "I think I want something to drink as well. It's been a long week."

"Go ahead," Falk said. "There's still quite a bit of that dry white left. The one you like, from Acheron."

"I've had my share of Acheron wines for a little while. Let me see what else we have."

She got up and walked back into the house to check the stock in the bar. None of the wines really appealed to her today, so she brought up the AI bartender's screen. After a moment of consideration, she selected her mother's old favorite summer drink, a strong pale-green cocktail made with aniseed liquor and fizzy water. When she got back to the patio with her freshly mixed and dispensed cold beverage, her father wrinkled his nose.

"*That* smelly stuff. I never could stand it. Tastes like medicine."

"I like it. Mama always said it was an acquired taste. People love it or hate it."

"Well, I never acquired the taste. But I don't have to drink it. How was the trip? Other than the indignities at the end, I mean."

"It was mostly fine."

"Mostly," he repeated.

"I think I may have mentioned my troubles with the Acheroni inability to give clear yes-or-no answers," she said. "But once I was used to their way of talking around something they didn't want to address, it wasn't so hard to get them to play along. But *gods*. Never make me spend another day in Gisbert's company, please."

Falk barked a laugh and looked out over the rows of flower beds behind the patio. "That bad, huh?"

"I know you picked him because he does what he's told. But he was a liability. I had to do all the footwork in the conference room. He spent the whole time either complaining about everything or sucking up to me. And he made us look like a bunch of rude boors. When he gets a few drinks in him, he turns into a pig."

"I didn't hire him for his tact, that's true. But he was always on his best behavior around me. It seems that my prolonged absence has lowered the standards."

"That's because you were in a position to fire him," Solveig said. "He was the senior VP on the trip. And he never left out an opportunity to act like it. Except when it came to doing the work, of course."

Falk looked at her, and for a fleeting moment she could see the spark of the old, familiar anger in his eyes.

"*Nobody* is senior to you in that place," he said. "Except for Magnus, and he knows who will take his chair when he retires. If Gisbert isn't smart enough to know his place, then maybe he has outlived his utility."

"I'm less than half his age," Solveig said. "And he has been a VP for a decade."

"And your family name is *Ragnar*," Falk said. "You outranked him the moment you walked into the building on your first day."

"Firing him may be a little harsh, Papa," she said. "It would be bad for morale among the other VPs. Make us look like we don't have our ship in order."

He shrugged and sipped from his glass.

"You're too forgiving. It's a quality your mother passed down to you. Along with a taste for that awful aniseed liquor."

She held his gaze with a neutral expression. This was supposed to be a training lesson, and she had no idea what his goal was, but for now she was just relieved he had chosen to engage in this work-related banter instead of blowing up at her over what she'd said to him on Acheron.

"All right," he said. "Then tell me the kind and gentle way to deal with Gisbert. Pretend you're sitting in the big chair at Ragnar already, and you have no one else to answer to. What do you do?"

Solveig considered his challenge. She knew what *he'd* do, of course, but she also knew that he expected her to put her own spin on things instead of just telling him what she thought he wanted to hear. As much as he'd elevated Gisbert for being a reliable yes-man, he wouldn't appreciate that property in his own offspring. The trick in dealing with him was always in fulfilling his expectations without making him think that she was trying for just that. It was a delicate dance, but she had been practicing it for a long time.

"Shuffle him around," she said. "Give him responsibility of a department that doesn't deal with external vendors or customers directly so he can't offend outsiders. Gradually reduce his influence. Make use of the fact that he delegates most of his workload anyway. Make *damn* sure it feels like a demotion. Ban him from any corporate function that includes alcohol. And if he doesn't get the strong hint and retire gracefully on his own after a few months in obscurity, I'd look into his corporate network records for an offense that merits termination with cause. There's always something if you look hard enough."

Falk grinned. It was the mirthless grin she knew all too well, the toothy one he employed when someone else had drawn a bad card from the deck.

"Not bad, Solveig. Not bad at all. It seems I underestimated your ability to weaponize your irritation."

He finished his drink and put the glass down on the side table slowly and carefully, as if he wanted to reinforce that he wasn't impaired in the least.

"When you get back to work, you should take your concerns to Magnus. Report what happened on Acheron. Propose to him what you just told me. You may find him in a receptive mood. And don't think for a second that you're being too harsh with Gisbert. Sometimes the rest of the executive floor needs to be reminded of what can happen when you let yourself turn into dead weight."

"Maybe I will," Solveig said and turned her glass in her hands. Then she took a sip to fortify herself.

Might as well go on the offensive, she thought. *He'll bring it up sooner or later anyway. Best to meet him on my terms.*

"I think we need to continue our conversation," she continued. "The one I cut short, when you called me on Acheron the night of that attack."

Her father didn't react visibly to her change of topic, as if he had been waiting for her to bring up the topic all along. Solveig reminded herself that he'd had two weeks to think about his own strategy. Still, she had expected him to be angry, and the lack of displeasure in his expression was somehow more unnerving than his anger.

"I've thought about what I said that night." He picked up his comtab and poked at the screen. She saw that he was ordering another drink from the AI bartender. "And I think that you were right. I was out of line."

Solveig was taken aback so thoroughly that she couldn't manage to keep the surprise out of her face.

"You had every right to tell me off," he continued. "Maybe it's because we never really spent much time together since you went off to school. But I let myself forget that you are a grown woman now. You can handle yourself. And you have the right to your own relationships."

The world has truly flipped upside down, Solveig thought.

"Even if I choose to go out with Detective Berg?" she asked.

Falk grimaced. "I think it's a big mistake. I still think he's just trying to squeeze you for back-channel information. But that is your call to make, not mine."

"Just like that? I can go out without Marten and his crew keeping tabs on me?"

He shook his head.

"Oh, they'll still keep tabs on you, Solveig. You're my daughter, you're the heir to the company, and you're probably one of the ten most valuable kidnapping targets on the planet. You can't just run out and act like you're some anonymous salary girl. But they'll be a little more in the background from now on."

Solveig looked at him quizzically, still fully expecting to walk into a setup any moment. *If something seems too good to be true, it almost certainly is*—she remembered one of her father's frequent aphorisms.

"Can I ask what made you change your mind on this?"

Behind them, the sliding door opened, and the serving robot came out onto the patio on silent wheels. It stopped in front of Falk, who took the prepared drink from the serving tray and watched the robot as it rolled off again.

"I don't want to drive you away, Solveig. I need you by my side. And because you are who you are, I know you would find a way to do what you want anyway."

The anxiety she had been feeling for the last few hours fell away, and it was like taking a deep breath after being underwater for too long.

Solveig picked up her glass and took a big sip to conceal the relief she was feeling, but from her father's little smirk, she knew that it wasn't fooling him.

"I know I can be demanding," he said. "But I'm on your side, daughter of mine. Never doubt that."

She smiled at him, still unsure what to make of this radical change in attitude, her father's unusual sudden mellowness.

If it's a ploy, let it be a ploy. For now, I might as well take advantage of the benefits.

"But make no mistake," he said with a smile of his own. "If he breaks your heart, I'll have him killed. Father's prerogative."

Solveig laughed, but her thoughts rushed back in space and time to a spot in an Acheroni diner three weeks ago where Aden had told her the reason for his flight from home, and a sudden cold trickle crept up her spine at her father's joke.

Chapter 9

Aden

The first sensation that returned to Aden was the sound of softly gurgling and sloshing liquid.

The second sensation was a particular smell, a scent that told him he was still alive. Medical centers on Oceana had a very particular olfactory profile, an airy blend of seawater and antiseptic cleanser that he had never smelled anywhere else.

He opened his eyes to soft, warm light. It came from the ceiling overhead, emitted from a few hundred invisible fiber-optic strands. His head felt like he was in the middle of the worst hangover of his life, but he knew it wasn't a hangover because he wasn't parched and dry mouthed. When he looked down at himself, he saw that he was in a medical cradle, swaddled in an autodoc suit that was connected to the cradle with a multitude of feed lines and sensor wires.

Over to the right of his medical cradle, Maya was curled up in a chair. *Zephyr*'s pilot looked like she was asleep, but as soon as he stirred and turned his head, her eyes opened and she looked at him.

"Welcome back," she said.

"I know this isn't Valhalla or any of that other afterlife shit," Aden mumbled.

"How can you be sure?"

"Because you're here," he said. "And you don't believe in any of that stuff."

"Doesn't mean I couldn't end up there by accident."

He tried to move his legs and arms. They were constrained by the tight autodoc suit and the cradle underneath, but it felt like they were responding the way they should.

"What are you doing here?" he asked.

"We have been taking turns guarding you. Decker and I."

A cold and clammy fear crept up his spine.

"What about Tess?"

"She's fine. They released her yesterday. We got a secure place off the grid. She's waiting for us there."

"Yesterday. How long have I been out?" he asked.

"Three days. You weren't ticking anymore when we hauled you out of the water. They had to restart you a few times. You're heavier than you look, by the way. Decker and I barely got you back to the surface."

"Henry and Tristan?"

She looked at the floor for a moment.

"Henry got the worst of it. They had to stitch his liver back together, but he'll need another. He'll be out for a good while."

She looked up and met his gaze.

"Tristan's gone."

He hadn't been prepared for the wave of grief and despair that washed over him. If he hadn't been in a medical cradle that supported all his limbs in a zero-gravity position, he would have slumped to the floor because he felt that all strength had suddenly drained from his muscles. He had been brought up in a household where showing emotion was a weakness, but there were unbidden tears burning in the corners of his eyes now, and he made no effort to blink them away. Maya watched him with the same calm and collected expression she always had on her face.

He had never seen her truly sad or cheerful. Whatever had happened to her, she had learned to keep a tight rein on her emotions.

"We were trying to save him," he said in a thick voice. "I tried to plug the wound. He wasn't gone long. Why the hell couldn't they bring him back, too?"

Maya shook her head.

"He was dead before you even got there. That piece of shit knew exactly where to stick the knife."

"Did they find him? That bastard with the knives. I dragged him down with me. Did they find his body?"

Maya shook her head.

"The rescue teams looked for a while, but he was gone. He got washed out to sea. Or he's some freak of nature who can hold his breath for twenty minutes."

"It should have been me," Aden said. "Not Tristan. He didn't deserve it. He never did anything to anybody."

"It should have been any of us," Maya said. "Look, we all agreed to take the contract. And then we all agreed to blow it off and hand that fucking contraband nuke to the Rhodies. We voted on it. We made that choice together. It's just that his face came up on top of the die when it stopped spinning."

"If we had walked in two minutes earlier . . ." he began.

"Then you'd be dead now, or Tess, or maybe all three of you. Stop thinking about it. There's no fate. There's no '*deserve.*' There's just random chance. And a universe that doesn't give a fuck about any of us. You start taking chance personal, you're on a fast track to losing your mind."

He wanted to be angry with her, to funnel his grief into another emotion to lessen the breathtaking intensity of it, but he found that he couldn't. Maya was just being Maya, aloof and analytical, pretending nothing could pierce that armor around her inner core. Or maybe she was right, and nothing ever truly did. Not for the first time, he found himself wondering what had happened to her before she became a pilot, what had caused her to keep everyone out of her orbit. Maybe it was a philosophy thing or a cultural difference he didn't understand yet.

No wonder she's such a good pilot, he thought. *All logic and numbers, with no inclination to let emotion get control of the stick. And spaceships don't try to become friends with you.*

"So what happens now?" Aden asked. "What do we do?"

Maya rubbed her buzz cut with one hand as she thought about his question.

"Ideally, we go find that bastard and his employers. Get our revenge for Tristan. But I think that's out of our league. The only one of us who's good with a blade is Henry, and he's in medical stasis waiting for a replacement liver right now."

She looked at him and shrugged.

"We make a pretty lousy crew of plucky rogues, to be honest," he said, and she smiled. It was a small one, a slight upturn of one side of her mouth, but it was more mirth than he had seen from her in a while.

"We'll get you out of here, and then we'll meet up at the safe place. That's as far as the plan goes right now. After that, we'll roll the dice again."

"I think my schedule is clear for that," he replied.

"The security police will want to talk to you, I think. They already squeezed me and Decker."

He tried not to show the alarm he suddenly felt.

"What did they ask you about?"

"What do you think? Somebody got stabbed and killed in their city. They want to figure out the why and how. Like they do. You'll be fine. It's the Adrasteia police, not the Gretian Blackguards. But remember—nobody in uniform is your friend. Not even the locals. Tell them what happened. No more, no less. It was all on the security sensors anyway."

She got out of her chair in one lithe and effortless move.

"I'll let them know you're up and ready to get out of here. Anything goes weird, hit the alarm on the cradle. I'll wait for you downstairs in the atrium."

Maya walked to the door and turned around when she reached it.

"And stop with this shit about wishing you were dead instead of Tristan. If he's in any of the gods-damned afterlives, you know what he's saying to you right now about that, don't you?"

Aden smiled weakly.

"He's telling me to pull my head out of my ass and be glad I'm still alive. And to find a good bottle and a pretty girl to wink at."

"Damn right." She flashed that little smile again. "You got to know him well enough in the end."

—

A med tech came in a few minutes later and disconnected Aden's autodoc suit from the medical cradle, then raised the cradle into a sitting position.

"How are we feeling?" he asked Aden.

"Like someone used my head for a punching bag," he replied.

"That's an aftereffect of the medical stasis. It will go away in another hour or two. You've had pretty extensive surgery. One collapsed lung, and the other was filled with water when you came in. They had to do a lot of work to get you breathing on your own again."

The tech took out a comtab and showed it to Aden.

"We got your personal data, but I'd like you to verify the details before we release you."

Aden looked at the screen, where the personal information of his purchased ID was listed: Aden Jansen, citizen of Oceana, born and raised on Adrasteia. He had memorized his social account number and the vital information of his fake life, of course, but the headache made it difficult to recall the data from memory quickly, so he just glanced at his name and image and nodded.

"That looks right to me," he said.

"Very well. We are sorry that you required our services, but glad that we could undo the damage that was done to you."

It's a very long way from being undone, Aden thought.

"Thank you," he replied. "Did you manage to rescue any of my things?"

"Unfortunately, we couldn't save your clothing. But your personal device, your ID pass, and the things you were carrying in your pockets are over there in the wet cell, in the top drawer of the cabinet next to the shower. You'll also find a set of basic garments in your size."

Aden breathed a sigh of relief. He didn't care about the clothes or the stuff in his pockets, but if he had lost his ID pass, getting a new one would have been a hassle. Regular citizens could just walk into their local government service station and have a new pass issued, but he didn't want to take the chance that the required checks would be more thorough than his bought identity could withstand.

"Thank you," he said. "Can you get me out of this thing so I can take a shower and get dressed?"

The hot water of the shower made him feel less sore and achy, but it did nothing to calm the uproar in his mind. Of all the members of the crew, Tristan had become the closest to him over the last few months, his recent fling with Tess notwithstanding. Tristan hadn't been quite old enough to be his father, but Aden had started to think of him as something of an older brother. He had died before Aden had ever found a fitting opportunity to tell him his true origin. Now he would never know if their friendship had been solid enough for forgiveness. He tried to remember the last thing he'd said to Tristan, but now he couldn't remember their final exchange. Knowing the older man's love of banter and ribbing, it had probably been something irreverent. That's what happened when people died unexpectedly, and their friends and family didn't have time to make their peace with it. It was like the universe had swallowed Tristan, and everything that was unfinished between them would remain unfinished forever.

Aden only noticed the new scars on his body when he dried himself off after his shower. One went down his left forearm, from a spot a few centimeters above the wrist all the way to his elbow. The other was much smaller, a thin red line under his rib cage on the left side of his body, the width of a ceramic blade. It looked much less dramatic than the long gash on his arm, but it had been the more serious injury by far. He inspected himself in the mirror while he was drying off. He was starting to look more like a spacer than a soldier, but his leaner build and the short red beard seemed like pretense to him now, like a costume that didn't quite fit right.

He opened the cabinet drawer and pulled out the generic outfit they had removed for him, off-white overalls and light-blue slip-on shoes. When he was finished putting everything on, he looked in the mirror again. The clothes reminded him unpleasantly of his old prison garb in the POW arcology on Rhodia. He collected his personal things from the drawer and stuffed them into his pockets.

When he walked back into the convalescence suite, someone else was standing in the room with the med tech, a short man with a stubbly beard who managed to look rumpled even though he was wearing a formfitting police bodysuit.

"I'll leave you to it," the med tech said. "You are officially discharged. You have subdermal medication dispensers that will stay active for a few days and then dissolve on their own. You should be well on the mend, but let us know if there are any issues or complications."

"Thank you," Aden said again. "I'm sure I'll be fine."

The tech nodded and left the room.

"Glad to see that you are back on your feet, Master Jansen," the police officer said. "My name is Constable Holst. I'm with the investigative team that is looking into the attack on you and your friends."

"Shipmates," Aden said. "We work together. We were taking a break planetside."

There were no chairs in the room to offer the constable other than the upright medical cradle, so Aden walked over to the window and indicated the space next to him with his palm turned upward, the Oceanian gesture of polite acquiescence. The view from the window was a corner of Adrasteia's busy inner harbor near the central island. Usually, the sight of the blue skies and calm seas had a pacifying effect on him, but right now he was too mindful of his circumstances to relax. He had to give enough information to the constable to evade suspicion, and not enough to raise questions, all while keeping his accent and mannerisms carefully controlled.

"I'm very sorry about your shipmate," Constable Holst said. "Master Dorn. We'll do all we can to find the man who is responsible for all that violence."

"I'll help you in whatever way I can," Aden said. "But I don't know how much good I'll be to you right now. I've been in stasis for the last three days. My brain still feels like mush."

"I completely understand. You want to tell me what happened in broad strokes? It's fine if there are some things you can't quite remember yet."

"We were planning to get together. The crew, I mean. It's a bit of a ritual when we're onshore. When Tess and I got there, we found Tristan dead in his bed with a wound in his chest. When we tried to summon help, we got ambushed by the man who did it. Everything after that is still kind of a blur. We fought, he stabbed us both, and then I managed to hurl myself off the balcony and into the water with him."

"You're certain the man who attacked you also killed your friend."

"He told us so," Aden said.

"And you know who he is?" Constable Holst asked.

Aden shook his head. "He calls himself Milo. But I'll swallow a liter of stasis fluid if that's his real name. He's an enforcer for the people we pissed off a few weeks ago."

"Tell me about that."

Aden considered his reply. Holst had almost certainly asked his crewmates already to get all the versions of the story, but he was reasonably sure that Decker and the others would have kept the nature of their contraband cargo a little vague. If they had told Holst about the nuke and Aden didn't mention it, he'd make himself suspicious with his evasiveness, but if they hadn't and he volunteered that information, it would turn a routine police investigation into a major news item on the networks in a few hours.

"We took on a cargo contract and defaulted on the delivery. After the supplier dropped the cargo with us, we had a strong hunch that it was illicit. So our engineer opened it. Then we contacted the nearest Alliance patrol and turned it over to them. RNS *Minotaur*, if I can remember correctly."

"Can you tell me what it was?"

"Military-grade weapon components," Aden replied. *And that's the understatement of the millennium.*

Constable Holst nodded. He didn't seem surprised, which confirmed to Aden that he had heard some variation of this information already.

"We refunded the advance fee to the client. But they didn't take it well."

"It certainly looks like they did not," Holst said. "I know it's probably a small consolation after what happened, but your crew did the right thing."

"It is a small consolation," Aden confirmed. "Tristan's dead because we made a bad call before we made a good one. But thank you."

"I know it's hard to think straight when someone is trying to stick a knife into you. But is there anything distinctive about this Milo you remember? Something that may help us track him down?"

"He's not from Oceana. I'm pretty sure he's Gretian."

"What makes you think that?"

"His accent," Aden said. "He doesn't really have one. But I have a Gretian mother. Something about the way he talked sounded familiar, so I started talking to him in Gretian to distract him."

"You speak Gretian, huh?" Holst said.

"Enough to know that he's a native speaker. He's fluent enough in our language, but he doesn't sound like he's from anywhere."

"Interesting. I'll pass that on. Anything else you can remember?"

Aden exhaled and shook his head.

"Nothing that comes to mind right now. He showed up, we talked, we fought, and then we were in the water. It all happened in a rush. And my adrenaline was through the roof."

"That is perfectly fine." Constable Holst pocketed the comtab he had been holding and flashed a curt smile. "I know there's a lot weighing on your mind right now, and you are still not fully recovered from your injuries and the treatment. But I would appreciate it if you could find the time to come see me at the justice center in a few days for a victim statement. After you've had time to clear your head."

It was a politely worded request, but something about the way it was delivered gave Aden the distinct feeling that his appearance was not optional, that Holst wouldn't just leave things alone if he failed to show. If Holst thought there was more to the story than what the crew had told him, he'd start digging deeper, and Aden knew that his fake ID pass would not withstand that kind of scrutiny. If he was lucky, they'd merely put him on a transport to Gretia instead of shipping him back to the Rhodians to serve a few more years for his POW parole violation.

"Of course," he said. "After I help bury my friend, if you don't mind."

"Absolutely," Holst said. "No rush at all. I will send the information to your comtab. Early next week should be more than fine if it's convenient. Contact me if you recall anything important before then."

"You can be sure of it," Aden replied.

"Good day, Master Jansen. And again, sorry for your loss and all you went through. We will make sure the man who did this ends up where he belongs."

Aden nodded and watched Constable Holst depart. When the automatic door closed behind the police officer, the room was so quiet that he heard his own heartbeat in his ears, beating a little faster than normal.

"Well, *shit*," he said into the silence.

Chapter 10

Idina

Inside the stricken Badger, the fire suppressant system went off again near the front of the vehicle with a sharp hiss.

"Sound off," Idina yelled. "Everyone okay?"

Her half section returned their affirmations one by one. In front of her, the deputy commissioner looked shaken but unhurt.

"Something went through the hull bottom in front," the Badger commander sent from his seat behind the forward bulkhead door. "Drive train's fried. We've lost a wheel or two. Running on the backup power pack."

"What did we hit? Explosives?" the deputy high commissioner asked. His voice sounded a quarter octave higher than before.

"Doubt it," Color Sergeant Sirhan said. "There was no bang."

"Whatever it was, it went through our armor somewhere," Idina said.

Sirhan nodded and tapped the controls on his comms cuff.

"Ops, this is Kukri One Niner. We've had hostile interface on the southbound lane of the bridge at Delta One Two. No injuries, but our ride is a mission kill. Request extraction and recovery team."

Idina scanned the feed from the overhead drone that was now circling their location. The Badger was nosed up against the low barrier dividing the transit lanes in the middle of the bridge. It sat almost perpendicular to the flow of traffic and blocked most of the roadway. There was smoke and fire suppressant pouring out of a spot in the right front of the hull. Twenty or thirty meters behind the wrecked Badger, she saw a hole in the road surface that was still smoking with the residue of whatever propellant the unknown device had burned.

"No contact," she said to Sirhan. "Traffic's stopped behind us. Nobody's shooting."

She turned to her troops in the hold next to her.

"Purple Section, disembark and secure the site. Don't let any civilians close to the armor. But keep your trigger fingers in check. Nobody shoots without clearance."

They unbuckled their harnesses and readied their weapons. When the tail ramp started lowering, Idina had an unwelcome premonition of gunfire ripping through the opening hatch and tearing them all to shreds before they had a chance to leave the Badger. But the ramp hit the green-colored roadway without incident. She was closest to the opening, so she rushed out and took up position to the left of the ramp to secure the egress of the rest of her small team. There was no obvious threat waiting, no insurgents in stealth suits advancing on them, no bullets bouncing off the armor of the Badger. It was a sunny, peaceful-looking day outside. They were stopped right in the center of the bridge span, dozens of meters above the river. Behind the Badger, the civilian pod traffic kept rolling up the bridge and slowly closing the gap the AI had made earlier.

Idina connected to the traffic network and overrode the bridge traffic controller manually with the military access code. The roadway underneath her boot soles changed from green to red, and the traffic stopped again. Her quick count showed at least a dozen transport pods on the bridge behind them, the closest one only fifty meters to the rear of the smoking Badger. In the Alon bubble of the passenger compartment, the occupant looked at her with anxiety on his face. She held out her hand, palm forward, in the universal "stop" gesture and shook her head at the passenger. Around her, the section had taken up their security positions, covering the Badger from all four corners. Idina walked toward the hole in the roadway that had blown open underneath their vehicle and carefully stepped close to it. It was a small hole for the outsized damage the vehicle had suffered, no more than the diameter of a dinner plate.

"Careful, Colors," Private Condry said from his corner of the Badger. "Could be a follow-up charge nearby."

She turned around and nodded her acknowledgment. Nearby, the Badger sat at a slight list. The front road wheel on the right side had been blown off the vehicle, and she didn't see it on the roadway anywhere, so she surmised it had been flung across the traffic lanes and over the edge of the bridge into the river. The second wheel stuck out of the wheel well at an angle, obviously wrenched from its mountings by the blast. Whatever had exploded underneath the Badger had ripped off the wheel, demolished the drive train, and almost flipped the thirty-ton vehicle onto its side. She turned back and gave the hole another look. The edges were blown out and looked melted. When she stood right in front of the opening, she could see that the explosive had punched cleanly through the entire upper layer of the bridge, fifty centimeters of steel, laminate, and solar cells.

"What have we here?" Idina murmured to herself.

She took a knee and touched the edges of the hole lightly with her glove. It was a familiar-looking penetration pattern, even if she usually got to see the entry instead of the exit.

"What do you see, Chaudhary?" Colors Sirhan asked over the comms.

"They used an anti-armor round," she said. "Explosively formed projectile warhead, large caliber. Maybe from a naval gun. Mounted upward under the road surface. Clever little shits."

She stood up and looked around again.

"Took away half the explosive power when it had to punch through that road top. But that way it was shielded from the drone sensors."

She walked back toward the Badger, suddenly feeling like there were hundreds of pairs of eyes on her.

"Section, stay on your toes. They had to blow it remotely. Means they're still out there. Maybe watching us right now."

The bridge was in the middle of an open area with long lines of sight. The nearest building was a residential cluster on the left bank of the river just as it made a turn. Half of the windows and terraces in that cluster were high enough to see the top of the bridge and the vehicles on it. She bounced a laser off the nearest windows: 475 meters. The little machine pistol she had in her hands was good for half that distance at best. At least a dozen terrace doors stood open in the pleasant late-summer weather, a dozen different vectors for eyeballs and gun barrels.

"How long for the QRF bird?" she asked Sirhan.

"ETA six minutes."

"Keep the VIP in the armor until then. We're too exposed up here to cover every angle."

"You got it. Stay close, don't take chances," Sirhan replied.

"I'm not going anywhere," Idina said. She looked back at the access ramp on the left bank, clogged up with civilian transport pods in orderly intervals. The right bank, their destination, was almost free of traffic now, but the Badger wasn't going anywhere, and the end of the ramp was over a hundred meters away, with no obvious cover beyond for another sixty or seventy.

"Colors, look," one of her troopers said and pointed behind her. She turned to see that one of the civilian pods was slowly rolling onto the red section of the bridge. The bridge AI had stopped all automatic traffic, which meant that the passenger had overridden his vehicle's AI and taken manual emergency control. The pod passed the row of standing traffic at walking speed on the inside of the travel lane.

You're either profoundly stupid, or you're about to make an explosives delivery, Idina thought. She disengaged the safety on her gun and walked toward the oncoming pod.

"Hold your fire," she sent to her section.

She waved at the oncoming driver with both hands, crossing them in front of her face emphatically.

"Stay back," she yelled. "Do not approach." Her helmet's AI translated her commands into Gretian and amplified them. But the driver either couldn't hear her, or he wasn't in the mood to listen, because his pod continued its slow drive up the ramp and past the waiting traffic.

"What in the hells is wrong with you?" she muttered. When the pod was past the front of the queue and still moving toward the Badger at slow speed, Idina raised her weapon and aimed it at the sensor lens at the front of the vehicle. She had taken up most of the slack on the trigger of her machine pistol when the pod finally came to a halt, less than thirty meters in front of her. She released the pressure on the weapon's trigger.

The pod's access door swung upward and back, and a Gretian man climbed out. He straightened up and walked toward Idina with unconcealed irritation on his face, oblivious or unconcerned that she was aiming a gun in his general direction.

"Stop!" she shouted. "Do not come closer. This is an Alliance military emergency."

He kept walking as she reeled off her canned warnings, and she finally raised her weapon and aimed the targeting laser at the middle of his chest.

"Is my translator software broken? Stop, or I will shoot you."

He looked down at the green chevron on his chest. Three more appeared one by one until his tunic looked like a novelty fashion item for safe nighttime exercise. The civilian looked past Idina, and the realization that he had several automatic weapons aimed at his vital organs finally seemed to sink in. He halted his advance and glared at Idina.

"You cannot just shut down the bridge!" he shouted at her. "There are people with a purpose here. People who have to be on the other side."

"Someone set off an explosive charge. Our vehicle is disabled. The Gretian authorities will direct you once they arrive."

"There is plenty of space to the side!" he said.

Idina shook her head in disbelief.

"No one gets to come within thirty meters of that vehicle. You may work out your transportation problem with the police when they get here. Now please return to your pod and do not come any closer to us with it."

That did not seem to mollify the civilian. He was a ruddy-faced man in his middle years, wearing business clothing, and clearly used to getting his way most of the time. Idina could tell that without the guns pointed at him, he'd walk right toward her and try to shove her out of the way, an approach that a few Gretians had tried on her in the past to amusing effect. Realizing that he had limited options for defiance displays, he kicked the road surface and threw his hands up in exasperation. The passengers in the pods behind him were watching the show with apprehension, undoubtedly cognizant of the fact that they were in the line of fire if their fellow citizen decided to do something stupid.

If only Captain Dahl were here, she thought. *She'd have him shut up and back in that pod faster than I can put my weapon on safe.*

"You people have been here long enough," he said. "This is ours, not yours. Our roads. Our bridges. Paid for by our public funds. You cannot just act like you own the planet now. Go home. Leave us be."

Idina found that her shallow well of patience had run dry somewhere in the middle of his little speech. There was a place and a time for occupation disputes with civilians, but the center of a bridge right after an insurgent trap was not it. But before she could voice that thought and order Privates Arjun and Raya to help the man back into his conveyance, there was a dull crack overhead. She looked up to see the surveillance drone falling from the sky, trailing debris and smoke as it plummeted toward the ground.

"What in all the hells . . ." she said. In front of her, the Gretian civilian followed her gaze and looked at the falling drone, dumbfounded. Then the significance of the event burned through the surprise that had slowed down her brain momentarily, and the jolt of adrenaline she felt made the top of her head feel like it was about to blow off.

"Section, take cover," she shouted. "The ambush is still in progress."

Behind the angry Gretian civilian, his pod took a hammer blow from something unseen that rocked it sideways and sprayed a cloud of composite and Alon shards in every direction. The civilian staggered and fell to the ground face-first. Idina felt bits of debris shrapnel tearing into the cloth layer above her spidersilk armor and turned away from the blast. When she looked back, the civilian was still on the ground, motionless.

"Incoming fire, direction unknown. Get me a fix on that firing position if he shoots again."

The PDS emitter on the nearby Badger came to life and blotted an incoming projectile out of the air fifty meters away from the vehicle. The fragments from the round hit the armor like sharp-edged hail, and Private Raya, who was covering from the left rear of the Badger, cried out in pain as something made it through his soft armor.

"They're shooting from the east," she shouted. "Get behind the right side of the armor. Badger chief, we could use some ballistic radar."

"The emitter is out, Colors. And the PDS is going to suck the backup cells dry in about ten shots."

"Gods-damn it. Sirhan, tell the QRF squad that we're immobilized and under fire, and to hurry things along a little if they can."

"Already on it," Sirhan replied.

Behind Idina, another civilian pod blew to pieces in a cloud of silver-white shards. She looked over at the residence building to the east, frantically trying to spot a muzzle flash or the propellant plume from a crew-served weapon. Whatever it was could take apart a civilian transport pod in a single hit, but she knew the devastation a rail-gun projectile left in its wake, and this wasn't quite it.

The nearby civilian groaned and moved his arm, trying to find purchase to raise himself off the ground. Idina looked over at the armor, then muttered a curse. She could make the dash behind the Badger in four seconds by herself. Playing combat medic would probably get her killed. But even though the Gretian had been belligerent and hostile, it didn't mean he deserved to be left out in the open to bleed to death while some unseen attacker fired at Alliance troops and Gretian civilians without discrimination. She rushed over to him in a low run and turned him on his back, then grabbed the collar of his tunic to use as a handle. Then she dragged him back toward the Badger with every bit of strength she could muster. Any moment, that unseen gun would fire, and she'd be blasted in half by the shell, dead in an instant because she just had to be noble. But when the gun fired, it tore apart yet another transport pod farther down the roadway. The insurgent gunner seemed to be spreading out his target selection to cause maximum confusion and carnage, and it worked all too well. The other pod passengers were now in full panic. Some of them left their vehicles and ran down the road to the access ramp that led back to the left bank of the river. Several tried to turn their pods around under manual control, which was an insane thing to do under fire.

Private Arjun ran out from his cover behind the Badger and grabbed the civilian as well. Together, they hauled him behind the bulk of the Badger's armored right flank. As Idina dropped to the ground with the Gretian, the Badger's Point Defense System fired again, breaking up another cannon shell headed for the vehicle, and the shrapnel splattered the far side of the armored personnel carrier.

"Does anyone have eyes on that gods-damned gun mount?" Idina shouted.

"Nothing on infrared, Colors. Whatever they're shooting, it's cooled and suppressed."

She aimed her weapon around the corner to look at the residential building in the distance without having to stick her head into the line of fire. Then she cycled her helmet's sensor filters through every possible mode. A gun big enough to take apart a travel pod in a shot or two would generate a muzzle flash big enough to be clearly seen on thermal imaging or infrared even at this range. She waited a few seconds. To her left, another pod took a hit to its front and spun around ninety degrees, crashing into a second pod in the process. The scene on the bridge was now complete mayhem. Civilians were running down the roadway or cowering behind transport pods, every bit as clueless about the source of the fire as Idina's section and their multimillion ags' worth of fighting gear. Still, there was no telltale thermal bloom from a gun muzzle, and the firing sound was so dulled and muffled that it sounded like someone beating a hanging carpet with a broom.

Not a rail gun, she thought. *Not heavy enough to get through the Badger's armor or PDS network. But sure as hell big enough to wreck the shit out of these civvie pods. It's a heavy machine gun, with a suppressor and a cooling setup. And they're firing it in single shots so they won't overwhelm the cooler and show themselves on thermal imaging.*

A familiar whirring sound reached her ears, and she looked to the left to see a Gretian police gyrofoil swooping out of the sky from the north, position and emergency lights blinking. It made a half circle above the bridge approach and pulled into a near hover above the scene. Frantically, Idina tapped the controls on her cuff to switch to the Joint Security Force guard frequency.

"Gretian police unit, get back to altitude! We are under heavy fire from the buildings to the east. You are right in their sights."

She received no acknowledgment on the guard channel, but a moment later, the police gyrofoil tilted its rotors and turned to reverse its course. There was another dull thumping sound from the direction of the residence towers, and something shattered the Alon bubble of the cockpit and made the gyrofoil lurch sideways violently. Idina clenched her fists. She had spent months on patrol in one of those units, and they were only armored against fire from small-caliber weapons, the type a determined criminal might employ. They were not built to stand up against military-grade firepower. She watched in helpless horror as the gyrofoil made a sharp right descending turn, engines whirring at full power. It hurtled toward the embankment on the north side of the river and smashed into the ground at a forty-five-degree angle with a sickening crash. The wreckage cartwheeled for a few dozen meters, spewing chunks of Alon and white laminate armor everywhere. Finally, it came to a rest, and Idina knew from the looks of the smoking hull that there was no point going out there under fire to look for survivors.

"Shakya, tell Ops to get in touch with the Gretians and have them keep their flying units away from this bridge." Her last word was drowned out by the high-energy discharge of the Badger's PDS as it swatted another incoming round.

"Understood. ETA for the QRF bird is two minutes."

Gods-damn these flight times, she thought. *Trying to pacify a city of a million from a single base on its outskirts.*

"Standing by to return fire at your word," the Badger's commander sent. The gun mount on the vehicle had swiveled around, and now the tri-barrel cannon and the stubby grenade launcher tube on the mount were pointed at the residence building, slowly panning in small arcs to acquire a target.

"Do not use that cannon," Idina said. "That dual-purpose shit will go right through the building."

"You want to keep playing target out here without shooting back?"

"I want to not end up in the system-wide news tomorrow for killing fifty civilians by accident," she replied. She turned her weapon around the corner again and looked at the open doors of the building, a dozen black holes staggered across five levels and a hundred meters of facade.

"Use the nonlethals," she said. "Foam rounds and shit balls. Put a couple through every open window over there. The gun's behind one of those."

"That won't kill anyone, Colors."

"That's the point. But we'll make a mess inside. Gum up the sensors and the aiming device on that gun. I'd rather we pay for a cleanup than a bunch of funerals. Do it, Sergeant."

There was a moment of silence on the channel. The gun mount stopped its swiveling motion as the commander readied the grenade launcher. Then the stubby tube began pumping out nonlethal grenades. The mount zipped from target to target with AI precision, three grenades per window. The nonlethals were slow, and Idina could see the big projectiles in flight as they arced toward their targets. One by one, each window received a mix of grenades that sailed right through the dark rectangles and into the rooms beyond. A few times, one of the grenades missed the target door and splattered against the Alon facade nearby, and the AI immediately sent rapid follow-up shots to account for the missed delivery. Idina allowed herself a moment to breathe. She looked to the right to see both Private Raya and the Gretian civilian on the ground, and Private Arjun tending to both with medical packs.

The hidden gun fired again. This time, the round did not hit anything in particular. It smacked into the divider between the travel lanes, fifteen meters to Idina's left, kicking up a cloud of concrete dust and leaving a crater the size of a fist.

"Keep firing," Idina said. "It's working."

"All those shit balls," Private Condry said. "That's going to make a fucking mess."

"They can be glad it's just shit balls," Idina replied. Four months ago, she wouldn't have hesitated to let the Badger commander reply with live cannon fire, collateral damage be damned. But Captain Dahl had been right—someone wanted the Alliance and the Gretians at each other's throats again, and peppering an apartment building with armor-piercing explosive rounds would do a great deal of progress toward that end.

They heard the low whoosh of the combat gyrofoil's rotors a few moments before it appeared. It popped up from low level above the river to the east and roared toward the residential towers. Even from this distance, Idina could see the gun turrets rotating as the ship's AI searched for targets. They approached the building from the side, away from the firing angles offered by the river-facing terraces and circled the rooftop. A few moments later, lines deployed from the craft, and a full platoon of QRF troopers roped down to the roof.

"They've stopped firing," Private Khanna said. He was still in his overwatch position behind the damaged front right corner of the Badger.

"They've done enough damage," Idina replied.

From the left side of the bridge, smoke poured from half a dozen destroyed or damaged transport pods. The scene was still complete chaos as the civilians were practically climbing over each other to get off the bridge. On the west side of the river, the wreckage of the Gretian police gyrofoil was smoldering and discharging the energy from its damaged power cells in bright sparks. Idina wondered if she knew the officers who had just died in that craft. She hadn't been on personal terms with most of the Gretians except for Dahl, but she was sure she would remember their faces if they had been with her joint patrol contingent before.

"Tell Ops to let the Gretians know one of their police units is down," she sent to Sirhan. "Multiple casualties on the northern end of the bridge. They need to get all the rescue and medical they have. It's a slaughterhouse down there."

She set her weapon to safe and let it drop from its sling to hang by her side. It had been worse than useless for this encounter, and she cursed herself for her failure to dress for the worst-case scenario.

I'll never leave the Green Zone without hard armor and a battle rifle again, no matter how aggressive the brass thinks it looks, she vowed.

A sudden rush of anger overcame her, and she walked to the back of the Badger and punched the hatch control. Inside, the deputy high commissioner was still in his seat, flanked by his security detail. He looked a little pale and unsettled.

"How are we back here?" she asked.

Colors Sirhan raised a thumb in reply.

It was never a wise move to speak one's mind in front of high-ranking officials, even if they didn't wear a uniform. But right now, she was so livid that she didn't care whether they stuffed her on a transport back to Pallas this afternoon or stripped her in rank all the way back to private. She walked over to the anti-shock seat across from the VIP and opened a screen in the air between them. She panned the point of view around so it faced the carnage down at the bridge access ramp, then turned the screen to put it in front of his face.

"There's your closer look at the situation on the ground right now, sir. None of this would have happened if we had taken a combat gyrofoil this morning. We'd already be halfway to Camp Unity by now."

He seemed to shrink in his seat a little. His eyes flitted from her to the screen and back, but he made no attempt at a reply, clearly rattled by what he saw. Some things looked simple and straightforward from the comfort of a distant office, but like a fractal painting, the details only came into view as the distance decreased.

"No disrespect intended, sir. But you may want to trust the judgment of your security detachment next time. They've been in this business for a long time. If that charge had gone off a half second later, it would have gone through the middle of this compartment and we would all be dead right now."

She waved the screen away and got out of the seat again.

"I have a rescue to coordinate and a bridge to clear. The QRF team will be here shortly to get you back to base, sir. Colors Sirhan, I'll see you and the team back at the barn."

She climbed out of the Badger and stomped down the back ramp with steps that were a bit firmer than strictly needed. When she glanced back, the DHC looked like he had taken a sip of something nasty. Next to him, Color Sergeant Sirhan gave her an almost imperceptible nod of silent approval.

Chapter 11
Dunstan

The cabin of *Hecate*'s commanding officer was twice as big as those of the other crew members, but it still felt like it was the size of a modest supply closet. Dunstan was used to bigger ships by now, and on *Minotaur*, he'd had two cabins, one for regular rest time and a smaller day cabin right next to the AIC. His new home for the next few months didn't even have its own wet cell, just a small combination zero-g toilet and sink that popped out of the wall when summoned via control panel. Everything was shiny and new and ultramodern, just crammed into half the space he'd had on his old frigate.

I never thought I'd miss the luxuries of that old bucket, he reflected as he stretched out on his bunk. For the last few hours, the crew had been storing fresh provisions in every available nook and cranny on the ship for the three-month deployment, and he had been part of the human chain, passing back an untold number of boxes and canisters. Now his arms and shoulders ached from the extended upper-body workout, an unwelcome reminder that he was four years from fifty and no longer the strong, young junior officer he used to be.

"Ops to commander," the voice of his first officer said from the overhead comms.

"Go ahead, Ops," he replied. *Hecate* was too small to have an Action Information Center, and he knew it would take him a few days to get used to the change in nomenclature.

"Supplies are secured, and all departments report ready for getting underway," Lieutenant Hunter said.

"Very well. Let Rhodia One know we are ready for undocking and request a departure slot. I'll be up in Ops in a minute."

"Affirmative," the first officer replied. Dunstan still wasn't used to hearing a Gretian accent on a Rhodian warship, and he suspected it would take him longer to get used to that than to saying "Ops" instead of "AIC." He swung his legs over the edge of the mattress to sit up and promptly bumped his head on the storage closet that was overhanging the entirety of the bunk.

"Gods-damned stealth boats," he muttered and rubbed the top of his head. "Way to make me feel like a midshipman again."

He got up and zipped his shipboard overalls back up to the collar, then checked himself in the mirror by the door to make sure he looked like someone who had business giving orders. It was his second full day with his new crew, and he still had to rely on name tags when talking to most people outside of the operations room even though the ship only had five officers and twenty-three enlisted on it.

From the topmost berth deck where the commander's cabin was located, it was a short commute down a narrow ladder to Ops. He stepped off the ladder and walked over to the upright gravity couch where Lieutenant Hunter was sitting and sipping from a stainless mug with a safety lid. On a larger warship, the first officer to see the CO coming into the AIC would announce his arrival to the whole deck, but standard protocol didn't work on a ship of *Hecate*'s size. The smaller warships were run in an almost egalitarian fashion, with little pomp. They had their own rituals, and Dunstan was quickly acquiring them again after years on larger ships.

"I have the deck," he said to Lieutenant Hunter. She got up from the command couch and moved over to the nearest seat on the right.

"Commander has the deck," she acknowledged.

He nodded at the coffee she was still holding.

"Smells good. Any more where that came from?"

She tapped her comms link.

"Galley, Ops. Can you run a cup of coffee up here for the CO, please?"

"Ops, aye. Be up in a second."

The operations deck was almost cozy. *Hecate* only had five officers, and four of them had their action stations here. The fifth one, the chief engineer, was in charge of the ship's reactor and propulsion systems and ran his department from the engineering deck all the way at the bottom of the ship. Unlike *Minotaur*, there was no half deck overhead for the pilot stations. Instead, the conning station was set up at the front of the operations deck, two gravity couches on either side of a center console, facing an array of screen emitters and backup readouts. As small as the ops deck was, the situational display projecting from the top bulkhead was easily twice as large as the one on *Minotaur* had been, and the resolution of the hologram was much higher. It was still hard to believe that *Hecate* was the most expensive ship the Rhodian Navy had ever built, but the ops center was the most modern one Dunstan had ever seen.

Behind Dunstan, the mess specialist on watch came up the ladder, walked around Dunstan's gravity couch, and placed a stainless mug into the receptacle on the couch arm. Dunstan nodded his thanks. He picked up the mug, which was engraved with the ship's name and her crest, the triple-headed goddess from Old Earth mythology. The coffee was strong and flavorful, rivaling the best he could make in his own kitchen. Dunstan hummed with satisfaction and placed the cup back in its holder.

"The board is green, and we are waiting for final undocking clearance from Rhodia One, sir," Lieutenant Hunter said.

Dunstan nodded. Then he tapped his own comms link to initiate an all-hands address.

"*Hecate* crew, this is the commander. In a few minutes, we'll be undocking for our first combat patrol. I know there has been speculation about what we're going to be doing out there with this shiny new ship, so let me set everyone straight."

To his left, Lieutenants Robson and Armer, the communications and weapons specialists, turned their couches slightly behind their consoles to listen to what he was about to say. He knew that Robson was the most junior member of the operations team, but even she was a senior lieutenant like Armer. There were no new midshipmen on this ship, no junior lieutenants, and no enlisted crew members fresh out of tech school. Everyone was at least one rank above where they would be if they were doing the same job on any other ship in the navy, including Dunstan.

"I'll get right to the point I know you all care about the most. This is not going to be a scrap hunt. We are not going on antipiracy patrol. We've been tasked with bigger things. We are going to track and neutralize the people who have been setting the trade routes on fire for the last few months. The people who managed to get a nuke through our planetary defenses. They call themselves Odin's Ravens, as you know. Brothers and sisters to Odin's Wolves on Gretia. We're going to go out and clip their wings."

There were no exuberant cheers, but Dunstan saw satisfied smiles on the faces of Robson and Armer, and there were at least a few approving whistles coming up the ladderwell from the decks below.

"That's not to say that we won't deal with pirates if we happen to come across them. But we're not going to be out there to play police. We'll tag them and call in the nearest Alliance guns to deal with them. There's no place for prisoners on this ship anyway. We have bigger prey to hunt. So let's get on with it. Commander out."

He terminated the transmission with another tap on his comms link.

"How was that?" he asked. "Too long, too short, just right?"

"Just right, I think," Lieutenant Hunter said. "All they need to know and nothing they don't."

"I don't think this crew needs much in the way of motivational speeches," he said.

"Did you really take a frigate up against a heavy gun cruiser, sir?" Lieutenant Armer asked from the tactical station.

Dunstan nodded and took another sip of coffee before answering. "With *Minotaur*, three months ago," he confirmed. "I'm sure you've read the reports."

"We ran the scenario in the sim a bunch of times for training, with the same parameters. We got turned into scrap four times out of five. The fifth time, we were dead in space and had to take to the pods."

"They had us in every way. Size, armor, gun barrels, firing rate, caliber. Frigate's not made for that sort of close-range joust. But their point-defense AI hadn't seen an update in four years. Ours was up to date. We wiggled around through their gunfire long enough to get a missile into their stern. They decided to break it off at that point and run."

"If the fight rides on AI, it won't be a contest," Lieutenant Robson said. Dunstan looked over at her and grimaced.

"I'm happy you're confident about that, Lieutenant. We took just two hits from those two-hundred-millimeter rail guns, and they damn near broke my old ship in half. And she was four times the size of this one. That's a day I don't care to relive."

"Have you read much Old Earth military history?" Lieutenant Hunter asked.

"I have," he replied. "Mandatory reading at the command academy."

"Back when the navies of Earth were fighting each other in steel hulls on the surface of their oceans, there was an arms race with battleships. They were super expensive. More like national prestige objects than weapons systems. And then one nation designed a ship with so many smart innovations that it made all those other expensive battleships obsolete overnight."

"*Dreadnought*," Dunstan said. "I remember that. But I think she became obsolete in a few years' time. After everyone else had caught up."

"Everyone had access to steel and gunpowder back then. And *Dreadnought*'s superiority was all in her gun layout and her engines. Easy for others to copy," Hunter said. "This ship isn't like that. Nobody else can put anything like it into space. If they have the tech and the shipbuilding skills, they don't have access to enough palladium. If they have the palladium, they don't have the ability to build a ship around it. We're the only ones in the system who can do both."

She nodded at the tactical station and Lieutenant Armer.

"We don't look like much on paper as far as weapons go. Just a dual thirty-five-millimeter gun mount and a single missile tube with six birds. But that's not our big gun."

Lieutenant Robson looked up from her station.

"Rhodia One just sent our undocking clearance. We are go for undocking and pattern entry, fifth in line to depart."

"Very well." Dunstan leaned back in his chair and slipped into his harness. "Sound maneuvering stations. Number One, initiate undocking sequence at your discretion."

Lieutenant Hunter talked herself through the checklist. "All supply lines retracted. The hull is clear. No personnel present in the caution zone. Initiating undocking sequence."

The docking pad was a giant airlock that turned on its base to rotate the ship outside the station hull. It was a slow turn, just one degree per second, and they sat through the three-minute rotation silently, looking at the screens showing the external view. Dunstan watched as the space dock's interior gradually slipped from view until the ship stood in darkness in the space between the inner and outer hulls of the station.

"Docking rotation complete. Dock is depressurized. Opening outer dock hatch."

The outer hull opened in front of them, revealing the busy space around Rhodia One. Dunstan couldn't see the planet's surface because the military section of the station faced away from it to prevent easy observation of coming and going traffic from Rhodia's surface. But this was a station where hundreds of ships arrived and departed every day, and it would be hard to stay unnoticed with an unmarked ship that looked like nothing else in the fleet.

"Once we're off the boom, it'll be about twenty minutes before there are some beauty shots of us somewhere on the Mnemosyne," Dunstan said.

"I would not bet on that, sir," Lieutenant Hunter said. "Permission to stretch the regs a little?"

Dunstan raised an eyebrow.

"Does that stretch have the potential to endanger my crew or ship?"

"Negative, sir."

"Permission granted," he said, his curiosity kindled.

Lieutenant Hunter tapped her comms.

"Engineering, Ops."

"Ops, go ahead."

"Would you bring the reactor up to thirty percent, Lieutenant Fields? I need a bit of extra juice for a little technology demonstration in Ops."

"Affirmative. Going to thirty percent power output."

Hunter leaned back in her chair and brought up a screen and expanded it in front of her face until it covered a 120-degree arc, matching the view they had from the open docking hatch. Then she projected a control panel and let her fingers fly across the screen, touching data fields and entering instructions. On her screen, dozens of icons were in her field of view, each overlaid on a ship's position lights in the distance. Next to each icon, there was a short data readout with the hull number and the vital information about the ship. Lieutenant Hunter tapped another control field, and all the icons on the screen went from white to green in a ripple that took two seconds at most.

"Handshake complete," she said. "AI core utilization is at eleven point one percent."

She looked over at Dunstan and smiled dryly.

"And now comes the fun part."

She spent a few seconds paging through data fields, then selected one and flicked it up onto her wide-screen viewer, where it multiplied and seemingly went to every icon on the screen at once.

"And *done*."

Lieutenant Hunter picked a ship icon from her screen and moved it over to the situational display on the top bulkhead of the ops center, then expanded it. It showed a ship standing in the opening of the space dock, just like they were right now, but it looked nothing like *Hecate*. Instead, it was an orbital patrol corvette, with weathered hull paint and blinking running lights.

"I just picked a ship at random out of the ones in our field of view. It's a merchant. RMV *Thornbird*. This is what their optical sensors are showing when they look in our direction."

Dunstan leaned forward in his chair. "Tell me how you just did that."

"Our AI core connected to their comms system and hacked past their firewall to take control of their ship systems. It's overriding their sensors to show them what we want them to see, not what's actually in front of them. Just a beat-up little patrol corvette about to launch for a watch."

"You hacked into their ship in that short amount of time?"

"Not just theirs," Hunter said. "Every ship in our field of view right now." She checked her data readout at the bottom of her viewscreen. "Fifty-two in total."

"We hacked into the AI cores of *fifty-two* starships in five seconds," Dunstan said.

"That's affirmative, sir. Three point nine seconds, to be precise. Seven of them are warships, and their firewalls are much better than those on the merchants."

"Good gods." He looked at the image on the viewscreen. Everything was right about the corvette the AI had placed in their spot for the merchant vessel's sensors: the lighting, the reflections, the scraped and faded paint scheme. It looked as real as any ship Dunstan had ever seen with his own eyes.

"They'll figure it out if they have a physical viewport over there and get close enough for eyeballs. But from beyond visual range, we are whoever we say we are."

"There are fifty-two ships out there who now see that same image when they look at us?"

Lieutenant Hunter shook her head. It was obvious that she enjoyed his reaction.

"They're all seeing a *different* ship. The AI created separate entries for each target ship."

She picked another ship icon off her screen and flicked it over to the situational display, where it resized itself and slid next to the image from RMV *Thornbird*'s sensors.

"That's one of the warships, RNS *Halberd*. To them, we are the civilian luxury yacht *Sun Empress*. And if they check their Mnemosyne data, there'll be a full record. Flight plan, crew manifest, passenger list, recent movement. All generated on the fly by our AI and squeezed into the legit entries."

"I've never seen anything like it," he said.

"Nobody has, sir. I've been working with this hardware since we started the shakedown cruise. And I don't think I've ever taxed the AI core past twenty percent utilization. It's a paradigm shift."

She removed the sensor images from the main situational display.

"Do you want us to keep up the masquerade while we depart, sir? We can put them back to normal in half a second. The AI cleans up after itself when I drop the tether. Deletes the fake records and restores everything to the way it was before. Like we were never there."

Dunstan shook his head.

"Let's stay secret for a little while longer. At least until we're out of visual range of the station. Give your AI a bit of a workout."

"This is child's play for that core," she said.

Dunstan shook his head and grinned. "You sure know how to sell this ship, Lieutenant."

"Once you're used to what she can do, you start thinking of *combat power* in different ways, sir."

Overhead, the zero-g alert sounded, and the docking boom began to lower the ship into launch position. The gravity couches on the ops deck followed the movement precisely, lowering their occupants into an inclined position to prepare for the imminent loss of gravity. Dunstan felt the familiar floating feeling in his stomach as the ship moved away from the station and its gravmag field. Then they were at the end of the docking boom, and the ship rotated around its dorsal axis into launch position.

"Ready to release docking clamps on your mark," the helmsman said.

"Stand by on thrusters," Dunstan replied. "Release on my mark. Three—two—one—mark."

"Release confirmed, standing by on thrusters. We are loose from the station."

"Lateral thrusters, five-second burst, bring up the main drive and go to maneuvering speed. Take us out to departure lane Delta Three," Dunstan ordered.

"Aye, sir."

Hecate moved out into the traffic pattern for her assigned vector. All around them, Rhodia One was as busy as ever, dozens of ships maneuvering into position to dock or depart, thousands of lives and billions of ags' worth of cargo from all over the system. There were a dozen ever-changing transit lanes between the planets, many hundreds of millions of kilometers, and an almost infinite volume of space between them. Keeping all this commerce safe from pirates and the new insurgency had been an impossible task with the postwar navy. Recommissioning old ships had been a stopgap, and building new ones took a long time.

Maybe we needed that paradigm shift, Dunstan thought as he sipped his coffee and watched the traffic all around them. *A new way of thinking, instead of doing the same thing over and over and expecting different results. I suppose we'll find out if this works better than the old guns-and-missiles approach.*

He turned the coffee mug in his hands and looked at the ship's crest engraved into the stainless steel.

"You know your Old Earth military history, Lieutenant Hunter," he said. "What about your mythology?"

"I know some, sir. We had to slog through a lot of the classical stuff at university. But my degree is in AI development and mathematics. I'm more the engineer type."

He held up the cup and turned it so she could see the crest.

"Hecate," he said. "What did you learn about her?"

Lieutenant Hunter shrugged. "Greek goddess of the night, I think."

Dunstan nodded.

"She's the guardian of roads and crossroads. Protector of travelers," he said. "And the goddess of witchcraft and magic. I've been on a lot of ships over the years. But I think this is the first one I've served on that has a fitting name."

Chapter 12
Solveig

When Solveig stepped out of the skylift capsule, she saw Anja waiting and at the ready by the executive reception, her ever-present compad cradled in the nook of her arm.

"Good morning, Miss Ragnar," Anja said and fell into step next to Solveig as she headed for the Alon archway that separated the hallowed halls of the executive floor from the rest of the building. The nearest set of doors slid sideways to admit them.

"Have you recovered from the trip yet?" Solveig asked her assistant.

"Not quite," Anja admitted. "How about you, Miss Ragnar?"

"It was fun, but I don't want to see the inside of that ship again for a good while. I just skipped two weeks of running, and this morning it was like I was starting from scratch all over again."

"The hardest part for me is getting used to the daylight rhythm again," Anja said. "I wake up too early or go to bed too late for a few days after." She pulled her compad out from underneath her arm.

"Sorry to pack your schedule on your first day back in the office, but the director would like to have you in this morning at nine for a post-trip update. And there are three more meetings that I tried to space out over the day as much as I could. Legal, finance, and the security debriefing."

"It's fine," Solveig assured her. "I didn't come into the office to sip tea and stare out of the window all day."

She crossed the executive floor, returning greetings and respectful nods along the way. On most days, she still felt wildly out of place here. She was the only one with an office up on the executive floor who was under the age of forty, and everyone here who was close to her age was an assistant or someone from corporate security. Nobody had ever said it to her face, and she was sure that none would even hint at it in her presence, but everyone knew that she would not be up here yet if she weren't her father's daughter. She knew she'd have to prove herself every day, until their politeness came from genuine respect and not just from the fear of getting thrown out, and that was not a process that could take place in just a few weeks or months.

Her office felt almost palatial after spending the last few days on the VIP deck of the corporate yacht. When she walked in, the room's AI recognized her presence and set the temperature and lighting to her preferred levels. Anja stopped at the threshold of the office door the way she always did, as if there was an invisible force field in the door that only Solveig was allowed to step through.

"Your meeting with Director Pettar is scheduled in thirty minutes. Is there anything you need this morning?"

"Just some tea, please," Solveig said. "A strong one, from Pallas. Or some North Coast blend."

"I'll have some brought to you," Anja replied.

"Thank you, Anja. I'll call you if I need anything else."

Anja nodded and walked off to put in the tea order. Asking her assistant to bring her a beverage still made Solveig feel like a bit of a pompous ass, but the one time she had gone to the refreshments lounge herself to fetch her own, it had caused a bit of anxiety among the lounge staff because they thought she'd been overlooked somehow. Nobody up here got their own food or drink, and it had taken a while for her to understand that it wasn't the status thing she had thought it was in the beginning. The executives were expected to spend their attention and time on the important work, and taking five minutes to go fetch some tea could turn that five-ag mug of leaves and hot water into a five-hundred-ag one in the long run.

She walked over to the window and looked outside. The gouged Alon panel damaged by the shrapnel from the insurgent bomb explosion on the square below had been replaced by the maintenance team in her absence. On Principal Square, the daily demonstrations were in full swing again, but this time with a different tone than before. In the spring, it had been reformers versus loyalists, people ready to move on from the old ways against people who wanted the old order and the traditional institutions back. Now it was almost all anti-Alliance rhetoric. For the first time, Solveig looked at the crowds and felt some sympathy after the treatment she had received by the Rhodian marines, who were exercising power because they could, being harsh because it was fun.

Solveig sat down at her desk and settled into the chair as it shaped itself around her. She started to make the hand movement that would turn on her usual array of screen projections, but then she lowered her hand and closed her eyes with a deep breath, enjoying the momentary calming silence in the room.

Her personal comtab knocked its polite "incoming message" notification against her wrist. She raised it to look at the screen. It was a message from Berg.

Dinner?

She smiled and considered her response. Tonight she had planned to begin holding her father to his declaration that he would let her have her own social life from now on. Maybe it was time to test the veracity of the statement a little ahead of schedule.

She sent a node address in reply.

You can vid call on this node.

It took a few moments for Berg to reply. Solveig smiled again as she imagined him scratching the back of his head in confusion. She had been communicating with him only over encrypted text to keep their relationship off Falk's radar. He didn't know yet that the secret was out.

Are you sure about that? he finally asked.

Positive.

There was a chime at the door, and one of the lounge attendants came in with a mug. He walked over to her desk and set it down in front of her gingerly and with professional smoothness.

"Thank you," she said.

"You're most welcome," he replied and withdrew from the room.

"There is an incoming comms request," her room AI said.

"I'll take it at the desk," Solveig said. She opened a screen and looked at the originating node ID: DET. BERG, STEFAN, SANDVIK POLICE (CRIMINAL DIVISION).

Time to take this one above ground, she thought.

Solveig enlarged the screen and tapped the green ACCEPT/ANSWER field.

"Good morning," she said when she saw Berg's face. He was peering at her with some degree of disbelief, as if he had expected to fall for a prank. Behind him, people were walking around between desks and data stations, and she heard the low din of office conversation.

"And a good morning to you," he said. "Did you really just give me your official business node and tell me to comm you at the office via video?"

"I believe I did," she said.

"Your office is much nicer than mine," he said. "I don't even get walls."

"Unearned privilege," she replied. "You know how it is with us stuck-up plot-holder families."

"I feel like this relationship just received an upgrade. This is the first time we're talking over vid comms."

"Let's just say there has been a realignment," Solveig said.

"Okay," Berg said with a smile. "Mysterious. But whatever it is, I won't complain. It's nice to see you."

"And it's nice to see you," Solveig said. "And I'd love to have dinner with you tonight. But I have some family business back at home once I leave here. Some more realigning."

"I see." He did a demonstrative little pout. "How about lunch, then?"

She shook her head.

"Sorry. Four meetings today. I won't be able to duck out long enough to make it to the noodle place on Savory Row."

"Are you just going to skip lunch?"

"I'll have something here at the office. We do have a canteen here, you know."

"Why don't I come over and join you? I'll be running errands in that area today anyway."

"You want to come over and eat in the canteen at Ragnar Tower," she said with a smile.

"Sure. If you're forced to eat there, I'll endure it with you."

She laughed. "It may not be as profound a sacrifice as you think. But why not? If you have the time. And you won't get in trouble for it."

"Only if you're going to try to bribe me in my official capacity. And I actually end up accepting the bribe."

"I'll do my very best to spare you the temptation. Although the beef fillet with herb butter can corrupt the strongest wills."

"Beef fillet with herb butter," he repeated. "What kind of canteen serves that sort of lunch?"

"Unearned privilege, remember?" she said, and he laughed.

"Come to the main reception at noon. I'll put you on the visitor list for today. Someone will get you and take you up to the executive level."

"I'll be there at noon," Berg said. "Looking forward to it."

"As am I," she said and ended the connection. This was the first time she had used her corporate node for a conversation with Berg, and everything they had just said would be stored in the security data banks. If Marten still had his orders to keep her father in the loop, Falk would know about their lunch date before it even happened. Her office had glass or Alon walls on two sides, and she hadn't bothered to darken the glass panes facing the executive floor for privacy. Anyone walking by would have seen her comms screen.

I guess we will see tonight whether you meant what you said, Papa, Solveig thought.

Meetings, as far as Solveig was concerned, were the biggest drain of productive time in the company. Nothing that was ever said in a one-hour meeting couldn't be summarized in a far more efficient message brief and sent over the Ragnar network, which could track to the millisecond when a document was opened and filed, and even to what degree it was read. But old traditions died hard, so she resigned herself to burning half her productive daytime hours by sitting in a room and exchanging phrases and sentiments that seemed to be all but ritualized at this point, like traditional Acheroni theater performances.

"It's good to see you home, Miss Ragnar," Magnus Pettar said when she walked into his office. He got out of his chair and walked around his desk to greet her, doubtlessly to avoid making her think he was treating her like any other underling even though that's what she was.

"It's good to be home," she said. "That was a long trip. A little longer than anticipated."

"Yes, it was unfortunate that we scheduled it when we did. But who could have known about that unfortunate business taking place on Rhodia at the same time?"

He led her to his desk and gestured at one of the chairs in front of it.

"Please, make yourself comfortable. Can Lars get you anything?"

"No, thank you," Solveig said. "I just had my starter tea a little while ago."

"I, too, need a little chemical boost in the mornings to be at my best," Pettar said. "But I am more of a coffee man myself."

He walked around his desk and sat down in his chair, which was the same executive leather monstrosity that had been behind that desk since her father had occupied this office. She suspected that Magnus had kept her father's furniture and declined to put his own touch on the president's office because he was the sort of man who would assign a totemic sort of power to the relics of the past. Or maybe he thought her father would be pissed off when he somehow clawed his way back into control and found that his chair and desk had been moved to the basement. The wood of the president's desk had been hewn from an ancient oak that had grown on the Ragnar estate since shortly after the family became plot holders, three hundred years after the landing and seven hundred years before Solveig was born.

"I hear you did amazingly well in the negotiations with Hanzo," Magnus said. "They especially commented on your excellent language skills."

"They are too kind," Solveig replied. "They used those language skills against me half the time. You never say exactly what you mean in Acheroni. I had to get a little blunt at times to get our point across."

Magnus laughed.

"You are your father's daughter, that's for sure."

"My father wouldn't have taken half the noise from them that I had to endure. Of course, they never would have made him. I'm too young to be an authority figure to them."

"You still got the concessions we needed out of them," Magnus said. "Thirteen percent rate decrease for the graphene quota for the next five years. That will save the company hundreds of millions in the near term."

"Yes, but everything above our contractual quota went down only three percent," she said. "And even the big concession was kind of a backhand."

"Oh? How so?"

"Thirteen is an unlucky number in their culture. When you sound it out in Acheroni, it sounds like their word for 'ruin.' You settle for twelve just to avoid thirteen even if it's not tipping the equation in your favor. But they wouldn't budge on fourteen, and I sure as hells wouldn't take twelve if I could get thirteen. It's not an unlucky number to me. But it was a veiled insult for them to offer it."

"Well," Magnus said. "Ruin. I did not know about that. But you got us the sort of break we were hoping for. And we will absolutely revisit those terms in five years. Who knows what the system economy will look like at that point?"

You've been dealing with the Acheroni for twenty years and you didn't know about that, Solveig thought. *How in the hells did Papa think you would be a good stand-in for him?*

"When we do revisit those terms, I'd be happy to be part of the delegation," she said. "But I will want to pick the team myself."

Magnus leaned back in his chair and steepled his fingers.

"Yes, I have heard that some of our people didn't behave in a way that reflects the best ideals of Ragnar."

"You have."

He nodded and flashed a curt and entirely humorless smile.

"Rest assured that appropriate corrective measures will be taken."

He got his marching orders from Papa already, she thought. *And he's trying to tell me what he thinks I want to hear. Everyone in this place is still under his sway. Except for me.*

"Let's talk without pretense for a moment," Solveig said. "I didn't like the way Gisbert embarrassed us in front of our hosts. But I wasn't the one who put him on the delegation as my minder. I could have done the job without him there. I probably would have done a better job, all things considered. So he had a lapse of judgment. But so did someone else. And accountability always goes up the ladder."

Magnus's smile faltered a little.

"My father built all of this," she said. "And we all benefit from his foresight and hard work. But he's not infallible. None of us are. We all screw up sometimes. If we fired everyone who does, there'd be no one left here on this floor."

Magnus looked at her as if he was unsure whether it was appropriate to reply the way he intended. She hadn't fully understood the sway her father still held over everyone here until just now, as she gently dressed down the president of the company without pushback. Here she was, a twenty-three-year-old woman in her first year on the job, telling a sixty-year-old career executive the way things were—and the way they would be going forward. Solveig knew that she would not have any of this power without the specter of her father hanging above Ragnar Tower at all times. But she would be damned if she didn't use it to make things happen her way while she could. One day, they would maybe fear and respect her like they did her father. In the meantime, power by proxy would have to do.

"Let's not overthink it," she said with a smile. "It wasn't a huge deal, so let's not make it one now."

There was a long pause between them, and Solveig felt a whole lot of gears and levers moving under her feet as it stretched on.

"Of course, Miss Ragnar," Magnus finally said. "Like you said, let's not overthink it."

"I'm glad you feel that way, too," she replied with a gracious smile. "I just don't want to assume the worst of someone who has always been loyal to my father."

"I understand completely, and I agree."

She looked at her father's handpicked replacement across the table, and a realization hit her.

This is all as much of a ritual as those Acheroni plays. He can't fire me, ever. He can't even contradict me except in gentle, inoffensive terms. He knows Papa's purpose for me, and he knows his place. I could tell him to fire Gisbert right now or make him the director of operations, and he'd do either without question. His entire authority rests on my willingness to participate in the play. I'm already in the chair behind that oak desk, and he fucking knows it.

"Well, good," she said. "I'd hate to cause hard feelings. Maybe we should have a few tweaks to company policy regarding off-world trade missions."

"I think that's a brilliant suggestion, Miss Ragnar," Magnus said. "You can be sure I will take it under advisement."

I'm sure you will, she thought. *And I'm sure you thought this meeting was going to go a different way.*

"I have a few more things to attend this morning," she said. "If you don't have anything else for me right now, I'll get back to the office if you don't mind."

"By all means," Magnus said without hesitation. "Don't let me keep you. You did fantastic work on Acheron. I think Ragnar has a bright future with you in our ranks."

"You're too kind," Solveig said. But when she got up and shook his hand, she could see the concern in his eyes, the fear that he may have irritated her. And as much as she hated herself for it, for just a moment she allowed herself to enjoy the satisfying rush of power she felt.

Chapter 13

Aden

The sea was calm, and the ocean wind was blowing gently, and it was the kind of perfect day on Oceana they used in the network advertisement to lure tourists. For the first time, Aden wished for some gray clouds and a little bit of drizzle, to match the weather that was in his soul right now. But he knew that Tristan had loved days like this one, and that the ocean here on his home planet had been his favorite refuge in the system, the place where he would return to feel renewed. Now he had returned one last time, and he'd forever be a part of it after today.

They were on a sail-powered yacht somewhere in the middle of the ocean, many hours out of Adrasteia. Above the gray ironwood planks of the deck, a multitude of brilliantly white sails billowed in the wind, driving the ship through the calm waters with the flapping of the composite cloth and the creaking of the ropes and pulleys as the background noise, accompanied by the sound of the waves and the water splashing against the hull.

Aden was sitting on the top deck, where a luxurious seating arrangement was sheltered from the sun by a computer-controlled umbrella that moved with the ship and the changing daylight. Tess, Maya, and Decker were sitting with him, all at arm's length from each other, each lost in their own thoughts. They were all appropriately dressed for an Oceanian funeral, light and flowing white fabrics that reminded Aden of the shirts Tristan used to wear when they were off the ship. There were drinks on the low table between them, but the glasses had barely been touched since an attendant had placed them there.

So much is going to remind me of him, he thought. *And I was only on the ship for a little over three months.*

"Everything about this is wrong," Maya said. "Henry isn't here. We're dressed like this. And we're all moping."

"Tristan would have wanted us to do our service in some seedy dive on Pallas One. Or on that beanstalk elevator he kept going on and on about," Tess replied.

"He'd want us to laugh and talk shit about him, and then get so drunk we can't walk," Decker added. The Oceanian formal clothes looked particularly good on her, Aden decided. They were all used to seeing each other in flight suits and whatever they chose to wear on their planetary outings. Captain Decker looked like a different person in those flowing clothes, with her blonde hair tied into an elaborate braid that crowned the sides of her head and then came together in the back, where it fell all the way to a spot below her shoulder blades. With her blue eyes and her fair skin, she was the stereotype of an Oceanian.

"I have a feeling that Tristan is going to prank us in some way before the day is over," Aden said. "One final time. Just to get the last word in."

"How long are they keeping Henry in stasis?" Tess asked. Decker shrugged and looked off into the distance.

"They didn't have a vat-grown liver that was suitable for a Palladian. Now they are waiting for one from Pallas. Depends on when they find a donor or a vat copy over there. Probably a few weeks." Decker looked at Aden. "How are you feeling?"

Aden touched the side of his chest where Milo's knife had found its way through the ribs to one of his lungs.

"Still sore. And I can't take full deep breaths yet without it hurting. But I'm fine. Better than Henry or Tristan."

"I hope you drowned that piece of shit," Tess said.

"They haven't found him yet," Aden replied. "That resort is pretty far out from the leaf. And the current is going out to sea at that spot. He's probably a quarter of the way around the planet by now. Feeding the fishes and the trilobites somewhere in the equatorial current."

"The police found one of his knives," Maya said.

"I knocked it from his hand right before we went over the edge. I think it landed on the balcony."

"Too bad it's evidence. I'd like to keep it. Just in case he's not dead and I'll ever get a chance to return it. Right into his throat."

"He was not joking about his skills," Captain Decker cautioned. "He almost killed four of us. You should hope he's dead. For more than one reason."

"What did he say to you?" Tess asked Aden. "When you were speaking Gretian with him."

"Aden was speaking Gretian with him?" Maya looked at him.

"I thought he had a Gretian accent," he explained. "I tried to distract him by asking him a question. It was the only thing I could think of at the time."

"What did you ask him?" Tess wanted to know.

"Whether he learned Oceanian in the military. It was too good for a language school. Too smooth and fluent. You have to go to a government school for that. Diplomatic service, military, that sort of thing."

"And did he tell you any details?"

Aden shook his head.

"He was vague about it. But I'm sure he used to be an operative. I mean, there are lots of good language schools out there. But how many people do you know who went to one of those and then went on to be experts in hand-to-hand and knife fighting?"

"War's been over five years," Decker said.

"People have to make a living," Maya said. "War may be over but fighting skills are always marketable. So he's a ronin."

"Ronin," Aden repeated.

"A samurai without a master. A sword for hire."

Someone ascended the staircase from the lower deck and approached them. He was dressed in vestment robes, and a shawl with a repeating wave pattern hung around his neck and reached almost all the way down to his ankles.

"We have reached the place for the ceremony," he said to them. "We can begin whenever you are ready."

"Thank you," Decker said, and he nodded and walked away again.

"I didn't realize we were going for a specific spot on the ocean," Maya said.

"Tristan was born on Meander," Decker replied. "It's the only city that changes latitude over the course of the year. To simulate seasons. The other ones all stay in the middle of the temperate zone. This is where Meander was on the day and hour Tristan was born. He wanted to be back here after he died."

"Well." Tess got up from her seat and straightened out the flow of her garment. "Then let us go and give the man what he wanted."

They gathered on the stern of the ship, where a semicircular platform jutted out over the water. The platform was big enough for all of them without feeling crowded. Other than the priest of the Church of the Ocean, there was only one person who wasn't a *Zephyr* crew member, and he stood at the back of the little crowd, keeping a respectful distance. Aden glanced at him from time to time as the priest went through the beginning of the ceremony. The other man was an older fellow, round faced and a little portly, and he wiped his balding head frequently with a small silk towel that glistened with moisture.

Tristan's ashes were in a little white bowl on a small dais right in front of the platform's guardrail. They all took turns walking up to the dais. The Oceanian way to say goodbye was a low-key and private one. Everyone said their last words to their friends and relatives quietly, with the rest of the small congregation six meters behind. Captain Decker stepped up and said her words, then took some of the ashes out of the bowl. She held out her hand and let the wind blow them out of the palm of her white glove and off the stern of the ship. She walked back to the group, and Tess took her turn.

Tess's flowing white tunic had no sleeves, and the vivid colors of the tattoos on her arms stood out against the almost monochrome setting, providing a vibrant contrast. She walked to the dais and did her own version of the ritual, holding the handful of ashes up in front of her face and whispering to it. Then she extended her hand over the edge of the platform and turned it upside down in a slow and steady motion to disperse the ashes.

Next came Maya, who looked slight and small in her Oceanian tunic. When she walked past, Aden saw with surprise that she had tears streaming down her cheeks. It was the first time he had ever seen a profound expression of emotion from her, more than she had shown in all of the three months he'd been on the ship. Unlike the others, she knelt before the dais and said a prayer before she took her handful of ashes. She spoke briefly, then scattered them into the winds with a slow wave of her hand that looked like she was bidding Tristan a final farewell.

Then it was Aden's turn to walk up to the dais. It seemed like he could feel the weight of the looks from the others on his back as he made his way to the little white bowl with measured steps. The small pile of gray ashes in the center of the bowl looked like nothing that reminded him of Tristan.

"I'm sorry," he said. "I'm sorry you are gone. And I'm sorry I never got to tell you the truth about me. Maybe we would have been friends still. I'm sorry I'll never get to find out."

He took a handful of the ashes and held them in his fist.

"I won't say we will meet again someday because I know you didn't believe in that sort of thing. Thank you for your kindness. I'll take that ride down the beanstalk to Pallas one day and think of you all the way. Goodbye, Tristan."

Aden let the ashes trickle into the breeze from the bottom of his fist, slow at first and then faster as he opened his hand gradually, until they were all gone except for a smudge of tiny grains that stuck to the palm of his glove. It seemed like a wholly inadequate way to say farewell to a friend, but he supposed there was no ceremony that could lessen the hurt of the loss, knowing that someone who was breathing and laughing and smiling just a little while ago was now gone from the universe, transformed into energy and gas molecules and a little pile of calcium and carbon dust.

When he returned to the group, the unknown stranger took his turn. He walked to the dais, spoke a few quiet words, and sprinkled a little bit of Tristan's ashes over the edge of the railing. On his way back, he looked at the group and offered a brief smile.

The priest had the task of scattering what remained, which he did with solemnity. He carried the now empty bowl past them, covered up by one of the ends of his vestment shawl, and disappeared in the covered lounge behind the stern deck.

They stood in thought for a little while. The stranger offered no word of condolence or explanation, obviously intent on not intruding. Then Maya wiped her face and walked over to the lounge as well. After a few moments, Tess followed her. With the fellowship of the crew temporarily broken, Aden turned to the stranger.

"Are you kin to Tristan?"

The stranger shook his head and wiped his forehead with the silk cloth he had pulled from his pocket again.

"Augustus Bosch. I was a friend of Tristan's. He has no living family." He looked at Decker, who had walked up next to Aden.

"I'm sorry," Aden said. "Did you know him for a long time?"

Bosch nodded. "Thirty-five years. We went to school together. I was also his solicitor for the last thirty years or so."

He offered his hand to Captain Decker, who shook it.

"Ronja Decker," she said. "I am the captain of *Zephyr*. Tristan was a member of my crew."

"Yes, I know," Bosch said. "I came to pay my respects to Tristan, of course. But you are part of the reason why I am here."

"Is that so?" Decker asked. She exchanged a look with Aden, but he couldn't tell from her expression whether that fact concerned her in any way.

Bosch nodded solemnly.

"Can we find a cool place to sit? Inside, perhaps? You, me, and the rest of your crew, I mean."

They gathered around a lounge table on the panoramic deck of the yacht. The attendants brought everyone drinks, and one of them put platters of light snacks on the table, which nobody touched.

"I told him a while ago that he was getting a bit too old for this business," Bosch said. "Flitting around among the planets. Drinking in bars on orbital stations with that rough crowd."

"That's what he enjoyed," Aden said.

"Oh, I know. Much better than you may think."

He looked at each of them in turn.

"I am Master Dorn's solicitor. As such, I am also the executor of his will, which he has requested to make known to you as soon as possible after his passing."

"Tristan had a will," Tess said. "The man who carried all his stuff in a single bag."

"Those were his worldly possessions," Bosch said. "They did not reflect the totality of his holdings."

"His holdings," Decker repeated. "You mean his cut of *Zephyr*'s operating profits. Whatever he stashed away over the years."

Bosch looked at Captain Decker, and there was a little smile playing in the corner of his mouth. Whatever he was about to tell them, he was clearly enjoying the opportunity to do so.

"I am not just here on Master Dorn's behalf. I am also here to act as the official agent for the Zephyr Consortium."

Decker let out a breath and sank back in her chair.

"Here we go. I was wondering when we'd hear from them. The ship's not served a contract in a month. If we don't count the one that got us all here today."

"Captain Decker," Bosch said. "Tristan Dorn was the sole proprietor and stockholder of the Zephyr Consortium."

Maya coughed up the sip of beverage she had just taken.

"He was *what*?" Decker said.

"He owned the consortium. All of it. He was your employer. He went to great lengths to keep that a secret."

"I'd say he fucking did," Tess said. "That cheeky little bastard."

"I'm afraid you are right," Bosch said to Aden. "Being out in space among you all *was* his joy. It was what he wanted to do with his life. But he did not want to be thought of as anything but ordinary."

"Tristan was never ordinary," Aden said.

Bosch rewarded his statement with a smile. He shook his arm to clear the fabric of his tunic from his wrist device and tapped it to activate a screen in front of him.

"It is the will of Master Tristan Dorn that upon his death, the ownership and legal liabilities of the Zephyr Consortium are transferred in full to the surviving crew serving upon OMV *Zephyr* at the time of his passing, to be divided equally. That includes all consortium shares, accumulated operating profits, and of course the ship itself."

They all looked at each other in utter disbelief. Then Maya let out a laugh that morphed into a sob.

"You have got to be joking," Decker said.

Bosch shook his head.

"If Tristan were here, he could confirm to you that I am not generally the joking type."

"*He* was the consortium?" Tess asked. "All this time?"

"He set it up when he purchased the ship three years ago. He was very adamant about keeping it anonymous."

"All this time," Tess repeated. "He kept us in the dark for *three years*. While we were chasing contracts and hopping from spaceport to spaceport, our boss was chopping peppers and brewing coffee in the galley."

"As often as we got drunk together, I am amazed that he never let any of that slip out even once," Decker said with a smile. She looked at Aden. "Remember when you said you had a feeling Tristan would prank us one last time? This is the biggest one he's ever pulled."

"And he didn't even get to see our faces this time," Tess said.

"What about the liabilities?" Decker asked Bosch. "How much will we still owe in payments on the ship? And how does the consortium account look?"

"The ship is paid off already," Bosch said. "Master Dorn purchased it outright from Tanaka Spaceworks as a special order. The title is free and clear. And as for the consortium finances—"

He brought up a page on his comtab screen and let it float into the middle of the table for everyone to see.

"It's not a vast fortune. The operating costs of the ship are considerable. But as you can see, it's not a trivial amount either, even after splitting it five ways. If that is what you choose to do."

"I shouldn't be in the equation," Aden said. "I've only been on the crew for a little over three months. I haven't earned a share."

"Master Dorn's will does not name anyone directly. Nor does it specify any other conditions, like length of employment. It merely says that the ship and the consortium are to be divided among the individuals who are members of the crew at the time of his death. You may refuse the inheritance share, of course. But you are eligible."

Bosch closed the screen and folded his hands in his lap.

"I realize that none of you will want to rush such a momentous decision. And there is absolutely no rush. The docking fees and business dues are being covered by the consortium account. Just be aware that the account will run dry eventually. If your intent is to liquidate the consortium and divide the proceeds, you should probably act as soon as you come to an agreement to maximize your respective shares."

He got up and nodded at the group.

"I am sure you have some talking to do after getting that surprise sprung on you. I will leave you to it. You have my contact information on your comtabs if you need advice or legal guidance. Good day, and my heartfelt condolences."

They watched as Bosch walked off to the other side of the panoramic lounge, where he sat down in a chair that faced the sea on the port side of the ship.

"So what do we do now?" Decker said.

"What are the options?" Maya asked. "Not that I am in the state to make any sort of decision right now."

"Well, we can do what he mentioned. Sell the ship and dissolve the consortium. Pay the obligations and then split what's left five ways."

Tess shook her head. "I'm not a fan of that idea. She'll sell in a minute, and for a lot. But we'll never find another ship like her."

"And then some rich asshole is going to use her for showing off," Maya said. "Maybe turn the galley deck into a bar. Paint over all your drawings on the engineering deck."

"Or worse, some smuggling outfit gets their hands on her and runs half a ton of stims per week past the Rhodies and the Oceana navy at eighteen g," Tess added. "With a military-grade Point Defense System."

"I see you two aren't in favor of selling the ship," Decker said with a wry smile. "Not that I would have guessed otherwise. What about you, Aden?"

"I'm not sure I want a vote in this," he said.

"You get one whether you want it or not. You heard the man. Even if you vote to forfeit your share. You could ask to be paid out for yours. I know I'd never be able to talk these two into selling the ship even if that's where my mind was. But we could buy you out if you want the money."

Aden shook his head. "If you turn everything into cash, I don't want a share. Split it between the rest of you. Or give it to Henry."

"Tristan would have wanted you to have it," Decker said. "Even if he didn't name you directly. You know how he was."

Aden looked out of the window next to their table. Outside, the sun was glinting on the water, and the breeze was whipping the crests of the waves into white foam. He imagined Tristan's ashes sinking below those waves right now, returned to the cycle of life and death, and the sadness and sorrow he had been feeling all day amplified until it seemed bottomless.

"He loved the ship," he said. "Even with all his talk about not getting attached to things. He wouldn't want us to sell her off. But he didn't want to tie us to her either. That's why he didn't say we have to keep her."

He looked at the others. "I don't care what the lawyer says. I don't have a right to an equal voice on this. But if you decide to sell her, I don't want a share."

"The other option is to keep going," Decker said. "We do what we've been doing all along. Find new contracts, keep the consortium going. Maybe hire someone new, eventually."

"That's my vote," Tess said immediately.

"Mine as well," Maya said.

"I don't really want to go back to flying bulk freighters," Decker said. "And the money from the consortium share would run out sooner or later. I'm really bad at sitting on my ass."

"If we keep going, I'll take the share," Aden said. "I'll stay on."

"Well," Decker said. "That didn't take very long to settle."

"What about Henry?" Aden asked.

"Oh, I am pretty sure he's going to want to keep the ship," Decker said. "But if he has a change of heart, we can buy out his share." Her facial expression left no doubt that she considered that possibility highly unlikely.

Tess let out a long breath. "I was worried I'd have to arm wrestle you all for the old girl. I sure as hell couldn't have bought anyone out. Rest assured that I am not secretly wealthy."

"So now what?" Decker asked. "We've decided to keep it all together. What do we do now?"

"We find a safe place and ride this out," Tess suggested.

Maya leaned back in her chair and wrapped her arms around the backrest.

"I don't know about you all," she said. "But the place where I feel safest is docked up there right now." She nodded at the transparent ceiling of the panoramic deck. "Nobody can sneak in. And if there's trouble coming our way, we can run away from it at eighteen g."

"We have to dock somewhere at some point," Tess said. "And then we have to watch our backs again."

Decker reached into her pocket and pulled out her comtab. She rested it on the tabletop in front of her and spun it slowly with one finger.

"I still have those coordinates," she said. "And the contact node for the handover we were supposed to do."

"You want to go *after* them?" Tess asked.

"They killed Tristan. They killed our *friend*. They damn near killed the rest of you. I would love a chance at payback. We can wait until they pick us off one by one. Or we can bring some trouble their way."

"We're not a warship," Maya said. "We don't even have the space for a weapons mount. Even if we could get a permit for one in a hurry."

"We don't need to be armed," Aden said. "We just need to call someone who is. Someone who's motivated to find people who trade in black-market nukes."

Decker looked at him and nodded. "That was my thought, too."

Tess groaned and let her shoulders droop. "Please tell me we're not about to vote ourselves into a terrible mess again."

"I think we're in the mess already no matter which way we turn," Aden said. "Maybe the best thing we can do right now is to make sure *they* get some of it on them, too."

Chapter 14

Idina

The QRF's big combat gyrofoil descended above the bridge and roared to its southern end, gun turrets turning and scanning for targets. The access ramp on the south side was clear of traffic now. Every civilian with a bit of sense had taken manual control of their pod when the shooting had started and cleared the area at a high rate of speed. The northern end of the bridge was pandemonium, a smoking mess of destroyed transport pods and mangled bodies. Some people were trying to free others from wrecked pods. Others were in headlong flight, abandoning their own pods and running away from the scene as quickly as they could.

"How are they doing?" Idina asked Private Arjun, who was still tending to Private Raya and the injured Gretian civilian.

"They'll live, but we need to get this man off the bridge. There's only so much I can do with these medpacks."

On the south side of the bridge, the gyrofoil lowered itself to the ground. The big tail hatch opened, and several heavily armored QRF troopers rushed down the ramp and started to run up the bridge toward her position. She walked out to meet them.

"I have two injured over there for medical evac," she said. "And the DHC is in the Badger and waiting for exfil. You want to get him out of here and back to the Green Zone before they spring another fucking surprise on us."

"Medical is on the way with several birds," the lead QRF trooper said. "The combat flight has to stay on station for fire support."

"Then at least get the VIP out of the damn armor and into your bird," she said. "He's safer there than on the middle of the bridge."

The QRF team lead nodded and signaled his men, and they ran up to the Badger and lowered the tail ramp. A few moments later, they had the deputy high commissioner and his security detail between them, covering him from possible incoming fire with their armored bodies from all directions. They made their way down the bridge to the southern end and ushered the VIP into the back of the combat gyrofoil.

"Cover me with the remote mount," Idina said to the Badger commander. "I'm going to see what I can do on the other side. Arjun, stay with the wounded. Khanna, Condry, with me."

Her two remaining section members left their guard positions and joined her as she walked down the bridge toward the northern end. She could see the anxious expression on Khanna's face as he looked at the carnage in front of them. Pallas Brigade soldiers were the toughest young men and women in all the worlds of the system, but he had just received his kukri not too long ago, and she knew that he had never seen the carnage of battle, never witnessed what a large-caliber automatic gun could do to unprotected human bodies.

"Khanna," she said, and he looked at her.

"Don't dwell on the dead," she told him. "Help the living. And scratch the rest from your memory."

He nodded. "Yes, Colors."

"Go and get all the medpacks you can grab out of the armor."

"Yes, Colors." He turned and ran back to the Badger.

The first pod she reached was jammed up against the divider barrier between the travel lanes. She took one look and knew there was nothing anyone with a medpack could do. The explosive grenade had hit the passenger compartment head-on through the canopy bubble and exploded within, and it was hard to tell how many people had been inside. Not every pod in line had been hit directly, but most of them had been sprayed with shrapnel from the ones that had, and the few undamaged pods were jammed in with the disabled and shattered ones. The next pod she reached had a wounded civilian inside who was slumped in his seat. She pulled the emergency release of the pod's door and yanked it open.

"Help me with this one," she told Private Condry.

Together, they pulled the man out of the pod and lowered him to the ground, where Idina bent over him to check his vitals. He had a pulse, and she couldn't see any obvious major wounds, so she left him for the medical teams and went to the next pod. Private Khanna came running up from the direction of the Badger, multiple medpacks in his arms.

"We're going to check these pods one by one," she ordered. "If they're too far gone, don't waste your time. Get out the ones who look like they can be patched up."

On the north side of the bridge, some brave civilians had started to check the pods there for wounded people as well. She took two of the medpacks from Khanna's arms.

"Bring the rest to those people down there, they will need some of them. I'll go down the line with Condry."

Khanna nodded, his face pale underneath his helmet, and ran off to do as she had ordered. Idina looked over at the residence tower where the insurgent firing position had been set up. Even with a whole platoon of QRF troops, it would take a while to clear every room in that building, and there was no guarantee that there wasn't a second hidden gun about to cut loose and add to the carnage. Whoever was behind Odin's

Wolves had shown the ambush skills to target rescue crews before. The second bomb at the demonstration three months ago had taken out many more people than the first one, which had only been set off to lure the rescue pods and gyrofoils to the scene.

If I had set this ambush, that's what I would have done, she thought.

It was tactically unsound to stay on the bridge in full view of the building. But until the rescue crews and the rest of the security forces got here, her little half section of soldiers were the only Alliance presence among dozens of dead and wounded civilians, and she was not going to run back to her armored box and hide in it to leave them out in the open alone.

Some of the pods she checked were empty, their occupants having fled down the bridge on foot when the shooting had started. Idina felt profound relief whenever she checked a pod's interior and saw nothing inside except for hastily scattered relics of everyday commutes—dropped comtabs and spilled food or beverage containers. She worked her way down the line mechanically, without allowing herself to rush just to get through the unpleasant task. One of the pods she checked had a hatch that would not open even after she pulled the emergency release, so she had to force her way into the vehicle by using her kukri to cut into one of the numerous shrapnel holes in the pod's skin and expand it with her blade. The civilian inside was lying on the floor of the cabin, in front of the passenger seats. It took her the better part of a minute to cut away enough Alon to be able to wedge her way through the opening she had made. When she finally got into the pod and checked his vitals, he didn't have a pulse. She rolled him over to see that a piece of shrapnel had torn deeply into the side of his head right above his ear.

Overhead, another Alliance gyrofoil appeared. It circled the bridge twice as if to ascertain the situation. Then it descended and landed on the embankment on the north side of the bridge, close to the burning wreckage of the Gretian police gyrofoil. Idina heard the sound of emergency signals coming from the direction of the city now, rescue and medical pods making their way to the bridge on the surface roads.

"The JSP put all the companies on alert," the Badger commander sent. *"And they're sending a full battalion from Unity."*

"Tell them to hurry up," Idina replied. "We've got our asses hanging in the breeze here."

"ETA for the medical birds is two minutes."

When she reached the next pod, she met Private Condry, who had worked his way up the line from the other side. There were two passengers in the cabin, a man who was obviously dead and a woman who was still alive and conscious. When they pulled her out of the broken pod, she groaned and mumbled some words that Idina's translator software couldn't parse.

"Why would they do this?" Condry asked when they were putting medical gel dressings on the woman's wounds. "Why would they kill their own people? It makes no sense."

She looked around at the chaos surrounding them. The air smelled like burned composites and gun propellant. The sound of the emergency signals got louder with every passing moment. Soon, the bridge and its approaches would be swarmed with emergency personnel and Alliance soldiers. She was sure that the ambush hadn't quite gone as planned, but it had achieved its goal nonetheless. This part of the city would be paralyzed for a while, and all of the Alliance's military resources in it would be tied up while they secured the area and looked for insurgents that were most likely already long gone, if they had been here for the ambush at all. Gun mounts could be remotely controlled, after all. In the countryside, a data link would be quickly detected and pinpointed to a source. In the electronic clutter of a modern city where everything and everyone was connected to the Mnemosyne, it was impossible to detect in time and very difficult to identify after the fact, buried as it was in the many data streams from a hundred thousand connected devices nearby.

"This is the point," she said. "The chaos. They want us to know that we're not safe anywhere on this planet. And they want their own people to know that, too. Show everyone that we can't keep control."

"QRF team found the gun," the Badger commander sent. *"Twenty-five mil. Cooled and suppressed. Ammo cassette empty. No shooters on site."*

"Fantastic," Idina replied.

They win again, she thought. *They lose one gun mount. But they get weeks and months of instability and fear in return. We can't keep this up.*

For the first time since she had set foot on Gretia, the thought crossed her mind that the occupation was a hopeless task, that the Gretians were every bit as unwilling to be conquered as the Palladians had been.

—

The team had left in the morning, but by the time the military gyrofoil put down on the landing pad in the Green Zone to get Idina and her half section back to the base, the sun was setting beyond the Sandvik skyline, giving the city a vivid background of orange and red.

When the engines had stopped and the doors and ramps were open, Idina unbuckled her harness and got out of her seat. She checked her weapon to make sure it was safe. Next to her, privates Condry and Khanna did the same. Khanna had a familiar look in his eyes, the unfocused long-distance stare common to soldiers who had just seen more violent things than their brain was prepared to process.

"That was a rough first day, Khanna," she said.

He looked at her and nodded.

"Do you ever get used to it?" he said. "Seeing the bodies, I mean."

She shook her head curtly.

"You don't *want* to get used to it," she replied. "And stay away from people who say they are. They're either full of shit, or they have a circuit crossed in their heads."

They walked down the ramp and onto the landing pad. Idina felt a tiredness that seemed to have seeped all the way into her bones. She had scoffed at the medical assessment a few weeks back that had made her commanding officer want to send her back to Pallas, but as she planted her boots back on solid ground, it felt like this planet's gravity had increased by a good 10 percent since they had left this morning.

The Green Zone was noisy and busy this evening. As Idina led her half section back to the Palladian embassy, they passed armored vehicles seemingly on every corner. A whole platoon of armor was deployed in a line right in front of the commemorative arch, positioned to block each of the archways. Overhead, several gyrofoils kept an eye on things from above. It was an immense show of force, but she knew that it was security theater, intended to make the high commissioner and all the government civilians feel safer. No insurgent with half a brain in his skull would attack the fortified Green Zone head-on, especially not after putting it on full alert with the earlier ambush. The armor would be gone in another day or two once the panic had settled, and the gyrofoils would waste a lot of time and power circling overhead.

"What now, Color Sergeant?" Khanna asked her when they walked up to the security lock at the main entrance of the embassy.

"Now you turn your weapon in at the armory with the rest of us. Did they assign you a room yet?"

"Yes, Colors."

"Then you'll go there right after, stow your gear, and come down to the mess hall to get some food. And then you're going to hit the rack for at least eight solid hours. You've been on your feet for too long today."

"Yes, Colors," Khanna said. She knew that he would follow her orders right up until the food part, but that he wouldn't be able to go to sleep just yet, not after what he'd seen and done today. She was willing to bet her kukri that if she walked into the enlisted lounge in a few hours, he'd be in there with the rest of the section, seeking comfort in company, trying to process the events. And if he slept at all tonight, she knew his dreams wouldn't be pleasant.

They filed through the security lock and headed downstairs to the armory, where they unloaded their weapons and handed them in for safe storage. When her troopers placed their disposable ammunition blocks on the armorer's counter, she saw that all of them were still fully loaded and sealed. Between all of them, they hadn't fired a single round today.

—

Taking a shower in her quarters and putting on a clean uniform did a little bit to restore her, but her stomach reminded Idina that she hadn't eaten anything since the sparse breakfast before her run. She put her kukri belt back on and went downstairs to the mess hall.

Tonight's food selection was limited, but she was pleased to find spicy stew, and the kitchen had set up a big thermal keg of hot water and several rows of metal mugs next to it. The mugs held fermented millet, and when combined with hot water, they made a hot beverage that was slightly sour and moderately intoxicating. She took a bowl of stew and filled one of the mugs with hot water, then looked around for a place to sit and eat while her drink was brewing. The mess was still busy, most tables occupied with new soldiers she didn't know, reinforcements from Camp Unity that had arrived today in the wake of the emergency. Idina spotted some troopers from her section at a table in the back of the room, and she made her way toward it. Almost every table seemed to have several screen projections hovering above it, and troopers were loudly discussing what they were seeing while eating their dinners. The atmosphere in the room had an angry note that she hadn't noticed when she had walked in, distracted by her hunger and the menu at the counter.

"What's going on?" she asked her section as she put her food on the table and sat down.

"These fucking people," Corporal Rai said. He reached over to the screen that was floating slightly to his right above Private Condry's meal tray, brought it over until it was between them, and turned it a little so she could see what was going on.

"We're on the system news," he said. "Well, you are. You and the team that was on the bridge today."

"Eight civilians dead and fifteen wounded," she said. "Of course that would make the system news."

"Just watch," he said. "Restart from time marker zero zero," he told the screen, and it flickered and scrubbed back through the footage it had shown so far. It was a wide-angle view of the bridge, shot from a distance, and it had the slightly unstable quality of a comtab recording that was taken at magnification. From the angle and aspect, Idina guessed that it was taken from one of the windows of the residence tower where the insurgents had set up the gun. Their Badger was visible in the center of the bridge, but something about it didn't look right. It was standing sideways and blocking most of the road, so she knew it was after the explosive ambush had detonated and disabled the Badger, but there was no smoke coming from the vehicle or the hole in the roadway.

"Watch," Rai said again and pointed.

"What the fuck," Idina said. On the screen, the weapons mount of the Badger was not turned toward the recording device, as it should have been for most of their stay on the bridge. Instead, it was aimed toward the north side of the bridge, where the civilian pods were lined up in the traffic jam. As she watched, the gun mount fired a single shot, then another. Down by the north end of the bridge, pods started shattering one by one.

"That's not right," she said, anger welling up inside her. "We didn't fire a shot from that mount. And sure as hells not at the civvies. What is this shit?"

"It popped up on the 'Syne about an hour and a half ago. Looks like someone tweaked it to make it look like we're the ones who killed all those civvies."

"Fuck," she said. "Is this on all the networks right now? Are they spreading this garbage?"

Corporal Rai shook his head.

"They're all showing the real thing. This is just floating out on the 'Syne. But it's generating a shitload of chatter."

"Of course it fucking is," she grumbled.

"Who's going to believe that shit?" Condry said. "Everyone's showing what really happened. All they have to do is watch the networks. It doesn't matter."

Idina watched with growing fury as the Badger on the screen kept firing at the line of pods at the end of the bridge. The AI tweaks were flawless. Everything looked *right* to her. If she hadn't been there and known better, she would have thought this was reality. The gun recoiled correctly, and the puffs of propellant smoke from the muzzle dispersed realistically. Even the little shockwave from each shot's muzzle concussion was visible briefly after the weapon fired.

"Most of them won't believe it, Condry," she said. "But some of them will. The ones that are already thinking that way. They'll believe it because they want to believe it."

She pinched the screen to make it disappear. The hot water in her metal mug hadn't steeped for long enough to make the fermented millet brew very strong, but she brought the drinking tube to her lips and took a long sip anyway. She looked at Condry.

"And it does matter. Even if only one in five hundred of these people think we committed that massacre, that's a hundred thousand on this planet. And if only one in five hundred of *those* are dumb or angry enough to join the insurgency?"

She let her spoon drop back into her stew and frowned.

"Then they got two hundred new recruits from this tonight. With thirty minutes of work and a basic AI editing algorithm. Think about how long it takes *us* to get two hundred new troopers."

Her troopers looked at her in silence. From the neighboring tables, animated conversation spilled over to theirs.

"You saying we're losing, Colors?" Corporal Rai asked.

Idina shook her head.

"We don't lose, Rai. We're the Pallas Brigade. But we're not winning either. If we don't find a way to root those fuckers out, they'll keep doing this shit. They'll try to wait us out. And then we'll be in this place forever."

Idina dunked her spoon into the stew only to find that most of her appetite had dissipated even though her stomach was still growling.

Chapter 15
Dunstan

"That one," Lieutenant Hunter said and pointed at the situational display to pick a ship out of the line of nearby traffic. "Let's go with her. She's a Starlink passenger liner. They've got way better sensors on them than the merchies."

"All right. Commence when ready," Dunstan replied.

They were on the third day of their patrol and a few ten thousand kilometers outside of the Rhodia–Oceana transfer route, gliding along with the flow of traffic toward Oceana. Most of the commercial ships on the route, freighters and passenger vessels alike, chugged down the parabolic at one g as well because it was efficient and provided regular gravity to the ships without requiring the use of expensive and energy-hungry gravmag arrays. The drive plume of a civilian ship burning its fusion rocket at one g made the ship visible on infrared from a long way off, and the IR spectrum of *Hecate*'s tactical display showed a long line of little flares in the darkness of space, strung out along the transit corridor like bright jewels on a dark velvet cushion.

"Waiting for uplink. Uplink established. Initiating handshake. AI core at three percent load. And there's our downlink. Firewall penetration took zero point one nine seconds. Like trying to stop the Galloping Tides with a leaky hand bucket."

Lieutenant Hunter brought up a screen and positioned it in the middle of the ship's situational display. It cycled through a variety of sensor feeds while she worked her console for a few moments. The spectrum on the viewscreen shifted to the familiar color palette of an infrared sensor.

"All right. We're going to borrow their array just for a moment, and then we'll be out of there. They won't even know unless someone happens to be using the manual array controls right now and wonders why it's turning left while he's steering it right."

She worked the controls, and Dunstan watched as the coordinate readout in the lower left of the screen changed.

"That's us right now," she said.

"I don't see a thing," Dunstan replied.

"Precisely," Hunter said and allowed herself a little smile. "They're running a pretty good commercial-grade IR sensor over there. Not quite as good as military hardware, but ten times better than what your average merchie or pirate has bolted to their hull. And it's not picking up our drive plume. They would start to see something if we got ten thousand klicks closer or kicked the burn up past one g. But right now we're not there. And we don't even have to coast ballistic."

"That is the most efficient stealth nozzle I have ever seen," Dunstan said. *Hecate*'s drive plume was practically nonexistent, even though the drive was accelerating the ship at almost ten meters per second squared. Whatever the engineering division had done with the hydrogen-cooled exhaust nozzle and its geometry, it worked like black magic.

"Well, the efficiency drops off a cliff when we really go hard on the throttle. Past two or three g, we are just as bright as anyone else in a hard burn. But someone would have to have really good palladium-core sensors and be closer than ten thousand klicks if they want to even start to pick us up at one g."

"And if we're that close, we can always brute force it and hack their sensor feed."

"Precisely." Lieutenant Hunter pulled the screen projection back toward her and disconnected the data link.

"They have their sensor control back. What do you think of this ship so far, sir?"

Dunstan shook his head with a smile.

"Well, to be completely honest with you, she makes me feel like I'm a midshipman again," he said, and some of the other officers on the operations deck chuckled.

"Everything is upside down and backward from where it was on any other ship I've had. I feel like I have to relearn my trade all over again. And I've been in the fleet for twenty-seven years."

"I had the same problem at first," Lieutenant Armer said from the weapons station. "We all did. On the shakedown cruise, we basically had to write the manual as we went."

"There's nothing in the fleet like this ship," Lieutenant Hunter said. "This crew has been working with her for six months, and we still haven't figured out her limits."

Dunstan leaned back in his chair and looked at the situational display. It was scaled out to represent a bubble of space around *Hecate* that was twenty-five million kilometers across. Every ship with an active Mnemosyne link inside that bubble was represented by an icon and a movement vector. He could tap on any ship's icon and bring up all its essential data: name, registry, crew list, cargo manifest, current speed, acceleration, heading, remaining fuel capacity, and a hundred other parameters that were readily available even if they were irrelevant from a tactical standpoint. The amount of information at his fingertips was dizzying, and it was easy to get lost in the sheer volume of it. *Hecate*'s sensors were excellent, by far the most advanced and capable in the fleet as far as he could tell. But to Dunstan, the truly awe-inspiring part was that she didn't even need her own sensors to keep an eye on eight thousand trillion cubic kilometers of space because she was able to use everyone else's.

No wonder the admiral told me to keep this ship out of the wrong hands at all costs, he thought. *Give me ten of these, and I can control the whole system.* The idea unsettled him in a way he couldn't quite define.

"All right, people," he said. "We know we can hack every merchie in sight and play with their systems. We can pretend to be anyone. We can sneak everywhere unseen. Now let's figure out how to do something useful with all those skills."

He looked around on the operations deck.

"As you said, you've been working with this ship and her systems for six months. I've only been in command for less than a week. Absent any better input, my plan is to continue this patrol just the way we've been doing for the last two days. We shadow the civilian traffic and wait for things to go sideways. That's a very small pebble to find on a very large beach, but it's the way my mind is still calibrated. If any of you have an idea that takes into account all the shit I don't yet know about this ship, speak up now, please. There are no wrong answers."

There was a moment of silence in the compartment. Then his first officer looked at Lieutenant Robson.

"How do you feel about trying out Cassandra, Robson?"

Lieutenant Robson shrugged.

"I think it's as ready as it's going to get. Could be a search for a black cat in a dark cellar. But if it doesn't work out, we're no worse off."

"I agree," Hunter said. "And if it does work, we'll blow some minds back at fleet command."

"Cassandra," Dunstan repeated. "Want to tell me what that is?"

"It's an AI routine Robson coded a while back, sir. We haven't had time to test it yet because it wasn't done before Commander Stone left. Core-level routines require the commanding officer's approval to run. It's not exactly a standard piece of software."

"And what does that AI routine do, Robson? Explain it in terms a crusty old relic like me can understand."

Lieutenant Robson took a long breath before she replied.

"Well, in broad terms, sir, it's a predictive pattern analyzer that helps us find the bad guys."

"If I give you permission to run it, is there a chance it will endanger the ship or the crew?"

"Negative. It's just a subroutine. I can isolate one core and run it on that. Worst thing that can happen is that it takes up all the utilization on the core and forces us to purge and reset it."

"All right," Dunstan said after a moment of consideration. "Do it. You have your CO approval. Impress me."

"Aye, sir," Robson replied.

She unbuckled her harness and got out of her chair.

"If I may, Lieutenant Hunter."

The first officer brought up a screen, moved it off to the side, and authorized access. Then she got up and swapped places with Lieutenant Robson.

"All yours."

Robson moved the screen to her eye level and started tapping her control panel. The data readouts on the display might as well have been Acheroni spelled backward and upside down for all the sense Dunstan could make of them. She worked with focused intensity for a few minutes.

"Core Three is sandboxed," she finally said. "Routine is loaded and ready to execute. Executing in three . . . two . . . one."

She tapped a confirmation field on her panel. For a few moments, nothing happened that Dunstan could see. Then the situational display slowly changed. Colored blotches started to appear on hundreds of locations inside the sphere, popping into existence and then slowly spreading out like paint dropped on a porous surface: green, yellow, orange, and red.

"Core utilization at forty-eight percent," Robson said. "The core is actually breaking a sweat for a change."

"That's a pretty sight," Dunstan said. "But tell me what I'm looking at here."

"The AI is querying the data from every ship in real time right now over the Mnemosyne. Origin, destination, tonnage, type and value of cargo, that sort of thing. But also their entire movement history. Where they've been in the past, and how often. How much time they usually spend docked on turnaround. Public records of the crew, and their movement history. And the ship's sensor data. Everything their sensors have seen since they left their last few ports of call. Even the stuff that the crew didn't notice or log as unusual. All the comms traffic they've sent or received or even just overheard on passive."

Robson highlighted a few of the colored blotches that had sprouted on the situational display.

"Right now the AI core is busy collating all that information and cross-checking it against known pirate patterns and previous attack locations. It's generating a real-time probability map for future pirate attacks. Green means a prediction for a safe zone segment. Yellow means slight risk. Orange is elevated risk. Red means a high-risk zone. It's also assigning a risk value to each individual ship based on all those factors. Pirates aren't interested in bulk ore freighters, for example. But they like smaller ships that ferry high-value goods that are portable."

She flashed a clipped little smile and shrugged.

"That's why we named it Cassandra. Like the oracle from mythology. It knows the past, it can see the present, and it predicts the future. At least as far as pirate incursions go."

"There are a few thousand ships out there right now," Dunstan said. "Spread out over twenty-five million kilometers. You're telling me that this ship's AI just pulled all that data from them and processed it just since you pushed your commit button."

"It's still pulling the data, sir," Lieutenant Robson said. "Processing it and integrating it into the map overlay. Fifteen hundred times per second. It'll keep doing that until we cancel the subroutine."

"And that takes half of one-quarter of our processing power."

"Affirmative, sir."

Dunstan looked at the display and its overwhelming amount of information. The Alliance navies did the best they could with what they had, but there simply weren't enough warships around to respond to every merchant distress call and get there in time to protect them. But if they knew where to focus their patrols and commit their limited resources, they wouldn't have to try to be everywhere at once.

"If we had one of these on station at all times, we could direct the battlespace," Dunstan said. "Tell the other ships where to lurk, where to patrol, which merchies to shadow. We would be their eyes and ears."

"Information," Lieutenant Hunter said. "The biggest gun of them all. We can do the patrol work of a dozen cruisers."

Dunstan got out of his chair and walked up to the tactical projection. He looked at the many little chains of light that were crossing the void, thousands of individual ships, each with dozens or hundreds of people on them, each unaware of the fact that *Hecate* was watching them with the knowledge of where they had gone and where they were going.

"All right, Lieutenant Robson. You have managed to impress me."

Robson smiled at the compliment.

"Now that we have all this information, what do we do with it? How do we start to turn that into a workable tactical doctrine?" Dunstan continued. "Because we're still just one ship."

"Well," Lieutenant Hunter said. "If we know where we're likely to see trouble, we also know where we don't need to be."

Dunstan nodded.

"Filter out all the green-coded low-risk ships, and every ship that's in or near a green zone regardless of their threat rating. Can you do that?"

"Affirmative," Robson said and turned her attention back to her console. A moment later, at least a third of all the ship icons on the situational display disappeared.

"Now drop the yellow-coded ships."

The display changed again, now considerably less cluttered than before.

"Get rid of everything except the orange- and red-colored ships that are either inside or near a red risk zone."

Most of the remaining ship icons went away, and the few that remained were scattered all over the orb in no particular pattern.

"How many does that leave us?"

"Thirteen ships, sir."

He looked at the display and chewed on his lower lip in thought.

"We have to start somewhere," he said. "We can play guard dog and patrol the transfer lane all the way to Oceana and back. We can insert ourselves in the pattern, pretend to be a luxury goods merchie, and hope that we make a tempting enough target."

"Or," Lieutenant Hunter said.

Dunstan pointed at the nearest red zone, a small blotch of crimson hanging in space a few million kilometers away.

"Or we can creep right into the middle of that spot, turn off our drive, and see if something interesting happens when those high-value merchies pass through."

The officers on the operations deck exchanged glances and smiles.

"I can find no particular fault with that plan," Lieutenant Hunter said. "Worst-case scenario is that we spend a few days twiddling our thumbs as we watch the traffic go past without incident."

Dunstan returned to his chair and sat down.

"All right. Let's see how good that algorithm is at predicting the future. Of course, you know the problem with Cassandra's predictions, Lieutenant Robson."

"What's that, sir?"

"Her prophecies were always right. But Apollo cursed her so that nobody ever believed them."

Robson shrugged.

"I just thought it was a good name for the program," she said. "It doesn't have to be prescriptive."

Dunstan laughed. "No, I suppose it doesn't. Number One, let's bring her to the new heading. Keep a low profile, one g."

"Aye, sir," Hunter replied. "Helm, come about to 330 over 40, Mark 9."

The only indication of their changing heading and attitude was the situational display, which rotated to keep itself oriented in relation to the ship's direction of travel. Dunstan watched the spherical projection gradually turn as the ship's cold-gas thrusters fired to correct their course. He still felt a little dazed by the impact of the technology demonstration he had just received from Lieutenant Robson. With the power of the AI core harnessed by Cassandra, they were all-seeing and all-knowing, an omniscient deity that could slip on whatever face it wanted to show, or glide into the shadows and be nobody at all.

This ship is the most dangerous thing anyone has ever put into space, he thought.

Chapter 16

Solveig

"Miss Ragnar?"

Solveig looked up from her compad to see Anja standing at the threshold.

"There's a visitor for you at the executive reception. Would you like me to greet him for you?"

Solveig checked the time and flinched a little. She'd let the morning get away from her, and now there was no time to prepare herself for lunch with Detective Berg unless she made him wait for her at the reception at the risk of appearing like the upper-class executive snot she tried hard not to be.

"Gods, no," she said. "Thank you, Anja. I'll go get him myself. He's a personal guest."

She got out of her chair and walked over to the door of her restroom. The outside of the door was a mirror, and she checked herself briefly to make sure she hadn't spilled her tea onto her suit this morning without noticing. When she looked over at Anja, her assistant had the hint of a smile on her face.

"That will be all, Anja," Solveig said. "And I'm stepping out for lunch, so hold all comms for an hour unless the building starts to burn down around us and I don't notice."

"Yes, Miss Ragnar." Anja turned and strode off toward her own office.

Solveig walked across the executive floor toward the reception. This was the first time she was meeting Berg in the open, and for a few moments she questioned the wisdom of having invited him to come up to the executive floor right away. Everyone would be able to see them, and there would be no more room for plausible denial. It was against every instinct she had acquired while spending her childhood playing hide-and-seek with her father and his lackeys. But then she saw Berg standing at the reception, casually leaning against the counter with one elbow on the countertop and one leg crossed over the other at the ankles, and it was surprisingly easy to suppress that nagging doubt when she looked at his green eyes and the way his shirt fit him just right.

"It's good to see you again," she said when she walked up.

"It's good to see you as well," he said, smiling. "I don't know about you, but Mnemosyne messages are a poor substitute for seeing someone's face in real life. Even if they are instantaneous across a hundred million kilometers."

"I will have to agree with you on that," Solveig said. She glanced at the executive receptionist, who was looking at her array of screens and pointedly not paying attention to the exchange. "Are you ready for lunch?"

"Very," Berg said. "I was running a bit late this morning, so I haven't actually had any breakfast. If you don't count the coffee from the dispenser at the office."

Solveig made a face. "Coffee isn't breakfast. Come on, then. Let's get some food into you before you fall over and I have to explain myself to your boss."

He ran a hand through his unruly brown hair and laughed.

"He'd probably send you a letter of civic commendation. It seems I annoy him a lot."

—

The executive canteen took up one of the building's corners, and it afforded a fiftieth-floor view of Sandvik on two sides of the room. Detective Berg paused in the doorway when they walked in and looked around in awe.

"You call this a canteen," he said.

"It's probably a bit nicer than the ones in police buildings," she admitted.

"A bit."

The attendant led them to one of the choice tables near the corner of the room, where the view was unobstructed. Solveig nodded her thanks and took a seat, and Berg sat down across the table from her in a slow and careful manner, as if he was afraid to break something or make an untoward noise.

"And you get to eat lunch here every day?" he asked.

"I usually get them to bring it to my office," Solveig replied. "I don't like to complicate things."

"Well, I appreciate that you are taking the time today. I was only mildly serious about coming to join you for lunch. As soon as I said it, I feared I might be imposing. But I am glad you took me up on the suggestion."

The executive canteen sometimes served as a room for larger functions, so it was much bigger than it needed to be to accommodate the lunch crowd on this floor. The room was mostly empty, but a few of the deputy directors and various assistants were sitting at some of the tables, and Solveig was keenly aware of the glances in her direction. She didn't usually eat here because she liked to be by herself, and she had certainly never eaten here with company from the outside. The administrative assistants at all levels of Ragnar were the most efficient network for the spreading of gossip, and she knew that if her lunch date wasn't common knowledge already, it would be by the time she was back in her office.

"Did you really have errands to run in the area, or did you go out of your way just to have lunch with me?" she asked.

"Well," he said with a smile. "I didn't have an errand when we talked earlier. So, I picked one that would give me the excuse for the detour."

They picked up the ordering compads that displayed the menu choices for the day. Berg let out a low whistle.

"You were not making a joke about that beef fillet with herb butter," he said.

She felt strangely embarrassed by his awe at the selections.

"Can I ask you a favor?" she said.

"Of course." He lowered his compad and looked at her.

She hesitated for a moment to gather her thoughts into a coherent request.

"I'm the daughter of the man who used to own this company," she said. "I went to Sondstrom Academy when I was eleven. I spent seven years there. Then I went to the university for five years. And now it's four months after graduation, and I'm in a nice office here on the top floor."

She put her comtab back on the table and made a vague gesture around the room.

"This is what I know. This is my default. I know it's not how most people get to have lunch at work. But I haven't been out in the real world enough to know any different. So please let me know if I ever come across as an entitled little brat. Because I don't think any less of anyone for doing lunch at some little hole-in-the-wall place on Savory Row. Truth be told, that's what I'd prefer most days anyway."

Berg smiled and shook his head.

"You do not come across that way. And I don't think any less of you for getting to eat here instead. Or for having an office with a great view. Although I will say that I am jealous you got to do your tour of authentic Acheroni noodle joints."

Solveig laughed. "That was worth the trip. Even if I had to pay a heavy price for it. Corporate meetings for days. And lots of business meals and receptions where the only people in the room within ten years of my age were the servers."

"Still," he said. "You got to see Acheron. I'd put up with some boring meetings to get to see the place in person."

"You've never been?"

He shook his head. "Never been off-world. It's hard to find the time with my work schedule. And whenever I do have the time, I never have the funds. Junior inspector salary, you see."

She opened her mouth to apologize for staying on the subject of relative privilege, but his smile told her that he wasn't offended, so she swallowed the words.

We really are from two different worlds, she thought. *Even if we live in the same part of the same planet.*

They put in their food orders, and an attendant came to collect the order compads.

"Our canteen has a food line," he said. "They don't serve you at the table."

"I wouldn't mind that at all. Sometimes I don't know what I want until I see it. And I am absolutely not above carrying my own meal tray."

"I didn't think you were," he said. "But it's a major downgrade from this arrangement. The food is pretty okay, though."

"I'd like to try it," she said.

He laughed. "Oh, no, you wouldn't."

"Sure," she pressed on. "Why not? You came to have lunch here. I'll come have lunch with you. Do they allow you to have visitors for mealtimes?"

"There's no rule against it," Berg replied. "Not that our police headquarters canteen is a major culinary destination in the city, mind you. People tend to pay extra to not have to eat there."

"I am serious. I will carry my own tray and eat all the food I pick. No special treatment. Are you in the office tomorrow?"

Berg laughed again and leaned back in his chair.

"All right. If you absolutely want to have the experience of eating mediocre food among a bunch of foul-mouthed civil servants, I will not deny you the opportunity. I am indeed in the office tomorrow."

"Good," she said. "Then that's settled. Noon?"

"Any time you want," he replied. "I'll be there anyway. Once you get there, you'll have to ask for me at the front desk. I'll have to come downstairs and sign you in."

"Are you sure? I wouldn't want to pull you away from anything important."

"Honestly, there isn't much I wouldn't let you pull me away from," he said.

They smiled at each other, and Solveig felt a fluttering in her chest that was only partially due to the good-looking young police officer sitting across the table from her, or his obvious reciprocation of her interest in him.

I didn't have to cover my tracks this time, she thought. *I'm sitting out here with him in plain sight. And tomorrow I will go see him at his office, without having to look over my shoulder.*

A comtab in his tunic pocket hummed a soft but insistent-sounding alert. He frowned and pulled it out to look at it.

"Forgive me for being impolite," he said. "This is my duty device. I have to acknowledge the message."

"Not at all," she said.

Berg looked at the comtab without making a screen projection, and his frown deepened. He looked up after a few moments, clearly unhappy.

"I'm afraid I really have to be rude and desert you for lunch. There's an all-hands-on-deck emergency order from headquarters. I have to go and report in."

"Is everything all right? What happened?"

He hesitated for a moment before responding.

"Someone bombed an Alliance military vehicle. Out on the southern loop bridge. Operations says there are civilian casualties."

"Gods," Solveig said. The rush she had been feeling a few moments earlier dissipated as fast as it had come. "Another bombing?"

Berg stood up and tucked the comtab back into his tunic.

"I'm afraid so. Would you please excuse me? I'm very sorry I have to run off on you like this, believe me."

"No apologies needed," she said and got out of her chair as well. "Your duty is more important. I will see to it that they get you downstairs quickly."

They hurried across the room, drawing curious glances from the sparse lunch crowd. Outside, she led the way to the executive reception.

"Detective Berg has a police emergency and needs to get out of here in a hurry," she told the receptionist. "Could you clear the VIP skylift for him and make sure someone from security meets him at the bottom?"

"Of course, Miss Ragnar."

"Thank you," Berg said when the VIP skylift arrived. He brushed her hand with his as he walked past her and stepped onto the platform. The brief, unexpected touch of his bare skin on hers almost made Solveig jump.

"And I really am sorry. I was looking forward to our lunch. And not just because of that beef fillet with herb butter."

"Please stop apologizing," Solveig replied. "I'm not offended in the least. And I will see you tomorrow. Hopefully we can do a repeat without any emergencies. And if there is one, you'll be at work already, right?"

"Right," he said. "Sorry for all the apologies. I will see you tomorrow."

He smiled at her as the skylift doors closed between them.

With Berg gone, she no longer had any desire to sit in the executive canteen and eat lunch by herself, so she went back and told the attendant to have her meal brought to her office. Then she made her way back across the floor, disappointed and excited at the same time. Next to her office door, Anja was waiting, compad in her arms as usual.

"Was that the policeman from a few months ago?" Anja asked.

"It was," Solveig confirmed. "But he wasn't here for work. He was paying a friendly visit. Have you seen any news bulletins come across the networks?" she asked before Anja could continue her probing.

"I have not," her assistant said. "Did something happen?"

"He got called away for work. Something about a bomb on the southern loop bridge. They called everyone in, so it must be big."

She walked into her office and tapped the controls for the viewscreen projector at the head of the room. The screen popped into existence across most of the wall next to the restroom door, displaying a slowly spinning Ragnar company logo.

"Vigdis, show me the network digest," she said.

The room AI dutifully changed the screen to a grid layout that showed the feed from a dozen different network streams. Most of them were showing the same scene from various angles and distances—a bridge spanning the Duna River where it finished its wide loop around Sandvik to the south. There was a big, many-wheeled military vehicle on the road in the middle of the span, and smoke was wafting from its front and side.

"Ber—the *detective* said there are people hurt," Solveig said to Anja, who had walked into the room behind her and was now watching the digest grid with one hand on her mouth.

Several of the feeds showed a wider angle of the bridge. On one side of the river, there was a mess of transport pods in a haphazard column, and some of them were smoking as well. There were people running around on the bridge, but the distance was too great to make out who they were or what they were doing.

"Gods, what a mess," Solveig muttered.

"I don't understand it," Anja said next to her. "Why do they keep *doing* this? They'll only make these Alliance soldiers come down on everyone that much harder."

"Maybe that's why they keep doing it," Solveig replied.

"Well, I don't like the occupation. But I really don't like feeling like I could get blown up at any time on the way home. Just because I'm in the wrong spot at the wrong time."

Solveig glanced at the window that had been replaced after shrapnel from an explosion on the square three months ago had torn a deep gouge into the Alon. She had been standing not too far away from that spot at the time.

Her personal comtab trilled an incoming vidcom request. Her heart did a little jump in her chest when she thought of Berg. But when she brought up a screen between her thumb and index finger to see the sender node ID, the disappointment was amplified by mild dread.

"Would you excuse me, please?" she said to Anja, who snapped back into her professional self and turned to leave the room. Solveig walked over to her desk and opened a screen, then flicked the comms request from her comtab over to it.

"Hello, Papa," she said.

Falk was in his office back at the estate. He looked tense and concerned, but she couldn't see any anger on his face, and she allowed herself to relax a little.

"Are you watching the networks?"

"I have them on right now," she replied. "Someone lit off a bomb on the Duna bridge down south. But that's a long way from here. Are you sure you're allowed to call me at the office?"

"If it's a family emergency. That's why I connected to your personal device and not the office one. Is anything going on in the city?"

She looked out the window. On the far end of Principal Square, protesters were gathered just like almost every day now, but there was no sign of danger or chaos. In the distance, halfway across the park, the blue shimmer of the security barrier marked the beginning of the government Green Zone. Beyond, there was some activity, but it was too far away for her to make out clearly. As she watched, two gyrofoils climbed into the sky from somewhere behind the Green Zone and turned to head east at low altitude.

"There's some military traffic in the air over by the Council Hall, but that's it."

"What are your plans this evening? Are you staying late?" Falk asked.

I don't think you've ever asked me about my workday plans instead of telling them to me, she thought.

"Not today, Papa. I was going to come home right after my last meeting. I wanted to talk to you about a few things."

"I see," Falk said. "Are you taking the company bird? Because I'd really rather not see you in a pod on the road today. I'd feel much better if I knew you were a thousand meters up in the air on the way home."

"Don't worry. I was going to take the gyrofoil all along."

"Good." He sighed with visible relief. "What is it that you wanted to discuss?"

She hesitated for a moment. The subject would be a tricky one on a normal day. Right now, with her father on edge because of the bombing, it didn't seem like a good thing to bring up, not if she wanted concessions out of him. But she could tell that making him wait until tonight would only increase his anxiety again, and she didn't want him to be three strong drinks into his evening already when she got home.

"It's a pretty long way from the house to work," she said. "I spend a lot of time in the air or on the road. I was thinking it may be a good idea for me to get a place in the city. Closer to Ragnar."

"You want to move out of the house," he said matter-of-factly, and for a second she thought she detected a spark of the old anger in his face.

"I don't want to move out," she replied. "It would just be a place for during the week. I'd still come home on the weekends. It would save a lot of time and money. I ran some numbers. The monthly rent for a little suite would be less than what it costs to run that gyrofoil for three flight hours. That's just a week of commuting time."

Improbably, Falk laughed.

"Of *course* you ran the numbers," he said. "You've never asked for more privileges or new things without presenting me with a detailed cost-benefit analysis to make your case, you know."

"If that's the case, I got it from you," Solveig said. "But we can talk about that tonight, Papa."

He rolled his eyes in mock exasperation and shook his head.

"But you're not asking for a privilege," he said. "You're twenty-three now. You're beyond asking. And I need to recognize that. I meant what I said the other day. You're an adult, and you're the vice president at large. You don't have to ask me for permission anymore. You want to stay in the city during the week, you can start looking for a place. Not that you haven't picked out a dozen suitable ones already."

For the second time this week, Solveig was momentarily disoriented by the mental whiplash of her father expressing a sentiment that was diametrically opposed to the one she had expected to come out of his mouth. It took her a moment to realign herself mentally, and from the little smile in the corners of his mouth, she could tell that he knew and that it amused him.

"I still wanted to get your blessing," she said. "Make sure you don't think it's a stupid idea. Or that I am ungrateful for what I have already."

"I'm not going to lie. I'd rather see you home. I don't care how much the stupid little gyrofoil costs per flight hour. That's a few drops in a very big bucket. But you're young, you want to see what it's like to be on your own, and you want to be closer to the nightlife. I get it. You may find it hard to believe, but I was twenty-three myself once."

He leaned back in his chair and raised an index finger.

"*But.* There are some things you won't be able to negotiate."

"And what are those?" she asked.

"You want your own place, *you* pay for it. Even if it's one of our company properties. Which it *will* be. Because Marten will want to make sure the security arrangement is airtight. And you will get a shadow for protection whenever you are off company property. They won't be breathing down your neck at all times, but they'll be nearby wherever you go, just in case."

"Agreed," Solveig said quickly. "On all points."

Falk laughed again, flashing his perfect teeth.

"See? We didn't have to save this for tonight after all. I hope you're still planning to come home on time, though. We could have dinner and look at rental properties together."

Solveig felt as if she'd had several strong drinks in the canteen with Berg that were just now starting to take effect. There had to be calculation and intent behind her father's sudden and profound change in attitude, but for all her knowledge of his personality, she couldn't begin to figure out his motivation right now.

"Of course. I'll be home at six," she said. "Dinner sounds good."

"See you then. Love you," Falk said.

"I love you, too," she replied, and he terminated the link.

Solveig stared at the blank screen for a few moments.

One careful step at a time, she thought. *But I'll be damned if I know what the hells just happened.*

Chapter 17
Aden

Zephyr wasn't a large ship, but with only the four of them on board, it felt unnaturally empty.

The feeling was enhanced by the way they were spread out after they had undocked and set a course for the transfer lane to Rhodia. Maya was in the pilot station at the very top of the maneuvering deck. Tess was all the way at the bottom of the ship in her engineering shop, and Decker split her time between the command couch on the maneuvering deck and the airlock deck whenever she wasn't in her berth. With Henry still in stasis at the medical center on Adrasteia, that left only Aden. Normally, he'd spend much of his time down on the galley deck, keeping Tristan company and learning how to set up a mise en place in a starship galley where things could go to zero g unexpectedly. But Tristan was gone, and the galley deck was cold and silent now, bereft of the smell of chopped herbs or the sound of Tristan's idle humming as he was turning packaged meals into something that didn't offend his culinary sensibilities. That left the medical and sanitary deck, and Aden spent some time there to clear his mind while taking inventory of medpacks and dry soap. Tristan had been the ship's medic as well, but he had never spent much time on the medical deck, so the surroundings didn't remind Aden of his friend everywhere he turned. The grief that had abated just a little when they had seen Tristan off to his resting place together seemed to be amplified again by being back on *Zephyr* without him.

He was in the middle of refilling a dispenser in the shower capsule when the ship intercom hummed.

"Everyone, can I see you in the galley?" Decker's voice said.

Aden finished his task of topping off the sanitation dispenser and stowed the refill bladder in its place in the storage locker next to the shower capsule. After a few months, double-checking locks and latches had become almost second nature, and he was pleased that his muscle memory now had him perform the motions without conscious input from his brain. He wasn't a spacer yet, but he was slowly turning into one, and much of his progress was due to Tristan's tutelage.

He went over to the ladderwell and climbed the two decks to the galley. Decker and Maya were already sitting at the crew table. There was a green away bag in the middle of the table, and Aden's stomach did a little lurch when he recognized it as Tristan's. He walked over to the table and took his usual chair. After a few moments, Tess came up from below as well and joined them.

"I sent the message to that Rhody captain," Decker said. Her blonde hair was tied back in a tight, precise braid that looked like she had spent a lot of time getting just right. "I asked him to meet with us to lead him to the people who gave us that nuke. But I want to let you all have your final say on this before we get the reply."

"Four votes," Maya said. "What if we deadlock? Henry can't vote from his stasis chamber."

"We all have an equal share in this now. But if you vote to risk the ship, you're not just voting to risk your part of it. So we'll have to remain unanimous on this. And hope that Henry forgives us for going over his head when he wakes up."

"If we're still around at that point," Tess said.

"If we're not, then Henry gets the consortium money by default. Even without his share of the ship in the mix, he won't have to look for a new crew for a long time," Decker said.

"If we go through with this, we will be at the mercy of the Rhodies. If they decide to not follow along with our plan, we won't be able to do anything about it. They can detain us and impound the ship."

"We can outrun anything in their navy," Maya said. "If we meet up with them and they start talking about handcuffs, we can just throttle up and get the hells out."

Decker nodded.

"We could get away in the short term, no doubt. But right now the Rhodies are still giving us the benefit of the doubt because we volunteered that nuke. If they want to arrest us and we go evasive, we'll never be able to cross into Rhodian space again. And they'll probably put us on an Alliance-wide arrest bulletin. There'll be nowhere left to go, no place where we can just fill up and lay low."

"They won't," Tess said. "There's no risk in this for them. We're going to offer ourselves as bait. All they have to do is come and collect. They're still trying to find whoever dropped that nuke on their planet. If they figure the odds on this are higher than zero, they'll jump on it. I say we go."

"I agree," Aden said. He wasn't wild about the idea of depending on the goodwill of the Rhodian military again, hoping that the bigger stakes would be enough to outweigh his parole violation and legal status if the Rhodies made an issue of them. But staying on Oceana meant that he'd have to talk to the police about Tristan's death eventually, and he was certain the attendant background check would result in his arrest and deportation.

"So do I. Three yes votes, then," Decker said. She looked at Maya. "What about you?"

"Ah, hells." Maya leaned back and shoved her hands into the pockets of her shipboard overalls. "We've taken it this far. No sense in sitting around and waiting for other people to make things happen."

"Can we run everything with four people?" Aden asked.

"We're short our first officer. And we don't have a medic anymore. But we have a pilot. We have our engineer. And we have a comms specialist," Decker replied.

They sat in silence for a few heartbeats.

"Well," Tess said. "If we're going to run off to do dumb things again, I should make sure that the Point Defense System works the way it should."

"What about *that*?" Maya asked and nodded at the bag on the table.

Decker let out a slow breath.

"Those are the things Tristan had with him when he went planetside. The police released them to me. He didn't have any next of kin. And I didn't want to throw it away. Or put it in some storage locker that nobody's ever going to claim. It's all that's left of him."

Aden stood up and reached for the bag. He pulled it across the table toward him and unzipped it. Inside, there were a few pieces of clothing, the lightweight linen shirts Tristan liked to wear when he was on leave. A jacket was rolled up and tucked into the space next to the shirts. Aden touched it with his fingertips and found that it was made of soft suede. There were a few little containers of various cooking ingredients—herbs and spices, all neatly labeled. Underneath the spice bottles, Aden saw something familiar. He reached into the bag and pulled out a few of the spices to get at the object, then pulled it out of the bag. It was Tristan's knife roll, his beloved cooking knives that he had taken everywhere even if he hadn't planned on using them. The others looked at the knife roll in his hands in utter silence.

Aden gathered the spice and herb containers and walked over to the galley counter. He put the containers down one by one until they were lined up in a tidy row. Then he put the knife roll down, opened it, and spread it out on the counter. All of Tristan's knives were there, from the large all-purpose blade to the little paring knife. The water stone Tristan had used to keep them sharp was in its little pouch in one corner of the knife roll.

"He said it took him twenty years to get his cooking knives exactly how he wanted them," Aden said. He looked over at the table to see that the others were all watching him.

It felt wrong to see the knife roll out on the counter without smelling any cooking preparations. Aden opened one of the herb containers and shook out a little bit of basil. The scent of the herb made him smile despite the sadness he felt.

He'll never use these again, he thought.

"I think these should stay in the galley," he said. "It feels like they belong here."

"He kind of made you his understudy, didn't he?" Decker said. "I think you were in the galley with him most of the time when there was cooking going on."

"He showed me how to do a few things," Aden said. "He said there were ten things everyone should know how to cook. I think we got up to number seven on that list."

Decker nodded at the knife roll.

"You're their custodian now. Nobody else knows how to sharpen them anyway. And if you can cook seven things, that's six or seven more than the rest of us know."

Aden picked up the basil leaves and stuffed them back into their container. Their smell remained faintly in the air in the galley.

"All right," he said. "Just don't expect me to be up to Tristan's level in six months, please."

Maya shook her head and smiled dryly.

"If we're still around in six months, I'll gladly put up with an overseasoned dinner here and there, Aden."

Decker's comtab beeped, and she waved her hand to make a screen and read the incoming message. She sat up straight, and all the levity disappeared from her face. They watched silently as she read the text on her screen.

"There's our response from the Rhody commander," she said finally. "They're giving us rendezvous coordinates to meet up and consider our request for assistance."

"That's not a *yes*," Tess said.

"But it isn't a *no* either," Decker replied. "They want to see just how willing we are to prove that we're the good guys."

She looked at what was left of her crew at the moment.

"We're sticking our necks out here. But we're doing it to bring the hurt down on the people who did this to Tristan and Henry. If any of you have second thoughts, now's the time to mention those."

"Not me," Tess said.

Aden ran his fingertips over the handles of Tristan's knives. He looked at Decker and shook his head.

"Well, let's go and burn some fuel, then," Maya said.

"I want to get there before the Rhodians so we can see what's coming our way. They are trying to gauge how sincere we are. They can't blame us for doing the same," Decker said. "Lay in a course and let's all strap in for a fifteen-g burn."

"That's burning some fuel, all right," Maya chuckled.

—

The rendezvous point the Rhodian commander had transmitted to them was nowhere near any current transfer lane. It was out in deep space between Rhodia and Oceana, many hours away from any commercial traffic. Three hours into their speed run, they reached the halfway point of their plotted trajectory, and Maya flipped the ship around for the deceleration burn.

"If we really don't like what we see, there's no way they can stop us from leaving," Tess said a little while after they flipped. The maneuvering deck had been mostly silent for the journey, with everyone lost in their own thoughts or engaging in busywork for distraction. The absence of Tristan and Henry in their usual couches to Aden's left and right seemed to suppress any levity or casual conversation. To Aden, it was as if the mood on the ship had been calibrated for the six people who had been on board when they docked at Oceana, and now the ship was running out of balance, like a turbine that had shed several blades, still functioning but operating well below its normal efficiency level.

"Are you sure about that?" Aden asked. "What if we get there and they have four or five ships converging on us from different directions?"

"They don't have a ship in their fleet that can match our acceleration," she said, her voice laced with mild contempt. "They can't catch and board us."

"They have guns and missiles," Aden reminded her. "They can just go 'Halt or I'll shoot.' What's the acceleration on a ship-to-ship missile?"

"A hundred, a hundred and twenty g," Maya supplied from the flight station above their heads. "Some of the new shit may be able to pull two hundred or more."

Aden looked at Tess and shrugged. She just shook her head and rolled her eyes slightly.

"*If* they threaten to shoot us, and *if* they're not bluffing, then they have to get one of their missiles past our PDS. While we're hauling ass at fifteen g plus. I'm not saying it's impossible. But they'd have to be damn close, get damn lucky, or put a fuck ton of missiles into space in a really short amount of time."

"And if they manage all of those at once, it's just not meant to be our fucking day," Maya said.

Maya had calculated the deceleration burn to end a few thousand kilometers early so they could flip the ship around and point the bow sensors at the rendezvous area ahead of their arrival. When they turned around and cut the drive to coast the rest of the way without a thermal plume to mark their position on infrared, everyone on the maneuvering deck tensed while the passive sensors looked at the space in front of them.

"No visual contacts. Nothing on thermal. Nothing on infrared. No radio chatter," Tess declared. "Looks like we beat them by a lot."

"That works for me," Decker said. "Get us right into the center of the coordinate and hold station with cold thrusters. Let's see what comes our way. Passive gear only."

"You got it," Maya said.

"Tess, make sure that we can go from zero to haul ass in a second if we have to."

"Affirmative," Tess replied. "Reactor is on standby for full output. I've got my fingers on the power slider. Just give the word, and we are going to launch like a missile."

"Let's hope I didn't misjudge that commander," Decker said. "He seemed like a level-headed man. If he wanted to lock us up, he had plenty of opportunity when we were on his ship and their marines were on ours. But we are here now. We'll have to dance to whatever tune he is bringing."

Aden hadn't been nervous about this meeting when they had made the decision. He'd only been mildly anxious when they had arrived at the coordinates the Rhodian commander had sent. But as the hours ticked by while they were floating in the darkness, his mind spent the idle time going through all the ways in which this plan could end badly, and the tightness he had started to feel around his chest seemed to clamp down just a little harder with every passing minute. He knew his crewmates well enough by now to tell that they were getting increasingly tense as well the longer they were waiting out here with their station lights blinking and their ID transponder broadcasting their presence into the void.

"It's been seven hours," Tess said at some point and started to unbuckle her harness. "Still nothing on passive. Even if they show up at the edge of our detection range in the next few minutes, it'll be a few more hours before they get here. If nobody minds, I'm going to get a meal and a shower. And maybe half an hour of bunk time."

"Go ahead," Decker said. "If there are surprises, I'll sound the alarm."

The comms console next to Aden came to life with the two-tone trill of an incoming transmission. The unexpected sound made him jerk upright in his chair.

"Incoming tight-beam comms," he said in disbelief. "Someone's hitting our comms array with a low-power tight-beam."

Tess fastened the buckles of her harness again and looked at her screens.

"There's nobody out there in tight-beam range. I don't see how that can be right."

"Answer the request," Decker said. "Put it on the overhead."

Aden accepted the connection.

"OMV Zephyr*, this is RNS* Hecate*. We are coming up on your starboard bow. Keep your drive cold and maintain your current aspect, please."*

Aden exchanged looks with Decker and Tess.

"*Hecate*, *Zephyr*. Confirm hold current aspect and momentum."

"Coming up on our starboard bow?" Tess said. "What the fuck. There isn't anything off our starboard bow."

"You heard them, Maya," Decker said. "Let's not get jumpy and give them a reason to dislike us."

"Keeping station," Maya confirmed. "No sudden moves. So much for seeing them coming, huh?"

"*Hecate*, we don't have you on our sensors. What is your distance and bearing?" Aden asked. *And why the fuck aren't you showing on our gear?*

He got the answer to his question a few moments later. Out in the dark void off their bow and slightly above their current inclination, a set of position lights started blinking in the distance. An alert chirped on Aden's screen, and he looked at the source.

"They just swept us with fire-control radar."

"They're inside of a hundred kilometers," Maya said. "Well inside."

"Fifty-five and closing," Tess confirmed. "How the hells did they get so close to us without getting picked up?"

She focused one of the optical arrays on the position lights in the distance and magnified the image.

"That's not the frigate that took on the nuke," Aden said.

"Looks like our Rhody commander got himself an upgrade." Tess enhanced the image, but even at this short range, the hull of the Rhodian warship remained indistinct. It seemed as if the hull swallowed the flash from the position lights as soon as they left their emitters.

"If their bow and stern blinkers are anywhere near their actual bow and stern ends, they're not quite sixty meters long," Tess said. "Still a lot bigger than we are. But nowhere near the size of a frigate."

"Under fifty kilometers now," Maya said. "If we decide to run and they launch at us, we may not be able to zap what they're throwing our way."

"Then let's not give them a reason to launch," Decker said. "Is that tight-beam link still open, Aden?"

"Affirmative," he replied.

"*Hecate*, this is *Zephyr*, Captain Ronja Decker, requesting to speak with Lieutenant Commander Park over vidcom link."

"Zephyr, *wait one.*"

A few seconds later, a new screen projection opened in front of Decker. Aden felt an unwelcome spike of anxiety when he saw the craggy features and the light-blue eyes of the Rhodian Navy officer who'd held their fates in his hand a few weeks ago when they had delivered a nuclear warhead to him. The background of the image was comprehensively blurred out by the Rhodian ship's comms AI, a clear sign that the Rhody crew did not want anyone to see the interior of that ludicrously stealthy ship, not even an accidental glimpse of a console or data screen.

"Lieutenant Commander, I will say that I was hoping I wouldn't see you again for a while, if ever," Decker said.

He raised one shoulder a little to bring one of his rank sleeves into the image frame.

"It's 'commander' now, actually. They saw fit to give me another stripe." He flashed a brief and awkward smile.

"It looks like they gave you a new ship, too. What happened to your old one?"

His smile disappeared again. "Decommissioned and on the way to the wrecking yard. Damaged beyond repair. We had a disagreement with a heavy gun cruiser."

"Sorry to hear that," Decker said. "I hope your crew came out of it okay."

"No casualties, thankfully. But I am sure you didn't ask me out here personally to catch up on old times, Captain Decker. You mentioned a lead. I hope it's worth the reactor fuel we both burned to get here."

Decker closed her eyes briefly and exhaled.

"After we gave you that nuke, we went to Acheron for a ship overhaul. While we were planetside, the people who hired us to deliver that cargo sent one of their enforcers. They demanded our ship in exchange for the value they lost. I have a set of coordinates to deliver *Zephyr* so they can seize her and claim a salvage title."

"I hope you didn't consider that," Commander Park said. "You'd end up air locked in the middle of nowhere. You know that."

Decker nodded.

"We had that suspicion. That is why we decided to head home to Oceana and wait them out."

Park flashed his curt smile again. "And I am guessing that didn't work out too well."

Decker shook her head slowly. "They killed one of my crew. And another one is still in the medical ward."

"I told you this when I let you go," Commander Park said. "I told you that the sort of people who smuggle nuclear arms are not the kind that will be happy with a refund and a heartfelt apology. I'm surprised they didn't kill you all."

"It wasn't for a lack of trying," Decker said.

"You should have brought this to the Rhodian Navy the moment you got those coordinates. Not run off and played hide-and-seek with a black-market arms cartel."

"That was right after the nuclear attack on Rhodia," Decker replied. "You know how hot tempers get after something like that. We were sure the first Rhodian Navy unit we came across would just haul us in and lock us up."

"You are probably correct. But you'd still have all your crew, Captain. And I don't take pleasure in pointing out that fact. But I am sorry for your loss."

There were a few moments of silence between Decker and the Rhodian commander.

"This will stay with me for the rest of my life," she finally said. "We can't turn back the clock on this. But we can try to serve up the people who did this."

"You want me to help you with a revenge mission," Park said. "That's why you wanted to meet out here."

He laughed and shook his head. "This is a Rhodian Navy warship. We're not guns for hire."

"We lost one man," Decker said. "You lost how many people? Thirty-seven thousand? If there's a chance the same people are behind both, why wouldn't you want to get your hands on them?"

"Oh, I would love to," Commander Park said. "Even if they're not the ones who dropped that nuke. Chances are they know the ones who did. Maybe they even sold them that warhead. And even if they had nothing to do with Rhodia at all, they still need to be shut down. Nuclear weapons threaten the stability of the whole system."

"Then let us help each other. I'm not saying we're out here purely out of unalloyed altruism. But I don't see why that should matter to you. We play the bait. You get to reel in the catch. We all get what we want."

"What do you propose, Captain?"

"We go to the coordinates they gave us. We'll do as we were told. Turn on our emergency beacon, launch our emergency pod, then see what comes our way. And you'll be right behind us to deal with them when they show up."

"Once they realize you crossed them again and there's a warship coming in to spoil their salvage, they'll blast you to shreds," Park said.

"Then we'll see if our Point Defense System was worth the money," Decker said.

Commander Park chuckled and shook his head again. "I think it's a terrible idea for you to assume that sort of risk. There is absolutely no guarantee that we will be in a position to prevent them from taking your ship or blowing it up. You have no idea what's going to be waiting out there. But you seem to be strongly determined to keep disregarding my well-meaning advice."

Captain Decker held the commander's gaze.

"I want payback," she said. "And so do you. It's not the noblest motivation, I know. But I'll be damned if it's not a satisfying one."

Commander Park smiled. To Aden, it didn't look like an amused or humorous smile. It looked like the satisfied expression on the face of a killer who has finally gotten a glimpse of an elusive target.

"Yes," he said. "It most certainly is. Send your data and the coordinates, and I'll review them with my first officer and the rest of the command crew. Maybe we can fine-tune things a little. But, *Captain*?"

"Yes, Commander?" Decker replied.

"Understand that I can't guarantee your survival. But if these people kill you, I'll try to make sure you don't have to wait long for them in the afterlife."

Chapter 18

Idina

The chirp of an electronic alarm stirred Idina from her sleep, and she sat up in her bed and blinked. At first she thought that her wake-up signal had gone off, but the time projection on the ceiling above her bed showed 0915 hours, almost two hours before her scheduled alert.

"Room, cancel blackout," she said. The windows, which had been completely opaque, slowly became transparent again until they let in the full daylight. Idina blinked and looked for the source of the continuing chirping. Her duty comtab sat on the small utility table on the other side of the room, and she got out of bed to answer the incoming comms request.

"Go ahead," she said to the device when she sat down at the table. A small screen materialized above the comtab.

"Good morning, Chaudhary," Color Sergeant Norgay said. "Sorry for the intrusion. I know your watch doesn't start until noon."

"It's all right, Norgay. What's the emergency?"

"The deputy high commissioner would like to see you in his office this morning."

Here we go, Idina thought. *He's had some time to process what happened, and now he's bristling because he got chewed out by a lowly color sergeant.*

"Any idea what he wants?" she asked.

Norgay shrugged. "No idea. He just asked me to tell you to stop by at your convenience."

"At my convenience," she said. "Now's convenient, I guess. I'll be over in fifteen."

"Thanks, Chaudhary. I'll pass it on."

She terminated the link and sighed. The DHC wasn't a military officer in her chain of command, but he was the second-highest Palladian authority on Gretia, one of the ten people who were in charge of every aspect of the occupation, military and civilian alike. If he wanted her disciplined or thrown off the planet and sent back home despite the troop rotation freeze, he had the power to do it. She had run her mouth out of turn, and now she'd have to bear the consequences.

Might as well get it over with, she thought and looked around for her uniform.

When Norgay led her into the office of the deputy high commissioner fifteen minutes later, the DHC was standing at the window, with his back toward the door. His office had a great view of the park and the Sandvik skyline beyond. It was another sunny autumn day out there, and the only thing spoiling the scenery was the blue shimmer of the security barrier in the distance.

"Sir, Color Sergeant Chaudhary is here for you as requested," Norgay said.

The deputy high commissioner turned his head and waved her in.

"Good morning," he said. "Thank you for coming over on short notice. I know you aren't on duty yet."

Norgay left and closed the door behind him. Idina walked over to the window and joined the DHC.

"Not a problem, sir. We're on call all the time anyway. What can I do for you?"

A pair of combat gyrofoils came in low from the direction of the city. The DHC watched as they soared overhead and disappeared from view above the building.

"You've been with the JSP company for a while, right?"

Idina nodded. "I got assigned to the JSP in the spring. My platoon did patrols with the Gretians right up until they suspended the JSP teams after the nuke attack."

"I noticed that you don't have any reservations about speaking your mind. Do you think we made a mistake when we stopped patrolling with the local police?"

"Absolutely," Idina said without hesitation.

"Would you care to expand on that?"

She took a deep breath before she answered.

"The JSP cooperation was the most successful thing to come out of this whole occupation. It took us years to get a good working relationship going. We had intel on the ground, from people who know their neighborhoods. We built trust with them one day at a time, one patrol at a time. And then we pissed it all away because we just had to make a big show of force. We did exactly what these Odin's Wolves bastards wanted us to do."

"You think we are going the wrong route with the strict blockade."

"We're accomplishing nothing with it. Other than pissing off whatever part of the population here wasn't mad at us before. If they all decide they don't want us here anymore, there aren't enough boots we can put on the ground to keep the peace. Not without their help."

The deputy high commissioner smiled and shook his head.

"You certainly don't hold back, Color Sergeant."

"With all due respect, sir, but why are you asking my opinion? I'm not a general. I'm not even an officer. I'm just an infantry sergeant. I had no word in that decision."

"I asked Color Sergeant Norgay which of the troopers he knew in the Green Zone had the most experience working with the Gretian police, and your name came up."

"Well, sir." Idina shifted her weight uneasily. "All that experience went out of the window when the high commission decided to suspend the JSP and reassign us all to diplomatic security."

"I had no voice in that decision," the DHC said. "I only got here a few days ago. But I agree with you that it may have been hasty and ill-advised."

He nodded at the Sandvik skyline in the distance.

"I'm going to meet with the Gretian police command this afternoon. We are going to discuss the possibility of resuming the JSP cooperation. I'd like you to come along with your section for added security. And because you may be able to share your experience and perspective. Show them that we're willing to act in good faith. Maybe we haven't used up all their goodwill."

Idina did a little double take, and the DHC smiled at her reaction.

"That would be the most useful thing anyone has done since this whole mess started," she said. "I have to say that this is not what I expected when I walked in."

"You expected to get dressed down."

"It wasn't my place to criticize your decision yesterday, sir. I was speaking in the heat of the moment. I apologize."

"I misjudged the situation on the ground," he said. "And you were right. Even if your criticism was a little blunt. The next time you have an issue with my judgment, please ask me aside and voice it in private."

Maybe I misjudged you after all, Idina thought.

"Understood, sir," she said. "Of course I will come along with my section. I know a few people over there. Who knows? It may lighten the atmosphere if they see a few familiar faces."

"Good," he replied. "Color Sergeant Norgay tells me the transport is scheduled for 1300."

"We will be on time." She hesitated. "Uh, are we going via surface or gyrofoil?"

The deputy high commissioner smiled and shook his head.

"The security assessment says it's safer to fly. I think I will take that advice this time."

—

In the briefing room at the embassy, her platoon stood ready when she walked in five minutes before the official start of the watch briefing. Idina looked at her group of young troopers carefully, trying to spot telltale signs of stress or fatigue after yesterday's events and the long evening that had followed. She had expected at least one or two sick calls today, but when she did a quick head count, every section was at full strength.

"Good morning, Fifth Platoon," she said when she had taken stock. "Yesterday was a big, steaming pile of shit."

Some of the troopers in the room chuckled or nodded in agreement.

"I'm glad to see everyone reporting in this morning. But I want to remind you all that there's no shame in sitting out a patrol or two after a day like that. We're not machines. I don't want to send out anyone who has a light trigger finger because they're strung out. Section leaders, report any concerns with your people to me after the briefing and before we arm up downstairs."

Her section corporals voiced their acknowledgments.

"The security situation is a little spicy after what happened yesterday," she said. "Drone coverage has been doubled. Gate guard has been doubled as well, and they've assigned armor to the buffer zone. I don't expect anyone to try and force the gate because that would be a suicide run. But the brass are jumpy right now. They want to see lots of troopers with rifles between them and the barrier.

"Which brings me to today's patrol assignments," she continued. "Red and Blue sections pulled perimeter patrol yesterday, so today Purple and Green get the honor. Yellow Section has the gate guard. Blue Section, rooftop overwatch. And Red Section gets the field-trip assignment today. You're going to do executive protection for the DHC with me."

The troopers of Red Section exchanged guarded looks.

"He's going out again today?" Corporal Shakya asked. "After what happened yesterday?"

"And we are going with him," Idina confirmed. "But this is good news. We're taking the combat bird this time. And we are heading into the city. To talk to the Gretians about kicking off the JSP patrols again. Looks like somebody upstairs recognized that it was a little hasty to pull the plug on those."

There were general sounds of approval in the room. Garrison duty was boring, and guard duty was the most tedious garrison duty of all. Troops who were assigned to do long stretches of it always lost much of their edge and motivation. The police patrols with the JSP were riskier than patrolling the inside of the Green Zone perimeter, but Idina liked that it was never boring work, that no two shifts were ever the same, and she knew that most of her platoon felt the same way.

"We'll be added security again. We make sure the DHC gets there safely and then makes it back to the Green Zone again. He has his regular crew, so we're just there in case something goes sideways. Which is not likely because we are going to the Gretian police HQ. You all know that place is a citadel."

She checked the time on her comtab.

"Right. The good news for Red Section is that we have an extra half hour to get ready. We'll grab weapons and kit after everyone else is done. Any questions?"

The section corporals shook their heads. Idina nodded and put her comtab away.

"Very well. Red Section, stick around for a minute. All other sections, go and gear up. Assembly out front at 1200 hours. And keep your heads out there, people. You're all professionals at this. Stay calm and cool until there's a really good reason not to be."

The bulk of the platoon filed out of the room behind their section leaders. Idina distributed encouraging nods as her troopers passed her on the way out. Then the briefing room was empty except for her and the eight troopers of Red Section.

"We have an extra thirty minutes, so if any of you need to hit the head or grab something from the mess hall, go ahead," Idina said. "We will be out for the rest of the day."

"Do you expect any trouble, Colors?" Corporal Shakya asked.

She shook her head.

"The DHC wants us along because the Gretians know a bunch of us. He figured it might make things a little more cordial."

He nodded, seemingly relieved.

"But we're still going to gear up just like the rest of the platoon," she said. "Medium armor and battle rifles for everyone. None of that low-profile soft armor and sidearms business like yesterday."

"Don't you think the DHC will find that look a little aggressive?" Shakya asked.

"I don't give a shit if he does, Corporal. Gyrofoils can get shot out of the sky. And I don't ever want to get caught in the open again without hardshell around my body and a long-range weapon in my hands."

If the deputy high commissioner thought Idina's team overdressed for the mission, he didn't show it when they boarded the gyrofoil together. Only Color Sergeant Sirhan, the leader of the DHC's primary two-man protection team, gave her a raised eyebrow when she took her seat across the aisle from him and stowed her rifle in the weapons bracket next to her. She returned his gaze and shrugged a little, and he grinned. Both main bodyguards wore soft armor again, hidden away under their regular uniform tunics. Idina's section, in contrast, were all clad in standard medium-weight infantry armor, the ideal compromise between protection and mobility.

The gyrofoil they had boarded was a reconnaissance version, fitted with big windows covered with Alon bulges that afforded an almost perfect all-round view of the craft's surroundings. They lifted off from the Green Zone's landing pad and climbed straight up at full power to remain in the protective envelope of the IBIS emitters on the government quarter's perimeter. Idina watched as the Green Zone receded underneath the gyrofoil, a heavily guarded enclave that looked smaller and more inconsequential the higher the ship climbed.

The flight to the Gretian police headquarters took them across the center of the city, where the corporate high-rise buildings stood in a tight cluster around Principal Square. Even from a thousand meters up, the crowds on the square were evident, concentrated on the side that faced the park and the Green Zone.

It's not all of them, Idina reminded herself. *It's not even most of them.* The majority of the city's population was not down there on the square and waiting for passing Alliance vehicles to vent their anger upon. Most of the civilians were down in the streets and in those office buildings, going about their daily business, not caring too much who set the rules as long as they had food and security and opportunities for leisure. The ones who cared enough to take to the streets were only a small fraction, and it was easy to forget that fact when the Alliance soldiers only dealt with that loud and hostile group. They all needed the JSP patrols to resume, if only as a reminder to everyone that both sides really were pulling on the same rope.

The Gretian police headquarters was part of a large semicircular complex on the western edge of the city's center. Idina had been here numerous times in the course of her JSP patrols with Captain Dahl, and she knew the general layout of the police section well by now. The inside of the semicircle had dozens of landing platforms for patrol gyrofoils jutting out of the side of the building, and from the air, the arrangement of landing pads looked like a giant cascading staircase. The combat gyrofoil descended above the Gretian government complex and landed on one of the large platforms that made up the lowest level. Idina saw curious faces peering out of the nearby windows as the huge war machine settled on its skids, dwarfing the Gretian patrol gyrofoils parked nearby.

The Gretians came out to greet them as soon as they stepped out onto the platform. Idina didn't recognize any of the police officers in the small group that was waiting for them, but she could tell by their insignia that they were all high ranking. She kept her distance as Color Sergeant Sirhan introduced the deputy high commissioner to the Gretian brass. When the higher-ups walked off toward the platform's access doors, she motioned for her section to follow. Inside, the access door led out onto a wide catwalk that overlooked the atrium from three tiers up. In front of her, Colors Norgay slowed his step a little to let her catch up with him while the VIPs strode on toward the nearby skylift, still exchanging introductory pleasantries through their translator buds.

"They're going to have their chat upstairs at the top tier," Sirhan said.

"You want us to shadow you and wait outside the conference room?"

Sirhan shook his head.

"No need. You can stand by down here. Kapoor and I can handle the bureaucrats if they get testy." He grinned at the apparent ludicrousness of the idea. "Take a break and get some tea. I'll let you know when we're coming back down."

"You're in charge," Idina said. "We'll keep an eye on things."

He nodded and turned to hurry back to the group of VIPs, who were stepping onto the skylift that had just arrived.

Idina turned toward her section.

"You've been here before. You know where the canteen and the toilets are. We're going to stand around and look important for a bit."

Down in the lobby, a small group of Gretian officers in green-and-white patrol skin suits caught Idina's eye. One of them was a woman who wore her hair in a familiar-looking silver-colored braid, and Idina smiled to herself in recognition.

"I'm going to go downstairs to get some tea from the canteen," she said. "Shakya, put someone out by the gyrofoil. I'll be right back."

—

Down at the refreshment counter in the lobby canteen, she felt out of place for the first time as she chose a tea mix from the dispenser, keenly aware that most of the people sitting down for their breaks were shooting her curious glances. When her cup was full, she withdrew it from the machine and walked off hurriedly, trying not to rattle her rifle against her armor as she did.

The group of officers she had spotted earlier was still standing in the same place near the large reflecting pool in the center of the atrium. One of them spotted her as she approached and pointed her out to the others. When the woman with the silver braid turned around, Idina was briefly convinced she would be someone else, that her wishful thinking had led her to misidentify a stranger. But the face she saw was a familiar one, and she felt a swell of relief and joy.

"Sergeant Chaudhary," Captain Dahl said with a smile. "What in all the worlds are you doing here? I thought you were long back home on Pallas."

"I was supposed to be," Idina said. "I was already on the shuttle. But then they canceled all troop movements when Rhodia was attacked. Now I'm stuck here for a while still."

"Well, I cannot say that I am too sorry about that. It is very good to see you again." Dahl offered her hand, and Idina shook it in the Gretian way, to the amused glances of Dahl's colleagues.

"It's good to see you, too," Idina said. "How have you been these last few weeks?"

Dahl looked back at her fellow officers.

"I will be along shortly, right after I catch up with my friend here."

The Gretians nodded and walked off without hurry, chatting among each other as they crossed the atrium toward the entrance vestibule.

"Things have been a little tense lately," Dahl said. "I did not anticipate they would end our joint patrols so suddenly. On the bright side, I did not have to get used to a new Alliance patrol partner."

"If that's the good side of things, then I bring bad news. One of our Alliance commissioners is upstairs to talk to your bosses about resuming the JSP patrols. It appears someone agreed that it was a dumb and hasty decision."

"Is that so?" Dahl smiled. "That would not be so terrible, I suppose. If that were to happen, are you going to be on patrol with us again?"

"Gods, I hope so," Idina replied. "Right now I'm either supervising gate guards or I am babysitting bureaucrats."

"So you did enjoy the police work we did together. And you kept telling me that you did not have the right temperament for the job."

"I still don't think I do. But at least it's never boring."

"And that is precisely why I have been wearing this uniform for as long as I have," Dahl said.

From the landing terrace above, Idina heard the engine sound of another arriving gyrofoil, muffled by distance and multiple layers of building. Even in the middle of a new interplanetary crisis and increased civil unrest, the police headquarters didn't seem much busier than before. Patrol units were arriving and leaving at a steady, seemingly unhurried pace. In the canteen where she had just gotten her tea, people were eating their lunches and chatting with each other. There was a sense of quiet, determined purpose to it all that she realized she had missed, something she hadn't felt since they had assigned her to the Green Zone and given her military busywork for the sake of appearances. Dahl and her colleagues had no crisis of purpose, no doubts that the work they were doing was making a difference for the planet.

Outside, the engine sounds from the landing gyrofoil increased sharply in volume and pitch. Dahl looked up at the ceiling of the atrium.

"Colors—" someone from her section shouted on the tactical channel. Idina felt her next heartbeat all the way in her throat. For a moment, time seemed to stand still around her.

There was a resounding, ear-splitting crash from high above the atrium, the bright, sharp breaking of glass and the tortured scream of bending steel. A fraction of a second later, the entire building shook so violently that Idina and Dahl had to hold on to the side of the reflecting pool's marble edge to keep from losing their balance. The lights in the atrium went out all at once.

Then the world blew apart around them.

The explosion was far beyond *loud.* It felt world ending, like someone had just dropped a nuclear charge at her feet and granted her three seconds of immortality so she could experience the primal force of the unleashed energy to the fullest before disintegrating. The shockwave knocked her down and ripped the rifle from her shoulder. All around her, bits and chunks of debris rained down from the atrium's ceiling, leaving huge holes that belched fire and dark smoke. She saw Dahl on the ground nearby and crawled over to shield the other woman from the rain of glass and steel shrapnel with her hard-shell armor. Next to her, the water of the reflecting pool sloshed over the edges of its retaining wall in big swells, spilling on the floor and drenching her and Dahl. When Idina's earpieces gradually restored her hearing after filtering the sound of the explosion, she heard people shouting and screaming, accompanied by a chorus of alarms going off in every direction. She looked up to see that the black smoke from the explosion was already clouding the semidarkness of the unlit atrium.

"We need to get out of here," she said to Dahl. "Are you still with me?"

"I am here," Dahl said in a voice that sounded like she had just woken up from deep sleep. "I think something just blew up in a big way."

"That fucking gyrofoil," Idina said. "Someone stuffed it with explosives and flew it into the side of the building. Come on. The ceiling is going to come down on us."

She helped Dahl to her knees. The Gretian police captain coughed sharply and wiped her face with the back of her skin suit's sleeve. Nearby, Idina saw her rifle in a puddle of water that was spreading steadily. She staggered over to it and picked it up. There was still a constant rain of debris coming from the ceiling, bouncing off the floor or splashing into the reflecting pool.

"Red Section, sitrep," she said into her headset. "Talk to me, troopers."

For a moment, there was silence on the channel, and the thought that she may have lost another section to an ambush made her nauseated with fear. Then someone shouted a curse into the tactical channel.

"Fuck," Corporal Shakya said. *"We just got it in the face, Colors. Are you all right?"*

"I'm fine. Give me a head count."

"I think Patel is gone. He was out by the ship. The whole platform collapsed. We're all wounded up here, but we can move."

"Good," she said. "Find a way to get down here. We need to get out before the building comes down on us."

"What about Colors Norgay and the DHC?"

Idina activated the sensor screen of her helmet, turned on the infrared filter, and tilted her head up to look at the floors above the atrium. There was a ragged hole in the building where the ceiling had been, and the entire side of the structure where the landing pads had been was now wide open to the outside. She could see hundreds of fires burning in the darkness on the shattered remnants of multiple floors. As she watched, a stream of burning fuel ran down from one of the floors and cascaded onto the marble of the atrium fifty meters away, where it set the debris of a smashed and overturned corner seat on fire. Somewhere high up in the building, a secondary explosion went off, but it sounded weak and feeble after the earthshaking bang of the first one. She switched to the platoon-level channel Norgay would be monitoring.

"Norgay, come in."

There was no reply. She repeated the challenge two more times, but the channel remained ominously silent. Idina toggled back over to the section.

"He's not on the network. Either his comms gear is out, or they're gone."

"We can't leave them behind, Colors," Corporal Shakya protested.

"We can't go up there," Idina said. "The whole side of the building is gone, and whatever's left is on fire. If their kit is busted, they'll make their own way out somehow. Norgay knows his business. Now get down here with your section. Acknowledge."

"Affirmative," Shakya said after a moment of tense silence. *"Red Section is on the way."*

Next to Idina, Dahl coughed again. The air carried the acrid smell of burning fuel and melting polymers. Somewhere in the distance, a fire-suppression module released its contents with a loud hiss.

On the other side of the atrium, a loud alarm began to blare. Idina looked up to see that it was coming from the entrance vestibule, where the access control arch had started to blink in an insistent red to match the cadence of the alarm noise. Through the smoke and the falling debris, Idina saw the outlines of several people rushing into the vestibule from the outside. For a moment, she thought they were part of some rapid response team or maybe a returning patrol unit coming to help. Then she saw that everyone in the group was wearing military-grade armor and carrying bulky weapons. Several people were crossing the atrium toward the vestibule to escape the building, but instead of stepping aside to make way or helping, the first newcomer aimed his rifle and opened fire at the officers rushing toward the exit. The harsh staccato of automatic gunfire cut through the din of alarms and shouts.

"Contact," she shouted into the section comms. *"Entrance area, multiple shooters!"*

Her rifle came up almost as if it were moving of its own accord. She used the low edge of the reflecting pool's wall as a rest for her left elbow and took aim. The newcomers—she counted four—were moving like a well-drilled fire team, spreading out and covering each other as they passed out of the vestibule into the lobby. For a few moments, she couldn't get a clear shot on either of them because of the people in the atrium who were now scattering in all directions before the gunfire. She watched in horror as one of the Gretian officers pulled out his own sidearm and fired at the closest attacker, then fell to a quick burst from the rifle of one of the others. Idina selected the armor-piercing ammunition feed, aimed her targeting reticule at the one whose armor had just shrugged off the round from the fallen officer's sidearm, and fired a three-shot burst. The attacker collapsed, dropping his own rifle as he went down.

Next to her left ear, a gunshot boomed. She turned her head to see Dahl, both hands holding her sidearm, squeezing off another shot with careful aim. Idina shifted her aim to the next attacker. They were quickly recovering from the surprise of taking return fire from a heavy weapon. She grabbed Dahl and yanked her down behind the cover of the wall just as one of them fired a burst their way, and the impact of the rounds nearby sprayed them with water and chunks of rock and marble. Behind Idina and Dahl, something in the canteen had caught fire in a major way, and the flames were billowing out of the door, bathing this part of the atrium in flickering red-and-orange light.

The gunfire kept coming. From the way the sound of the bursts started diverging, Idina could tell that the remaining attackers were spreading out and covering each other, taking turns firing and moving.

Three left, she thought. *They have to split up to get both sides. Pick the side that has less firepower.*

She switched her sensor filter to Sonic/Acoustic. In the noise and the chaos of the atrium, it was an imprecise way to locate her attackers from behind cover, but the gunshots were loud enough to show as a little light bloom on her screen even through the thick marble of the retaining wall. Two of them were moving off to the left to flank her from that side, which left one on the right. Idina motioned to Dahl to stay low and cover the left. Then she got up into a crouch and rushed right, glad for her low and stocky Palladian build.

When she came around the right side of the reflecting pool, the gunman closest to her still had his rifle aimed at the spot where she had opened fire initially. He saw her movement out of the corner of his eye and brought his rifle around, but she had hers aimed at him already, and her burst caught him in the middle of his chest plate and spun him halfway around. Idina fired another round into the side of his helmet as insurance, and he slumped over sideways. With her cover two steps behind her and her momentum going the other way already, she shifted her aim toward the remaining two attackers. For the second time since they had rushed into the place, she had taken them by surprise, but just as before, their reaction time spoke of excellent training. They shifted their stances as she took aim, and she knew that she wouldn't be able to drop them both before at least one of them got off a burst.

A short but intense fusillade of fire rang out from Idina's left, multiple automatic rifles set to burst fire. She could see the bullets tearing through the armor of the two remaining gunmen in a dozen places, and they fell where they stood, crumpling to the ground in the particular way bodies did when they were already dead before they hit the floor. On the other side of the reflecting pool, in the firelit space between the edge of the pool and the canteen, Corporal Shakya and three of the Red Section troopers stood in firing stances, scanning the atrium for more attackers.

"Four down," Idina sent on the section comms. "That's all the ones that came in through that door. Keep that vestibule covered."

She approached the fallen gunmen with her rifle at the ready. They were wearing medium hardshell armor suits with ballistic liners underneath, just like her own section. The armor was of a style she didn't recognize, but it looked modern and in excellent shape. If she had told her section to gear up like they had done for the escort mission yesterday, their small-caliber submachine guns would not have been enough to punch through that armor reliably, and she would have been dead on the floor in the first few moments of the attack.

Shakya didn't waste time making the trip around the reflecting pool. He just stepped over the chipped retaining wall and walked through the hip-high water, then climbed out on her side, his rifle never wavering from its aiming point somewhere between the two nearest dead attackers.

"Fuckers came geared for a massacre," Shakya said. "Looks like they didn't expect to end up in an infantry battle."

"Well, they got one," Idina said. "Now let's get the hells out of here before the place falls down around us."

On the other side of the pool, Dahl stood up, her gun still in her hand and held at low ready. She looked a little shaken, but not as rattled as Idina would have felt in her spot, wearing only a light ballistic skin suit and carrying a service pistol with ammo that was only good for soft targets.

"We got them," Idina called out to her.

Somewhere inside the building, a burst of automatic fire rang out, then another. A few quick single shots followed in reply. The Red Section troopers reoriented themselves to face the direction of the new threat. Dahl checked her pistol and started rushing toward the sound of the gunfire.

"*Wait,*" Idina shouted.

Dahl stopped and looked back at her.

"Bad idea," Idina said. "You're not geared for that fight."

"That is my job," Dahl replied. "I have to do it. No matter how I happen to be geared."

Idina looked over at Corporal Shakya.

"Sounds like the massacre's still in progress," she said. "Want to go even the odds a bit?"

Shakya shrugged and checked the ammunition status of his rifle.

"Might as well. Beats walking perimeter patrol."

They gathered around Dahl, who looked slight among all the armored troopers even though she was taller than most of them. Somewhere in the bowels of the station, there was more gunfire, handguns trading shots with military rifles.

"If you are sure about this, then let us not waste time," Dahl said.

They moved out toward the sound of the gunfire together.

CHAPTER 19
DUNSTAN

"It *is* a pretty ship," Lieutenant Armer said. "I've always had a thing for those Acheroni-built composite hulls. That one must have cost a bundle."

They were looking at a viewscreen that showed a close-up image of *Zephyr*'s bow section. The little speed yacht had flipped around for her deceleration burn a few hours ago, and her drive plume was no longer obstructing the direct view of her hull. Even at ten thousand kilometers, the optical sensors combined with *Hecate*'s otherworldly AI gave them such a clear image that they could count and identify all her antenna arrays and sensor bulges.

"It's light, and it's fast," Lieutenant Robson said. "But it's almost all graphene matrix and a composite skin. They're brave to take that ship where they're taking it. If they take a hit from anything more powerful than a socaball, they'll crumple like a paper lantern."

"Speed is armor," Dunstan interjected from the command chair. "That's what they teach at the space warfare command school, you know. If they can't hit you, it doesn't matter how thick your hull is."

Lieutenant Hunter shook her head with a smile.

"With all due respect, sir, but that's old-school talk. If we really needed to blow that ship out of space right now? I would let Armer use fifty percent of the AI core capacity for the gun mount. The AI would calculate two trillion aim lead points per second. Unless they can travel back in time, we'd have them shot in half with the first ten-round burst."

"Old-school talk," Dunstan said. "You're saying it's pre-*Dreadnought* thinking."

She rewarded the reference with a grin.

"Pre-*Dreadnought* thinking. Exactly."

Hecate was in a precise pursuit trajectory controlled by the navigation AI. They were following in *Zephyr*'s shadow to keep what little thermal emissions the warship's stealth nozzle dissipated hidden behind the much larger thermal bloom from the civilian ship's drive. If someone in the target zone were to look their way, they would only be able to see a single bright flare coming toward them. They were well off any current low-energy transfer lanes. A few ships were on direct brachistochrone trajectories, willing and able to spend the fuel and gravmag energy to make multiple-g runs through the interplanetary space for urgent cargo, but even the closest one of those was a few million kilometers away, lawfully broadcasting its ID and location on the Mnemosyne as it went. If there were other ships in this part of space, they were coasting with their transponders off and their Mnemosyne nodes deactivated. Anyone they would run into out here was likely to be a smuggler or a pirate.

"Decelerating right on the numbers. Thirteen minutes until we cut the burn," Hunter said. "Prepare to switch to internal heat sinks as soon as the drive shuts down."

"Prepare for internal heat retention, aye," Lieutenant Armer replied.

"Tell me again how long those will last," Dunstan said.

"Depends on our output, sir. With the drive off, it's just the environmental heat from our bodies, the energy the hull absorbs from the sun, and whatever the core puts out. If we don't need to fire up our main propulsion, we can go for two or three days before we have to start ejecting heat sinks."

"Let's hope we won't have to hide out here for that long." Dunstan looked at the situational display. There was nothing special about this corner of interplanetary space, no asteroids or natural anomalies to hide behind. But it was a long way from the regular shipping lanes, and if someone was lying in wait out there, they would see incoming traffic from a long way out.

"Give me a fix on the nearest Alliance unit in the area," he ordered.

Lieutenant Robson checked her display.

"We have two light cruisers roughly equidistant at three million kilometers. RNS *Cerberus* and ONS *Pelican*. At maximum design spec acceleration with deceleration burn factored in, four point three four hours for *Cerberus* to get here, and four point one four hours for *Pelican*."

"Good. We'll call on them if we need space for prisoners. Any civilian traffic that may get in the way?"

"Negative, sir. The closest commercial traffic is five million kilometers out and burning at five g for Oceana. We have the neighborhood all to ourselves."

"Very well. Number One, let's get ready for business. Call the ship to action stations."

Lieutenant Hunter picked up the hardwired handset for the low-power ship comms.

"Action stations, action stations. All hands to battle positions. Assume vacsuit state alpha. Set EMCON condition one. Ship-to-ship action imminent. This is not a drill."

Everyone on the operations deck reached for their vacsuit helmet to follow the first officer's directive. Dunstan put on his own helmet and sealed it to the collar of his pressure suit. If the ship took a hit and their compartment lost atmosphere, the visor of the helmet would seal in a blink and switch his air supply to his seat's built-in oxygen feed. It was an action he had performed a thousand times or more in his long career, but the simple act of tightening the seal and double-checking it always felt like stepping into a fighting ring, preparing to give someone a bloody nose or receive one.

Now we are just waiting for the bell to ring and the round to start, he thought.

"All hands, prepare for zero-g maneuvering," Lieutenant Hunter announced ten minutes later. "Main drive shutdown in ten seconds."

Dunstan felt the familiar lightness in his middle when the ship's fusion drive throttled back to standby mode. *Hecate* had a gravmag array like all warships, but stealth mode meant making as little electromagnetic noise as possible, so the ship would remain at zero g while they were drifting silently.

"Main drive is idling," the helmsman said. "Acceleration zero meters per second squared. Velocity three hundred fifty meters per second."

"Flip us around," Hunter ordered. "Sensors, stand by for passive sweep."

Hecate turned 180 degrees with its dorsal thrusters to point her bow into the direction of travel again. A moment later, the tactical display updated with the feed from the passive sensors. Ten thousand kilometers ahead of *Hecate, Zephyr* was still decelerating, radiating their thermal signature like a miniature star in the darkness of the interplanetary void. If the fusion-drive plume masked *Hecate* from the target area, it also worked to shield that portion of space from their passive sensors. *Zephyr* was plunging down a deep, dark well without knowing what was waiting at the bottom, in a ship that was unarmed and unarmored. *Hecate* was going in after them, ready to hand down a rope, but there was no way of knowing if they would be able to get there in time to make a difference if things went very wrong.

Revenge is a strong motivator, Dunstan thought. *That's why we are all here, after all. They want to get payback for their dead friend. With all the righteous talk of law and justice, everyone on this ship wants to get retribution for our quarter million dead and wounded. And whoever Odin's Ravens are, they were justified in their own minds for dropping that nuke. We're all just kindling new grudges even as we are settling old ones.*

"EMCON is under AI control. All sensors are in passive mode. We are rigged for full stealth," Lieutenant Robson said.

"*Zephyr* is coming out of her burn as well. Distance is now twelve thousand five hundred kilometers," Armer reported.

On the tactical screen, the icon for the little Oceanian courier looked lonely all by itself. Unlike *Hecate*, they hadn't turned off their active emissions on purpose, and their transponder was sending out the ship's ID once every second: OMV-2022 ZEPHYR. They wanted to make sure to be seen, to signal to whoever was waiting that they had no subterfuge in mind. A few minutes later, the icon for *Zephyr* changed to a pulsating orange.

"They've turned on their emergency beacon," Robson said. "Now we wait and see if someone comes to sniff the bait."

"Well, that didn't take long," Lieutenant Hunter said less than an hour later. A new icon had materialized on the tactical screen, eight thousand kilometers off their port bow. "Contact, designate *Sultan-1*. Heading right for the emergency signal at a quarter-g acceleration."

"Any chance they're a random merchie coming to check for a salvage opportunity?" Dunstan asked.

Robson shook her head. "They're not squawking any ID. We picked them up on passive when they lit their drive. They've been parked out here all still and quiet. Probably took the last forty-five minutes to decide if the coast is clear."

"If that's just some shady scrapper looking for an easy payday, they've picked a bad time and place."

"This isn't anywhere near a brachistochrone trajectory between any of the planets right now," Hunter said. "They have no reason to be out here. Could be that they just happened to be in the area. But that would be a fantastic coincidence."

Dunstan watched as the icon labeled UNKNOWN steadily moved toward the spot where *Zephyr*'s emergency beacon was sending out its automated message once every seven seconds. To a passing military ship or an honest merchant, it would constitute an obligation to render assistance. Any ship that was found to have detected an emergency beacon and failed to investigate without a good excuse or explanation was subject to having its operating license pulled and her captain prosecuted. To a freelance scrapper or a pirate, a beacon would represent the possibility of a lucrative wreck to salvage. A claim on a wreck with half a ton of palladium in it could keep a small salvage outfit in the black for a year or two.

On a normal day during a routine patrol, Dunstan would have been happy to bust a scrapper who was coasting dirty, but today he was hoping for much more consequential prey.

For the next twenty minutes, they watched the plot. The unknown ship wasn't rushing in to snatch the bait. Instead, they reduced their burn, then counterburned to finish the approach to the "crippled" *Zephyr* on cold-gas thrusters. In the middle of the other ship's return to a nose-first course, an alarm signal sounded at Lieutenant Robson's station, and the icon for the unknown ship lit up with new identification and position data.

"They went active on their radar," Robson said. "Nine-gigahertz band, one and a half kilowatt. That's commercial civilian gear. Not a military piece of hardware."

"Checking the neighborhood for lurkers," Dunstan said. "Any chance at all they're getting a return from us?"

Robson shook her head.

"Not with that gear at that range, sir. At eight thousand klicks, you couldn't get a hit from our hull with a good military set at a hundred times the wattage."

The distance between the newcomer and *Zephyr* decreased slowly but steadily. *Zephyr* was playing her part, pretending to be dead in space. They would have picked up the radar sweep from the incoming ship, but *Hecate* and *Zephyr* had kept radio silence ever since they'd started their burn many hours ago, so there was no way for *Zephyr*'s crew to know for sure that *Hecate* had followed them and was lurking in wait according to plan. Dunstan tried to put himself into the head of the other captain, knowing that someone was coming to steal her ship and probably flush her out of an airlock, and putting her trust in someone who had almost arrested her the only time they'd met.

I don't know if I would have made that leap of faith in her place, Dunstan thought. *Not even for revenge.*

On the tactical screen, the icon for the unknown ship changed to a blue lozenge shape, and an ID tag appeared next to the symbol.

"And they *just* went legit," Robson said. "They turned on their ID transponder. OMV-1519 *Morning Star*," she added, with skepticism in her voice.

"They have to squawk their ID so *Zephyr*'s logs can pick it up," Dunstan said. "For salvage claim disputes. First ship to get there gets to make the claim. Check the ID with the Mnemosyne data, please."

"Already on it, sir." Robson had a data screen floating next to her console, and her fingers were flying across the input fields. "OMV-1519 *Morning Star*. Pleasure cruiser, five thousand tons, certified for two hundred passengers. Rhodian built, served as an interplanetary tourism ship until the war. Registry says she was sold to a civilian investor group on Oceana three years ago. The flight plan database says she left Oceana One over four weeks ago."

"That's a really long pleasure cruise. Check the drive and EM profiles on file. If that's the same ship, they're a long way from home for no good reason."

"How long before we spring the trap, sir?" Hunter asked.

Dunstan looked at the distance scales on the tactical screen.

"I want to let them know we are here before they get close enough to *Zephyr* to be able to do something stupid when they realize they are burned. Are we in certain intercept range?"

"If that's really OMV-1519, they can do five g at the most," Robson said. "They were in our certain intercept envelope the second we spotted them on passive. If they make a run for it, we'll be on top of them inside of ten minutes."

"All right. Let's spook them. Give me a tight-beam link so we don't broadcast our presence to the entire neighborhood. Who are we pretending to be?"

Robson thought for a moment while she worked her control screen.

"How about RNS *Hades*?"

"*Hades* it is," Dunstan said.

"Go ahead on tight-beam, sir."

Dunstan cleared his throat and tapped his comms button.

"Attention, *Morning Star*. This is the Rhodian Navy ship *Hades*. Are you receiving us?"

Lieutenant Hunter flashed a wry grin. Anyone whose comms array just got hit by a focused comms laser knew good and well that the sending party was aware of their presence and exact location. They would not be able to remain silent and feign ignorance unless they pretended their comms gear was broken, and every skipper knew that failure to answer a navy challenge would result in seeing the challenging ship come alongside in short order. The other option was to turn and flee, but that was tantamount to admitting illegal activity.

"Hades, *this is* Morning Star. *We receive you loud and clear, but we don't have you on our sensors."*

"We are nearby, *Morning Star*. You want to explain why you are cruising through interplanetary space without a valid transponder squawk?"

"Hades, *our transponder is on and broadcasting. We are on course to reply to an emergency beacon off our bow. Are you transmitting that signal?"*

"He knows good and damn well that the tight-beam is coming from somewhere else," Hunter said.

"He's weighed his options and decided to feign ignorance," Dunstan replied. "He knows he's fucked now. But he doesn't want to turn and run because he doesn't know if we can catch him."

Dunstan tapped his comms button again.

"That is a negative, *Morning Star*. Maintain course and bring your velocity to under ten meters per second. We will be alongside shortly for an inspection."

"Hades, *copy. Any reason for the inspection? We were just checking on that emergency beacon."*

"*Morning Star*, let's just save each other time and drop the pretense. You only turned on your transponder five minutes ago. We've been tracking you for a while."

"That must be a sensor malfunction on your end, Hades. *We've been squawking proper ID since we left the station. We have our ship's autolog to back us up. But go ahead and do your inspection. We've got nothing to hide. Maintaining course and reducing velocity as ordered."*

Dunstan looked over at Lieutenant Hunter, who raised an eyebrow.

"They're determined to keep up the theater, it seems."

"They probably figure they'll take their chance with the courts and hope their rigged autolog gets them off. Or they have a mysterious data bank malfunction right as we board. I've seen that one tried more than once," Dunstan said.

"They are reversing thrusters and slowing down as ordered," Robson reported.

"Drop the tight-beam."

"Tight-beam connection terminated, sir."

"Bring the drive on line and let's go for an intercept," Dunstan said. "One-quarter g, no more. They're looking hard for us right now. I don't want them to see a thing. Once we're close enough for network access, it won't matter what switches they flick over there."

"Aye, sir. Bringing the drive on line. Setting thrust for one-quarter g, steady as she goes."

"We'll have to flip and counterburn in twenty minutes if we don't want to overshoot them," Lieutenant Hunter said.

"How close for the network takeover to work, Lieutenant Robson?"

"Depends on their equipment, sir. If they still have the factory systems integration, we shouldn't have to be much closer than ten or twenty thousand."

"Start the hack as soon as you think we're close enough. We'll cut the burn halfway but don't turn the ship just then. Once we are inside their systems, we can turn around and counterburn. At that point it won't matter if they see our exhaust on IR."

"That will be plenty of time, sir. I'll be in long before we have to flip."

"Very well," Dunstan said. "Weapons, go to standby on the missile launcher. Make sure you have an updated firing solution if things go to shit and we have to throw punches. Could be they decide to let us get close and then stitch us up."

"I've had a passive solution running on that ship since we spotted it," Lieutenant Armer said. "Going to standby on the missile launcher, aye."

"Sir, once I am in their AI core, they won't even be able to flush their toilets unless we allow it," Lieutenant Robson said. Hunter grinned and shook her head.

Morning Star seemed to be who she claimed to be through her transponder. As *Hecate* decreased the distance on her intercept trajectory over the next twenty minutes, the optical sensors on the warship's bow brought the other ship into ever-sharper detail on the viewscreen Robson had overlaid on the tactical plot. If this was a clandestine Odin's Ravens unit, it didn't strike Dunstan as a particularly suitable platform for the job. It was a sleek and elegant hull, but it was built for sightseeing, not piracy. Many of the decks had large wraparound Alon windows, to allow passengers to see planets and moons with their own eyes instead of through a viewscreen connected to an optical feed. Alon windows were highly resilient and impact resistant, but they were still transparent slabs mounted onto big holes in the hull. Any opening in a spaceship's hull was a weak spot and a potential failure point in a fight.

Maybe we're mistaken and you really are only out here to have your rich guests view the stars, Dunstan thought. *I guess we will see in a few minutes.*

On the tactical plot, the positions of the three ships were now the corners of a roughly equilateral triangle. *Zephyr* was floating in space at just a few dozen meters per second. *Morning Star* was drifting toward *Zephyr* at the same slow rate.

"Did they really come in dumb like this?" Dunstan said, more to himself than the rest of the operations crew.

"What was that, sir?" Hunter asked.

He gestured at the plot.

"This feels a little off, Lieutenant."

"How do you mean?"

"The *Zephyr* crew gave us the coordinates for the nuke handoff a few weeks ago, right? We showed up and the other ship ran. We gave chase and ended up running into a gun cruiser. They'd planned for the chance that they'd get crossed. Now they know that crew over there has crossed them once already. And now they just show up with another ship and no backup."

"You think there's a trap waiting for us out there."

"I think the odds are better than even, Lieutenant."

"With respect, sir, this is not some antique prewar frigate. They saw you coming, and they had time to run. That ship right there doesn't even have the faintest idea where we are right now. We're a hole in space," Hunter said.

Dunstan looked at *Morning Star*'s icon creeping across the plot and bit his lower lip in thought.

"I know you are right," he said. "But let's not get overconfident. The last time I let that happen, I ended up with a wrecked frigate."

"Crossing inside of a thousand kilometers now," Armer announced.

Dunstan stared at the plot, trying to divine the immediate future from the limited information on the display. The passive sensors were telling him that the coast was clear, that the only ships out here other than *Hecate* were *Zephyr* and the Oceanian pleasure cruiser, but he knew the limits of passive sensors all too well. As long as they didn't use active radiation, *Hecate* was invisible, but the difference in their own awareness was like the difference between walking into a brightly lit room while fully awake and stumbling into a dark basement while wearing sunshades.

I'm not going to let myself fall to the bottom of that well without knowing what's really waiting down there, he thought.

"Take us out of EMCON and get us into that ship's AI," he said. "And send a message to *Zephyr* to turn off their emergency beacon. It's too much background noise right now."

"Aye, sir," Robson said.

"Stand by on active sensors. On my mark, give me a 180-degree active sweep."

"Ready for active sensor sweep."

"Three. Two. One. Mark."

Hecate's powerful active sensor array swept the space in front of the ship in a wide cone. Dunstan looked at the tactical screen to follow the progress of the scan.

"Getting a blip of something at 290 by positive 10—never mind, it's gone now," Robson said.

"Define 'blip,'" Dunstan said. An electric sort of trickle was working its way up his spine to the base of his skull. "And be quick about it."

"Like a sensor echo. It was there for half a second and then it went away."

"Isolate that location and do an active search at full sensor power."

"Aye, sir," Lieutenant Robson said without taking her eyes off her control screen.

"I've seen that sort of echo before," Dunstan said. "Back at the internment yard, three months ago. Then again above Rhodia, right before the nuke dropped. Active search now, Lieutenant."

Robson tapped a field on her screen. At the same moment, an alarm trilled on the tactical screen, and two red icons appeared as if she had just summoned them with her control input.

"Bandit, bandit," Lieutenant Hunter called out. "Missile launch, 290 by positive 10, distance 441 kilometers."

"New contact," Robson shouted a moment later. "Active return—290 by positive 10, distance 480. Designate *Sultan-1*. Burning hard and away."

Another icon materialized on the display behind the missiles, rushing in the opposite direction. Dunstan had seen this precise pattern before when the attack on Rhodia had commenced three weeks ago. When he opened his mouth to shout a command, the anger he felt squeezed his throat and forced his voice into a growl.

"Hammer that piece of shit on active. It's a stealth hull. Don't let him get away. Bring up the drive and lay in an intercept course."

"Point defenses are online," Armer said.

"Those aren't meant for us," Hunter said. "They're headed for *Zephyr* and *Morning Star*. Twenty-five seconds to impact."

"Tight-beam to *Zephyr*," Dunstan ordered.

"Go ahead on tight-beam, sir."

"*Zephyr*, you have ship-to-ship ordnance coming your way. Get the hells out of there right now. Twenty seconds."

"We see it," Captain Decker's voice replied. She sounded remarkably calm for someone who had a few hundred pounds of high explosives or maybe even a tactical nuke headed for her unarmored ship at one hundred gravities. *"Point defense is active. Going evasive."*

On the tactical screen, *Zephyr* rapidly increased the gap between herself and *Morning Star*. She was burning her main drive at full throttle now, leaping from a virtual standstill to a twenty-g sprint in just a few seconds. It was an astonishing rate of acceleration, one that he'd never seen another ship match, civilian or military. He knew the crew were trying to create extra milliseconds for their Point Defense System, the only right move they could have made in this situation.

"Fifteen seconds," Robson called out.

"I have a firing solution on the bogey," Armer announced. "They're moving off at seventeen g. We need to move if we want to catch them, sir."

"Knock me those missiles out of space, Lieutenant Robson."

"Brute-forcing the guidance systems," Robson said. "AI core at thirty percent. I've got control of one." Her fingers were a blur on her control screen. "Overriding and detonating."

One of the missile icons disappeared from the tactical display. The second one rushed toward the two civilian ships.

"Squash one," Robson said. "Bandit-1 is history. I can't get a solid lock on Bandit-2. Seven seconds. That one is headed for *Zephyr*, sir."

"At least they have a PDS. I hope it's a good one."

Sorry we couldn't do more, Captain, he thought as he watched the missile icon rush toward the icon for *Zephyr*. The fast little courier was running the sprint of her life, not to evade the missile but to give her PDS's AI the needed time to calculate a precise intercept. The red missile icon raced toward the blue ship icon, closing the distance relentlessly. When the red icon was almost on top of the blue one, it blinked once and disappeared.

"They got it," Robson said in disbelief. "Their PDS shot it down, two seconds out."

Dunstan watched *Zephyr*'s icon, expecting it to blink and leave the plot forever as well, but the little courier kept up its trajectory, still accelerating at an unheard-of twenty and a half gravities. As he watched, the pilot came off the throttle, and the acceleration value next to the icon fell: eighteen, sixteen, ten, then five.

"Tight-beam for *Zephyr*," Dunstan said.

"Go ahead on tight-beam."

"*Zephyr*, *Hecate*. What is your status?"

"We got our tail singed a little, I think," Captain Decker's voice replied. *"But the PDS worked as advertised."*

"I'd say it did," Dunstan said.

"I'm rather glad. I'd hate to have to haggle over a refund." Despite the joke, Dunstan heard the stress in Decker's voice, and he doubted that she still felt as calm as she had sounded earlier.

"*Sultan-1* is hotfooting it out of here at seventeen g," Lieutenant Hunter said. "They'll be out of engagement range in twenty seconds."

"Standing by on missiles," Lieutenant Armer said.

Dunstan shook his head. "Weapons hold. We need evidence, not glowing debris. Come to new heading for intercept and open her up all the way, helm. All ahead flank."

The ship vibrated as the main drive lit off at full throttle. Up ahead beyond the top bulkhead, Dunstan knew that the gravmag system was pouring megawatts of current into the palladium rotors to counteract the gravitational effects of the acceleration from the fusion rocket. Even with the gravmag system at full spin, it still felt like someone had come into the operations compartment and sat down on his chest.

"Passing through eight g," Hunter said, her voice strained. "Ten. Twelve."

"They're doing seventeen, sir," Armer said from his couch. "We can't catch them in a stern chase."

"They have to keep their throttle open if they want to get away," Dunstan replied. "We follow them for as long as we can keep them in sight. Give the AI as much data as it can get. Maybe we'll get a good prediction of where they're going."

"Aye, sir."

"Thirteen g," Hunter said. "Fourteen. Come on, you little beast. Let's see what you've got."

On the tactical screen, an alarm beeped, and one of the ship icons started flashing orange.

"*Morning Star* has activated her emergency beacon," Lieutenant Robson said.

"Get them on comms."

"*Morning Star*, *Hades*. What is your status?"

"Hades, Morning Star. *Whatever exploded off our stern sent a bunch of high-speed debris through our stern section. We have lost propulsion and our reactor power. We need immediate assistance.*"

Dunstan allowed himself a grim smile.

"We're a little occupied, *Morning Star*. The missile we intercepted off your stern was sent to wipe out evidence. You're damn lucky you only lost your drive. Take that into consideration when the next Alliance ship comes alongside to take you into custody in a few hours."

He terminated the comms link without waiting for a reply.

"Can I get a visual on *Morning Star*? Something tells me we can't take them at their word."

Lieutenant Robson opened a screen and flicked it over to the main tactical display. They were still close enough to the civilian liner to get a high-definition visual of the hull. They were trailing frozen air and venting gas into space from multiple spots on their stern section, and hundreds of shrapnel holes of various sizes were evident in the outer skin.

"Contact the two Alliance ships we spotted four hours away. *Cerberus* and *Pelican*. Tell them to make haste to *Morning Star*'s location and secure the ship and crew."

"Aye, sir," Robson said.

"Fifteen and a half." Hunter was grasping the armrests of her gravity couch so hard that Dunstan could see the whites of her knuckles. "We're as wide open as we're going to get. She's got maybe another quarter g in her. We're not going to catch them."

The unknown stealth ship opened the distance between them with frustrating ease. It wasn't a huge head start, and the acceleration advantage wasn't decisive yet, but it would get the other ship far enough away in a few hours to let her cut her main drive and drift back into stealth to lose her pursuer. Dunstan was absolutely certain by now that this was the stealth unit that had smuggled a nuke through Rhodia's planetary defense belt and then launched it at the planet to devastating effect. It was the same ship that had started the scuttling of the Gretian internment fleet a few months ago, the event that had signaled the rise of this insurgence on land and in space. This was their best chance at catching this ship, and he was going to stay on their tail as long as he could.

"Keep her open, Number One. If they get away, we may never see them again."

On the tactical plot, the icon for *Zephyr* had changed course, and the civilian courier was accelerating again. They were a few ten thousand kilometers off the starboard stern of *Hecate*, but they were catching up rapidly.

My kingdom for a ship with a thrust-to-weight ratio like that, Dunstan thought. The acceleration number next to *Zephyr*'s icon was once again climbing rapidly into numbers that were unobtainable for any fleet unit ever built. They blew through fifteen g, then accelerated past sixteen and seventeen.

"Tight-beam from *Zephyr*, sir," Lieutenant Robson said.

Dunstan tapped his comms screen.

"Hecate, *they're pulling away from you,"* Captain Decker sent. *"We can keep pace with them. Let us take the lead and attach ourselves to their ass. We can relay their position back to you, and you can come and collect them once they're out of fuel or they're tired of running. They won't be able to shake us. We have at least two g on them."*

"You seem to have a real obsession with volunteering your skin today, Captain," Dunstan replied.

"I can hold a mean grudge," Decker said. *"It's a character flaw. Look, we're going to stay on them anyway, and you won't be able to do a thing about it unless you're willing to launch a missile at us. So I suggest you take advantage of our obsession while the opportunity is developing in front of you."*

"I want that ship," Dunstan replied. "Whatever it is. The people who are flying it killed almost forty thousand Rhodians. If you can help me get them, I'll be happy to give you my absolution. In fact, I'll make sure you'll never have to pay docking fees at Rhodia One again."

Decker laughed.

"I'll hold you to that. You people overcharge shamelessly, you know."

"That's beyond my pay grade," Dunstan said. Decker's voice sounded like she was now squeezing out sentences in between fast, shallow breaths. He glanced at her ship's icon on the tactical screen and saw that *Zephyr* was now a fraction of a percentage from twenty-one g of acceleration.

"We will keep our connection open," he continued. "May the gods be with you, Captain."

"I don't think the gods are interested in our little disagreements. But we will both get our payback today, Commander. Zephyr *out."*

The Oceanian courier was now well past *Hecate* on her intercept course, gaining thousands of kilometers on the Rhodian warship every second. With a fast scout like this one, there was very little chance for the stealth attacker to slip back into anonymity. If they couldn't hide, they'd have to surrender or turn and fight at some point.

"That's one lucky ship today," Dunstan said to the command crew. "Let's hope their luck holds just a little while longer."

"Call me a pessimist," Lieutenant Hunter said. "But I really hope those people are just running because they're scared. And not because they're the ones playing bait right now."

Chapter 20

Solveig

"Look, I warned you ahead of time that this would be a step down from your usual lunch fare," Berg said.

Solveig looked up from the offerings at the lunch counter and realized he was taking her smile as incredulity. She laughed and shook her head.

"I told you I'd be fine with this. I was just looking at the curried sausage bowls. Gods, I haven't had one of those since my first year at university."

Berg still looked at her as if he was trying to figure out whether she was joking, so she took one of the dishes from the counter and put it on her tray to demonstrate her sincerity. Now it was his turn to laugh and shake his head.

"Curried sausage," he said. "The classic peon lunch."

She took a little tray of fried yam sticks and covered the yams with squirts from the red spice sauce dispenser, then the white cream sauce, making the traditional lattice pattern across the sticks with the lines of condiment. Then she placed the side dish next to her sausage bowl and shrugged at Berg.

"You are not joking. You *have* eaten this before."

"I told you I don't really belong on that top floor. I do my own laundry, I wash my own dishes, and I like curried sausage."

He put the same meal choices on his plate and replicated her move with the condiments, adding a little swirl of mustard sauce with a flourish at the end. The canteen was busy, with a roughly equal contingent of uniformed officers and plainclothes detectives sitting down for their lunches. Some of them shot her curious looks as she walked past with Berg, who was greeting people here and there as they went. There were some smaller tables free in the back of the room, and Berg walked over to one of them. Five steps behind them, Solveig's bodyguard Cuthbert followed, looking conspicuous and out of place in his business tunic and without a meal tray in his hands.

"There's no table service, I'm sorry to report. If you want more, you need to get back in line. And when you're done, the tray goes over there." He pointed at a rack along one of the walls.

"Just like university," Solveig said.

"Is he not going to sit down?" Berg said with a glance at Cuthbert, who was taking up position with his back to the nearby wall, far enough away to give them privacy but close enough to jump to her side if it was required.

"He's going to stand there and look stern while we're eating," Solveig said. "I told him that I probably don't have anything to worry about in the middle of the police headquarters. But he didn't want to wait outside in the nice weather."

"How long have you had bodyguards assigned to you?"

Solveig shrugged. "I can't remember a time where I didn't have one. They were kind of hands-off at university, though. I only had to let them know whenever I was leaving the campus. They kept their distance in the residences and the lecture halls."

"That must have made dating a little awkward, I imagine. Going out to eat with someone, and there's a big man with a gun and a frown sitting nearby and watching everything that happens."

"I didn't date much at university," she said. "But the ones I did go out with were usually really well behaved."

Berg laughed. "I bet they were."

Solveig tried a bite of her curried sausage. Berg watched for her reaction as she did.

"Better than the ones in the canteen at the university," she proclaimed. "But still a canteen version. Not as good as the ones from a proper sausage shop on Savory Row."

"I concur. It's just good enough that it keeps me from blowing my whole lunch break on a dash down to the Row. But sometimes one of us goes out and brings back orders for the other people in their office pod."

He glanced over at Cuthbert, who was standing with his back against the wall and his arms folded across his chest now.

"So that time I ran into you in that noodle shop, did you manage to ditch your shadow, or was he just hanging way back?"

She smiled and took a bite of the fried yams, which were as barely okay as the sausage.

"Sometimes I like to slip the leash for a little while. I've been playing cat-and-mouse games with the security detail since I was little. You wouldn't believe how much I know about network security and anonymity layers."

"You would be great for our information forensics division, then," Berg said. "They're always looking for people. Just think—you could eat like this every day." He gestured at their food trays.

Solveig laughed. "A tempting proposal. I'll consider it if the whole corporate executive track doesn't work out for me."

"You seem to be doing just fine in that field, Miss Ragnar."

She shook her head lightly.

"We're having our third meal together. We've been talking on the Mnemosyne for weeks now. I don't know where this is going to go from here. But I think that once you have more than one meal together outside of work, you must be on a first-name basis. *Solveig*," she said. "My first name is Solveig."

She was aware that he already knew her first name because he had investigated and interviewed her before in his official capacity. She knew his first name because he had left a calling card with his full name when they had first met. But going to first names was an important formal step in the hierarchy-based and class-conscious Gretian culture, especially between an upper-class corporate heir and a low-level civil servant. She hated that it was already so ingrained in them, that they were both so used to the convention that she had to make the offer because of her higher status.

"Solveig," he repeated. "I'm Stefan. And I think this is our two-and-a-halfth meal. Technically speaking. I never did get to try that beef fillet."

"Let's correct that as soon as we can," Solveig said. "You got the short end of the stick so far. At least I got some curried sausage."

At the nearby tables, some heads turned, and Solveig followed their gaze. At the beverage station by the entrance of the canteen, a female soldier was filling a drink container from one of the dispensers. She looked out of place with her dark skin and her dull green armor. As she filled her cup, she shrugged her shoulder to move the rifle she had slung over her shoulder out of the way of her elbow. Stefan turned to see what was going on.

"Pallas Brigade," he said. "I wonder what she's doing here. In full battle gear, no less. The joint patrols have been suspended for weeks."

"Maybe they are starting again," Solveig said.

"Everything is possible, I suppose." He turned around and redirected his attention to the food in front of him once more. Solveig watched the Palladian soldier as she finished drawing her beverage. She was a short, powerfully built woman. When she was finished, she glanced around the room, and Solveig briefly made eye contact with her. The Palladian's expression looked a little sad and tired. Then the woman turned and walked out of the canteen, holding her beverage mug in her armored fist.

"I have a confession to make," Stefan said.

"Isn't that usually what you make other people do?" Solveig said with a smile.

"Occasionally." He grinned. "When the day goes well. But now I'm on the other side of the table."

"So what secret are you going to spill?"

"I was just thinking about the day we met at the noodle shop in Savory Row. And I must tell you that ever since you gave me your node address that evening, I've never quite stopped thinking about you."

Solveig laughed even as she felt her face flush.

"That sounds terribly distracting, to be honest."

"It is. But it's a welcome distraction."

He leaned back in his chair a little and smiled. Then he blew one of those unruly curls of hair out of his eyes, and her heart felt like it was doing a jaunty little extra beat.

"I'm not usually that daring," she said. "But it felt like the right thing to do at the time."

Somewhere outside, there was a new sound cutting through the everyday hum of activity in the building, the powerful and insistent whine of gyrofoil engines that were increasing thrust quickly. Stefan looked up at the ceiling, and she saw irritation and a bit of puzzlement on his face.

"Someone's forgotten how to—" he began.

Above their heads, it sounded like the sky over the city was splitting apart in one cataclysmic spasm of thunder.

The building seemed to rise and buck her out of her chair. Solveig felt a sharp pain across the side of her forehead. Then she was face-down on the floor, and her ears felt like someone had shoved a rusty nail through both of her eardrums. She tried to gather her breath for a scream, but found that there was no air left in her lungs, and she rolled over to gasp for oxygen. The lights in the room had gone out, and the air smelled like smoke and burning fuel. All around her, people were shouting and screaming in the darkness.

Solveig sucked air into her lungs. It stung her throat and felt like she had just inhaled hot smoke. A strong pair of hands grabbed her by the arm. She struggled for a moment until she realized that it was Cuthbert, attempting to help her up. He got her to her feet and shouted something at her, but she couldn't quite make it out among all the noise and the ringing in her ears. He kept one arm wrapped around her and started to pull her with him. The table where she had been sitting was turned over onto its side. Stefan Berg was struggling to get to his feet next to it, using one corner of the table for leverage. She pulled away from Cuthbert and grabbed Stefan by his arm to help him.

"We need to leave, miss," Cuthbert shouted and reached for her again.

"Help me with him!" she yelled back. To her relief, he didn't try to argue. Together, they helped Stefan to his feet, and Cuthbert kicked the table aside to clear the way for them. The emergency lighting around the exit cut through the smoke and the semidarkness like a pulsating green beacon. She had Cuthbert on one side of her now and Stefan on the other as they rushed across the room toward the way out, navigating around fallen chairs and flipped tables. Something had caught fire along one of the room's walls near the door, and the flames intensified and roared up toward the ceiling, where they fanned out.

"What happened?" Solveig yelled at Stefan and Cuthbert. "What is going on?"

"Someone flew a bomb into the building," Stefan shouted back. *"In a gyrofoil."*

Out in the atrium, pieces of the ceiling were raining down onto the floor, some of them on fire and bursting apart and spreading burning chunks across the marble. Ahead of them, people were rushing toward the main exit vestibule. Solveig looked up and saw that half the building was gone, blown apart and dashed to pieces, floors open to the atrium or pancaked onto each other at steep angles. There were fires everywhere she looked. On the other side of the atrium, the security ring around the vestibule blinked red, and an alarm started to wail.

"Wait!"

Cuthbert yanked her back roughly, and she yelled. Before she could voice her protest, she saw that he had his gun out. He pushed her back into the doorway of the canteen just as gunfire sounded from the entrance, shockingly loud even among the din of the yells and the dozens of alarms. In front of them, people were scrambling to get away from the entrance now. Solveig caught a glimpse of bulky, armored figures wearing helmets and carrying large rifles, walking into the adjoining lobby and aiming and firing their guns in methodical and almost clinical fashion. Then Cuthbert and Stefan had her turned around and back inside the canteen, where the smoke was now thick enough to obscure the back of the room.

"Back door, straight ahead," Cuthbert shouted. *"Go, go, go!"*

He had a high-powered light on his pistol that sliced through the smoke and the semidarkness when he turned it on. Cuthbert aimed the bright focus of the light at the back of the room, where a set of double doors was framed between two meal tray racks that had spilled most of their contents all over the floor, carpeting the area in front of the door with shattered plates and dirty utensils. Behind them, the gunfire in the atrium continued, punctuated by screams and shouts. Stefan had drawn his service sidearm as well, and he was moving in a way that told her he was shielding her from behind.

They reached the double doors in the back. Cuthbert kicked them open and dashed through the opening, weapon at the ready. Inside, the canteen's scullery was in total disarray. Solveig followed into the room and stepped into water that was pooling all over the floor. Overhead, a water line had broken, and the spray soaked all three of them before they were halfway into the room.

"I don't know this building," Cuthbert yelled at Stefan against the blaring of the alarms. "I just saw these doors earlier. Get us to an exit."

Stefan pointed at another set of doors at the far end of the scullery. "Out through there and straight ahead. I'll lead."

Cuthbert nodded and gestured for Stefan to go ahead. When the policeman was past him, he took over the guard position behind Solveig, shielding her from the direction of the canteen. There was more shooting from the atrium, but it had a different rhythm to it now, two distinct sets of rapid-fire weapons, interspersed with the weaker report from a smaller gun firing single shots.

Stefan opened the next set of doors only slightly and scanned the space beyond with his weapon at the ready. He shouldered one of the doors aside and waved them on.

"This way. Stay behind me."

They rushed out into a long, dark corridor that was only sparsely illuminated by the strips of green emergency lighting running along the walls near the ceiling. The acrid smell of smoke was stronger back here, and the air felt hotter. Solveig had never been claustrophobic, but the idea of going deeper into a dark building that was on fire made her feel a wild, fluttering sort of panic in her chest. She looked to the left and right and saw that the rooms on either side were storage for food and kitchen supplies.

"We need to hide somewhere," she said.

"We need to get out of here before this building falls down on our heads," Cuthbert replied, urging her on from behind.

Behind them, a new and intense barrage of gunfire came from the direction of the atrium and the canteen, making Solveig jump and lending added urgency to Cuthbert's statement.

At the end of the corridor, Stefan turned left but stopped in his tracks. Solveig came to a halt behind him and saw that the path to their left was blocked by a collapsed ceiling.

"This way," he said and led them to the hallway on the right. "We have to go around this mess. Stay behind me."

"If I tell you to get down, you *drop*," Cuthbert told her. "Just like the security drills."

This is nothing like the security drills, Solveig thought wildly. She'd had her biannual refreshers with the corporate security division for as long as she had been able to walk on her own, but now she realized that she had taken them too lightly, and that she had not been prepared for the sheer terror she was feeling now. Whoever these people were, she knew they weren't here to kidnap her for ransom, that they weren't aware of her at all beyond the fact that she was a convenient target.

At the end of the hallway, Stefan led them to the right and into a small skylift lobby. The doors of the skylift capsules were closed, and red lights were blinking on their control panels. To the right of the skylift bank, there was a door, outlined in pulsating green emergency lighting. Stefan briefly touched the door, then yanked it open, and another alarm went off to join the chorus of the dozens that were already wailing in every part of the building.

"Down two floors," he said. "That's the garage for the surface pods. We can get out of the building through there."

They rushed into the stairwell and down the first flight of stairs. When they reached the landing of the floor below, one of the stairwell access doors on that level burst open, and both Stefan and Cuthbert had their guns up and aimed at it in the fraction of a heartbeat. Solveig yelled as Cuthbert pushed her down roughly with one hand, but her shout was drowned out by gunfire that was cataclysmically loud in the confines of the stairwell. The ear-splitting reports from the pistols were followed by the brief rolling thunder of an automatic burst.

When she looked up again, a body was writhing on the landing, clad in the same armor she had seen briefly on the men that had burst into the atrium. Cuthbert ran up to the prone attacker, shooting as he went. The armored man got back up to one knee and tried to renew his grip on the rifle he had almost dropped. Cuthbert kicked it out of his hand, and it slid across the landing and clattered down the nearby staircase. Then he bodychecked another man with his shoulder and sent him sprawling on his back, following him as he went down. When he was on top of the attacker, he pulled on the underside of the man's helmet where it was sealed against the soft armor covering the neck, wedged the muzzle of his pistol into the gap he had created, and fired three times. The other man convulsed once and went still.

"Go to all the hells," Cuthbert panted in the near darkness. "You and your fucking armor. Detective, go grab that rifle, see if it has a biometric safety."

Stefan went down the staircase and retrieved the weapon, then checked it.

"No bio-lock."

"Good. We'll need that if we run into more of these assholes. Fucking hardshell. I'm not getting close in with a pistol like that again."

Somewhere on the floor on the other side of the open door, a burst of gunfire rang out, and Solveig heard the muffled screaming of several people. A targeting laser flickered in the darkness, followed by another short rifle salvo and more screaming.

"They're going from room to room in there," Cuthbert said. Stefan tried to push his way past him, but Solveig's bodyguard grabbed him by the collar of his tunic and pushed him back.

"You go out there, they'll shoot you, too," he said. "There's too many, and they're wearing armor. You want to be stupid, go ahead. But leave the rifle so I can get *her* out of here."

Stefan glared at Cuthbert but made no attempt to push past him again. Somewhere in the staircase above them, they heard footsteps and scattered voices, several people making their way down the stairwell. Beyond the doorway, rifle fire cut through the noise again, short bursts followed by single shots. Cuthbert grabbed Solveig by the arm and guided her down the staircase.

"We have got to go, *now*."

He led the way with the light from his weapon, pulling her along with him as he went down the stairs. Behind them, Stefan followed, guarding their backs. Solveig couldn't even begin to estimate how much time had passed since the explosion had knocked her out of her chair in the canteen. She was running for her life in the dark with no control over what was happening to her, utterly powerless and at the mercy of others.

Above them, the footsteps and voices reached the landing they had left just moments earlier. Solveig saw Stefan tensing behind her as he took aim at the stairs to his rear. A door flew open with a loud bang, and there was a brief swell of shouting before the sound of gunfire drowned out every other noise in the staircase. Cuthbert rushed ahead to the door at the end of this landing and kicked it open. The sounds of the gunfire drifted out into the space beyond and echoed off unseen walls and corners.

Stefan rushed her through the door after Cuthbert, who was standing with his gun at the ready and scanning the room for threats. The pod garage was a cavernous space that was filled with rows of patrol and emergency pods, neatly lined up in their recharging spots along the walls and down the middle of the hall. The vehicle lock in the back of the garage was fifty meters away, bright daylight and fresh air beckoning beyond.

"Hand me the rifle," Cuthbert said and held out his free hand. Stefan looked back at Solveig and hesitated.

"Hand me the fucking rifle *now*," Cuthbert repeated over the din of the gunfire reverberating in the staircase from the landing above. "I can put that to better use than you. Get her out of here. I'll keep them bottled up."

"Cuthbert, *no*," Solveig protested. He looked back at her and shook his head.

"I'll be right behind you, Miss Ragnar. Now get her the fuck out of here," he addressed Stefan. Then he raised the rifle to his shoulder and took up position next to the door.

"Come on," Stefan said and pulled her away. "We have to go, now."

"Cuthbert," she shouted, but her bodyguard was already focused on the task he had set for himself, to kill the people who were coming for his charge. She felt ashamed for every time she had thought of him as a nuisance, merely one of Marten's snitches, an inexperienced understudy who was only by her side to keep an eye on her for Papa.

Stefan rushed her over to the nearest row of pods and crouched behind the cover they provided.

"Can you run?" he asked. She nodded, even though she wasn't sure her legs would fully obey her right now if she tried. He pointed down the row of pods and toward the vehicle lock that led outside. On her sunny running track on the estate, she could cover that distance in ten seconds.

"When I tell you to run, you run that way, and you don't stop," Stefan said. "There's an exit ramp that leads up. Once you're halfway up the ramp, you'll be out of sight and out of the line of fire. Do you understand?"

She nodded. Over by the doorway, Cuthbert squeezed off a burst of automatic fire into the darkness beyond, and she heard yells and shouted commands from the stairwell. Then there was a furious exchange of gunshots. Cuthbert moved to the side in a crouched stance, away from the doorway and the wall, firing off shots in rapid succession. Solveig watched him stumble as some of the return fire found its mark, but he gathered himself and kept up his barrage.

"Come on," Stefan yelled and pulled her to her feet again. They dashed down the row of police pods toward the vehicle lock. When they were halfway there, a loud alarm Klaxon sounded, and a security barrier descended from the top of the lock. Stefan shouted in wordless frustration and tried to pull Solveig along faster, but Solveig could see that the barrier was coming down too fast for them to make it out in

time. It settled on the ground with a dull thumping that had a sound of finality to it.

"Gods-damn it." Stefan pulled her between two of the pods and pushed her down behind cover. By the door at the front of the garage, the gunfire had increased to a wild crescendo. Then it stopped, and the sudden silence was scarier to Solveig than the sounds of the gunshots had been. She peered out from behind the cover of the pod to see Cuthbert on the ground, the rifle loosely in his grasp. Someone in armor stepped next to him and kicked the rifle away. Then he aimed his own weapon at the prone Cuthbert and fired a short burst into his chest. She opened her mouth to let out the scream of horror and disbelief that was welling up in her like an explosion, but Stefan stifled it with his hand and pulled her back down. The suppressed wail she managed to produce was still enough to draw unwelcome attention. She heard a few terse commands and then footsteps heading their way.

"Two left," Stefan said in an insistent whisper. "We can't get out, so we have to go through them. Stay down."

He peeked around his side of the pod, gun at the ready. As soon as he did, several shots rang out, and Solveig screamed as they tore into the pod and showered them with bits and pieces of broken laminate and glass. Stefan returned fire with his pistol, but his shots sounded woefully inadequate compared to the booming thunder of the rifles. There was another salvo of automatic fire. One of the rounds tore through the pod's skin, so close to Solveig's head that she could feel the hot sting of the projectile as it streaked past her cheek and smacked into the pod behind her. Stefan groaned and doubled over, then slumped on his side on the ground in front of her, dropping his weapon. The fire was relentless now, a steady rhythm of shots hammering away at their cover and tearing through the alloy hull of the police pod.

She picked up Stefan's pistol, but as soon as she had her hand wrapped around the grip, a little sensor strip above the trigger guard turned red, and the trigger retracted into the body of the weapon, denying her the use of the gun. When the next salvo rang out, she felt a blow against her back that drove the breath from her lungs. She dropped the gun and fell over Stefan, covering his upper body with hers.

I'm going to die, she thought, and a strange sense of calm came over her. *I'll never see Aden again. But he knows that I love him. And at least I won't die alone.*

She tried to sit up but found that her back muscles were no longer obeying her. Solveig steadied her breath and concentrated on the feeling of Stefan's body underneath hers, the smell of his hair, the memory of the way his cheeks had flushed a little when he had told her that he hadn't stopped thinking about her since their first meal together.

The attackers were shouting now, but she couldn't make out what they were yelling through the gunfire, and she didn't want their words to be the last thing she heard, so she let the noise pass through her. Another fusillade of gunfire thundered in the confines of the garage, short bursts of rapid fire that had a different cadence. Then the gunfire stopped. For a moment, everything was quiet, and only the echo of the gunshots was ringing in her ears. She did not dare to look up, didn't want to see the muzzle of the gun that would put an end to her existence, everything she was and would ever be, erased by someone who neither knew her nor cared about the thread he was pulling from the fabric of the universe forever.

"We've got wounded over here," someone yelled right next to her.

The voice was that of a woman. Solveig jerked her head up and looked toward its source. A Gretian police officer was crouching at the end of the pod they had used for cover. She had a pistol in her hand, and a trickle of blood was running down her cheek and dripping onto the braid of silver hair that was hanging over her right shoulder. Behind her, Solveig saw soldiers in Alliance armor spreading out in the garage, weapons at the ready. Nearby, one of their attackers was sprawled out on the concrete floor of the garage a few dozen steps away, ragged holes in his armor that were still smoking from the impact of whatever had pierced the plating.

"Are you all right? Can you get up?"

Solveig shook her head and coughed, and the taste of blood filled her mouth. It felt like her lungs were no longer able to hold any air. She heard an alarm Klaxon, and when she looked at the source of the sound, she saw daylight pouring into the garage as the vehicle lock's security barrier raised itself again, but it all sounded distant and muffled.

"You will be all right. The rescue crews are on the way. *I need some extra hands over here,*" the woman shouted over her shoulder at someone else.

Solveig looked at Stefan, who had his eyes closed. In the light that was coming in from the outside now, he looked very pale. She put her hand on his chest to see if he was still breathing, but her fingertips felt numb, and she couldn't sense any movement from him. She coughed again, and when she managed to force some air into her lungs again, she saw that her cough had sprayed blood all over the chest of Stefan's tunic.

Several sets of strong arms grabbed her and carefully pulled her off Stefan. She tried to struggle, to remain with him, but there was no strength left in her body. Someone placed her on the ground and rolled her on her side. The wound in her back hadn't hurt at first, but now it felt like someone was prodding her back with a red-hot steak knife. Then someone placed something cold and sticky on the spot where the pain was centered, and the agony subsided to tolerable levels of pain within moments. But whatever they had put on her back had no improving effect on her lungs, which still felt like she had to will the air into them with every breath. All around her, people were talking now, but she couldn't make sense of anything they were saying, and their voices sounded thin and distorted.

If I close my eyes now, I'll never open them again, she thought, but she found that the thought didn't scare her anymore. Stefan was lying on his back just a few meters in front of her, his eyes closed, looking like he was merely peacefully asleep.

I'm sorry, she thought as she drifted into unconsciousness. *I am so sorry.*

Chapter 21

Aden

"This is definitely a nosebleed ride," Maya said from the flight station.

Aden could only muster a grunt in agreement. As far as he could see, none of them actually *had* nosebleeds yet, but the ship was running at over twenty g of acceleration, and the gravmag generator was hitting the limits of its compensating abilities. He didn't know how many g they were feeling in their gravity couches by now, but he knew the number was a fair bit above one g because he could barely lift his head away from the headrest, and his chest felt like someone was pushing on it with both hands.

The ship they were pursuing was still well ahead of them, but *Zephyr* had a speed advantage, and the distance had shrunk to a mere one thousand kilometers since Maya had opened up the throttle all the way and set a pursuit course.

"A stern chase is a long chase," Decker said. "I really hope our invisible friends are able to keep up, or we're going to have our asses hanging out in the breeze when we get to wherever these people are going."

"I can't see shit through our drive plume," Tess replied. "But we still have a data link going. From the ping, they're about ninety thousand kilometers behind now."

"This may not be the smartest thing we've ever done," Maya said.

"We left 'smart' well behind the moment I sent the Rhodians our message," Decker said. "Now we have to see this through."

On the navigation plot screen, the icon for the unknown ship forged ahead, still at seventeen g, its drive plume a bright signal flare that was pouring out infrared and electromagnetic radiation like a high-powered transmitter. The other ship had counted on its speed to increase its distance from the Rhodians quickly, then return to ballistic flight and become invisible again once they had opened the gap sufficiently. But with *Zephyr* giving chase and more than matching their speed, they would have to keep running until one of them ran out of reactor fuel. In the meantime, *Zephyr* was gaining on them every second, broadcasting their position back to the Rhodian warship and anyone else who was in the sector.

"I don't want to get too close," Decker said. "I want some reaction time. Just in case they have more missiles and decide to fire one down their wake at us."

"We'll overtake them in four and a half minutes if we keep burning the way we're going."

"Back us off to match their acceleration, keep the gap constant for now. Aden, if we still have that comms link, ask our Rhody friends what they know about the weaponry on that bird."

Aden checked the link and sent a connect request, which was accepted promptly.

"*Hecate*, we are backing off the burn a bit so we won't overshoot them. Do you have any intel at all on the armament that bandit is carrying?"

"If that's the same one we've run into three times now, they've launched two missiles every time and then run away," the reply came from the Rhodian commander. *"If I had to bet, I'd say someone fitted that ship with two missile tubes and no easy reloads. But there's no way to know if they don't have a gun mount tucked away somewhere."*

"I doubt it," Decker commented. "Slugs are cheap. If they had a cannon, they would have sent some rounds our way already, just to make us dodge."

"We will keep our distance, *Hecate*. They're not going to disappear again."

"You are doing just fine. Keep relaying your telemetry and your sensor data. We are going to keep up as best as we can."

"Copy that, *Hecate*. We'll keep the link active." Aden ended the connection.

"Burning at seventeen g." Maya's voice didn't sound strained in the least. The weight on Aden's chest seemed to lift just a little bit. *Tristan would have hated this. He didn't care for high-g runs,* he remembered.

"We got some reactor juice to spare now," Tess said. "We could make ourselves even more of a nuisance and turn on all the active gear. Maybe we can get a preview of where they are heading."

"Wherever that is, it'll be out in the middle of nowhere," Maya said from above. "We are a long way from anything. The closest transfer lane is over a million klicks off."

"Do it," Decker told Tess. "Go active on the bow sensors. Make their threat detectors go off. Maybe they'll do something stupid. They don't know for sure we're not armed."

"I wonder if they know we have company trailing behind us," Aden said.

"Not likely. We can't see them through our own drive plume. In fact, I doubt we could detect them even if we weren't throwing out that heat flare. That is one stealthy ship," Tess replied.

Aden watched her as she brought up another screen and activated the bow array with a quick and practiced series of taps on the input fields.

"Bow sensors are hot. Commencing active sweep. Distance to bandit is nine hundred fifty-one kilometers, decreasing at fifty meters per second."

"We have the drive blowing at seventeen g and the sensors transmitting at full power," Decker said. "Any hobbyist with store-bought astronomy gear can probably pick us up all the way from Hades right now."

Tess chuckled.

"I can pipe in some Acheroni dance tunes from the Mnemosyne over shortwave comms if you want. Maybe go all in and turn our docking lights on, too. Make it a party."

"Henry's going to be angry when he finds out what he missed," Decker replied.

I was wrong, Aden thought. *Tristan would have loved this reckless rogue business, high-g or not.* The idea brought a smile to his face.

On the navigation plot, the icon representing the fleeing ship seemed to hang in space nine hundred kilometers in front of them, their speeds matched to tens of meters per second. It seemed pointless to Aden for the other ship to be burning its fuel like this, knowing that their pursuers could match them gravity for gravity, but people did irrational things when they knew they were being chased.

They were another half hour into the chase when Tess muttered a curse from her gravity couch, where she was looking at data on multiple screens.

"What's on your mind, Tess?" Decker asked.

"I took the time to do some millimeter-wave and laser mapping," Tess replied. "It's kind of tricky through the noise from their exhaust plume, but our aspect angle has been stable for a while now. Look at the radar mapping of our bandit's hull," Tess replied. "And then check out their drive signature."

She flicked copies of her screens to the central navigation screen, where they arranged themselves around the main display.

"Does that look familiar to you?"

Decker looked at the images silently for a few moments and let out a low whistle.

"I'll be gods-damned."

"What is it?" Aden asked. "What are we looking at here?"

"That," Tess said, "is what *we* look like when you map our hull with radar and a laser. And that's more or less what *our* drive signature looks like. That thing is a Tanaka model two thirty-nine."

"One of the other few two thirty-nines they made," Decker said. "I've never seen one of them out and about on the trade routes. I've always wondered who ended up buying those."

"Why aren't they as fast as we are?" Aden asked.

"When the consortium—when Tristan had this ship fitted, he went for low mass. The only thing we have that adds extra weight is the PDS. But that only added a few hundred kilos," Tess explained. "Everything else is as light as possible. Right down to the furniture in the galley. If they are doing three g less at full burn, they added a bunch of hardware to their stock configuration."

"Two missile tubes, for example," Maya contributed. "That shit is heavy. And whatever stealth layers they added to the hull. They probably have two hundred tons on us at least. Unless they're holding back."

Decker shook her head. "I don't think they are. I think that if they had the speed, they'd use it right now."

She looked over at Tess.

"The Rhodies are going to be interested in that data. They've been looking for this thing for months."

"I'll send it to them," Tess said.

On the navigational display, an alarm chirped. On the outer edge of the sensor cone, a new icon appeared on the screen, then three more in quick succession.

"Now it gets interesting." Tess checked her screens. "We got some hard returns here. Four confirmed contacts, distance ninety-eight thousand and dropping at a hundred klicks per second."

"Shit. Now we know where they were running, I guess. Let the Rhodies know we are heading for company. We're making a huge blind spot for them with that drive plume," Decker said.

"*Hecate*, we are relaying sensor data," Aden sent. "We have four contacts at ninety-eight thousand, dead ahead."

"Zephyr, acknowledged," the response came. *"You may want to tweak your trajectory soon."*

"Turn us around, Maya," Decker ordered. "Full counterburn. Open her up as wide as she'll go. Slow us down."

"We won't be able to stop in time," Maya said even as she wrapped her hands around the control sticks to follow the command. "We're going way too fast. If they have guns or missiles, we'll end up in someone's firing arc no matter which way we burn right now."

"Just do it," Decker said. "Aden, open the comms link to *Hecate*."

"It's open," Aden replied. "Go ahead on voice."

"*Hecate*, we are doing a full counterburn. I suggest you do the same while we give you a nice big thermal bloom to hide behind."

"You know you won't get out of range even at full burn," *Hecate*'s commander said.

"No," Decker said. "But neither will they. You should be able to get into range before they even realize you're coming in behind us."

There was a moment of silence in the link.

"You're aware that trap may close on you, too, Captain."

"Yes, I'm aware," Decker replied. "If they swallow the bait, just make sure they end up squirming on the hook. We'll try to stay out of the way and put our point defense to work. Now I suggest you turn and burn, Commander. Time's running short."

"Affirmative."

On *Zephyr*'s navigation screen, *Hecate* duplicated their maneuver a few ten thousand kilometers away until both ships had reversed their acceleration vectors. With the sensors now pointed away from the ships they had detected, *Zephyr*'s AI updated the plot by placing small spheres of uncertainty around the icons, representing the area of their possible presence based on the data from last time they had been actively spotted. Aden watched as the spheres around the icons expanded slowly with every passing minute.

"When we are five thousand klicks out, you turn the ship around," Decker told Maya. "We'll go right through them and hope they hit each other if they start shooting. Tess, you turn on the PDS and the active sensors that very second."

"You got it," Tess said. "Let's hope it's just a quartet of shit boxes like that *Iron Pig*."

"So do I." Decker checked the tightness of her harness straps. "Either way, I hope that Rhody ship is as good as they seem to think it is."

"We will find out soon," Maya said. "Nine minutes until we cross inside of five thousand K."

The feeling of weight was back on Aden's chest now, and he grasped the ends of his gravity chair's armrests and closed his eyes. It was a reckless thing for them to do, hurtling themselves into the midst of a group of unknown ships just to help the Rhodians, but it felt good and right to be acting instead of reacting, to claim the initiative even if it seemed rash. Whatever happened next, they would have the other side on the defensive for the first time, even if only for a few minutes.

"We are really burning through reactor pellets," Tess said. "Fuel is down to forty-five percent. I've never seen the gauge drop that quickly. The way we're flogging her, we're going to need to put in for another overhaul when we're done with this business."

"We can buy more fuel," Decker replied. "If we come out of this with an overhaul as our biggest worry, I'm going to mark it as good fortune and pay the tab gladly."

To Aden, the next few minutes ticked by much too slowly and way too quickly at the same time somehow. It felt like an exquisite form of torture to have time to reflect on the danger they were hurtling toward without a way to avoid it. But every minute that passed before they reached the danger zone was one where he was still alive, still drawing breath. It was something that he had stopped taking for granted after the events of the last few months, where he'd had more close scrapes than in his seventeen years of military service.

He looked over at Tess, who glanced in his direction and flashed a smile before returning her attention to her screens.

If we don't come out of this, there are worse ways to die, he thought.

—

"Thirty seconds," Maya announced, her voice slightly vibrating from the resonance of the fusion rocket blasting at maximum power.

"Active sensors and PDS are on standby," Tess said. "Ready to reroute the power output."

"We will be on our own for a little while before the Rhodies get here. Let's try to still be around when they do," Decker said. "Maya, Tess, it's all on you now. Dodge what you can and blast what we can't."

Aden looked at the navigation screen that was floating between them in the center of the maneuvering deck, expanded to fill the available space. The little *Zephyr*-shaped symbol in the center of the plot was almost touching the outer bubble of the computer's probability zone for the new contacts. There was another bubble that represented the possible locations of the ship they had been chasing, but with no contact updates from the active sensors in ten minutes, the prediction zone was so large as to be useless from a tactical standpoint. If they had resumed their burn, they would now be well out of range for active detection.

"Ten seconds," Maya counted down. "Stand by on PDS for turn on my mark. Three . . . two . . . one. Mark."

The center display rotated through a full 180-degree arc in just a second or two as Maya brought the nose of *Zephyr* around to point at the threat. At the same time, she cut the main drive, and the acceleration numbers next to *Zephyr*'s icon plummeted.

"Bow sensors are online. Active sweep commencing," Tess called out.

In front of *Zephyr*, the uncertainty bubbles around the unknown ship icons disappeared as the bow sensors lashed the space ahead with active radiation. The four icons blinked and shifted position into a diamond-shaped formation, just a few thousand kilometers in front and slightly below *Zephyr*'s trajectory.

"Keep the active sweep up. I want to clutter their sensors as long as we can so they won't see what's behind us," Decker ordered.

"Well, hello there," Tess said to the screen, where one of the icons now had a familiar name popping up next to it. "If it isn't our old friend, the *Iron Pig*."

"What the fuck is that thing," Decker said. Aden didn't have to guess what she meant. Next to *Iron Pig*, a much larger contact was at the tip of the formation, at least three times the mass and length of the cobbled-together smuggling freighter they had encountered weeks earlier. On Tess's consoles, several warning sounds went off.

"Whatever it is, it's sweeping us on active," she said.

"Bend our trajectory as far away from that as you can, Maya," Decker said. "I don't have a good feeling about that ship."

"I got visual. Putting it on the main display." Tess flicked a screen over to the navigational plot, where it expanded and arranged itself on the periphery of the screen. It showed a chisel-shaped prow aimed at them, and a long and lethal-looking hull behind that very clearly belonged to a capital warship.

"Rail-gun mounts," Tess said. "Fuck."

"A lot of rail-gun mounts," Decker confirmed. Aden's stomach did a little lurch at the sight of the batteries on the unknown ship's hull.

"Database says it's a fucking *Gretian*. GNS *Sleipnir*. Seventeen-thousand-ton heavy gun cruiser. How the hells can that be? Their navy's gone. Captured or destroyed."

"Someone managed to tuck that one away for a rainy day, I guess," Decker replied. "Keep us out of the firing arcs of those things, Maya."

"Three thousand klicks and closing. We're going to cross their engagement zone no matter what," Maya said. She sounded tense, an emotional note Aden wasn't used to hearing in her voice.

The other two icons on the plot now had ID tags next to them, but with the presence of the huge gun cruiser in the picture, the information was almost irrelevant to Aden. They were both smaller commercial designs, a freighter and a fuel hauler, and even if the pirates had refitted them with weapons, they didn't represent a tenth the threat of the Gretian ship, purpose-built to engage and destroy other vessels.

"You want me to burn or what?" Maya asked.

Decker shook her head without taking her eyes off the plot. "It's not going to make a difference. Better to keep them lit up on active. Let the sensors see what's coming."

They hurtled along their trajectory, closing the distance with every passing moment. Aden saw that their course would take them just fifty kilometers past the gun cruiser. He wasn't trained in space warfare, but one thing he had learned was that fifty klicks on the ground went a much longer way than the same distance in space, where missiles and rail-gun slugs could bridge that range in just a few seconds.

"They're accelerating and spreading out their formation," Maya said. "Maybe they think we're about to nuke them."

"They're clearing the fields of fire for that cruiser," Decker replied.

"Shit," Maya muttered.

Over by Tess's position, another warning signal beeped on one of her screens.

"They've locked onto us with their fire-control sensors," Tess said. "If you have any tricks up your sleeve, use them now, people. Shit is about to fly our way."

Aden turned on the comms transmitter and selected the universal emergency frequency, then turned the transmitting power to maximum.

"Hold your fire, you fucking idiots," he said in Gretian. *"You're locking up a friendly."*

Tess and Decker looked at him in surprise, and he shrugged in response.

"What did you tell them?" Tess wanted to know.

"That we're one of theirs," Aden said. "Couldn't think of anything else."

There was no reply on the emergency channel, and the alarm for the target lock kept chirping on the screen in front of Tess. A second, much louder alert sounded over by the main screen, where several small objects launched from the cruiser and rushed to intercept them on their trajectory.

"Incoming fire," Maya shouted. "Rail-gun slugs. Sixteen seconds to impact. Going evasive."

"Guess they didn't buy it," Tess said. "Setting PDS to automatic mode."

Maya took the ship through a series of rotations and hard burns to alter their trajectory. The rail-gun projectiles streaked ahead to the point in space where they would have been without the corrective burns. Aden let out a breath when the salvo passed a few kilometers in front of them.

"Don't start celebrating," Maya said. "Those are just ranging shots. The next round will be a bit harder to dodge."

True to Maya's prediction, another round of slugs left the cruiser, rippling out from the ship's icon one by one in short intervals. She turned the ship again, counterburned, then flipped the bow into a different direction and burned the main drive.

"Staggered ranging shots now," she commented in a matter-of-fact voice. "Their targeting AI is trying to get dialed in."

The center display spun madly as Maya continued her series of random turns and burns. When the salvo passed, it was still a clear miss, but Aden saw that some of the slugs from this group had come much closer to *Zephyr* than the previous one.

"We're inside of a thousand kilometers. This is going to get bumpy, I'm afraid," Maya said.

"I can't believe they're wasting that much energy on us," Aden said. "We must have pissed them off somehow."

"We're broadcasting their position and ours to anyone within a million klicks," Tess replied. "They want to shut us up as quickly as they can. Where are those fucking Rhodians?"

Decker checked the main display. "No telling. We lost them when we came out of the burn and turned around. They can see what's going on unless they've gone blind and deaf. We're not exactly subtle out here. And neither is that Gretian."

"I don't think he cares much about subtle right now," Aden said as he watched another staggered swarm of rail-gun slugs separating from the warship and heading their way at tens of kilometers per second. Just a moment later, another salvo followed, then another.

"Three broadsides coming in," Tess yelled up at Maya.

"I see them," the reply came.

Aden grabbed his armrests again as Maya spun the ship through another round of evasive maneuvers. She was working with her whole body now, both hands on their respective control sticks, feet on the pedals for the cold thruster controls. She weaved *Zephyr* through the barrage like a dancer sidestepping punches from a boxer. This time, Aden heard the high-energy discharge from the Point Defense System reverberating through the hull. One of the rail-gun slugs had crossed into *Zephyr*'s inner defensive zone despite Maya's maneuvering ballet, and the closest PDS emitter fired a megawatt of tightly focused energy at it and blasted it into tiny fragments.

"Hard kill on one," Tess said. "Keep doing what you're doing. Everything's still in the green."

Another salvo headed their way from the Gretian cruiser. Decker groaned at the sight of the staggered phalanx of sensor returns on the main screen.

"They've thrown fifty or sixty slugs at us already. They really want to see us dead."

"No missiles yet," Aden said.

"They won't waste one, now that they know we have a PDS," Tess replied. "Too easy to shoot down outside of a hundred klicks. But you can bet your ass they'll keep those tungsten slugs coming."

"This one's going to be close," Maya warned from her station above.

The grid on the navigation screen spun around again, first one way and then another, until Aden had thoroughly lost his reference points. *Zephyr* twisted and squirmed her way through the oncoming storm of projectiles once more. The PDS emitter fired again, then a second time. There was a sharp, ugly noise from belowdecks that sounded like a hammer coming down on a tablet full of silverware. All the lights on the maneuvering deck went out for a heartbeat, then returned. The navigation screen flickered and disappeared. At the same time, Aden felt the strangest and most unpleasant sensation, like his body was being pulled into two different directions by a pair of giant hands. He felt a brief and intense wave of nausea that made him retch. Then the feeling dissipated, and he looked around, dazed.

"What was that?"

"Reactor just went out," Tess said. She let out a wordless shout of frustration. "So did the drive."

The navigation screen projection returned, showing a grid that was slowly spinning around them. All the ship icons on the plot had little uncertainty bubbles around them again, signifying they were out of date and getting more so with every passing second.

"Sensors are down. PDS is down. Main drive is down. We're running on the backup power bank," Tess said. Her control screen had returned, and she used it to check the status of the stricken ship.

"The reactor is out," she said. "Integrity breach, magnetic confinement shutdown. We got nicked by a slug, or maybe some shrapnel from the PDS intercept."

"Can you bring us back online?" Decker asked.

Tess shook her head even as she unbuckled her harness to get out of her gravity couch.

"I'll go below and see. But if the confinement field collapsed, there's a hull breach and a hole in the torus jacket. That's nothing we'll be able to fix outside of a good repair yard."

"Give me something up here," Maya said. "We're coasting ballistic right now."

"You only have the cold-gas thrusters and whatever runs off the power cells," Tess replied. "Sorry."

Tess floated out of her couch and pushed off toward the ladderwell at the back of the maneuvering deck. She grabbed one of the ladder rungs and pulled herself against the ladder.

"If anyone wants to take to the rescue pod, I won't think less of you," Decker said. "Any of you. We're done for the day, I think."

"Not in this lifetime," Tess replied with conviction. "I'm fixing this ship or I am going to turn to stardust with her."

She looked at Aden, and he shook his head.

"Not going to claim I'm not scared shitless," he said. "But I don't want to be the only one in that pod."

Maya let out a long breath up on her piloting platform. "I didn't just inherit one-fifth of this ship to let these people have her."

"So stop talking nonsense, boss," Tess said in a gentle tone. "I'm going to go do my job now. If we get blown up before I come back up, it was the best fucking time of my life to fly with you all."

She pushed off her ladder rung and disappeared belowdecks before anyone could reply.

"Well," Decker said. "That settles that, I suppose. We're all a bunch of idiots."

"We already had that settled before the shooting started," Maya replied. "Can I get the passive array up, please? Not that I can dodge a lot with the thrusters. But if there's something coming I could be avoiding, I'd like to be able to see it."

Decker turned on her control screen and started tapping input fields. A few moments later, the navigation screen updated with a blink and shrunk the bubbles around the other ship icons to half their size. Aden realized that without the active array, there was no way to tell if the cruiser was launching another salvo at them. *Zephyr* was coasting ballistic now, an easy target for even the most rudimentary gunnery AI, defenseless without her PDS emitters.

"Attention, all ships," a voice sounded over the emergency channel. It was that of a woman, and despite the telltale echo of a multilingual translation, Aden could tell that her original voice was Rhodian with a Gretian accent.

"This is the Alliance warship Hecate. *Cease all active sensor and weapon use immediately, or you will be disabled or destroyed at our discretion. You have twenty seconds to comply. There will be no further warnings."*

Above their heads, Maya let out a celebratory little whoop sound, a sentiment that Aden found he shared wholeheartedly right now.

On the main navigation screen, the bubble around *Sleipnir* disappeared as the Gretian warship started an active sensor search of the area. One by one, the other pirate ships came out of their uncertainty bubbles as they lit their drives to maneuver, until the screen showed all four ships without any margin of doubt as far as the passive sensors could tell. Despite her active broadcast, there was no sign of *Hecate* on the plot, no indication that *Zephyr*'s sensor AI had picked up the faintest trace of the Rhodian ship's presence.

"We're not dead yet," Decker said. "That's a plus."

"About fucking time they got here," Maya said. "Took them long enough."

Sleipnir was burning her drive at one g now, accelerating away from her companions, her active sensors flooding the space in front of her with megawatts of radiation in search of a target for her rail guns and missiles. Aden watched the cruiser's progress on the plot, profoundly glad they were moving away from *Zephyr* and focusing their attention somewhere else.

"They think the Rhodies are bluffing," Aden said.

"Wouldn't you?" Decker asked.

"I would," Maya said. "You don't turn off your guns just because someone says so. Not until you know they can kick your ass in a fight."

"That Rhody commander is either the gods-damned system champion at bluffing, or his ship really is that good," Decker said. She was trying to sound nonchalant, but Aden could hear the relief in her voice, and he realized that all of them had mentally prepared themselves for their imminent deaths just a few minutes ago.

The acceleration number next to the Gretian cruiser rapidly decreased, then showed a zero with a question mark next to it, and the AI uncertainty bubble started to expand around the icon again immediately.

"They killed their drive," Decker said. She switched control screens and scrolled through a few panels, then flicked another screen over to the main display. It showed a visual of the Gretian cruiser. *Zephyr* was just a few thousand kilometers away right now, looking at the Gretian warship from a stern angle, and the screen came on just in time to show the fusion drive plume at the stern of *Sleipnir* extinguish. Then the rail-gun mounts on the hull swiveled around slowly until they faced roughly astern. Aden felt a brief swell of panic until he realized they weren't aiming at *Zephyr*, but at some point well behind and below them.

"What the hells is he doing?" Maya asked.

They watched as one of the mounts fired a single round. A moment later, one of the rail-gun turrets on the other side of the ship fired a round as well, then another. Decker took control of the optical sensor array and swiveled the viewpoint to track the direction of the slugs the Gretian cruiser had just launched.

"They're fucking shooting at their own ships," Decker said.

In the center of the sensor screen, the patchwork freighter they knew as *Iron Pig* was floating seemingly motionless in space. As they watched, the rail-gun slug from *Sleipnir* streaked into the picture and blew into the stern section of *Iron Pig*, tearing through the hull plating and blowing off huge chunks of alloy and laminate. Almost instantly, *Iron Pig* began trailing frozen gas and debris from its stern. Decker switched the array's focus to the unknown fuel hauler that was the target of *Sleipnir*'s second shot, only to see an expanding ball of fire and debris where the ship had been floating in space just a few moments ago. If the gunner in control of *Sleipnir*'s rail battery had meant to disable the propulsion section just like they had on *Iron Pig*, it looked like their aim had been off just enough to hit one of the fuel storage segments of the hull instead. The passive array flipped to the location of the fourth ship, the freighter of unknown make or name. In this instance, the aim had been true if the shot was intended for the propulsion unit. The stern of the freighter was in tatters, its drive cone messily amputated by the impact of the tungsten slug.

One by one, three automated emergency beacons popped up on *Zephyr*'s navigation screen.

Maya barked a laugh.

"Did that just happen?"

"They just blew up one of their own fleet and crippled two more," Decker said after a moment. "If that's what you mean."

"Just like that."

"I don't think it was just like that," Aden said.

The emergency channel came to life again with the same Gretian-accented voice.

"Belligerent ship Sleipnir, *or* Valravn, *or whatever the hells your name is these days. You are probably aware by now that we are in full control of your ship's systems. Your life support will go offline in three minutes. We will vent all your available oxygen into space. You are advised to order your crew to the rescue pods and abandon ship. Ignore this warning at your peril. We*

will be more than happy to take inventory of your corpses if you do. Odin's Ravens end today. Remember Norfolk-9."

When the transmission ended, there were a few heartbeats of silence on the maneuvering deck. Then Maya let out a throaty chuckle.

"Gods-*damn*. That was cold. Remind me to never cross those Rhody bastards."

For the next minute and a half, nothing happened. Then an automated emergency beacon popped up next to *Sleipnir*'s icon on the plot. Another followed, then a third and a fourth. A few minutes later, several dozen beacons were blaring their distress calls in the space around the Gretian heavy gun cruiser. Aden felt a laugh coming on, and even though it didn't feel proper and appropriate in these circumstances, he let it out. Maya joined in from above, with a merry and bright laugh he had never heard out of her before. Decker merely shook her head with a grin.

"The luck of drunks and fools," she said.

In the rear of the maneuvering deck, Tess's head popped up above the rim of the ladderway hatch.

"You're fucking *laughing*. Will someone tell me what the hells just happened?"

"Don't ask how, but we won," Decker replied. "That is, the Rhodies won. Without firing a single gods-damned shot of their own."

CHAPTER 22

IDINA

The garage smelled like the inside of a busy shooting range. Idina lowered her rifle and looked around, but there was no more movement except for that of her own troopers, clearly marked in blue outlines on her helmet's display. She walked over to the assailant she had just dropped with a three-round burst to the back from twenty meters away. He had fallen to the ground and rolled over faceup, and now was lying motionless next to his rifle. As she stepped close, Idina raised her weapon again and fired another burst into the middle of his chest, just for insurance. Then she kicked the rifle out of his reach.

"Clear," Corporal Shakya said on the section comms. "Two down over here. Two more bodies by the door."

"Secure that doorway," Idina said.

"Yes, ma'am."

"We have some wounded over here," she heard Dahl yelling. Idina looked over to the Gretian woman and saw that she was kneeling behind one of the shot-up patrol pods. She walked over to the pod. Dahl was bent over a young woman in civilian clothes who looked like she was in rough shape. They were exchanging words, and when the young woman tried to answer Dahl, she coughed up blood. Next to her, another civilian was faceup on the ground, motionless.

Over by the exit, an alarm Klaxon blared, and the security gate started to open.

"Cover that exit," she ordered. Two of her Red Section troopers took up cover behind patrol pods and aimed their weapons at the expanding crack of daylight underneath the opening gate.

"The QRF bird is overhead," Corporal Shakya said. "They're putting a whole platoon on the ground right now."

"QRF Leader, this is Colors Chaudhary," Idina sent on the tactical network. "Do you read?"

"We got you on tactical, Colors. Go ahead," the QRF commander responded tersely.

"I'm in the pod garage on the sublevel with what's left of my JSP section. We have engaged and neutralized multiple hostiles, but there may be more in the building. Be advised they're wearing battle armor and carrying infantry weapons."

"I need some extra hands over here," Dahl shouted over her shoulder in front of Idina. She moved next to her partner and saw that she was trying to pull the wounded female civilian away from the motionless man. Together, they picked her up and moved her out from between the pods. Dahl gently rolled the woman onto her side to evaluate the extent of her injuries. There was a bullet hole in her back, a hand's breadth underneath the right shoulder blade. It was oozing bright-red blood.

"Pulmonary hemorrhage," Dahl said. She pulled a medpack from her belt and flipped the pouch open with a quick and practiced motion. Then she placed the gel sealant over the wound and spread it out to seal it.

"I need more," Dahl said. "For this one and him over there."

Idina took her own medpack out and handed it to Dahl.

"Shakya, come here and give me your medpack," she ordered. The corporal rushed over and complied, and she passed his pack on to Dahl as well.

"These people need to get to a medical center—and fast," Dahl said.

"QRF Lead, we have a lot of civilian casualties down here," Idina sent on the tactical channel. "We need medical personnel and evac units right now."

"They're sending everything they have," the QRF commander replied. "But we have to clear the building first before we let them run in there. Sit tight and wait until we get to you. QRF out."

"Fuck all the gods," Idina said.

"I can't hear any more shooting upstairs," Shakya said from his nearby covering position. "Maybe we got them all."

She did the math in her head.

"They had a four-man team upstairs in the atrium. How many do we have down here?"

"These two we just drilled. One more inside the door. That's three."

"Makes seven. Maybe one got killed by one of the Gretians upstairs. Two fire teams, two entrances?"

"If there's a third team, they're laying low. But that wouldn't make sense. They were going to sweep through. Kill everyone left standing. Get the hells out before backup arrives."

She walked over to one of the dead attackers and prodded him with her boot. The armor he was wearing looked vaguely familiar. It was clearly Gretian, but she had never seen this specific pattern before, flat black, with an octagonal pattern laser-etched on the plating. It looked like it was somewhere between scout and light-assault armor in thickness and weight. Everything about it shouted "commando gear" to Idina.

Over by the door to the stairwell, another civilian lay dead. This one was a fit-looking man in a business outfit. There was a holster on his belt with a sidearm in it. One of the attackers' rifles was on the ground near the dead man's body. Inside the stairwell door, a body in commando armor blocked most of the staircase. Idina picked up the rifle and checked it to see that the ammunition feed was empty.

"Looks like he got one before they got him," Shakya said next to her.

"That wasn't really a fight he could win. They had armor and he didn't. And they outnumbered him. But he sold himself well."

"Went out like a soldier," Shakya agreed.

She went back to Dahl, who had finished applying the medical packs to the two injured civilians. The woman was unconscious now, and Dahl had placed her on her side in the textbook first aid position to keep her from aspirating her own blood. Dahl looked up at Idina.

"If she does not get to a trauma pod in the next few minutes, she will die. There is only so much I can do with these medpacks."

"They won't send in medical teams until the building is safe," Idina said.

"Then we have to get her out." Dahl pointed at one of the patrol pods nearby. "Those extended units have collapsible stretchers in the back with the emergency equipment."

"Pop one of those things open and get us a stretcher," Idina ordered the nearest trooper. He dashed over to the row of pods Dahl had indicated and opened the back hatch. A few moments later, he returned with a long bundle wrapped in orange fabric. He handed it to Dahl, who opened it and extended the stretcher with swift and sure movements. Together, they carefully lifted the unconscious woman onto the stretcher, and Dahl inflated the restraints that would keep her on her side and breathing properly.

"Out that way," Dahl said and nodded at the garage exit. "I will take the front. You take the back."

"Let me go in the lead," Idina said. "If there are QRF guns aimed at that gate, I want them to see JSP armor first."

Dahl nodded and swapped places with her.

"Shakya, watch our backs and bring up the rear," Idina ordered. "And keep an eye on that doorway back there."

She switched to the guard comms and slung her rifle across her back.

"QRF units, we are coming out of the garage gate on the lower level with a medical emergency. Five troopers, one Gretian JSP officer. If there's a trauma pod on scene already, have them meet us outside."

She grabbed the handles on her end of the stretcher and looked back at Dahl.

"Ready? On three. One—two—three."

They lifted the stretcher in one smooth movement. With the adrenaline that was coursing through Idina's veins and her Palladian physique, the woman they were picking up seemed to weigh next to nothing. When they started toward the gate, Idina's troopers formed up beside and behind them in a protective phalanx. They covered the fifty meters to the exit ramp in a quick trot that was as fast as Idina dared to go with the stretcher between her and Dahl.

Outside, the sky was swarming with gyrofoils and drones. At the top of the vehicle ramp beyond the exit, an entire section of QRF troopers had taken up covering positions, and Idina's stomach clenched momentarily when she saw eight rifle muzzles aiming in her general direction. An Alliance combat gyrofoil was hovering nearby, its gun pods fixed on the garage exit. If someone decided that her section's appearance was a ruse, her team and Dahl would die a quick and violent death.

"Don't anybody aim at anything," she told her team over the section comms.

One of the QRF troopers at the top of the ramp lowered his rifle and waved them on.

"Keep going," he shouted. *"Clear the ramp."*

They made their way up the ramp, careful to keep the stretcher level. The QRF section moved to let them pass through their firing line. Idina recognized the section leader, a sergeant from the JSP's Rhodian company.

"There's a trauma pod around that corner, twenty meters from the intersection," he said and indicated the direction. "Any of yours left inside?"

Idina shook her head. "Three of mine are dead. The DHC and his security team are gone, too. They were on the top floor. We were the only Alliance in there when it went up."

"Go," the Rhodian sergeant said. "Pod's waiting. We're going in to mop up."

Idina nodded. "Watch yourself. No telling how many civvies are left in there. This is all a big fucking mess."

"Isn't it always."

They rushed on with the stretcher. Behind them, the QRF section grouped up in fire teams and moved down the ramp into the garage, weapons at the ready. The police headquarters was all but gone from the fifth floor up, and black smoke was pouring out of the ruin, roiling into the blue midday sky. Overhead, the assault gyrofoil tilted its engine nacelles slightly to move sideways a few meters, kicking up dust and debris with the downdraft from its powerful rotors.

The trauma pod's medical crew met them as soon as they were around the next corner. The medics started working on the young woman on the stretcher before they even had her all the way to the pod. When they reached it, the medics took over the stretcher for the transfer.

Dahl shook her head.

"No injections, just two biogel medpacks. I think she got shot through a lung. She coughed up bright-red froth when I got to her."

"Understood. We will take it from here."

The medics loaded the stretcher into the trauma pod and climbed in behind it. The young civilian woman looked small and pale, and Idina wondered whether they had gotten her out here in time. She had seen strong young Palladians die on the battlefield in moments from injuries like that. But if she had learned anything about human bodies, it was that they could be frighteningly fragile and at the same time very hard to kill, and there was no way for her to know which way the life of the young woman on the stretcher would swing. They had done what they could, and now it was in the hands of the medics.

"What about the other one?" Idina asked Dahl. "The one that was next to her."

Dahl shrugged.

"I patched him up as well. But he was not conscious or moving. I do not think he will make it. This one was still teetering on the edge."

"What do we do now, Colors?" Corporal Shakya asked.

"We go back in there," Idina replied. "We're going to look for the others. Check your weapons and make sure you are topped off. We're going around to the front and going in from the atrium entrance."

"I will come with you," Dahl announced.

"I don't think that's a good idea," Idina said. "If there are any of those Odin's Wolves fuckers left alive in there, you can't do much more than scratch their armor with that pistol of yours."

"This is my home," Dahl replied. "These are my colleagues. My friends. I can no more stay away than you. If you wish to keep me out of that building, you will have to restrain me."

Idina shook her head.

"I have no desire to do that, Captain Dahl. None whatsoever."

Dahl nodded and checked her own weapon, then ejected the ammunition block and pulled a new one from her belt pouch.

"But if you're coming in there with us again, my troopers are taking the lead," Idina continued. "And that's not optional."

Dahl snapped the fresh ammunition block into her weapon and charged the gun.

"Take the lead, then. But be quick about it."

On the atrium level, every body in sight was on the ground and motionless, dead or grievously wounded. They moved through the atrium, sidestepping chunks of burning and smoking debris as they went. Above them, the remnants of the upper floors were a roiling inferno of fire and smoke, fanned by the air coming in through the huge hole the bomb had blown out of the side of the building.

Idina led her section up the staircase behind the canteen that was now ablaze from one end of the room to the other. They made it to the floor above before the way was blocked by burning debris. Above their heads, Idina could see that the staircase simply ended in a ragged and twisted jumble of torn steel supports before it reached the next floor. She turned to Dahl.

"Is there another way up?"

Dahl surveyed the scene above and shook her head slowly.

"This is the main stairwell. Maybe there is an emergency staircase left intact somewhere on the other side of the atrium. But I would not count on it. If we get trapped in one of those, we are finished."

"Colors," Corporal Shakya said. "If they're up there and they're not showing up on the network, they're beyond our help."

"Gods-damn it," Idina cursed. For a hot and angry moment, she was hoping for a few of the Odin's Wolves insurgents to show up in her field of view so she could vent her rage at them with her rifle.

"If the hallway behind us is still intact, we can get to the corner staircase that way," Dahl suggested. "We can go back to the lower level and sweep the floor from the southwest. Kill whoever needs killing, save whoever needs saving."

Despite her anger, Idina flashed a grin at Dahl's statement.

"You sounded like a Palladian just now."

"Let's go, Colors," Shakya said. "We're no use to anyone up there. But we may get some of the civvies out of the lower level before this whole place drops on our heads."

Idina looked at the faces of the troopers around her. She knew that she could order them into the fires above, and they would obey her without hesitation. But she had lost three of them already today, three young brigade soldiers who would never return to Pallas except in a burial capsule, and she wasn't about to add the rest of Red Section to that count without a hope of success in return. Above, the mortally wounded building creaked and groaned as if to lend its weight to Corporal Shakya's argument. She bit her lip and turned away from the destroyed staircase.

"Down that hallway to the southwest corner, just like the captain said. Shakya, take the lead."

The rooms on the lower level were mostly empty. This was the part of the building farthest from the explosion, and the people working in these had been able to escape. Idina's team cleared the floor room by room. Several of the offices were locked with security panels that would not accept Idina's Alliance override codes, and she had Dahl unlock them. It was obvious that people had left in a hurry during the evacuation, and whatever hadn't been knocked over by the explosion had been overturned or flung aside on the way out.

They didn't encounter the first bodies until they were in the offices closest to the atrium, where a row of large windows that separated the rooms from the hall beyond had been blown in and shattered. Half a dozen bloodied bodies were sprawled on the floor or slumped over desks. Some of them were obviously dead, staring at the ceiling with sightless eyes. Idina and her section fanned out into the room to check the others for signs of life while Corporal Shakya stood guard with his weapon at the ready. After five minutes of grim, silent triage, Idina knew that everyone on the ground in this room was beyond saving, killed by the flying glass or the concussion of the explosion that had thrown unprepared bodies against walls and furniture with immense force.

High above them, there was a loud and drawn-out shrieking and groaning, the noises of tortured steel. Then something large and hot crashed down into the middle of the atrium on the other side of the row of broken windows.

"All Alliance units in the building, this is QRF lead," a voice came over the guard channel. *"Abort your sweeps and get out. We have an imminent structural collapse. I repeat, get out now."*

"Affirmative," Idina replied. "On the way."

Next to her, Dahl was bent over a dead woman who looked to be maybe half her age. She threw aside the medkit she had been holding in her hand and let out an incoherent sound of rage.

"You heard the man," Idina said to her troops. "Red Section, leave everything and move out. Let's go, let's go."

She knelt down in front of Dahl and offered her hand.

"You too, Captain. You won't be able to get your vengeance if you die in here with them."

Dahl's dismayed expression did not change, but after a moment, she grabbed Idina's offered hand and allowed herself to be pulled to her feet.

Together, they climbed through the nearest window frame and dashed across the atrium, following the troopers of Red Section who were already halfway to the exit. All around them, the building continued its drawn-out, noisy death as they ran.

Outside, it looked like every Alliance unit on the planet had gathered. Idina didn't make it three steps beyond the threshold of the outer door before several troopers converged on her and Dahl, providing help to spirit them away from the police building as quickly as possible. To her, it seemed that her boots didn't touch the ground more than twice during the dash to the next intersection. Here, someone had parked three armored combat transports in a line to provide cover from the direction of the police building. Several medics rushed toward her and Dahl as soon as they cleared the barrier.

"Are you all right, Color Sergeant?"

"I'm fine," Idina replied. "A little singed, that's all. Check on the captain over there. She wasn't wearing hardshell." She indicated the spot where Dahl stood bent over, catching her breath. The Gretian woman waved them off.

"I am not fine," she said. "But I am not injured."

The medics moved on. Idina watched Dahl as she was getting her breathing under control. Over at the police headquarters, there was a sound like a deep exhalation, then a shrill screech of twisting metal. A part of the remaining section of the upper floors collapsed and fell inward in a shower of sparks that whirled wildly in the updraft from the fires. They observed the inferno silently.

"This is the end for them," Idina said after a while. "Odin's Wolves. They don't know it yet. But they've just finished themselves."

Dahl gave her a long look.

"I hope that is true," she replied. "But that is my home burning over there. My friends. My family. Right now I feel that the Wolves are winning."

"Colors Chaudhary?"

Idina turned toward the sound of her name to see a Rhodian QRF trooper trotting up and coming to a halt behind them.

"Yes, Private?"

"QRF Actual would like a word, if you have a moment."

Idina gave Dahl an apologetic look.

"Sure. Where is he?"

"At the incident command post, over there in the back of the C3 Badger." He pointed at the nearby vehicle.

"I'll be back," she said to Dahl. "Please don't leave before I've had a chance to talk to you again."

"I will be here for a while, I think," Dahl replied.

Idina nodded and went to follow the Rhodian private back to the command vehicle.

—

The commanding officer of the QRF company was a wiry little Rhodian captain with a jawline that looked like he chewed a bowl of steel bolts for breakfast every morning. He was standing at the back of the command Badger, half a dozen screen projections open in front of him that he didn't bother closing when she walked up.

"Color Sergeant Chaudhary, Pallas Brigade. You asked to see me, sir?"

"I did," the captain said. "Captain Shaw, Rhodian Army. You were with the deputy high commissioner this morning?"

"We were acting as augmentation for his security team."

"You were in the building when the bomb went off," he said. "We'll get the data from your armor, of course. But I wanted to get your assessment."

"My assessment," Idina replied, "is that they caught us with our pants down again. Someone had eyeballs on us the whole way from the Green Zone. That gyrofoil with the bomb arrived right after we got there. The DHC and his escort went up top to meet with the Gretians. We stayed down to keep an eye on things at ground level. And three minutes later, the place went up."

"I don't think so," Captain Shaw said. "Their ground element wasn't expecting to run into you. Maybe the timing was just coincidence. They wanted to cripple the police. You just happened to be there."

"We're still one step behind. We're always one step behind. And I've lost three more of my people to them. They're slowly grinding us down."

The captain nodded. "Insurgency basics. Damage the occupiers' morale, keep them in fear, erode their support back home."

"Well, it's working pretty well, sir."

"That's because we've spent the last six months reacting instead of acting, Sergeant." An alert went off on one of the screens in front of him, and he glanced at it and silenced it with a quick swipe of his finger.

"No offense, sir, but you really don't want to hear my opinion on that particular subject."

"Try me." He turned to face her fully and folded his arms in front of his chest. "You're not in the QRF. You aren't downstream in my chain of command. We're not even in the same service. Have at it."

If you insist, Idina thought.

"I should be out there looking for these people and hunting them down one by one. Instead, I've spent the last few weeks on babysitting assignments and fence patrols," she said. "That's a waste of time. Whoever decided to cancel the JSP missions is a fucking idiot. We need to root these Odin's Wolves bastards out from their home turf. We have absolutely no hope of doing that without the Gretian police. If we just keep doing what we've been doing, we might as well pack up and go home. All of us."

The Rhodian captain shook his head and smiled wryly.

"That is almost word for word what I told the general. Only he didn't ask my opinion before I offered it."

Idina shifted uncomfortably.

"It's the gods-damned truth, sir. Just because command isn't listening doesn't mean we should stop pointing it out."

"Fortunately, it looks like someone is finally listening, Sergeant."

Overhead, a medical gyrofoil roared past at low altitude, momentarily drowning out all the nearby noise and chatter, and they waited for a few moments until the craft had disappeared behind the nearest line of rooftops.

"You've got a bit of a reputation in the JSP," Captain Shaw continued. "I'm about to hand over the QRF command to someone else. I've been charged with putting together a new unit. And I want you to be a part of it."

Idina blinked in surprise.

"What kind of unit, sir?"

"A task force," he said. "Outside of the usual demarcations. I'm pulling in people from all over the place. QRF, special ops, field intelligence. Rhodian and Palladian, joint ops. I was hoping you could help me get some of the Gretians on board. You've done a bunch of work with them in the last few months. I figure you probably know a few who are up for the challenge."

Idina glanced back at Dahl, who was now standing next to a rescue pod and talking to the Gretian medics inside.

"I may know somebody," she said. "But my CO is already keen to send me home on medical retirement. I doubt he'll sign off on a transfer."

"If I put your name in the hat, that won't be a problem."

"People from all over the place," she repeated. "Doing what, exactly?"

"Crossing lines," he said. "Going out there and hunting down Odin's Wolves. With all the assets we need, and none of the shackles. No guard duty. No babysitting assignments. Just the best people from across all the services. We gather the intelligence, we analyze it, we do the tracking work on the ground. We decide which doors to kick in, and when. We've been fighting this on their terms. It's past time we started to play the game their way, don't you think?"

Over at the burning police headquarters, another section of wall collapsed. This one fell outward, tumbling down the front of the building and crashing onto the plaza in front of the main entrance lock. By now, there were firefighting pods all around the building, and several of them directed thick streams of foam at the burning pile of rubble from roof-mounted dispensers. Overhead, drones were dumping their own foam payloads into the middle of the conflagration. Somewhere in there, three more of her troopers were entombed in the structure, young men that had looked to her for guidance and leadership, three more names on a list that would remain carved into her brain until the day she died.

Nothing I can do will bring them back, she thought. *But maybe I can see to it that the list doesn't grow longer.*

"I think we should go and collect some pelts," she said.

Chapter 23

Dunstan

"Well, that worked better than I expected," Lieutenant Hunter said dryly.

On the screen projection above the tactical display, the Gretian heavy cruiser drifted through space, its drive cone extinguished. Dozens of escape pods were littering the area around the hull. As Dunstan watched the feed from the optical sensors, several more pods launched from the warship on the bright plumes of their ignited solid-fuel booster rockets.

"System says that was the last bunch of pods," Lieutenant Robson reported. "If there's anyone left on that ship, they have no way off now."

"They had their warning. Bring their life support offline. We'll keep it there until someone with a boarding team gets here," Dunstan said.

"Aye, sir. Shutting down life support on all decks."

"And keep us well clear of that hull. I don't want to be near it if someone's arming a nuclear scuttling charge over there right now."

The tactical display was dotted with the emergency beacons from the pods. Nearby, the two other Odin's Ravens ships were drifting, trailing long arcs of debris and frozen air from their damaged stern sections.

"Give them fair notice, Number One," Dunstan said. "Tell them to shut their mouths and sit on their hands."

Lieutenant Hunter nodded and tapped her comms screen.

"Attention, remaining ships," she sent. "We are still tracking you with some very big guns. Do not attempt to maneuver or use your communications gear. If you take any evasive or offensive actions at all, you will be destroyed without further warning."

Dunstan leaned back in his gravity couch and exhaled sharply. He knew from experience that it would take the better part of an hour for the adrenaline to ebb again, and that nothing he could do would get rid of the shakes he felt any sooner.

"Thirty-three pods," Hunter said. "And two ships with gods-know-how-many people still on them. We wouldn't be able to collect everyone even if we wanted."

"We may have just fought the most decisive engagement in the history of space warfare," Dunstan mused.

"If we had half a dozen of these, we could run space control for the entire system without breaking a sweat," Lieutenant Robson said.

"If we had half a dozen of these, we'd be broke," Dunstan replied. "But I don't think you are wrong, Lieutenant. How far out are the other Alliance ships in the sector? *Cerberus* and *Pelican*?"

"Two point one and two point seven hours at full burn, sir."

"Let them know we've captured *three* Odin's Ravens ships. And let fleet command know where we are and what we're doing. Those two ships may not have enough brig space to hold that many prisoners."

"There's one problem I never thought I'd have," Lieutenant Hunter said. "Having to deal with too many surrendering ships."

"I'm surprised they folded so quickly," Armer said from his station, where targeting markers for the ship's retractable gun mount were littering the screen.

"Dying for your cause is a pretty abstract concept, Lieutenant," Dunstan replied. "It becomes a lot more real when you're told you have three minutes to choose between a rescue pod and suffocation."

"They must know that we can still shoot those pods to pieces."

"They went into those pods because they know we probably won't. Because we're the Rhodian Navy." Dunstan looked at the cloud of emergency beacons surrounding the abandoned Gretian cruiser. "But it'll be over five hours before our backup gets here to collect all those pods out of space. I'll be happy to let these people sweat the probabilities for a bit. Get me a tight-beam to *Zephyr*. I want to see how they are doing."

"Our reactor took a hit," Zephyr's comms officer said over the tight-beam connection a minute later. *"All our high-power systems are out. We're running on the backup power cells."*

"Can you get it fixed on your own, Mr. Jansen?" Dunstan asked.

"Our engineer says probably not. She's still taking stock of the damage. But she thinks our torus jacket got holed in that last exchange. That's beyond anyone's field repair skills. You can't just weld a patch to it."

"I see." Dunstan exchanged a look with his first officer. "We have two Alliance ships on the way to render assistance. How long can you keep afloat on your backup power?"

"A good while. But there's no telling what else got bent when we took that hit. The captain says she'd feel much better if we had a power and oxygen umbilical connected to our ship as soon as possible."

Lieutenant Hunter made the hand signal to mute the feed, and Dunstan tapped the audio field.

"You know how classified this ship is, sir," she said. "We can't allow anyone through our airlock and let them get a good look around."

"I won't take anyone aboard, Number One. But we can probably justify a tow assist and some spare juice. Maybe have someone from our engineering section go over there and see if they can lend a hand."

"That's a risk, sir. Just noting my concern for the record."

"And I have made note of it. But if they need assistance, we're obliged to assist. And I'd say we owe them the help. After they played bait for us the way they did."

Lieutenant Hunter considered his words for a long moment. Then she nodded and shrugged.

"I suppose I can take one of the engineers across. But I'm going to let the master of arms post an armed guard by the airlock while we are connected."

"I have no problem with that." Dunstan touched the audio field on his comms screen again, and it changed from red to green.

"*Zephyr*, we will come alongside and run a supply line. If you prep your airlock for docking ops, I'll send someone over to help your engineer. Do you need medical assistance?"

"Negative, Commander. Just a nosebleed or two from the high-g pursuit."

"That is a very fast little ship you have there," Dunstan said. "I've never seen anything like it."

"I was going to say the same thing. We have absolutely no idea how you did what you did," Aden Jansen said.

"And that will have to stay that way. In fact, while you are under tow, you'll need to keep your sensors offline and trust our ears and eyes instead."

"That won't be a problem. We'll prepare for docking. Be advised that we are down to cold thrust only right now, so we're a little limited when it comes to rendezvous maneuvering."

"We'll take care of that, *Zephyr*. Sit tight. *Hecate* out."

Dunstan ended the connection and turned toward Lieutenant Hunter.

"I know what you are going to suggest."

"You do," she said.

"You'll hack their AI core and make sure their sensors stay cold. And when we cut them loose, we're going to wipe whatever data they have on us already. Including our encounter with those ships."

"That was my suggestion, sir," Lieutenant Hunter said. "Of course, it won't erase the knowledge in their heads."

"No, it won't," Dunstan conceded.

"And they're cargo jocks, flying a little hot rod. That kind isn't known for discretion. The next time they get drunk at a spaceport, they'll tell the story to half the bar."

Dunstan sighed.

"They're spacers. Most of them tell tall tales when they're drunk. At least they won't have sensor data to back it up."

Lieutenant Hunter nodded, but she didn't look like he had convinced her.

"Maneuver to rendezvous and commence docking operations when ready. Take whoever you need along with you to assess the situation," Dunstan said.

"Aye, sir."

"While you're over there, you may want to impress on them that it would be best if they forgot what they saw today," he added. "Make sure they understand that the alternative would be to keep them detained until this ship officially exists. And that may never be the case."

Hecate was a small ship for a deep-space patrol vessel, but docked alongside *Zephyr*, she seemed enormous. The Oceanian courier ship was a third the mass and not quite half the length of the Rhodian warship. Her origin as a speed yacht was undeniable, given away by her slender, graceful build and the size of her drive cone, which looked disproportionately large for a ship of her mass. The only indicator that she wasn't quite in her original configuration anymore was the pair of megawatt-class emitters for her Point Defense System, which were definitely not a common piece of technology on a civilian-flagged vessel. PDSs were military technology, and private permits for them were tightly controlled and difficult to obtain. But the permits for *Zephyr* had all checked out the first time he had encountered her with *Minotaur*. Whatever the cost of the system, it had paid for itself by saving the ship, if only barely. The hull section above the drive cone showed damage from shrapnel, but Dunstan knew what rail guns could do to a hull. The slug that had disintegrated into that shrapnel would have caused much more serious damage if *Zephyr*'s PDS hadn't blown it to pieces.

That ship and her crew had no business rushing headlong into battle, he thought. *That was almost suicidal recklessness, point defense or not.*

He checked the secondary mission clock projection on the bulkhead. They had been docked with *Zephyr* for over four hours, and Lieutenant Hunter had been over on the other ship with a few members of *Hecate*'s engineering crew for most of that time.

"Lieutenant Robson, what's the updated ETA for *Cerberus* and *Pelican*?" he asked.

The communications officer checked her display.

"Fifty-three minutes for *Cerberus* and sixty-one for *Pelican*, sir. The other inbound reinforcements are still ten-plus hours away."

"It's a bit of a trip from Rhodia One," Dunstan said. Fleet command had sent half a dozen more ships their way to secure the remaining vessels of the Odin's Ravens fleet. Even in an organization that was chronically short on ships right now, someone had managed to scrounge up a fair-sized task force to come out for *Hecate*'s catch.

"It's a shame they don't do prize money anymore," Dunstan said.

"What's that, sir?" Lieutenant Armer asked.

"Oh, they used to award money to the crew whenever they captured another ship," he replied. "Back in the Old Earth wet-navy times.

They'd split the worth of the ship and its cargo between the crew and the admiralty."

"I would not object to that at all," Armer said. He looked at the screen that tracked the Gretian gun cruiser floating in space a few thousand kilometers away. "How much do you think that ship is worth?"

"That was their last and most modern hull," Dunstan said. "Probably as expensive as our Nike-class ships. And those cost a little under thirty billion per hull."

"Thirty billion ags." Robson let out a low whistle. "Divided by twenty-eight. That would not be a bad bonus for our troubles."

"In all fairness, we would have to cut in the people on *Zephyr*, too. But I don't think fleet command would be too receptive if we floated the idea of prize money."

"Control, airlock deck. The first officer is back on the ship with the boarding party."

"Airlock, Control. Acknowledged," Dunstan answered. "Secure the airlock and prepare your deck for undocking."

"Aye, sir."

A few minutes later, Lieutenant Hunter climbed up the ladder behind Dunstan and stepped onto the control deck. When she sat down in her gravity couch with a low sigh, Dunstan saw that her shipboard overalls were dark with sweat stains.

"Every time I am on one of those civilian nutshells, I am reminded why we build warships the way we do," she said.

"What's the situation?" Dunstan asked.

"Their engineer had it right. The reactor torus ate some high-speed shrapnel. There's no way to patch it out here. They'll have to replace the whole unit. Maybe even the entire reactor assembly depending on the overhaul inspection they'll have to do once we get them to a space dock."

"I hope they are insured well," Dunstan said. A reactor replacement could put a ship out of commission for three months and easily cost a quarter of the original construction costs.

"That's not the end of it, though. I crawled around in that hull with their engineer for about three hours. Some of the power conduits got nicked, too. She is patching what she can. But there is no systems redundancy on that ship. They made a lot of sacrifices to get all that speed out of her."

"As you pointed out, Lieutenant, it's not a warship. It's not built to take hits."

"Someone's going to have to tow them all the way into Rhodia One," Hunter said.

"I guess that will be *Hecate*," Dunstan replied after a moment of consideration.

"Are you sure about that, sir?"

"We're already connected. Once the other Alliance units get here, there's not much we can do to help. We don't have the space to take in anyone from the escape pods. And we don't have marines to board those Odin's Ravens ships."

Lieutenant Hunter expanded the navigation window and let the AI plot a direct course back to Rhodia One.

"Twenty-five million kilometers. And they can't use their gravmag, so it'll be a one-g tow all the way. I guess we know what we're going to be doing for the next two days."

Seven hours later, *Hecate* was on the way down the track to Rhodia One, with *Zephyr* tethered alongside. A few hundred thousand kilometers behind them, the Alliance ships RNS *Cerberus* and ONS *Pelican* were collecting Gretian escape pods out of space. The reinforcement task force was coming down the track from Rhodia in the opposite direction, now three hours away and in the middle of their deceleration burn, and Dunstan decided to head belowdecks for a meal and a shower.

He was sitting at a table in the galley with a coffee and a fresh serving of lamb stew when Lieutenant Hunter climbed down onto the deck. She nodded at him and walked over to the serving nook to get a food tray of her own. The seating in the galley was tight quarters, only two booths with space for four people in each, and Hunter brought her food over to his booth and sat across the table from him. Dunstan was still learning the ropes of day-to-day life on a stealth ship, but by now he was accustomed to the economization of the limited space. He knew that Hunter was joining him to keep the other booth free as a courtesy to enlisted crew members.

"You can claim bunk time first," Dunstan told her. "You look like you've been awake for days."

She took a long sip of coffee and hummed softly with pleasure.

"No offense, sir, but you don't exactly look fresh either. You're the commander. You go first."

"I'll shake odds and evens for it with you. Pick one."

Hunter shook her head with a little smile. "Odds."

Dunstan raised his fist and flexed his fingers. "Ready? *One. Two. Three.*"

They shook their fists at each other in the cadence of the count. On three, they opened them. Dunstan had two fingers extended. Hunter had chosen two fingers as well.

"Evens," Dunstan said. "Looks like my luck is holding today."

"Well, you gave me a fair contest. I was going to check in with the department heads after my meal anyway. I may let Armer have the deck for fifteen minutes longer, though. I'm going to need a shower after that climbing tour."

"I'd never begrudge anyone the luxury of a shower. Just make sure we keep our eyes open on sensors. The ship that got away is still out there."

Lieutenant Hunter took a bite of her food and chased it with another long sip of coffee.

"Do you think that's all they have left?"

Dunstan shrugged. "We just captured what's without a doubt their best warship, plus company. Two supply ships in attendance. And that fuel hauler we blew up by accident. If that wasn't all of it, we probably got the bulk. Unless they have a secret invisible space station out there somewhere."

"Oh gods, I hope they do," Hunter said. "I hope this isn't over."

"I thought you didn't crave conflict anymore."

She stirred the stew on her tray with a spoon.

"This wasn't conflict. It was flicking a switch and turning off an unruly piece of gear. Whatever else they may have out there, we will find it. And with this ship, it won't even be a contest. Whoever designed this beast, I want to kiss them square on the mouth."

"We will find them," Dunstan agreed. "We'll bring these people to Rhodia One, and then we are going back out to look for what's left of Odin's Ravens. And maybe this ship will save their lives, too. I like the idea of ending fights without firing any ordnance. I think we've both picked through enough wreckage in our lifetimes."

Lieutenant Hunter nodded.

They continued their meal in silence for a while. Two enlisted crew members from the engineering department came up into the galley and sat down in the other booth, and a third one joined them a few minutes later. When Lieutenant Hunter was finished with her bowl of stew, she checked her wrist comtab for the time.

"Well, I better hurry up with that shower. Watch change is in twenty, and then there'll be a line."

Dunstan nodded. "See you in a few hours, Number One. Sorry you lost the odds and evens shake."

"As you said, your luck is holding."

She got up and carried her tray to the cleanup rack, then went over to the ladderwell and climbed belowdecks. Dunstan returned his attention to his lamb stew. In the booth next to his, the enlisted crew members were having a muted conversation, but he could tell they were moderating themselves because the commander was sitting behind them. He finished his stew and drained his coffee mug and got up to give the galley back to the crew. Even in the egalitarian atmosphere of a stealth ship, the boss was still the boss, and the enlisted and junior officers needed their occasional private spaces.

Forty more hours to Rhodia One, he thought as he climbed up toward the officer berth deck. *If my luck keeps holding, maybe I can get a day or two of surface leave for the crew before we head back out. Maybe get a chance to see Mairi and the girls.*

As he reached his cabin and unlocked the door, he realized that it had been a very long time since he had actually looked forward to going out on patrol again. This ship was a daring experiment, but the last few days had conclusively proven the validity of the concept. She was small and lightly armed, and she only had one shower for twenty-eight people, but she had just captured a heavy gun cruiser almost ten times her size without getting a scratch into her paint.

"Not bad," he said and patted the bulkhead next to the door. "Not bad at all. Let's see what else you can do."

CHAPTER 24

SOLVEIG

When Solveig opened her eyes, there was darkness all around her.

The pain she felt told her that she was still alive. She had no idea how long her mind had been floating in the nothingness. There had been dreams, but she couldn't remember any images or details, just darkness and all-consuming fear. Her mouth felt parched and dry, and she was feeling the worst headache of her life, a sharp, bright pain that radiated out from her forehead to the rest of her skull and spiked and ebbed with her heartbeats.

It took a while for her eyes to adjust to the lack of light. She concentrated on the rest of her body and tried to focus on each part in turn: arms, legs, chest, abdomen, hands, feet. Everything seemed to be there and working, but it all felt as if someone had beaten every square centimeter of her limbs and torso with a rubber mallet. There was another pain center, just a little less intensely bright than the one in her head. This one was on the right side of her back, radiating out to the front, and unlike the pain in her head, it remained constant with her heartbeats.

She turned her head to get her bearings. As soon as she did, the pain in her forehead turned from intense to blinding, and she let out a groan that sounded croaky to her ears in the silence. Nearby, a soft blue light came on in the darkness, and she heard the faint humming of an electric pump. A few moments later, something cold entered her lower arm and made its way up toward her brain. The wave of nausea that followed almost made her retch, but then the pain dissipated like a dusting of snowflakes on a sun-warmed rock.

She looked down to see that she was in a medical cradle, held in place by light-blue gel cushions that conformed to her body. The medical gel was cool and soothing. There was a medication port in her left arm with a tube and several probe wires connected to it. When she tried to move the arm, the gel reconfigured itself into a gentle embrace around her limb and kept it in place.

Still alive, she thought. *But where am I?*

The medication had taken away the pain almost completely, but it had also wrapped her brain in a fog that made everything seem distant and abstract once more. When she felt herself drifting off again, she did not fight it.

The next time she opened her eyes, the darkness was gone. Solveig looked around to see a familiar scene, the meadows around the Ragnar estate where her running path curved through the orchards and past the fishponds. The unexpected sight disoriented her a little until she figured out that the medical suite had a holographic projector AI built into the ceiling.

The suite was empty except for her medical cradle and the automatic monitoring unit next to it. Whatever meds the unit had given her when she woke up were starting to wear off again, but the dull aches she was feeling in her back and her head were not entirely unwelcome.

"Room," she croaked. "End the projection. And get me some water, please."

The hologram of her running track disappeared. A few moments later, a door opened nearby, and a woman in a medical tunic came into the room, holding a tray with a cup on it. The woman stepped next to the cradle and pulled out a stool from some crevice Solveig couldn't see.

"The autodoc told me you woke up," the doctor said. She looked like she was barely older than Solveig. The name on her white tunic identified her as D.MED LARSEN. "I won't do the thing where I ask you how you are feeling because I know the answer already."

"Thank you," Solveig said. Her tongue felt rough and dry and twice its usual size in her mouth. She nodded at the water cup on the doctor's tray. "Can I have some of that?"

"Yes, you can," Dr. Larsen said. "Small sips. Don't want you to aspirate. Your lungs took a beating already."

She held out the cup for Solveig. It had a lid with a thin stainless drinking tube in it, and Solveig wrapped her lips around the end of the tube. It took three tries for her to get suction going, but when the cool water finally hit her throat, it felt like the best thing she'd ever had to drink. She emptied the cup in the prescribed small sips, then leaned back and exhaled with relief.

"What happened to me?"

"Someone shot you, Miss Ragnar. There was an insurgent attack."

"I remember. I was in the middle of it, at the police building. Where am I now?"

"You're at Sandvik University Medical Towers."

"Where's Stefan? Detective Berg? He was with me when I got shot. He got hurt, too. Did they bring him here as well?"

"I'm not sure," Dr. Larsen replied. "There were a lot of casualties. We've been very busy over the last few days. But I can try to find out for you."

"Please," Solveig said. "He is with the police force." Then she parsed the doctor's statement.

"The last few days? How long have I been here?"

"Three days, Miss Ragnar."

Solveig felt a lightness in her head that she knew had nothing to do with medication.

"You know who I am. Does my father know I am here?"

"He has been staying in one of the family suites here since they brought you in. He asked to be notified as soon as you were awake."

Solveig closed her eyes and focused on her breathing. When she opened them again, Dr. Larsen was still there, holding the empty cup, looking at her patiently.

"Do me a favor," she told the doctor. "Wait thirty minutes before you let him know. I need to sort myself out before I talk to him."

"As you wish," Dr. Larsen said. "If the pain comes back, you have a manual override on the autodoc. Just tell it you are hurting."

"Thank you," Solveig replied and closed her eyes again to give the doctor a window to excuse herself. The pain was indeed starting to return in earnest, but she had no intention of dulling her senses with narcotics, not when her father was on the way to see her. She listened as Dr. Larsen left the room and opened her eyes again when she heard the door close.

There was a row of windows to her right, and a sliding door that led out onto a balcony. Her room was high up in the tower, and the view of the sunlit countryside beyond the Sandvik outskirts was beautiful. She was glad that her windows were facing out of the city instead of giving her a panorama of the skyline.

"Room, open the balcony door," she said.

The door slid open on silent tracks and let in a gust of temperate late-summer air. From outside, the distant noises of life in the outskirts drifted into the room. Solveig closed her eyes once more to calm herself with the smells and sounds of normalcy, and she quickly drifted off to sleep again despite her intentions to stay alert.

When she woke up again, it was to the sound of a familiar voice. She opened her eyes to see her father pacing out on the balcony, talking to a screen projection from his comtab in a low but intense voice.

"You know I don't believe a single gods-damned thing you are telling me, right?"

The voice of her father's conversation partner was just quiet enough through the Alon panes of the windows that she couldn't understand the other side of the exchange, but Falk sounded as white-hot angry as she had ever seen him. If he got loud, he was mad, and best handled with care. If he got quiet and focused like he was right now, his anger was nuclear fury, and anyone who got in his way would be incinerated where they stood. There was no bluster in him at the moment, just the intensity of a time that Solveig had thought to be long in the past. Hearing his voice like this sent a chill down her spine.

"No, you aren't being forthright. You are trying to float on excuses. You should know me better than that, friend. Give me what I want. I'm in the medical center at my daughter's bedside. My daughter who almost died because of this."

She listened as the other person spoke, but she could make out only disconnected sentence fragments.

"That is your problem, not mine. And it's going to be the very least of your problems if I do not have a head on a plate very soon."

Falk swiped the screen projection away with an angry gesture that looked like he was about to hurl his comtab off the balcony. Then he put his device away and turned to look out over the outskirts, running his hands through his hair as he stood at the translucent safety barrier.

When he came back into the room, he looked at her and did a double take, clearly expecting to see her still asleep.

"Solveig," he said. There was more emotion in his voice than she had heard from him in a long time.

"I'm still here, Papa," she said. The momentary flash of guilt on his face unsettled her.

He rushed over to her bedside and took her hand into both of his.

"I am *so* sorry," he said. "I am sorry I wasn't there for you. None of this should have happened to you."

"It shouldn't have happened to anyone," she said softly. "Cuthbert died. He tried to protect me. I would be dead without him."

"I know, Solveig. I know."

To her surprise, she could see tears welling up in the corners of his eyes, tears that he wasn't trying to hide or wipe away immediately as an unwelcome sign of emotional incontinence.

"Where is Stefan? He got me out with Cuthbert. They both saved my life together. He was right next to me when I got shot."

Falk flinched a little when she said "I got shot." He shook his head, and a tear ran down his left cheek. This time he reached up and wiped it away with the sleeve of his tunic.

"I don't know. I really don't. They brought you in by yourself. They said you had a fifty-fifty chance of making it through surgery. I came here straight from the house, and I have been here ever since."

"I want to know if Stefan is okay," she said. "I need you to find that out for me."

"I will," he said. "I'm sorry if something happened to him. I hope he is all right."

"It wouldn't be your fault," Solveig said. She felt a strange sense of calm now, a feeling of detached control she had never experienced around her father.

"You getting hurt is my fault," Falk said. "I never should have acted against my instincts. Letting you go off without a proper security escort."

"They weren't after me, Papa. They were just killing people randomly. They were shooting at anyone who moved. I am sure they didn't even know who I was."

"No," Falk said, and a familiar dark shadow flitted across his gaze. "I'm sure they had no idea. But they will."

She looked at him, her blue eyes probing his. There was something about his demeanor that made her feel a coldness at the base of her spine, a chill that was working its way upward, blotting out the pain in her lower back and chilling her to the core.

"What happened, Papa? What did you *do*?"

They had been in this position a thousand times, but always with reversed roles—him as the interrogator, trying to pry the truth from her whenever he had busted her for a transgression. She knew the momentary hesitation and the flicker in his gaze all too well. It was something she'd had to train to suppress over the years because he was an expert lie detector.

You've turned me into one, too, she thought. *Whether you meant to do it or not.*

"We'll talk about it when I get you home," he said finally. "I had them get the medical suite at the house ready for you."

Solveig breathed in and out, mindful of the simple act of inhalation and exhalation. There was so much that she had taken for granted, so many things that had never crossed her consciousness before. If she slowed her breath, she could slow her heart rate, and exhale her anxieties along with the spent air in her lungs.

"Papa," she said. "If you don't tell me the truth right now, I will not come home. Lie to me, and I will do as Aden did, and you will never see me again."

He flinched, genuine pain etching his face.

"I know that's not what you want. It's not what I want. But it's what will happen if you keep the truth from me. And I will know if you do. I know you too well."

He looked at her for a long time, conflict swirling behind those blue eyes of his. Then he got up and paced the room, one circle, in precise and measured steps. When he got back to her bedside, he pulled out the stool the doctor had used earlier, and sat down on it with a sigh that sounded tired and deflated.

"Very well," he said. "Just don't think too badly of me. Because everything I have done, I have done for us."

Solveig met his gaze, feeling calmer than she ever had in his presence.

"Tell me," she said.

Epilogue

Aden

"Call me a hopeless optimist," Tess said. "But I think we may just come out all right in this."

Aden used the heel of his hand to move the kitchen knife up and down in a rocking motion, chopping the peppers he had lined up on the cutting board on the galley counter in front of him. He still wasn't half as fast as Tristan had been at the same task, but he was getting better every time he tried it, and he found that he enjoyed the practice. When the peppers were cut into sufficiently small bits, he picked up the cutting board and scraped the chunks into the Palladian-style stew that was simmering on the galley stove. He wiped the knife on the edge of the pot and put the lid back on, in case the one-g acceleration provided by *Hecate* cut out suddenly. Cooking in a spaceship galley was a delicate dance of preparation and logistics more than anything else, and it was only now that he appreciated how easy Tristan had made the job look to the uninitiated.

"Maybe," Maya said. "We're still under tow. And our reactor is still fried. The Rhodies have us pretty much by the scruff right now."

"We helped them put an end to Odin's Ravens," Decker said. "If that doesn't count for something in their book, there's no fairness and justice left in the world."

Zephyr was under tow by *Hecate*, on a straight course back to Rhodia One, which was the space station nearest to the site of their fracas with the insurgent fleet. Back at the spot of their encounter, the Alliance ships *Cerberus* and *Pelican* were busy securing prisoners and taking inventory of the ships *Hecate* had captured in the span of three minutes. Aden still didn't have any idea about the precise capabilities of the warship that was now towing them back to Rhodia as a courtesy, but he suspected that he didn't have the technical knowledge to even begin to understand them. *Sleipnir* was the most modern ship in the Gretian fleet when she had been commissioned just before war's end, and *Hecate* had dominated her completely without even launching a single missile or rail-gun slug.

"We'll come out all right," Aden agreed. "But we didn't put an end to Odin's Ravens. That Tanaka two thirty-nine is still out there."

"They won't be able to dock anywhere without triggering red flags," Tess said. "You can't just be out there for months and years on end without ever coming back to civilization. They need fuel. Food. An overhaul. Sooner or later they have to go to a place with a dockmaster. One who has a list of wanted ships."

"They were able to resupply that seventeen-thousand-ton cruiser," Maya pointed out.

The other three crew members were sitting at the galley table that had seats for six, and whenever Aden glanced in their direction, the empty chairs were obvious markers of Tristan and Henry's absence. He rinsed the knife in his hand under the thin stream of water from the sink faucet, wiped the blade steel with a cloth rag, and put the knife back in its place in the leather knife wrap that had Tristan's initials on it.

"That was a dumb move on their part," Decker said. "Using that beast. Sure, it has a lot of guns. But it's a fucking warship. Anyone who came across it was going to see that. You can't just repaint a heavy cruiser and pretend it's an ore hauler. That Tanaka can pass for a pleasure yacht everywhere it goes."

Aden put his dishrag on the towel bar in front of the stove and walked around the galley counter to join his crewmates at the table. It didn't feel good to know that *Zephyr* couldn't move under her own power, but they were all still alive after dodging multiple broadsides of tungsten slugs, and Aden couldn't remember when his life had last felt as vivid and full of sensory details as it did right now.

"Zephyr, Hecate. *We are sixty minutes out from docking at Rhodia One,"* the intercom announced.

Decker leaned over to the control screen on the wall next to the table and tapped it.

"Understood, *Hecate*. Thank you for the long-haul tug service."

"Don't mention it, Captain. It's the least we could do."

"Damn right it is," Maya muttered under her breath.

"What do we do after we dock?" Aden asked.

"I don't know what *we* are going to do," Tess said. "*I'm* going to find a Rhodian shipyard that can fix a punctured toroidal confinement loop on a CriTech Model D-5 fusion reactor. And right after that, *I* am going to find a bar that serves single malt whisky, and *I* am going to get very, *very* drunk. You are most welcome to join me. But I am not making any plans beyond that right now."

"I do believe I will take you up on that," Aden said with a smile.

"We have an hour," Decker said. "Is that enough time for that stew to finish cooking?"

"Plenty of time," he replied.

"All right."

She looked at the galley space behind him, lost in thought. Then she saw that Aden was watching her and flashed a sad smile.

"I'll miss him forever," she said. "But I'm glad you were friends. That pot simmering over there. You, using his knives, chopping those peppers like he used to do. It feels like part of him is still around."

Aden tried to think of a fitting reply, something profound that would invoke Tristan's spirit and make her feel better, but there was nothing he could come up with of that would sound right to his own ears at the moment, nothing that wouldn't seem forced. Instead, he replied to her sad smile with one of his own, and he could see that she understood.

"Ten seconds until release," Hecate sent.

"Copy," Maya said. "Standing by on thrusters."

They were back on the maneuvering deck for the last phase of the docking process. *Hecate* had towed them to the inner junction of the station, and *Zephyr* would be able to limp to her assigned berth on her own with her cold-gas thrusters.

"Five. Four. Three. Two. Mark. Towing clamps released. You are clear to maneuver."

"Confirm towing clamp release, clear to maneuver," Maya replied. "Thanks for the lift."

"Good luck, Zephyr. Hecate *out."*

"Well, that was that," Tess said. "Nice fellows, all things considered. Although they could have shown up a minute or two earlier and saved us a fifty-thousand-ag repair bill."

"They could have shown up a minute or two later and combed through our wreckage, too," Decker contributed.

Maya took the ship into the inner ring and toward their docking spot with practiced precision. When they slipped into position in their assigned berth, she pushed the control sticks away from her and let out a deep sigh before turning her attention to her screen for the final docking process.

"Green light on the starboard airlock. We have a hard dock on the collar," she said. "Umbilicals connected, external power and air confirmed. Good to go, everyone."

"All right," Tess said and unbuckled her harness. "Rhodia One. We'll be here for a while. Let's go find someone to patch us up."

They got out of their gravity chairs and went over to the ladderwell to climb down to the airlock deck. It felt empty with just the four of them in the airlock, without Henry to take lead and Tristan to remind them for the fiftieth time where the good bars were located on the hospitality ring of the station. Tess waited until they were all in the lock, then punched the unlock code into the control panel for the outer hatch to open the way into the docking collar and the station section beyond.

At the end of the docking section, the usual security lock barred access to the main part of the station. They went through one by one, scanning their ID passes and stepping through the scanner array that checked everyone for illegal weapons or explosives. Aden went last, with the squirmy feeling he always felt in his midsection whenever he had to use his purchased identity to pass official muster.

When he scanned his pass, the screen turned its usual friendly shade of green, and he let out the breath that he'd been holding. He tucked his ID pass back into his pocket and stepped out of the lock.

"Major Robertson," a voice said next to him.

He turned to see two Rhodian soldiers in military police uniforms, and a feeling of dread washed over him. He hadn't seen a Rhodian MP since the day of his release from the POW arcology, and he would have known the reason for their presence at the security lock even if they hadn't addressed him by the name that belonged to his Blackguard identity. For a brief moment, he had the impulse to fight or run, but he knew that he would never make it off the station even if he managed to overpower or evade these two MPs.

His crewmates were already past the lock, twenty meters inside the station ring and beyond the one-way security barrier, waiting for him to emerge. Tess looked back at him with concern. The twenty meters between them had suddenly extended to half a solar system in width, and he knew that nothing he could do right now would let him bridge that gap.

"Yes," he said to the MP who had addressed him, replying in Rhodian. "I think I know why you're here, Sergeant."

The MP had a screen up above his hand that showed Aden's military ID in mirror image from his perspective. He was wearing a closely cropped beard now, but the man in the image was unmistakably him, and he decided to cut the proceedings short in front of his friends instead of trying to insist they had the wrong man, only to have his fake ID uncovered in a minute anyway.

"Major, you are under arrest. The charges are violation of your parole, illegal reentry into Rhodian territory, and the use of fraudulent identification."

Aden forced himself to look away from the security barrier where Tess and the others were waiting for him.

I always knew this would happen sooner or later, he thought. *I am who I am and I did what I did, and it was stupid of me to pretend I could just leave that behind like an old uniform. But gods, I wish they weren't here to see it.*

"I don't dispute those points in any way," he said to the MP sergeant. "Can I ask for the courtesy of delaying the restraints until I'm out of sight of my crewmates, please?"

The MP looked at him for a moment as if he was looking for a reason to deny the request, but it seemed that he couldn't find one in Aden's expression or his attitude.

"This way, Major," he said. "We can take care of business over there in the security room."

"Thank you, Sergeant. I appreciate that."

They marched him off, one man in front and one behind, to the curious gazes of the people in the station ring nearby. Tess came running up to the barrier, and Aden felt his face flush with shame.

"What's going on, Aden? Where are these people taking you?"

"Talk to Decker," he told her. "She knows. I'm sorry I didn't tell you."

The MPs had him ushered into the security office before he could hear her response, and the door closing behind him cut off all the sound from the station ring and the security lock. The MP sergeant was true to his word and didn't put the restraints around Aden's wrists until the door was closed. The shackles were lighter than he remembered.

They searched his pockets and the shore-leave bag he was carrying and emptied their contents on one of the tables in the room—his ID pass, his comtab, the spare sets of clothes, and his hygiene kit. He was glad he had left Tristan's knives in the galley instead of bringing them along because the prospect of getting them confiscated by the Rhodians would have been the one thing that could have tempted him into violence today.

"Looks like you are going back to the POW arcology for a while, Major," the other MP said.

"It does look that way," Aden agreed.

"You're being remarkably calm about that, I have to say."

Aden glanced at the windows of the security room, which looked out over a stretch of the inner ring's concourse. Hundreds of people were going about their business out there, catching shuttle connections or making souvenir purchases before their cruises back home. Just a few months ago, he had been one of them, worrying about where he would go and what he would do with his newfound freedom.

Just this morning, we were in a battle with a heavy gun cruiser, he thought. *And we lived through it, and I went on to cook a meal for my friends. None of this is going to be anything like running out of air in a rescue pod, or getting stabbed while fighting a professional assassin, or dodging rail-gun fire in a lightweight ship. I can suffer this with a smile. And the gods know that I need to do a little bit of penance.*

"There are worse things in life, Sergeant," he said. "Ready whenever you are."

Acknowledgments

This is the eleventh novel of mine to see publication since 2013. It is—in my completely objective and unbiased opinion—a good novel. But it's also the one that was by far the hardest to write. Not because the structure is inherently complex (although it took a fair amount of reshuffling color-coded sticky notes on a whiteboard to get the four interweaving storylines just right), but because of when it was written.

I began this book in the spring of 2020, right when the COVID-19 pandemic really started to take off. I blew my deadline for the draft by rather a lot because it felt like sitting down to write was about four times more difficult than usual. On top of the pandemic, 2020 was a singularly chaotic year for politics and civil discourse. All of this combined into what my agent, Evan, called "the blanket of cortisol" under which we were all laboring for most of the year. It turns out that it's extremely difficult to focus on creative things when your brain is soaked in stress hormones, and all your mental bandwidth is mostly needed to deal with the challenges of living through once-in-a-century kinds of events.

But it did get done—eventually—and whenever I read the completed manuscript, I can't tell that almost all the writing days were laborious ones.

I'll make this short instead of rattling off seven paragraphs of names, because so many people deserve my thanks at the moment that this book would be one thousand pages long if I listed them all. If the pandemic has made anything clear to me, it's that we are all interconnected, and that none of what we do is done in isolation, even if we're all sitting at home. Thank you to my family and friends, to my colleagues and acquaintances, and to everyone I have chatted with, emailed, Telegrammed, Zoomed, or FaceTimed in 2020. Thank you for staying home, masking up, taking care of your communities, and protecting the health of others. Thank you for maintaining friendships and for looking out for each other, for making sure that we all make it through the darkness together. I love you, and I am very much looking forward to seeing all of you again in person soon.

About the Author

Photo © 2018 Robin Kloos

Marko Kloos is the author of two military science fiction series: The Palladium Wars, which includes *Aftershocks* and *Ballistic*, and the Frontlines series, which includes, most recently, *Orders of Battle*. Born in Germany and raised in and around the city of Münster, Marko was previously a soldier, bookseller, freight dockworker, and corporate IT administrator before deciding that he wasn't cut out for anything except making stuff up for fun and profit. A member of George R. R. Martin's Wild Cards consortium, Marko writes primarily science fiction and fantasy—his first genre loves ever since his youth, when he spent his allowance on German SF pulp serials. He likes bookstores, kind people, October in New England, fountain pens, and wristwatches. Marko resides at Castle Frostbite in New Hampshire with his wife, two children, and roving pack of voracious dachshunds. For more information visit www.markokloos.com.